Thunder Moon

A JUDD WHEELER MYSTERY

THUNDER MOON

RICHARD HELMS

FIVE STAR
A part of Gale, Cengage Learning

GALE
CENGAGE Learning

Detroit • New York • San Francisco • New Haven, Conn • Waterville, Maine • London

GALE
CENGAGE Learning™

Five Star Publishing, a part of Gale, Cengage Learning.

Set in 11 pt. Plantin.

LIBRARY OF CONGRESS CATALOGING-IN-PUBLICATION DATA

Helms, Richard W., 1955–
    Thunder moon : a Judd Wheeler mystery / Richard Helms. — 1st ed.
        p. cm.
    ISBN-13: 978-1-4328-2533-1 (hardcover)
    ISBN-10: 1-4328-2533-X (hardcover)
    1. Police chiefs—North Carolina—Fiction. 2. Murder—Investigation—Fiction. 3. City and town life—North Carolina—Fiction. I. Title.
PS3608.E466T47 2011
813'.6—dc22   2011007684

First Edition. First Printing: June 2011.
Published in 2011 in conjunction with Tekno Books and Ed Gorman.

Printed in the United States of America
1 2 3 4 5 6 7 15 14 13 12 11

For Elaine

The most precious jewel has uncountable facets

PROLOGUE

The first settlers fell upon North Carolina's Bliss County from the Pennsylvania Colony in the early part of the eighteenth century, fifty years before independence was even a glimmer in the eyes of Philadelphia's revolutionaries.

They were drawn by the virgin, fertile rolling hills; by the warm sun and the moderate winters; and by land grants from the English throne. They wended their way south, following the lure of a new beginning in a rough-hewn land and the prospect of molding their own futures and destinies, and those of their children and grandchildren

One of them, my many-times-great-grandfather Tillman Wheeler, staked out a tract of a thousand acres between a stream that became Six Mile Creek, and a horse-worn dirt track through the forest that connected Bliss County with the mercantile center in nearby Parker County, a day and a half ride to the north. This track was called the Catawba Trail, after the cinnamon-skinned natives who first used it as a trading route.

As the years rolled on, Tillman's sons and grandsons and great-grandsons slowly pieced off parcels of his claim to settle various debts, until all my grandfather had left was the hundred acres he and my father farmed with a passion that verged on religious fervor.

I don't farm my land anymore. I own it, and I love it, for the memories it affords me of family warmth and mild winters and the steaming summers that flipped by like a riffled pack of cards until the day that evil landed in Prosperity like a fallen live electric wire.

ONE

Clay Steger loved it when other men refused to look him in the eye. He thrived on intimidation, and reveled in the fear he instilled in others.

Steger's mother had squeezed him from her womb on Christmas morning. She was dead by New Year's Day, after a hotshot bolus she'd squirted into her veins stopped her heart between beats. Steger was briefly taken by his father, whom his mother had never married or particularly cared for, but the father quickly determined that a mewling baby didn't fit in with his rambling lifestyle, and Clay Steger became a foster home baby before his eyes could rightly focus.

His story went more or less downhill from there.

They say that the vast majority of penitentiary inmates enter their majority with a juvie jacket that would choke an elephant. Clay Steger was no exception. From the time Steger could hold a broom or push a vacuum he had been some foster family's personal houseboy. Until, that is, he reached age ten and decided that indentured servitude didn't fit his life plan, and he broke a pool cue over the head of a four-hundred pound woman who had taken him in on the promise that he'd attend school for a change. She lived, though painfully, and filed assault charges against Steger in Juvenile Court, which led to his first trip inside. He was sent to the State Training School system for six months.

Six months stretched to five years. Being young and perceived as weak by the older youths, Steger was immediately targeted. Two of the older boys lured him into their room a half-hour before lights out one evening, with the intent of busting Clay Steger's butt cherry.

Instead, Steger walked out of the room ten minutes later, covered in spatters of blood, having left one of the youths blind in one eye and the other eating through a straw for six months.

Steger's juvenile record, by law, was wiped clean when he turned eighteen, just in time for him to start a fresh adult record for armed robbery, trafficking, and white slavery.

After his second trip through the joint, the way water finds its own level, Steger fell in with the Carolina Vulcans cycle gang in Morgan, the Bliss County seat. The Vulcans welcomed him with open arms, since he was their kind of guy—meaning the kind of lowlife who enjoyed violence more than sex and considered the opportunity to kick ass one of the primary perks of any job.

A little less than a year earlier, three of Steger's cycle jockey riding buddies had jacked up a Prosperity kid named Jaime Ortiz. They'd kicked and beaten him, flayed his face with a carpet knife, and then nailed him to a white oak tree with an eighty-penny nail through his palms. To this day Ortiz couldn't pronounce sibilant consonants very well, and he had a hard time adding two-digit numbers. The three guys who assaulted him had been caught in a raid on a Vulcans' meth lab several days later, and were now under the protection of the Aryan Brotherhood in Central Prison in Raleigh.

As often happens in corporate hierarchies, this development left Clay Steger high on the totem pole in the Carolina Vulcans, a position he relished and defended quickly and decisively when challenged.

Clay Steger drove a rusted-out Buick into Morgan to meet with a rep from the Tarheel Outlaws gang. The Vulcans and the Outlaws, who had engaged in a bloody Independence Day shootout a decade earlier, had patched up their differences—however temporarily—in the interest of making a lot of money off illicitly produced amphetamines. Steger, as the local Vulcans honcho, was the front man, charged with setting up the particulars of the gangs' underground commerce.

They were supposed to meet at a bar off Eisenhower Boulevard, the main four-lane drag in Morgan. When Steger stepped out of the car, he saw a man standing in the parking lot, waving his hands and shouting at the top of his voice.

"The Lord will exert His will on you, my heathen brothers!" the man exhorted a group of bikers who had gathered in front of the bar. "The wages of sin are death. Not the death of the body, which is but a transitory journey from the sins of the flesh to the Glory of the presence of the Lord, but true, eternal, unpardonable death of the soul!"

The preacher was dressed in black from head to toe—black shirt buttoned all the way to the neck, black twill trousers, black socks, and black wingtip shoes. The solitary submission to color was an ornate gold cross he wore on a heavy chain around his neck. His eyes were obsidian marbles that bore into Clay Steger as Steger joined his pals at the entrance to the bar. The preacher wore a black wide-brimmed hat that seemed hermetically sealed to his scalp. His chin was prominently pointed.

"What's with the roller?" Steger asked the biker closest to him.

"Just a Jesus freak. Come to save us from ourselves."

"I hear God made Man in his image," Steger said. "You think God looks like that?"

They all laughed, and were about to leave the man to his lonely asphalt lot crusade when the preacher dashed up to them.

"Blasphemers!" he cried. "You dare to question the wisdom of the Lord or the exhortations of His earthly messenger?"

"You better blow, brother," Steger said. "Time to dee-dee.

You run along, now, before you get hurt. We men have business to attend to."

The preacher then made what Steger considered a mistake. He reached out and grabbed Steger's arm.

"Don't you dare turn your back on the Lord!"

Steger grabbed the man's wrist, and twisted it. To his surprise, the preacher neither shrieked in pain nor even grimaced. He did release Steger's arm. Steger grasped the man by the front of his shirt, and hoisted him six inches off the ground. The prison tattoos on Steger's bare arms gleamed as if they had been lacquered on polished marble.

Then he tossed the preacher five feet, onto the hood of a parked car. To his surprise, the preacher rolled over to his side, hopped off the car, and pointed a long, bony finger.

"Vengeance is mine, sayeth the Lord!" he exhorted.

Steger didn't acknowledge the threat.

"C'mon, boys, let's go inside," he said, trying to keep his voice even. "We'll let the preacher here convert the cars for a while."

Two hours later, Steger left the bar, walking as steadily as his two rubbery legs and six cheap beers allowed. He slid behind the wheel of his rusty Buick and attempted to slip the ignition key into the slot. It wouldn't go.

"Wha'n hell?" he said, his voiced slurred by the alcohol.

"Super glue," a voice said behind him. "Don't it work great?"

Steger was drunk, but he could still marshal enough of his wits together to reach between his legs for the sawed-off Remington pump gun he kept on the floorboard under the front seat.

"Uh-uh," the voice said, and Steger felt something hard and cold press against the back of his neck. "You lookin' for this, boy?"

"What do you want?"

"Give me what's in your pockets."

"You robbin' me?" Steger said, incredulous. "You know who I am? The Vulcans'll be all over you."

"We'll deal with that later. Give."

The man in the back seat pressed the gun harder against the back of Steger's neck. Steger felt his heart roll like a storm sea in his chest. He had seen firsthand what a sawed-off load did to human flesh, and he was deathly afraid of it.

No fool, Steger reached into his pocket. He had a roll of twenties, and he lifted it up so that it rested on his shoulder.

"This is gonna get squared," he said.

"No doubt," the man said, as he took the roll of bills.

Steger felt the pressure come off the double barrel.

"You know who I am?" the man said.

"No."

"The Angel of Death," the man said.

He dropped the shotgun on the seat, grabbed Steger's forehead from behind with one hand, and rammed an ice pick deep into the base of Steger's skull with the other. Then he swept it back and forth, the way you'd pith a frog in biology class. Quickly, he pulled Steger's head back, and leaned forward so he could watch as Steger's pupils dilated and the light behind them faded into oblivion.

A mangy cat saw the man in black leave Steger's car. The cat's crusted eyes blinked at the flash of reflected light on the gold crucifix hanging from the heavy chain around the man's neck.

Two

Middle summer in North Carolina was created by God as an object lesson for those who don't believe that asphalt has a liquid state.

I sat in my office in the Prosperity Police Station, finishing the mid-July payroll records to submit to the town treasurer, so that my officers and I would get a paycheck on the fifteenth. I had a fan in the open window, which blew hot, blacktop-scented air across the middle of the room from the shopping center parking lot outside, and another smaller oscillating fan standing on the top of my filing cabinet to keep the air moving. Neither one seemed to be making a hell of a dent in the oppressive swelter.

I had lounged on the front porch of my house last night, sipping a Corona and listening to a Braves game as storm clouds gathered like converging ocean waves. I had enjoyed the rise in the wind and the first distant rumbles of thunder that grew and rose like the sound of desperately losing artillery. I had stayed on the porch until the storm was right on top of me, and only retreated to the safety of my den when lightning arced from the top of an ancient pecan tree a hundred feet from my steps, followed by the instantaneous whip crack of thunder and the tangy ozone smell of ionized air.

While I was enjoying my storm, a lightning strike had apparently hit the air conditioning unit behind the police station. Something critical inside was fused, and I had arrived this morning to an office that already resembled the ambience of a Turkish bath.

The HVAC repair company contracted by the Prosperity Town Council had assured me that they would send someone by sometime later in the day. It hadn't happened yet.

I finished the payroll and slipped it into a damp manila envelope, wrote the town treasurer's name on the outside, and dropped it into the OUT file on my civilian assistant's desk. Presuming that the treasurer hadn't decided to abscond to Bolivia with the town's money, my patrolmen and I were safe from starving for another month.

I was also free of all my administrative duties for the day. Being the Chief of Police in a three-cop town may sound like a lark, but I still had to fill out all the same personnel forms as they did in Pooler, the city of more than half a million to our immediate north.

I locked my office door and headed straight for the new cruiser, climbed behind the wheel, and kicked in the AC as soon as I turned the key. It took the compressor a moment to overcome its own understandable inertia, before the first wisps of blissfully chilly air blew from the vents. I had nothing to do for the rest of the day except patrol the back roads and make any number of rationalizations as to why I shouldn't pull over miscreants and venture back into the oven just to give them a ticket.

I needn't have worried. In the deep summer in Prosperity, anyone not in an office somewhere was already napping away the hottest part of the day, or was submerged in a pool trying not to parboil. I cruised the secondary roads around the town and saw very few cars, which was fine by me.

After a half hour or so, and several trips around the Prosperity perimeter, I became apathetic about the whole thing and decided to park the car and set up a speed trap. I chose a likely spot on the shoulder of a long open stretch of Niley Crook Road, where any conscious driver would see me half a mile before they really needed to slow from either direction. I put the cruiser in PARK, and settled back in my seat to enjoy the crisp recirculated air.

I had stopped at Gwen Tissot's Stop and Rob on Morgan Highway and had picked up a quart of spring water, from which I sipped as I listened to a local radio station and tried to stay awake.

After ten minutes, my two-way crackled to life.

"Officer down! Officer down!" someone yelled. "Fourteen hundred block of Arnie Hudson Circle! Officer down! Request assistance immediately!"

I recognized the voice of Stuart Marbury, one of my officers. Arnie Hudson Circle was an oiled dirt road about a mile from where I had set up my speed trap. I reached up and toggled the microphone on my shoulder epaulet.

"Chief Wheeler," I said. "I'm on my way. ETA three minutes."

I dropped the shift into gear and peeled away from the shoulder.

Before I even hit the asphalt, the chatter on the police bands jumped tenfold. I recognized calls from the Bliss County Sheriff's Department in Morgan, the county seat, and from the Mica Wells PD, five miles to the south of Prosperity. Everyone seemed to be getting in on the action.

I saw the rotating lights on the top of Stu's cruiser when I turned onto Arnie Hudson Circle from Morris Quick Road. Stu was crouched down at the driver's side door. A sheriff's deputy's car was parked a few yards away, its doors and windows shut tight.

I pulled up beside Stu, and shut off my car. After grabbing the riot gun from its rack next to my seat, I opened the door, rolled out onto the ground, and crabbed my way around to Stu, who leaned up against his door with his service pistol resting on his thigh.

"Give me the situation," I said.

"I received a call from this deputy, Roger Cord, from Morgan. He had to serve some papers on the guy in that shack over there, and he wanted some local backup. I met him here, and provided cover while he went up to the front door. I heard a shot from inside, and, . . . well you can see. There's a hole in the door you could toss a basketball through. Guy inside must have cut loose with a twelve gauge. Cord went sideways, behind those bushes in front of the house. I haven't seen him since."

Far off, I could hear the first wail of sirens. The sheriff's department had apparently alerted the rescue squad at the Prosperity Fire Station.

"Hey, Deputy!" I yelled. "Can you hear me?"

"I'm shot!" he yelled back. "Caught some of the spread on my right side. Don't know how bad it is. The bleeding isn't too awful, but I don't know what he hit inside."

"You just lie still! We're going to get you out of there."

I turned to Marbury. The back of my blouse was already clinging to my skin, as the merciless Carolina sun beat down on me.

"What kind of papers was he serving?"

"Eviction."

"Oh, great," I said. "You know who this guy is?"

"No."

I nodded, gritted my teeth, and ran bent at the waist around the end of the deputy's car. I could see a truck parked in the gravel drive of the wooden frame shack, parked nose-in. I memorized the license tag.

"This is Chief Wheeler, Prosperity PD," I said after turning the radio to the Bliss County Sheriff's Department frequency. "I need an ID on a car tag."

I read off the number, and waited for the clerk to punch it into the computer.

"His name's Luther Steele. Over." she said after a moment.

"I need everything you've got on him. DOB, family names, anything you've got. Understand?"

"Copy, Chief. The sheriff's on his way."

"We're not going anywhere."

I scrambled back to the Prosperity cruiser, where Stu sat behind the front wheel, probably the safest place to be, since there was so much cast iron and so many suspension pieces separating him from the shooter.

"How many rounds did he fire?" I asked.

"Two. The first one knocked the deputy into the bushes. The second just went off into the woods over here."

He nodded toward a stand of hardwoods across from Steele's house.

"You didn't catch any of the pellets?"

"Missed me by a mile. I was just here for backup."

"You're a starter now," I said.

The sirens grew louder and higher in pitch as the sheriff and the Mica Wells police cars drew nearer. They were joined by sirens of a different, more mournful sort, which I recognized all too well as the local volunteer fire and rescue service, and an ambulance. Over the years I had developed this subconscious association between their sound and some poor bastard having the worst day of his life. I hoped it wasn't in the cards to be mine.

"Gonna be a goddamned circus," I said.

Within a half hour, we had blocked off all of Arnie Hudson Circle. The sheriff and rescue boys had parked about a hundred yards down the road from Steele's house. Most of the officers and firemen kept a respectable distance, but the sheriff, a former high school teacher of mine named Don Webb, crouched next to the Prosperity cruiser with me and Stu.

"I want my man out of there," Webb said.

"Okay. Go get him."

"You know, Judd, I usually like you as a person."

"We haven't heard anything from inside the house since I got here," I said. "Stu said he heard two shots. The first one hit your guy. You don't suppose Steele parked the second one up under his chin, do you?"

"I don't get that lucky."

"Give me that data sheet you brought on Steele."

He handed me a metal clipboard, the kind the State Patrol boys use for writing out tickets. There was a computer printout stuffed underneath the spring-loaded clip.

I read for a second, then pulled out my cell phone. I dialed a number. The phone on the other end rang about five times before it was picked up.

I heard a tremulous voice on the other end, slightly slurred and full of adrenaline.

"Hello?"

"How you doing, Luther?"

"Who is this?"

"This is Chief Wheeler. I'm sitting out here behind the Prosperity police car."

"What do you want?"

"I want the deputy you shot. I'm not interested in charging the house or busting down your door, but you've got a bleeding law officer lying in your bushes, and he needs to get to a hospital right now. You understand?"

"I don't want none of you cops near my house!"

"That's not gonna shine, Luther," I said, trying to keep my voice quiet and level. "I want you to think about this real hard. Right now, you're only up for assault. If that deputy dies because you didn't let him get medical help, it turns into murder. You know what happens to cop killers in this state?"

"No."

"It isn't pretty. So, I'll tell you what I'm going to do. I'm going to drive this cruiser up to your bushes. You can watch me the entire time. I'm going to get out, unarmed, and I'm going to put Deputy Cord in my backseat, and then I'm going to drive back down the road to the ambulance. You're not going to shoot me. Got that?"

"I don't know . . ."

"Well, let me make it clearer for you. I'm coming to get that deputy. If you shoot at me, I'm putting you under a black flag. I'm the law in Prosperity, and I can do that."

"What's that mean, a black flag?"

"It means I'm clearing all the other law officers out here to open fire on you. You shoot at me, and they're going to unload every piece of ordnance they have on that shitbox you live in. When they're finished, your house is going to be nothing but a pile of splinters, and you'll be a big gooey spot right in the middle of it. Is there anything I've said that you don't understand?"

"And if I let you take the deputy?"

"Then we move on to the next step. We have to get through this one first. I'm coming on up, now."

I closed the phone and opened the cruiser door.

"You're nuts," Webb said. "You don't know what that idiot's gonna do."

"I know he isn't going to shoot me."

"How in hell can you know that?"

"I heard it in his voice. He doesn't want to die today."

"You heard . . ." Webb shook his head. "If that ain't the damnedest thing. You're gonna get your ass shot off, Judd."

"I don't think so. Just in case I'm wrong though . . . well, if he lets loose with that shotgun, I'd appreciate it if you'd blow him into the middle of next Tuesday."

Don Webb and I went back about a quarter century. He had been my high school history teacher before he retired and ran for Bliss County Sheriff. He knew when I was shitting him and he knew when I wasn't. He nodded solemnly.

"You be careful, Judd," he said.

I stood, slowly, and placed my riot gun on the rear deck of the sheriff's cruiser. Then I unbelted my Sam Brown, and laid it next to the riot gun. I turned slowly, my arms in the air, to show Steele I was unarmed.

Of course, he couldn't see the .32 strapped to my ankle. I wasn't about to throw myself into the hornet's nest without a little insurance. Better to have it and not need it than to need it and not have it.

I crouched and waddled over to Stu's cruiser, the three-year-old one that was due to be traded soon. If I got the new car messed up, I'd have a lot of explaining to do to the Town Council.

The car was still running. I slid behind the wheel, and dropped the transmission into drive. Slowly, I started up the driveway toward Steele's house. When I reached the gravel walk leading to the front stoop, I turned and drove across the grass. I ducked a little as I passed the front door. I had seen what a load of double-ought on full choke could do to a man. Things like that can kill your whole day.

I pulled up next to the bushes, and could see Deputy Cord lying between them and the house.

"You still with us, Deputy?" I called through the open window.

"Took you long enough. This hurts like a son of a bitch."

"Can you walk?"

"I can crawl."

21

"Then crawl over here and get in the car. The ambulance is waiting down at the road to take you to the hospital."

I watched him roll over. There was a dark splotch on the left side of his blouse, not much bigger than a football. It didn't glisten, which was good, since that meant he wasn't bleeding profusely.

He crabbed through the bushes, and pulled open the back door of the cruiser. After he hoisted himself up into the seat, I drove on back around to the road without waiting for him to close the door.

As the ambulance crew tended to him, I pulled out my cell and hit the redial for Steele's telephone.

"Yeah?" he said.

"You did real good, Luther. You want to tell me why you shot through the door in the first place?"

"What difference does it make? You guys are gonna take me out anyhow."

"That's one way it can go. If you toss out that shotgun and walk out with your hands up, I can promise you won't be harmed."

"I done been to prison twice, Chief. You know what that means."

"This isn't a three-strike state. You're confused."

"You know better. Three-strike or not, the judge is gonna lock me away for the max. I can't do that again."

"It's walk or come out toes up. Those are the choices."

I heard the click as he hung up the phone.

"Great," I muttered.

"What are you going to do now?" Stu asked.

"Call the power company. I want the electricity cut for this whole street."

"The other folks who live here are gonna raise hell, Chief."

"Can we deal with one crisis at a time?"

Two hours later, I was still sitting next to the old cruiser. The sun, directly overhead, toasted the phalanx of law officers who had assembled in front of Luther Steele's house. I was covered with a coating of salt and sweat. My hair was soaked through. My blouse was sopping.

One of the deputies crawled over to me and handed me an ice-cold bottle of water.

"Thanks," I said.

"Sheriff's setting up a canopy next to the fire truck," he said. "We're bringing in water and sodas. We should have some sandwiches soon. Maybe some watermelon. Gonna make a regular picnic out of it. There's this reporter over behind the barrier, says he wants to talk with you."

I looked over at the barrier the sheriff's deputies had assembled several houses down to keep people off Arnie Hudson Circle. Cory True, a reporter for the *Morgan Ledger Telegraph* stood there, trying to catch my eye.

"Tell Cory I'm a little busy right now."

"Ten-four. Chief, are we going to get this guy out?"

"Time will tell, Deputy. With his power out, that house will be getting pretty hot by now. By late afternoon, it will be like a sauna in there. Maybe we can sweat him out."

"If'n we don't melt first."

"There is that. Thanks for the water."

He worked his way back down to the barrier. I saw him speak briefly with Cory True, who tossed up his hands in frustration.

I heard an oscillating mechanical drone over my head and looked up, almost into the blazing sun. I could just make out a helicopter hovering over my car. I could tell by the markings that it wasn't Garfield, the nickname for the Pooler Police Department chopper over in Parker County. None of the law enforcement agencies in Bliss County could afford a helicopter. That meant it was one of the television stations.

"Perfect," I mumbled.

I picked up my cell phone and thumbed the redial again.

"What?" Steele said.

"Getting steamy in there?"

"Why'd you turn off my power?"

"Seemed like a good idea at the time. You toss out the shotgun and come to us, like a good boy, and I can have you in a nice air-conditioned car in about five minutes."

"I ain't ready to come out, Chief."

"Well, I have to tell you, I'm about ready to come in and get you. I'm not risking any damn sunstroke over the likes of you."

"You come in, and you'd better send in two ahead of you. You better make it two guys you don't like so much, 'cause I'll blow 'em both away."

"Luther, Luther. Talk like that isn't going to sound good at your trial."

"Ain't gonna be no trial, and you know it. The minute I set foot outside this house, those deputies are gonna turn me into cube steak."

"The sheriff isn't the law in Prosperity. I am. You won't be going to the Morgan Jail. I'll take you personally over to the station in Prosperity, and we can arrange for you to stay there until your trial if you like."

"I don't believe you."

"When was the last time you slept, Luther?"

"Yesterday. Why?"

"You were up all night?"

"My landlord called yesterday an' told me that he was kickin' me out. I figured the sheriff deputies would be by to serve the papers. I stayed up waiting."

"You know, the longer you go without sleep, the harder it's

going to be to stay awake."

"So?"

"So, it's just a matter of time. As soon as we know you're asleep, we'll be all over you like shit on a work boot."

He hung up the phone.

Stu leaned over and tapped me on the shoulder.

"The mayor's here. Says he wants to chat with you."

I looked over at the police barrier, where Kent Kramer spoke with Cory True. Kent had been elected mayor the previous fall, after the untimely demise of his predecessor.

"I'll be right back," I told Stu.

I scrambled over to the new cruiser and backed it down Arnie Hudson Lane to the barrier, then climbed out.

"Join me in the car, Mayor?" I said.

Kramer was intensely aware of the television news cameras, and wasted no time crossing the barrier to sit in the passenger seat next to me.

"Shut the door," I said. "You're letting the cold out."

He pulled the door closed and leaned back against the vinyl seat.

"How's it goin', Judd?"

"Not too bad. You?"

"I mean the hostage situation."

"There is no hostage situation. It's just one scared redneck with a gun, holed up in a shack. How's your boy doing?"

"They're redshirting him at Georgia Tech this year. He's working out with the scrimmage team as quarterback."

"I'm glad he made it somewhere."

Kent's son, Seth Kramer, had been the star quarterback on the Prosperity Glen High School team the year before, just as I had been twenty-five years earlier. He was a big, blond, straight-toothed kid who'd look great on the cover of a Wheaties box someday, if he didn't get arrested for raping some fifteen-year-old girl first.

I was betting on the arrest. Seth Kramer was a natural athlete but he still had a lot of work to do on his people skills.

"What were you telling Cory?" I asked.

"He wanted some background information."

"You had some to give him?"

"I had spoken with Sheriff Webb."

"Did you talk to the radio and television people, too?"

"A couple."

"Can I offer you a word of advice?"

"I suppose."

"Don't do that again. This is a police matter, and that makes it my command. How do you know that Luther isn't sitting over there listening to you talk about him on a transistor radio? You say the wrong thing, and you might make it necessary for me to kill him. I don't want to do that."

"I'm still mayor in this town."

"And I work for the Town Council. I mean it, Kent. Don't talk to any of the press until this thing is over. There'll be plenty of time to claim credit later."

"You can't talk to me that way!"

I dropped the car into drive and spun the tires a little as I drove back up to the old cruiser in front of Luther's house.

"What are you doing?"

"Giving you something to talk about."

"Let me out of this car!" he said, as he glanced cautiously at the front door of Luther's house.

"Sure. Of course, you're on Luther's side. I can't promise he won't take a pop at you when you open the door."

"Jesus!" he yelped, and leaned across the front seat, almost placing his head in my lap.

"I'm getting out," I said. "After I do, maybe you can just slide across and get out this side. Or, you can stay in the car.

I'm going to leave it running. Might be cooler in here."

I pushed my door open and half-rolled out onto the street.

"You coming?" I asked Kent.

"I'm all right here," he said, his voice muffled somewhat by the front upholstery.

I shut the door, eliminating—at least temporarily—one of my problems.

"I don't like the look of that," Stu said, pointing off toward the west.

In a matter of minutes, steamy clouds had gathered in the distance and were beginning to coalesce into an angry thunderhead.

"I'll just bet they fixed the air conditioning at the station too," I said. "Just in time for it to get fried again. How long you figure before that storm gets here?"

"Maybe an hour. I don't cotton to sitting out here against two tons of steel in the middle of an electrical storm, Chief."

"Good point. We need to find a way to settle this thing. We can look on the bright side, though."

"What's that?"

"The storm will ground that damn TV chopper."

I checked the information Sheriff Webb had given me again, and had an idea. I called the dispatcher in Morgan and asked her to task a deputy to make a pickup for me.

"What are you doing?" Webb said over my radio.

"Calling on a higher authority. I need to get Luther out of that house before this storm rolls over us. If we get pinned down in a cloudburst, he could sneak off before we know it."

Twenty minutes later, a sheriff's department cruiser pulled up alongside us and stopped. I leaned over and opened the passenger side door.

"Thanks for coming," I said, as I escorted an elderly woman

out. "I'm sorry we don't have a nice clean place for you to sit, but it's safer if you aren't in the line of fire."

She knelt next to me and smoothed her housedress.

"What's this all about?"

I told her. Then I told her what I wanted her to do.

"Give me the telephone," she said.

I dialed the number. She spoke for a few moments, as the wind whipped up around us and the trees in the hardwoods across from Luther's house began to sway ominously. I could taste the metallic edge in the air, like a rusty penny on the tongue, as the electricity began to build with the approaching storm.

I didn't hear everything she said, but after a couple of minutes she handed the telephone to me.

"Luther?" I said as I held it to my ear.

"Is it true what she said?"

"I'll stand by every word," I said, though I didn't have a clue what she had told him. At that point I'd have tongue kissed a copperhead to get him out of the house.

"Okay. Here's the way I want to do this thing. You drive up here in the car and park it with the passenger door next to my front stoop. That's my cover, see? I'll open the front door and crawl out to the car, and you drive me right to the Prosperity jail."

"You forgot something."

"What's that?"

"The hogleg."

"Oh. Yeah. Okay, as soon as I see your car, I'll toss it out the window next to the door."

"Break it down first. I don't want it going off by accident. You crack it and remove the shells."

"When I see your car."

"I meant what I said, Luther. You open up on me, and there

28

won't be enough of you left to pick up with a paintbrush."

"Okay. When are you coming?"

"Right now."

I told the woman to get into the deputy's car, and to stay low. After giving the deputy some instructions, I crabbed over to the old cruiser and climbed behind the wheel. I didn't bother to take off my Sam Brown this time, because I wanted Luther to know I wasn't playing games.

I pulled up the driveway, then began backing across the front of the house. Just as I reached the front porch, a window opened on the other side of the steps and I saw a shotgun fly out into the bushes.

So far, so good.

I pulled even with the front door and pushed open the passenger side door of the cruiser. Slowly, the front door of the house opened. I saw a wiry, scrawny, balding man the size of your average eighth grader slide out onto the porch almost on his belly.

"Come on," I said. "Storm's going to hit any minute."

He snaked across the front porch the way I'd seen actors do in old World War II movies, and climbed up into the car.

I hit the light and the siren as soon as he slammed the door. He crouched down below the window valance. We drove out to the barrier, which was quickly pulled aside by the deputies, and made our way through the gauntlet of reporters, law enforcement officers, and hangers-on, until we reached Morris Quick Road. Then I laid on the gas.

We reached the Prosperity Police Station in about four minutes.

The deputy arrived with the woman I'd summoned a couple of minutes after I patted Luther Steele down and placed him in one of the three holding cells.

I had her take a seat in my office, and then waited. As I expected, Cory True arrived only a minute or so later. I had already radioed Stu and told him to hold Kent at the scene for a little while, ostensibly to secure the area.

I allowed Cory into the office and locked the front door. Within minutes, the front of the police station was going to look like we were holding a rock concert.

"I'm giving you an exclusive," I told Cory. "Don't think it's because I like you. We both know better. On the other hand, I don't want to have to tell this story fifteen times, so I figure it's better if we do pool coverage."

I walked him back to my office, where the woman sat patiently, her hands folded in her lap.

"Cory, this is Selma Steele, Luther's mother. Miz Selma, Cory True of the *Morgan Ledger-Telegraph*."

"Pleased to meet you," Cory said, extending his hand.

She shook it tenuously.

"Miz Selma is responsible for getting Luther out of that house," I said.

"This is a story I want to hear." Cory pulled a miniature tape recorder from his pants pocket.

"I have Luther in the back, in one of the cells. He surrendered voluntarily, after Miz Selma talked with him on the telephone."

"Talked some damn sense into him," she added.

"Luther was brought up over in Tulip Springs," I said. "You know what it's like there. If the whole town has two nickels to rub together, they shoot craps for both of them. Moreover, most of the families in Tulip Springs are matriarchies."

"Run that by me again?" Cory said.

"The mother is the boss of the family. The boys grow up, get married, and move back in with their mommas. Their wives learn to live with it, because they know when Momma kicks off, they get to be Momma. Luther never got married, though. He moved out, but not far enough to break the apron strings. When I read that Luther's momma was still living over in Tulip Springs, I sent a deputy over to pick her up."

"Don't know what that boy was thinking," she said. "Luther never had a lot of sense, but I think maybe he done gone and lost what little he had. That boy never had the brains God give a billy goat."

"So what did you tell him to get him out of the house?" Cory asked.

She smiled. "I just told him that if he kept up this foolishness, I was gonna come in myself and give him a fair whoopin'. That boy may not be bright, but he sure knows enough to avoid a momma whoopin'."

"And he gave up?" Cory asked. "Just like that?"

"Not quite," she said. "I also promised him I'd make him chicken and dumplings and bring them to him here at the jail-house."

Outside, I could hear cars pulling up in the gravel parking lot of the station. Overhead, I heard the first rumble of thunder as the storm crossed over the Bliss County line and started to edge in on Prosperity.

"Luther shot a Bliss County sheriff's deputy," I said. "Word is that the boy is going to be all right, but even so I don't think it would be a good idea to transport Luther over to the county jail just yet. I promised him I'd let him stay here in the Prosperity station until his trial comes up. That was part of the deal."

I spent the next ten minutes giving Cory the details of the standoff, and then ushered him out the front door. I followed behind him. The sky was a roiling, swirling black mass over our heads as the cameras all lit up and flooded me with brilliance. I squinted a little as I faced them.

"The suspect was arrested a little over a half hour ago," I told the crowd. "He's being held pending arraignment. He gave

31

himself up peacefully after speaking with his mother. I've given all the details to Mr. True of the *Ledger-Telegraph,* and he will share them with you. Now, I'd like to suggest that you move to a safer location, because we are about to be hit with a gully washer of a storm, and I'd hate to see any of you fine folks come to harm."

I stepped back inside the station, and walked to my office. Selma Steele was still sitting there.

"Don't worry about Luther," I told her. "He'll be safe here. I would like to ask you one more favor, though."

"What's that, Chief?"

"Could you bring a little of that chicken and dumplings for me when you come back? It's been a long time since I had some good old Tulip Springs chicken and dumplings."

THREE

The good news was that the air conditioning had been fixed.

The bad news was that I got to enjoy it while I filled out a ton of forms. Because Luther Steele had been arrested in my department's jurisdiction, I had to complete the arrest papers for the Clerk of Courts' office over in Morgan.

I was halfway finished filling in the forms when my phone rang.

"Judd?" Donna Asher said. "When you have a moment, I'd appreciate it if you'd explain to me exactly what the hell you thought you were doing out there this afternoon."

Donna is an English teacher at Prosperity Glen High School. Somehow, the word *girlfriend* doesn't seem adequate for the role she plays in my life. I don't think the poetry of romance has coined the word that properly sums up our relationship.

"It seemed like a good idea at the time," I said.

Outside my office, I heard an electric snap and an immediate explosion of thunder as the storm rolled over the top of the station.

"How'd I look on television?" I asked.

"Who knows? The only pictures came from the helicopter. From there, you looked like a cabbage with hair riding around on an ox yoke."

"Yes. A devastatingly handsome cabbage, though."

"Don't change the subject. I was worried sick. You could have been shot."

"I wasn't. By the time I got there, Luther was more frightened than he was dangerous. I just worked on that a little to soften him up before I could get him out of the house."

"You thought this all through at the time?"

"Not exactly. It was more an instinctual thing. On the other hand, I have lightning sparking off all around the station. I am at much greater risk using the telephone than I was out on Arnie Hudson Circle. So, I'm going to hang up now. Are you coming over for dinner?"

"Around seven?"

"Seven sounds good."

In an hour or so, the storm rolled off toward the east. The electric explosions turned to distant rumbles and the sky brightened over the police station. Outside my office window, I could see streamers of foggy mist rise from the asphalt parking lot of the Piggly Wiggly. Even with the repaired air conditioner, my office felt sticky.

I heard the front door open and shut. Kent Kramer strolled into my office and sat across from me in one of the chairs. He didn't look happy.

"Something I can do for you, Mr. Mayor?" I asked.

"That was a dirty trick, Judd."

"You mean the car thing?"

"You know I mean the car thing."

"Then you're right. It was a dirty trick. Anything else I can do for you?"

"You want to explain what you meant by that stunt?"

I leaned my office chair back and stared at him.

"No," I said, finally.

"Come again?"

"I do not wish to explain myself."

I crossed my arms and waited.

Kent Kramer and I go way back. He was the first-string quarterback at Pooler High School about a quarter century back, at the same time I was the starting quarterback for Prosperity Glen. My team kicked the grits out of his team at their homecoming. He should have hated my guts. Instead, we became close friends. Events over the previous year had tested that friendship dearly.

After finishing college and not being drafted for the NFL, Kent followed his natural inclination to make people do what he wanted, and went into real estate. He had been very successful, during the years when I was a cop in Atlanta, and later when I had made an earnest—if futile—attempt to become a farmer. Kent had a ton more money than I did, but I had a feeling I had retained a somewhat larger chunk of my soul.

When the property tax refugees from next-door Parker County started spilling over into Bliss County, turning three-century-old farms into sprawling, sterile bedroom communities, Kent was quick to seize the advantage and turn developer. He made another ton of money buying farms dirt cheap and parceling them out in acre-sized lots for ugly houses on cheaply constructed cul-de-sacs.

The rural Bliss County I had known almost all my life was disappearing a hundred acres at a pop, and my long-time friend Kent Kramer was largely responsible.

He also wasn't used to being stonewalled.

"Suppose that idiot in the shack had decided to cut loose with his shotgun while I was stranded in your police car? He might have hit me."

"It was a calculated risk."

"I could have been killed!"

"That was part of the calculation."

I almost smiled at that point, but I worked really hard to suppress it.

"You're pretty cavalier with my skin, Judd," he said.

"Not really. On the other hand, if Luther had shot you, I imagine the Town Council would have found a suitable replacement for you in a week or so. There's no shortage of ambitious Republicans in Prosperity. Tell you what; let's settle it here and now."

I stood and walked around my desk to the door that opened to the three-cell holding tank.

"Hey, Luther," I said.

From the back cell, Luther said, "What is it, Chief Wheeler?"

"The mayor's dropped by to sit a spell. He thinks maybe you might have considered taking a shot at him today."

"I don't recollect shooting at anyone but that deputy, Chief. I don't recall actually thinking about it, either. Has my momma brought by any food yet?"

"I'll check in with her in a bit. Good chicken and dumplings takes a while, you know."

"That it does. How long have I been in here?"

"A couple of hours."

"Seems like longer."

"You just sit tight while I converse with the mayor, all right?"

"Sure thing, Chief."

I gently closed the door and crossed back to my desk chair.

"Seems you were pretty safe after all," I said.

FOUR

Donna and I sat on a wicker settee on the front porch of my house, and listened to the cicadas off in the cornfield. It was dusk, and it wouldn't be long before the mosquitoes ran us indoors.

When I got home that afternoon, I had lit the stone charcoal grill next to the house before changing out of my uniform into a pair of jeans and a Pooler Pythons T-shirt. Donna had arrived a few minutes later, and a few minutes after that I was again out of the jeans and tee. That's the nice thing about charcoal. It stays hot for a good long time.

I'd grilled a couple of thick bone-in pork chops, and some foil-wrapped onions, potatoes and peppers, and we ate at the picnic table with bottles of beer we pulled from an ice-filled bucket. By eight o'clock, the ambient temperature dropped below ninety, and a light breeze rose from the northwest, sweeping out the humidity, but not strong enough to deter the inevitable invasion of winged bloodsuckers.

Donna had arrived ready to spend the night. My son, Craig, was working for the summer at a resort in Myrtle Beach, in order to make some college money, so we didn't have to worry about being quiet or discreet. I liked it that way.

Donna is a former midlevel-ranked tennis star who retired from the sport because all the middle school rookies were kicking her ass, and she realized that—at twenty—she was way over the hill. She left the circuit to go to college and become an

English teacher. She's in the middle five-foot range, about a head shorter than me, with the tight, compact frame of an athlete who had kept up with training. A session with Donna could leave me breathless. Her ebony hair, streaked with just enough gray strands to make her look mortal, fell around her oval face with a precision not often seen outside salon ads as she stroked my hand. Hot as it was outside, that was about all the physical contact we could stand without air conditioning.

"So, how did I look on TV again?"

She chuckled.

"Big. Masterful. Brave. Manly."

"English teachers know all the best adjectives."

"Were you afraid?"

"I didn't give it a lot of thought."

"That man could have shot you."

"Luther? Not likely. He was scared to death, but after a while he could see how things had to go down. Either he was coming out of the house, or the house was going to come down around him. We weren't going to just go away. I could tell from the way he talked that he'd figured it all out. After that, it was mostly taxi work."

She slapped at her wrist.

"I'll be glad when fall comes, and we get rid of these damn bugs," she said.

"You and me both. Let's go inside."

Much later that night, I woke for no apparent reason, and couldn't get back to sleep right away. I listened to Donna's measured breathing next to me. I recalled a lot of other sleepless nights the previous autumn, when I had willed myself to stay awake in order to stave off the terrible dreaming recollection of my wife's death.

Those days were over. The dreams had disappeared right

after I found out who murdered Gypsy Camarena and left her body on the banks of Six Mile Creek. Since then, I had slept like a baby.

Mostly.

Donna had filled a lot of empty spaces in my life, but the hole left by Susan's death still lay open and gaping, raw around the edges like an avulsed limb. I supposed it always would.

That was okay. Some things should never be forgotten.

FIVE

I was sitting at my desk the next afternoon when the wreck happened.

The Prosperity Police Department—actually, not much more than a storefront with a reinforced back room for holding cells—was situated in a strip shopping center next to the Town Hall. Downtown Prosperity is at one edge of the town, right at the intersection of two highways that form a "T." Morgan Highway dead-ends into a state road between Pooler, in Parker County to the north, and Mica Wells, to the south.

A Mica Wells kid driving to her job in Pooler was fishing around in her pocketbook for her cell phone instead of watching the road, and ran the red light at the intersection. She rammed into a minivan that had just started to turn left toward Mica Wells, sheared off the front of the van, and sent her own car somersaulting into the parking lot of the Baptist church next door. Her car landed wheels-up. The minivan sat in the middle of the intersection, bowed in the middle and streaming fluids all over the tarmac.

I felt the crash before I heard it, a sort of pressure change in my chest that I had long since associated with destruction and ruined lives. I grabbed my hat and dashed out the front door of the station, almost before the car came to rest on its roof in the church lot.

A man with less experience would have lit out on foot to help, but I was the law in Prosperity, and I knew that someone had already phoned the Rescue Squad at the local VFD. I yanked open the door of the new cruiser, and hit the bubble top and the siren before pulling out of the parking lot to manage the scene.

I parked the cruiser in the middle of the intersection to warn oncoming drivers. Cars were already backing up on Pooler Highway and Morgan Highway in each direction. That was too bad. As soon as I could get control of the situation, I'd radio Stu Marbury or Slim Tackett, my patrol officers, to set up a detour around the intersection. First things first, though.

With the traffic stopped, I rushed to the minivan. The driver, a blond woman in her middle thirties, remained behind the wheel. She had struck her head on something. Blood streamed from a wicked gash on her forehead. I knew it looked worse than it actually was, since head wounds bled out of proportion with their severity. I reached into my back pocket and pulled out a clean handkerchief.

"Press this hard against your forehead," I told her. "The medics should be here in a few minutes."

She nodded, but I'm not sure she really understood. I grabbed the handkerchief, folded it into a pad, and pressed it against the laceration.

"Hold this tight," I told her again. She reached up and pressed it against her scalp.

"Are you hurt anywhere else?" I asked.

"I . . . I don't think so," she said, shakily. "What happened?"

"You were hit. You just sit tight, and keep that pad pressed against your head. You'll be fine. I'll be right back."

I turned just as I heard the first wails from the fire department trucks in the distance. A small crowd had gathered around the upside-down car in the church parking lot. I dashed across the intersection, even as I grabbed at the radio microphone on my epaulet.

"Prosperity Chief to Prosperity One," I shouted.

A moment later, I heard the radio crackle.

"Prosperity One, this is Slim."

"Come to the station. There's been a wreck at the intersection, and I need you to set up a detour."

"Ten-four. I'm about five minutes out."

I reached the overturned car. The group of people who had gathered around it parted, and I saw a teenage girl lying on the asphalt, on her back, being tended by a man in cutoff jeans and a sport shirt. I kneeled next to him. He had long blond hair pulled back and tied tight with an elastic band. On the inside of his left wrist was a blurry tattoo that I knew had been done in the joint. Normally, I would have been suspicious. Under the circumstances, however, he seemed to know what he was doing and I needed all the help I could get.

"She has a crushing injury to the rib cage," the man said after glancing at me. "Must have hit the steering wheel."

"You a doctor?"

"I was a Corpsman. Desert Storm. Her chest is filling up with fluid, and it's pressing on her lungs. She can't get any air."

"What do we do about it?"

As he spoke, he ran his hands along her ribcage.

"They call this a flail injury," he said. "She's broken three or four ribs. We need to roll her onto her side with the broken ribs, or she stands a good chance of puncturing a lung. Grab her by the belt, and I'll get her shoulders. We'll have to hold her in position until the medics get here. It's going to hurt her like hell, so it'll take both of us."

Together, we put her on her side. She screamed as her weight fell on her fractured ribs, but after a moment or two she seemed to begin breathing a little easier. By then, the Rescue Squad had arrived.

"Hold her for a moment," I told the man.

I stood and ran over to the first ambulance.

"The woman in the minivan has a cut on her head, probably a concussion, too," I told the paramedic. "The one in the church lot may have internal injuries."

A second ambulance pulled up to the scene.

"Okay, Chief," the paramedic said. "We'll take it from here. Do us a favor and keep us from getting run over, okay?"

"You got it."

I heard the siren from the second Prosperity cruiser as Slim pulled up to the scene. I ran over to him as she rolled down the window.

"We'll route the traffic on Morgan Highway onto Howard Shore Road."

"What about the traffic on Pooler Highway?"

"I'll divert the incoming traffic onto the detour."

"What do we do about the people coming north from Mica Wells?"

"I'll call the Highway Patrol, see if they can spare a trooper to turn people off onto Copper Mine." He rolled up the window, did a U-turn, and headed back down the Morgan Highway.

One of the paramedics rushed up to me.

"They both need a hospital, Chief. We can take the woman in the minivan to the hospital in Morgan, but the girl needs the Trauma Center in Pooler. We should be able to transport in about five minutes."

I looked over toward the overturned car in the church lot, trying to find the ponytailed man who had attended to the girl with the chest injuries. I saw the paramedics who were strapping the girl down to a gurney for transport, but the man was nowhere in sight.

SIX

Donna and I had been invited to a get-together at Kent Kramer's house before the dust-up with Luther Steele, and Kent hadn't called to withdraw the invitation.

We pulled up to the Kramer estate off Ebenezer Church Road, in one of the newly minted McMansion developments that had popped up like toxic toadstools all over the county. There were three or four cars already in the driveway, so Donna parked her Honda at the curb. One of the cars was a low-slung affair with ten-inch tires and three times more engine than it needed. It looked as if it begged to be wrapped around a tree.

"The high rollers are here tonight, apparently," Donna said.

"So I hear. Kent's trying to persuade a couple of the Pooler Python players to move here. He thinks they'll lure more city folk out to the hinterlands."

"Hinterlands?"

"I read it in a book."

"You read a book?"

We reached the front stoop and I pushed the doorbell.

"Could have been a comic book," I said.

Kent's trophy wife, Crystal, answered the door. She had been Pooler's candidate for Miss North Carolina some years before, and she spent more in personal upkeep each year than I had spent on my last two cars. Her hair was blond, her teeth were pearly, and the skin on her face looked as if it had been stretched like the head on a bongo. I figured if she had one more facelift, she'd come home with a goatee.

"Judd!" she said as she hugged me and then Donna. "I'm so glad you could make it. Kent's out back tending the grill. Can I get you and Donna some drinks?"

"Beer's fine," I said.

"Some white wine, if you have it," Donna said.

"Come to the kitchen. We'll set you right up."

A couple of minutes later, we were ushered out the French doors to the backyard. Kent had installed a stone charcoal grill next to his swimming pool. Eight or nine people were scattered around the pool. Kent's son Seth had returned from summer training camp for the evening. He saw me from the other side of the pool and sulked.

Kent stood at the grill, a glass of brown liquor in his hand, talking to two men. One, a black man five or six inches taller than I am, looked like he'd left his spandex tights and cape somewhere else for the evening. The other was almost as tall, but more sinewy. Kent saw Donna and me walk through the French doors and said, "Judd, Donna, come over here. Some people I'd like you to meet."

We crossed the concrete patio to the grill.

"This is our chief of police here in Prosperity," Kent announced to his guests. "Judd, Donna, this here is Jermaine Coltes."

"Wide receiver for the Pythons," I explained to Donna as I grasped the black man's hand.

"Duh," she said.

He shook Donna's hand, somewhat more gently than I'd imagine.

"And this is Steve Samples," Kent said, introducing the other man. "He was the Pythons' second round pick this year. We're expecting big things from him this season."

"Chief," Samples said as he took my hand.

"Mr. Samples."

"Please, call me Steve."

"Kent told us you played quarterback for the Tarheels," Coltes said.

"About a quarter century ago, for two seasons," I said. "Got hurt and rode the pine for the last two years of my eligibility."

"Tough break," Samples said.

"Not so tough. I just had to find another way in the world."

"Jermaine contracted to buy a house here in Prosperity," Kent said. "He's moving into Bliss Ridge, soon as it's finished."

"Welcome to our town," I said.

"I probably would have moved out here anyway," Coltes said. "But Mr. Kramer made me an offer I couldn't refuse." He smiled.

I didn't. I knew Kent too well to find the humor in it.

"How about you, Steve?" Donna asked. "Have you decided where to live?"

"We're still in training camp," Samples said. "I haven't made the cut yet. I probably shouldn't spend money before I start making it."

"We're letting him stay in a place here in High Shoals," Kent said. "There's a corporate house two streets over that changes hands every year or so. Steve's going to be the guest of Kramer Development while he's in training camp. Soon as he signs a contract, we're gonna make him a property tax payer."

He grinned and slapped Samples between the shoulder blades, as if they had just come off the field after a fifty-yard touchdown play. Samples smiled weakly. I'd seen that same look before, on customers at a used car lot.

"What are we grilling tonight?" I asked.

Kent gave me a sly, conspiratorial smile.

"You are in for a treat. This is a special occasion. It isn't every day that I get a huge NFL star to move into the neighborhood. I ordered these prime steaks from a place in New York called Lobel's. They're all-American beef, but bred from some of those Japanese Kobe steers. They call it Wagyu."

"No hot dogs, then, huh?"

"Listen to him," Kent said to his athlete guests. "Talks like a hayseed, but I can tell you guys the Chief here loves a good steak more'n his grandma, you can bet. No, Judd, we ain't gonna grill no hot dogs tonight. This is going to be an experience that'll put your taste buds on the critical list for months. After this, nothin'll seem good enough. And expensive? You have no idea. Nothin' but the best at the Kramer house, though."

I nodded, paid my respects to Jermaine Coltes and Steve Samples again, and wandered around the pool. Donna, as she tended to do, let me go. She doesn't like to spend too much time in anyone's shadow.

I walked up to Seth Kramer, who sat in a lounge chair and sipped a Coke. He was a huge kid, with clear skin, a Tom Swift buzz cut, and flushed cheeks. He regarded me like some kind of virus.

"Glad to see you aren't drinking beer," I said.

"Training."

"I hear the Yellow Jackets are going to be pretty stout this season."

"They'll be all right."

"Bet you reckon they'll be better next year, when you get to suit up."

"You don't think so?"

"Just passing the time of day, Seth."

"Well, pass it somewhere else, okay?"

I took another sip of the beer. It was getting warm. I didn't care. "I'm here as your father's guest, Seth. Don't make me feel unwelcome."

"He don't care. You're just here so he can show you off to his

47

Pythons buddies."

I glanced at Kent, who was apparently boring Coltes and Samples with some story about his glory days at State.

"He wants them to know he has the police chief in his back pocket," Seth continued. "Wants them to think they can do what they want in Prosperity."

I nodded. "Yeah, I know."

"Is he right?"

I finished off the beer. "What do you think?"

"I think you love him like a brother," Seth said. "But I never saw you let him push you around."

"And I try to return the favor."

"So why you lettin' him parade you around like he bought you?"

"Your dad and I don't do things the same way. Can't say I always agree with his methods, but right now he needs me to help him look good to his customers. Out of friendship, I'm willing to play along. We both know what's what." I drained my beer and glanced back at his father. "Besides, if the steak's as good as he says, I can live with it."

SEVEN

Years ago . . .

The boy woke before sunrise.

He heard his father in the kitchen, a rattling of frying pans here, the closing of the refrigerator door there, a spoon dropping to a Formica counter.

The boy dressed quickly, in the clothes his father had left for him at the foot of his bed. He washed his face and slicked his hair with water, and pulled on the P.F. Flyers he had picked out at the department store in town the previous weekend. They felt stiff and they pinched his feet, but his father had warned him that they needed to be broken in. Today seemed like a good opportunity.

The boy found his father in the kitchen, frying bacon.

"Up early?" the father said.

"I don't want to miss it," the boy said.

"Don't reckon you will. Bacon and eggs with grits for breakfast ought to hold you to lunch, eh?"

The father checked the grits simmering on the back burner of the stove. He held the proper preparation of good stone-ground grits as a reverent task, much the way he approached most of his life.

"When is she coming?" the boy asked.

"Hard to say. You know how she is. Could be early. Could be late. Do me a favor and set the table."

The boy pulled knives and forks and spoons from a drawer in the cupboard next to the hand-hewn oak kitchen table, and found napkins in the other drawer. With practiced speed, he assembled the

49

table for breakfast.

In a few minutes, the father placed bowls of eggs and grits and a plate with strips of bacon on the table between them, first taking care to protect the tabletop from heat with cast iron trivets that had been in his family for generations.

The father took his seat across from the boy. Eagerly, the boy reached for the serving spoon for the grits.

"Uh-uh," the man said.

The boy's hand froze in midair.

The man folded his work-worn hands in front of him, and bowed his head.

The prayer was a long one, a custom to which the boy had become accustomed. He was in a hurry, though. What if she came while they were still eating? She might not want to wait.

Presently, the father completed his thanks to the Almighty and, with a wink, signaled to the boy that he could take the first helping.

The grits were steaming, with a pool of melted fresh butter in a spoon-formed crater, and the boy almost burned his mouth as he took the first bite. He steeled himself and wolfed his meal, finishing just as the first orange rays of sunlight peeked over the horizon and began to illuminate the fields beyond the house.

He rose to run to the door, but the father stopped him.

"Ahem," he said.

The boy turned around. The father pointed at the boy's plate and milk glass.

His shoulders slumping, the boy picked up his plate, glass, and flatware and took them to the sink. He rinsed them off, and left them on the counter for his father to complete the cleaning.

"Now?" he asked.

The father tried to suppress a smile.

"All right, then," he said.

The boy dashed to the door, allowing the screen to slam behind him, and tossed himself onto a chair on the front porch to wait for his mother.

The father watched him through the window. He lowered his head again and prayed that—this time—she wouldn't disappoint the boy.

EIGHT

An errant fly had invaded my office. It flitted from one window to another, but when I opened the door it refused to leave.

To pass the time, I took potshots at it with rubber bands.

I had about fifteen bands lying around on the floor when someone knocked on my door.

"Come in," I said.

A young man opened the door and walked in. At first I didn't recognize him, until he turned a quarter of the way around and I saw the ponytail.

"Have a seat," I said.

He crossed the room to the visitors' chairs at my desk.

"I'm Chief Wheeler," I said, extending my hand. "I didn't get a chance to thank you for helping that girl at the accident last week."

"How is she?"

"She'll recover. I have a feeling she'd like to thank you herself."

"No need," he said. He glanced around. "You have a bunch of rubber bands on your floor."

"You weren't supposed to notice that."

"Sorry, sir. My name's Carl Sussman."

"How can I help you, Mr. Sussman?"

"I'm here pursuant to Article 27A."

I leaned back in my chair a little.

"I'm just a small town cop," I said. "I skipped law school. You want to remind me what Article 27A is?"

"It's the . . . uh, the registration law."

"The sex offender registration law, you mean?"

"That's right, sir."

"I think you've been misled. You're supposed to register with the sheriff over in Morgan."

"I've been there. He said I might want to drop by and have a word with you."

"Why's that?"

"I'm planning to live in Prosperity."

"I see."

About ten years earlier, the North Carolina Legislature had passed a strict version of Megan's Law, which required all convicted sex offenders to register with the local sheriff's department within ten days of their parole from prison, or upon moving, changing jobs, or even getting a tattoo. Anything that would change their identifying information had to be reported.

"You just got out?" I asked.

"A week ago."

"Have a job?"

"Not yet. Don't really need one, actually. I have money."

"Do tell."

"I'm . . . I was in the high-tech business. I kind of struck it rich during the dot-com boom. As it happens, I was convicted before the bust, and I liquidated my holdings and placed them into savings just before I went to prison."

"Lucky you."

"Yeah," he said, smiling just a little. "Who knew getting convicted of rape would make me a rich man?"

"You want to tell me about the crime?"

He looked at the floor as he said, "I made a lot of money. It all came so quickly. I went from this socially inept computer nerd to multimillionaire in a little less than a year. I had no idea how to cope. I bought this big old house, threw parties like there was no tomorrow. Something I learned, Chief, is that when you've got it all, everyone loves you. I started to think I could do anything. You can have so much money that you have to think up ways to spend it. I found a great way."

He laid a finger alongside his nose and sniffed.

"Ah," I said.

"Yeah. I got high one night. There was this girl at the house. I don't even know how she got there. She asked if she could have a hit. I gave it to her. Then I started thinking she wanted a little more than just the blow. Once the idea got in my head, nothing she could say would make it go away."

"So, she accused you of getting her high so you could rape her."

"That's right. Only, that isn't the way it happened. I did get her high, but only because she wanted to."

"That's dangerous talk for a rapist, I hear."

"No, no. I don't want you to get that idea. The rest of it was completely me. Getting her high had nothing to do with the rape. I just made up my mind and I went ahead and did it."

"She told you to stop?"

"I suppose. I don't really recall. I just remember wanting to do it and nothing was going to get in my way. Between the cocaine and the power trip I was riding, I just felt . . . you know. Entitled."

"I know."

"The police came the next day. They told me the girl had filed a complaint. I fought it at first, claimed that she was trying to set me up to get money from me. At that point, I suppose it was all about the money. They arrested me, put me in jail. My attorney had me out in a couple of hours. He told me he'd only represent me if I quit using coke.

"So I dried out. The further I got from the drugs, the clearer

I saw stuff. I realized that, in all likelihood, I had raped her."

"You pled out?"

"The judge allowed me to drop the charge to second-degree sexual offense. Some guys, I suppose, might have drawn probation and treatment. The judge, though, said she was tired of seeing rich young guys get off with slaps on the wrist. She sent me away for five years."

"So you were guilty."

"Yes."

"And the sheriff suggested you come here so I'd know you were living in my community."

"That's right."

"You know how the law works, right?"

He nodded.

"Just to be sure, I have to recite it for you. You're on the State Sex Offender Registry for ten years after you get out of prison. During the time you're on parole, you must see your P.O. as scheduled. Any time you change your address, you update your file with the sheriff. Any time you change your hair color, you update your file. You knock out a tooth, you update your file. You understand all of that?"

"I have it memorized."

"Where are you planning to live in Prosperity?"

He looked up for the first time since starting his story. "I thought I'd build a house. I took some community college construction courses while I was in prison. I bought a piece of land over off Morgan Highway. Used to belong to a fellow named Donnie Clift. Bought it from his estate."

"Yeah," I said. "Donnie killed himself almost a year ago."

"That's what they told me. There's a mobile home on the property. Is that where he . . ."

I nodded then said, "I hear it's been cleaned up nicely. Still and all . . ."

"It's okay. Compared to prison, it's like a palace."

"There's something else."

He cocked his head.

"The notification thing," I said.

He dropped his head again. "Oh."

"Yeah. Donnie Clift's place is still a little isolated, but there are a couple of neighborhoods nearby. According to the statute, I have to inform them that you've moved in."

"I understand."

"They may not take kindly to the idea of having a rapist as a neighbor."

He leaned back in the chair and sighed a little.

"Maybe I can win them over," he said.

NINE

I was sitting in the new cruiser, which I'd parked in an empty driveway off Howie Branch Road, with the AC cranked to infinity. The weatherman had made a lot of noise this morning about record high temperatures, and had warned everyone who didn't have to be outside that they might want to stay inside.

I had to be outside. That's where I do most of my work.

I had the radar unit propped in the passenger side window, and once in a long while I'd glance up from the Donald Westlake novel I was reading to see if it had captured any dangerous speeders. It was a nod toward working, since I hadn't actually seen a car pass in over a half hour.

Through my windshield, the world looked as if someone had trained a magnifying glass on it. The grass was parched, and the trees sat motionless, their image wavering a bit in the heat risers. The kudzu that had crept across the landscape and climbed the electrical poles like some kind of verdant tumor looked wilted and parched. I placed my palm on the driver's side window, and pulled it back quickly.

What I really wanted was to chuck it all, drive home, and spend the afternoon swaying slowly in the Pawley's Island hammock under the black walnut tree in front of my house. I checked my watch. I still had a couple of hours before going off duty.

I couldn't concentrate, so I tossed the book on the bench seat next to me, and dropped the cruiser into drive. Out of curiosity, mostly, I tooled up Morgan Highway, over Six Mile Creek, and turned onto Bostian Road. I pulled into a gravel drive that—until almost a year earlier—had belonged to Donnie Clift.

Carl Sussman had bought a used pickup truck. It was parked in front of Donnie's old mobile home, looking old and sad and hot. There was an empty trailer behind it. I could see the depressions from metal tracks rolling up behind the trailer.

I got out of the cruiser and listened. Back behind the trailer, I could hear a diesel motor running. I hiked back, and saw Sussman sitting on a Bobcat, clearing brush and tree stumps.

He was shirtless, with his hair pulled back and wrapped in a bandana. I could see the crude outline of a second prison tat on his right shoulder, under the shiny glow of the sweat that covered his torso.

He didn't see me at first. I stood and watched for a few moments. He turned the Bobcat finally, and caught sight of me standing in the shade of a longleaf pine. He switched off the ignition.

"Chief," he said after dismounting and walking over. "I'm not in any trouble, am I?"

"Guilty conscience?"

"No. After a while, though, you get used to being blamed for stuff you never even dreamed yourself doing."

"Getting ready to build?" I asked, nodding toward the Bobcat.

"Just clearing the ground. I have a heavy equipment guy coming in tomorrow to grade the foundation lines. Figured I'd save him a little time and me a little money by giving him a clear field to work with."

"What kind of house are you building?"

"Come on inside. I'll show you the plans."

He led me around to the front of the trailer and up the treated pine steps to the front door. As he pulled it open, a draft of cool air blew out into the heat.

"Feels good, doesn't it?" he said as we walked in. "After sitting unused for a year, Donnie's central unit was pretty much shot. I installed a couple of big BTU window units. I prefer them anyway. The sound helps me sleep at night. The plans are on the kitchen table. Want something to drink?"

"Whatever's easy."

He pulled a couple of canned Cokes out of the refrigerator, and handed me one. Then he yanked a handful of paper towels off a roll hanging on the side of the refrigerator and wiped the sweat from his face and shoulders. He dragged them across his chest and tossed them into the trashcan. Then he stepped by me to the table and unrolled the plans.

"I drew them up while I was in prison," he said. "Took a CAD course there."

The house he planned was basically a single-story farmhouse with an attached wraparound porch under a gambrel roof. It was about sixty feet long by forty feet deep. Behind the house, the landscape architecture called for a pool surrounded by a rock garden.

"It isn't much," he explained as he pointed out the highlights. "Mostly, I worked off of stock designs I was able to download from the Internet. It'll have a living room and kitchen, a couple of bedrooms and a bath, and this addition off the back of the house will be storage and a workshop."

"You plan to build this by yourself?"

"Have to stay busy some way," he said, grinning. "I can live in the mobile home while I build, so I'm not in a big hurry. I plan to install pulleys about twenty feet up in the trees, to hoist the assembled exterior walls by myself, and I figure I can stick-build the interior walls, what there are of them."

I pointed to the fireplace in the main living quarters.

"You take masonry in prison, too?"

"You bet. It's strange, Chief. I spent almost all my life as a computer nerd, except for my stint as a corpsman in Kuwait. Went into the joint and learned to use my hands. I think I like the hands thing better."

"More money in computers."

"Money got me in this situation. I can live the rest of my life comfortably on my savings. I figure I don't need to make any more. This seems more fulfilling."

"A workshop, you said."

"For building furniture."

"Something else you picked up in the joint?"

"No. Never made a stick of it there. Read about it, though. Thought I'd like to give it a try."

I finished the Coke and placed the empty can down on the table.

"Well, just wanted to drop by, see what you're planning to do with the place."

He pulled off the bandana and dropped it on the counter. He scratched his head vigorously.

"It's all right," he said. "I know you have to check up on me. I've had a couple of deputies swing by already. They aren't comfortable with the idea of a convicted sex offender living all alone in a trailer off back in the woods."

"Just part of the job. Nothing personal."

"Any more word on that girl? The one in the wreck?"

"She's pretty banged up, but I hear she'll make it."

"That's good to hear."

"You stayed pretty cool out there."

"Shoot, Chief, that was nothing compared to holding some guy's intestines in his belly while the Iraqi National Guard is peppering your position with mortar fire."

I turned to the door. "Sounds like an interesting story. We'll save it for another time, though. I'm still on the clock. You keep it in the road, Carl, and we'll have no problems between us. Understand?"

"Yes, sir," he said.

Ten

Jermaine Coltes dropped by Steve Samples's upscale corporate house in High Shoals around five in the morning, two days after the cookout at Kent Kramer's house, to pick him up for the drive to Newberry for training camp.

He hadn't been inside the house fifteen seconds before he lurched out the back door and vomited in the pool.

When his head cleared, he yanked out his cell phone and called 9-1-1.

I was sound asleep when my telephone jangled next to the bed. In a second, I sat bolt upright. Years of training had left me with an acute awareness of what it means when the telephone rings before daylight. I glanced at the clock and grabbed the receiver.

"Chief Wheeler."

"This is Sheila, the dispatcher at the Sheriff's Department in Morgan."

"What's up, Sheila?"

"We have a 9-1-1 call. Sheriff Webb said we need to bounce it back your way. The caller says some guy's been murdered. Here's the address."

I wrote it down and switched the receiver to my other hand while I slipped my watch over my wrist one-handed.

"Okay, go ahead and call the ambulance. Tell Don to send some CSIs and a few deputies to handle crowd control. I'll be at the scene before they get there, coming from Morgan. Thanks for the heads-up."

By now, Donna was awake, but she hadn't sat up. I looked back at her. She was staring at me from her pillow.

"I have to go," I said. "Dispatcher in Morgan says there's been a murder."

"In Prosperity?" she said. "That makes two in one year."

"Town's going all to hell."

I stood and began to dress in a freshly cleaned and pressed blouse and uniform pants.

"You'll be careful," she said.

I never understood why women said that. It wasn't as if I were headed into battle. Something about the presence of death, I suppose.

"I'll be extra careful. Go back to sleep. I'll probably be most of the day. We'll get together for dinner tonight, okay?"

She murmured something that might have been agreement, but I could tell she was already halfway asleep.

The house Kent Kramer had provided for Steve Samples was three rows over in the High Shoals development, on a street named Appaloosa Trail. It was a silly name for a street in Prosperity, but I guess after a while you start to run out of ideas.

I had my lights and siren blaring even before I left my driveway, and I could see houselights flicker on in my wake as I turned onto Ebenezer Church Road, roared past Kent's house, and jerked the cruiser around the next corner.

I saw Jermaine Coltes waving for me at the end of Samples's driveway as soon as I turned onto Appaloosa Trail. I pulled into the drive and silenced the siren, but left the bubbletop twirling.

"It's awful," Coltes gasped as I climbed out of the cruiser. "Blood all over the place."

"Slow down. Tell me what's happened."

Coltes was on the verge of passing out from hyperventilation. I sat him down on the curb and waited for him to get his breath.

"I came by to pick Stevie up for training camp," he said. "We were supposed to be back in Newberry by seven-thirty. When I went inside . . . Jesus, Chief, it's like somebody's been slaughtering cattle in there."

"Okay," I said. "We'll take a look in a second. How'd you get inside?"

"Stevie gave me a key. He's a real sound sleeper. Sometimes he doesn't hear the clock, or even the phone. He said I should come in and make sure he's awake, and if he isn't I ought to yank him out of bed."

"I see. And when you went inside you found . . . what?"

"There's a body in there. It might be Stevie. I couldn't tell. It has to be him, though, right? I mean, who else would be in there?"

Far in the distance, I could hear the first faint wails of the ambulance from Morgan, and I thought I could make out the higher-pitched, faster-paced woops of the deputies' squad cars.

"You stay here," I said. "I'm going to take a look. The rescue squad and some sheriff's deputies will be here in a few minutes. I'll be right back."

I left him shivering on the curbside and walked up to the front door. It was unlocked. I decided Coltes had opened it himself, since he hadn't said anything about it being unlocked when he arrived.

I pulled out my nightstick and pushed the door open with it. My nose crinkled immediately, some kind of instinctive reflex to the faint odor of iron and organic chemicals that had suffused themselves into the air. I immediately regretted knowing that all smells are caused by aerosol particles, which meant I was huffing up parts of whatever body lay beyond the vestibule.

I hit every light switch I could find with the stick. In stages, the house went from murky and shadowed to nearly blinding light.

The first thing I saw was a long ochre smear of blood along one wall of the living room, looking as if someone had dragged the entire torso of a gutted deer along it. I glanced at the floor, to make certain I wasn't tramping through any pools of blood there. The CSI team from Morgan would kick my ass if I screwed up their crime scene.

I found the nude body on the other side of the living room, sprawled on the floor of the kitchen. A heavy steel meat cleaver was buried by its point in the heart pine floor. I could make out the torso, legs, and a couple of arms, but the head had been worked over with the meat cleaver to the point that it was nothing but ragged meat and splintered bone. Blood spatters a foot wide arced up the side of the refrigerator and across the cabinets. The body had sprawled face-down. I couldn't tell for certain that it was Steve Samples, but the shoulders were broad and the neck was thick, the way I recalled Samples to have looked at Kent Kramer's. The rest was impossible to distinguish as human, let alone Samples.

Out front, I could hear the sirens doused as the first of the emergency vehicles arrived. I slowly backed out the way I had come, careful not to disturb the site any more than I already had. I met the EMTs at the front door.

"Nothing for you to do in there," I said. "I'm cordoning off the scene. You guys hang loose and wait until I release you. Got it?"

The first of the paramedics nodded and said, "What happened?"

I glanced back through the foyer at the smears of blood on the living room walls. It was the kind of scene that led me to wonder whether every two-legged creature really had shared a common ancestor.

"Good question," I said.

Clark Ulrich and Sharon Counts, two Sheriff's Department CSIs who had worked the Gypsy Camarena murder the previous fall, arrived five minutes later. Ulrich was tall and broad and blond, with a round moon face and open blue eyes. Counts was his physical antithesis, a wiry, razor-faced woman with straight mousy hair and the evidence of way too much sun as a youth etching her prematurely aging features. Her eyes always looked distant and empty. I suspected she carried two or three hard lives in her past, and she wasn't even middle-age yet. I think I'd heard her say ten words in the last year. All of them had been laced with regret.

"I went in long enough to establish that the guy was dead," I said. "I tried not to disturb any evidence. You guys might want to wear masks. I have a feeling there's still a lot of him floating around in the air."

"Thanks, Chief," Ulrich said before they waded in. As I had come to expect, Sharon Counts didn't say anything.

Five minutes later, Ulrich returned to the front door.

"You can send the Rescue Squad boys home," he said. "We're going to be a while. I'll get the Sheriff's Department's meat wagon here to take . . . that stuff to the M.E.'s office."

The sun was peeking over the tops of the pine forest surrounding Appaloosa Trail, hard and red and foreboding. Drawn by the lights and the sirens, most of the neighborhood lingered on porches and in driveways, waiting for a glimpse of the tragedy that had befallen one of their own. A few of the more fearless ventured up the street toward Samples's driveway.

I turned to one of the deputies who had been dispatched from Morgan.

"This is a crime scene, gentlemen," I said. "I want to cordon off the entire yard, from the curb all the way back to the rear property line. I want these people, except for the immediate next-door neighbors, a hundred feet away at all times."

"Yes, sir," he said, and started directing his partners.

Jermaine Coltes remained seated on the curb.

"Let's go sit in my car," I said.

He followed me to the cruiser. I opened the passenger side door and held it for him as he slid in, his body almost leaden. The car rocked slightly over to the right under his considerable weight. Like many football stars, Coltes was a beast.

I pulled out my aluminum duty folder, turned to a fresh page in the legal pad, and took out a pen.

"Tell me from the very beginning," I said.

"Like I said, we were supposed to be at the training camp at Newberry College by seven-thirty. Normally, we would've been there already, but Stevie and I had permission to stay off campus last night on account of we were doing a publicity thing over in Pooler."

"Where was this publicity thing?"

"Why? Is it important?"

"Not knowing is important."

"It was at the River City Athletic Club. It was their annual awards dinner for the high school standouts."

I wrote it down.

"Did Steve talk with anyone in particular there? I mean, to say more than passing the time of day?"

"Jeez, Chief, I don't know. Once we got there, we kind of got taken in different directions. They even sat us at different tables for the dinner."

"Did Steve drink?"

"Just a beer. Come to think of it, it was probably an alcohol-free beer. He said something about not wanting to take the edge off."

"What did he mean by that?"

"You know. He hasn't made the team yet. He's still in competition for his position. He didn't want to go groggy or anything, so he didn't drink alcohol."

"What about you? Did you drink?"

"Just a beer. Only one."

"No edge to take off?"

"My position is pretty safe this season, Chief."

"How did you and Steve get back and forth from the dinner?"

"They sent us a limo."

"What time did this limo bring you back?"

"I'm not sure. Not later than midnight, I know that."

I scribbled some notes down, slowly allowing a timeline to begin forming in my mind.

"Okay," I said, "So you got up this morning around . . . what?"

"Four o'clock. I set my clock for that, and I didn't hit the snooze."

"Must have been tough to hold yourself back at four A.M."

"Not so hard. You get used to early hours in training camp. I took a shower and got dressed."

"You didn't call Steve before coming over? Tell him you were on your way?"

"No. I had a key. He probably wouldn't have answered the phone anyway."

"Why's that?"

He looked over at me, momentarily panic-stricken. "Chief, I don't mean it that way."

"What way?"

"I don't mean he wouldn't have answered the phone on account of being dead or anything. I mean he wouldn't have answered the phone because he's such a sound sleeper."

"Relax," I said. "I'm not accusing anyone of anything right now. I'm just trying to pull all the information together that I can while everything's still fresh."

"You saw that body in there?"

"Yes," I said. "Yes I did."

"You think that was Stevie Samples?"

"I think it probably was. I didn't see his face."

"Who would do something like that to another person? He was hacked up like barbeque pork."

"How long were you inside the house?"

"Maybe fifteen seconds. I'm afraid I got . . . you know. Sick."

"Where?"

"In the pool. I saw that body in the kitchen, and I felt my stomach turn flat over. I raced out the back door to the pool to get my breath, but it was too late. There went my breakfast."

"In the pool."

"Yeah. It wasn't like I had a lot of time to think about it, Chief."

"So you got back around midnight, and five hours later you arrived here and found Steve chopped up."

"That's right."

"Did he say anything about expecting visitors last night?"

"Not a word."

"So you were the last person to see him alive."

"You mean besides whoever killed him."

I didn't say anything.

Coltes eyes grew wide.

"Chief. You don't think I'm a suspect?"

"Right now everyone's a suspect, except for me. I know *I* didn't do it. You could sure make my job a lot easier if you'd confess or something."

"Don't even joke about that."

"I was only half joking."

Someone knocked on my window. I turned my head to find Kent Kramer standing by the car. I cranked the window down.

"This is a crime scene, Kent. Please step behind the yellow tape."

"I own this house, Judd," Kent said. "I need to know what's happening. Why's Jermaine in the car with you?"

"Please," I said, trying to put a little more steel in my voice. "Step behind the yellow tape. I'm conducting an investigation, and I don't have time to talk right now."

"Hold on," Kent started. I suppose he said some more, but I couldn't hear it because I'd cranked the window back up.

"You can piss in his grits like that?" Coltes asked.

"Yes."

"He don't fire you or nothing?"

"He can't fire me. I work for the Town Council. Who did Steve hang out with here in town? I mean, besides you?"

"I don't know. He was so busy with training camp, trying to make the team, he didn't have a lot of time to get to know people. Most of the time, we stay in the dorms down at the college in Newberry."

I thought for a second.

"Samples is a cornerback, right?"

"That's right. He can also play free safety, but he isn't competing for that position on the team."

"Who is his primary competitor for the position at cornerback?"

"What? You think he might have been killed by one of the other players?"

"I don't know that he's dead, truth be told. All I saw was a lot of blood. If that is Steve Samples in there, I'd imagine there are at least a couple of cornerbacks in Newberry who just got bumped up the cut list."

Coltes shook his head. "I don't see it. Stevie was a second-round pick. By that point the teams aren't dicking over Upland Trophy winners. At best, he was going to be third string this year. Coach likes to develop his players, and Ryan Kiper is still in good shape."

Ryan Kiper was the Pythons' star defensive player. He was famous for his vertical leap, which had allowed him to lead the league in interceptions the previous season.

"So Kiper's going to be first string again this year."

"Yeah, and second string is pretty secure, too. That's what I meant. At best, Stevie would have been third string."

"So I want to look at the fourth and fifth best cornerbacks."

"I don't think so. The organization keeps a pretty tight lid on training camp. Once you arrive on campus, you're pretty much there until you get cut, or the team needs you to make an appearance somewhere."

"Like the one you and Steve made last night?"

"That's right."

"Okay. I'll check with the team officials, see if any other players were allowed off campus last night. Have you called to let the team know you won't be there?"

"Yeah. I called while the crime scene folks were inside the house."

"You didn't tell them Steve was murdered, did you?"

"Not exactly. I told them someone had been killed at his house."

"Who did you talk to?"

"Harve Lucanian. He's the offensive coordinator."

"I know. Give me his telephone number."

"Why?"

"I need to ask him to keep this under his hat until we know what's going on."

Coltes recited Lucanian's number and I wrote it down.

"So, besides you, Samples didn't have any friends here in

Prosperity?"

"Well . . ."

"What?"

"He knew the Kramers, of course. Mr. Kramer is putting him up while he's in training camp."

"Ah ha," I said.

"What?"

"Cop talk. That'll be all for now, Mr. Coltes."

"Please, call me Jermaine."

"Maybe after this whole thing is over. If you'd like to step out of the car, I think I can make time now for Mr. Mayor."

"That's twice in one week you've blown me off, Judd," Kent complained as he closed the car door. "I can't say I like it."

"You still don't get it," I said. "When I'm interviewing a witness, you don't figure in the picture, unless you're the witness. Which brings us to our current conversation."

"What?"

"Here's what I know right now. Someone was murdered in that house last night. The hot money says it was Steve Samples."

For a second, I thought Kent was going to cry.

"What happened?" he asked.

"It's too early to say. According to Jermaine Coltes, Samples didn't know many people here in Prosperity. He did know you. When was the last time you spoke with Samples?"

"Yesterday. Why?"

"What was the nature of the conversation?"

"He dropped by the house for a few minutes. He was out running."

"What time was this?"

"I don't know. Around five. I had just gotten home."

"Who else was at your house?"

"Crystal and Seth. Why?"

"Just being complete. What did you and Samples discuss?"

"There was a problem with the house. Nothing major. He had seen a water spot on one of the upstairs ceilings. He wanted to let me know so I could have it fixed."

"A water spot?"

"It's a new house. It happens. When they nail the roofing shingles in place, sometimes you get a leak. I told him I'd take care of it."

"Did he talk with Crystal or Seth?"

"I don't know. I excused myself for a few minutes. He might have talked with them then."

"Why'd you excuse yourself?"

Kent stared at me.

"Why'd you excuse yourself?" I repeated.

"To go to the bathroom, okay?" he said, irritated.

"For a few minutes."

Again the stare.

"All right," he said at last. "I'm having a little . . . trouble. You know. Prostate."

I nodded and made a note.

"You're not putting that in a report, are you?"

"Just a note," I said. "Might be important, might not."

"Now how in hell could something like that be important in a murder investigation?"

"Can't say. But it would sure be embarrassing if I ignored it and found out later it was a clue. I'm going to need to talk with Crystal and Seth."

ELEVEN

The CSI team was still raking through Steve Samples's house, looking for any small clues that might have been hidden in the carnage. The outside thermometer in the police cruiser had already hit the triple digits when I had turned into Kent's driveway. As I pulled myself out of the car, it was like stepping into a crematorium.

It was lunchtime. My breakfast had been a pack of nabs and a coke. I tried to stanch the rumbles from my stomach as I sat in Kent Kramer's living room with his son.

Seth Kramer always regarded me as if I'd shot his favorite dog.

At one level I could understand. I awoke every day with a subconscious expectation that the boy was bound to be arrested for some abomination before the sun set, and I probably treated him that way. Seth had many positive qualities, almost all of them physical. You could barely dampen the soles of your feet wading the depths of his soul, though, and you'd want to scrape them clean afterward.

I suppose I shouldn't have laid all the blame on him. He was, after all, brought up in a household that worshiped at the Altar of the Almighty Dollar. His mother, a sweet-natured woman whom Kent had met at college, might have tempered Seth's egocentricities. Unfortunately, she was as subject to the ravages of time as any of us, and after Kent acquired the bulk of his riches she didn't fit in with his self-image as a successful *bon vivant.* She had been ushered out, Crystal had been ushered in, and in some small way I suppose that event served as well as any to seal Seth's fate.

On the other hand, I have learned to be cautious when it comes to citing life circumstances as the cause of people's character faults. That was the way of the social worker. Sometimes, I had determined, we are what we are, and more often than not what we are is simply a matter of the fruit not falling far enough from the tree.

"Thought you'd be back at training camp," I said.

"Being redshirted, I don't have to be there as often. They'll work my ass off on the practice squad once the season starts."

"When do you move into the dorms at Atlanta?"

"Second week in August. You want to ask your questions? I have things to do."

I opened my metal duty folder and made a show of checking my notes.

"You know what happened last night," I said.

"No. I heard that someone killed Steve Samples."

"That's probably true. Someone was murdered at his house. The medical examiners will establish who it was, but nobody's seen Steve, so I'd say it's a good bet it was him."

"How'd they do it?" Seth asked, and I suspected that his curiosity was more than a little morbid.

"The deceased was bludgeoned and chopped with a meat cleaver. That's not for public disclosure, Seth."

"Whatever. You think I had something to do with it?"

"Why do you ask?"

"Seems you always suspect me of something, Chief. I reckon if a meteor hit this town you'd be rooting around my closet looking for a space suit."

"Well, not this time. Not yet, at least. I'm just talking with everyone who associated with Steve since he moved here."

"Why?"

"Because they know him better than I do. How did you and Steve get along?"

"He's okay. Hell, he's only four years older than me. He could be my brother. So, we got along all right."

"Besides the dinner here the other night, did you and he associate any?"

"I've been to his house once or twice. I'm telling you this because I know you're going to find my fingerprints there. Don't mean nothing. My dad owns the house, and I've been there a bunch."

"When were you there last?" I asked.

He stared at me. Then he shook his head.

"Sure. Okay. I was there last night. All right?"

"Why did you go last night?"

"Needed to borrow a meat cleaver."

He grinned at me, like he'd made a funny joke. I corralled my impulse to dump him on the floor and cuff him on general principles. Instead, I kept my face stony.

"All right, all right," he said, his face back to sullen. "No fuckin' sense of humor. I knew Steve was coming in from training camp to go to that awards dinner. He called and asked whether I'd like to come by afterward, watch a movie."

"What time did you get there?"

"About midnight."

"Did you watch your movie?"

"Yeah. I picked up a video of *Dawn of the Dead.* Steve likes horror flicks."

"So what time did you leave?"

"Around two in the morning. I was worn out on account of I had to do some work for my dad yesterday."

I made some notes on the pad.

"Did you and Samples do any drinking?" I asked.

"No. Well, I had a Sprite, and he had some iced tea, but no alcohol."

"Drugs?"

"No way! You have any idea how closely the NFL watches that kind of thing after that Ricky Williams shit? Steve wanted to make the Pythons team. He'd have put a gun in his mouth before toking up."

"The initial evaluation from the crime lab people shows that whoever got hacked in Steve's house last night was killed between three and four o'clock. Let me ask you something, Seth. Were you and Steve alone in that house?"

He looked over my shoulder at the door, as if he weren't certain whether to answer.

"Seth, this is a murder investigation. You don't want to get jammed up with an obstruction charge just because you want to be a stand-up guy."

"There was someone else," he said. "Actually, a couple of people."

"Who were they?"

"A couple of girls."

I nodded, acknowledging that we were venturing into all-too-familiar territory. Seth's procurement talents had been well established the previous year, when he had arranged for Gypsy Camarena and her friend Anita Velez to be the main attraction at a sex party with most of the Prosperity Glen High football team.

"Steve is a stranger around here," Seth said, attempting to defend himself. "He doesn't know anyone. A guy's got needs."

"Who were they?" I asked.

"Ann Koehler and Tracy Wall," he said. "I know them from last year."

"You have phone numbers for these girls?"

"I have them. Upstairs. Both girls live over in Morgan."

I wrote a couple of notes.

"Tell me everything," I said.

He looked around, as if some kind of exit portal might miraculously open in the floor. After a moment, he sighed and said, "It started the other night, at the cookout. Dad took Coltes into the house for a few minutes to show him some stuff from his own hot-shit football days."

I thought I noted a sneer in Seth's voice. Maybe I just expected it. Seth didn't seem to respect much of anyone or anything. It was the kind of personality flaw that was someday going to bite him on the ass.

"Steve looked bored. He started up a conversation with me. I guess I was the only person there close to his age. We started talking about high school ball versus college ball. Since I'm on the five-year plan at Tech, I figured I could pick his brain.

"Turns out Mr. Clean is a real horn dog. He told me that when he was playing at Texas he could get all the women he wanted, sometimes two at a time. Said that the people who ran the athletic dorm turned a blind eye when he'd walk girls in the door, because he was such a star. This is just between you and me, right?"

"Wrong," I said. "It all goes in the report."

"Hell, Chief, the guy's dead. Why go around draggin' through his dirt?"

"I didn't say the report was public record. But I do have to know what you talked about, and how these two girls wound up at his house."

"All right, okay. I should know by now you're gonna do what you're gonna do. So Steve tells me that the Pythons' defensive coach—"

"Lucanian."

"Yeah, him. Steve says this guy is real old school, runs a super-tight camp. Says girls weaken the legs, and he's imposed some kind of bullshit curfew. Steve told me he'd been at camp for almost a month with no pussy. What's worse, when they did let him come to the house here in Prosperity for a day or so, he didn't know anyone. He couldn't call an escort service, 'cause if he did it would be all over the newspapers the next day.

"I told him I knew some girls that like to party. He asked me if I'd arrange to bring them over next time he had a night off. He called me yesterday morning. Told me that he had to do the banquet in Pooler, and wondered if I could come around with some girls when he got home."

"Which you were happy to do."

"Hell, Chief. Steve Samples is in the *show*. How many chances do you get to make points with someone who can put in a good word for you down the road? I called these two girls, Ann and Tracy, and asked whether they'd like to spend time with a real pro football player. I could hear them get juicy over the phone. Neither one of them waited a second to say yes."

"What happened when you got there?"

"Like I told you, we watched a movie, and by the time it was over, it was like two o'clock. Steve said he had to get up at four-thirty, so we left."

"That's all?" I asked, in a tone that made it clear that I was certain it wasn't all.

"Well, Samples and Ann disappeared for a few minutes during the movie."

"How many minutes?"

"Hell, Chief, I don't know. A few. I suppose he could have knocked boots with her. If his dry spell had been as long as he said, he'd probably have gotten off pretty quick. It's not like I followed them and watched."

"Where did they go?"

"Upstairs. Just for a few minutes, like I said. Probably not more than ten, fifteen at the most."

"Did both girls leave with you?"

"Yeah. I took them home."

"And that was around two o'clock?"

"Yeah."

"Was there any drinking while you were there?"

"The girls had a couple of beers, but Steve only drank iced tea, like I told you. I drank Sprite, on account of training."

"Like at your house the other night."

"Exactly."

"Okay," I told him. "I need you to get those numbers for me."

TWELVE

The boy looked at the Timex watch his father had bought him for his last birthday. Nine-thirty-eight. It was July, and as humid as the inside of a sharecropper's boot.

His father had checked in on him around seven-thirty before heading out to the fields. Two hours later, the boy still waited on the front porch. His bladder was full, but he didn't want to run inside to pee. He was afraid he wouldn't be on the porch when his mother pulled into the driveway, that she might think he wasn't waiting for her, and she might turn around and go back.

Again.

The air was still and close. He could feel the heat of the day building into a palpable thing that began to seep through his clothes and pick at his skin. He ran his hand through his close-cropped hair. His palm came away soaked.

He didn't really understand why his mother no longer lived in the house. The explanations his father offered hadn't made sense. From what he could gather, the boy thought it sounded as if his mother had done something awful, but also that his father hadn't made her go away. According to his father, his mother simply decided she couldn't stay.

It was all more than a seven-year-old boy could be expected to understand.

Off in the distance, the boy could hear the diesel thrum of the father's tractor. There were stumps to be pulled, his father had told him at breakfast. There was no time to wait on the porch with the boy.

In the moments when the tractor was silent, the only noise that could be heard was the rise and fall of the cicadas' calls, and the boy's own labored breathing.

Every several minutes, he would hear a car in the distance, and he'd strain his eyes, trying to see as far down the highway as possible. His mother's car was blue, he knew, and he waited eagerly for a first glimpse.

Each time, the car was either not blue or it didn't slow as it approached the drive.

Ten o'clock.

If I had gone to the bathroom fifteen minutes ago, *the boy thought,* I wouldn't have to go now. The longer I wait, the more likely it is that she'll come while I'm peeing.

When he couldn't wait a second longer, he dashed through the screen door and down the short hall to the bathroom.

Moments later, he returned to his seat on the porch, relieved but fearful that he might have missed her.

THIRTEEN

By the time I left the Kramer house, the sun was high overhead, and beat down on me like a fiery cudgel.

I sat in the cruiser and waited for the air conditioning to kick in. The back of my uniform felt tacky and steamy. I didn't dare touch the steering wheel, at least until the vents had blasted it for a couple of minutes.

Back at the crime scene, I parked next to the Bliss County CSI truck and waited. I knew better than to check in on the sheriff's crime scene people. If I so much as placed one foot inside the doorway, they'd run me out like mockingbirds protecting the nest.

I pulled out my cell phone and, after checking the phone numbers Seth had given me, called Ann Koehler. A woman who sounded considerably older than the girl Seth had described answered the call.

"This is Chief Judd Wheeler of the Prosperity Police Department," I said. "Could I speak with Ann Koehler, please?"

"Why? What's happened?" the woman asked.

"Who's speaking?"

"This is Betty, Ann's stepmother. Is she in some kind of trouble?"

"I don't know. Could I speak with her, please?"

"I'm afraid not. She didn't come home last night."

I think I might have raised my eyebrows. On the other hand, what with the heat and all, I might not have been willing to

83

waste the energy.

"Are you certain?" I asked. "I just spoke with a young man here in Prosperity who said that he dropped her off at her home around two-thirty."

"Well, if he did, she was gone again by six. That's when I got up to go to the bathroom and checked on her."

"Miz Koehler, I'm going to leave you my telephone number. When Ann comes in, could you have her call me immediately?"

"Of course. Can't you tell me anything?"

"I need to get some information from her about where she was last night. I need to corroborate another person's story."

"So she's not in trouble with the law?"

"Not yet. Please have her call me."

I had better luck with Tracy Wall. She was the only person at her house, and I caught her asleep.

"Uh-huh," she said drowsily as she picked up the receiver.

"Tracy Wall, please?"

"This is Tracy."

I introduced myself. She apparently woke up very quickly and said, "The police?"

"Yes. I need to ask you a few questions. Will you be at your home this afternoon?"

"I don't plan to leave before five o'clock. I'm on the closing shift at Waffle King."

"I hope to be able to get by long before that," I said.

As I was about to say goodbye, I thought of something else. "By the way, is Ann Koehler there with you?"

"No."

"Have you seen her since about two-thirty this morning?"

"No."

There was an uncertainty in her voice. I couldn't tell whether she wasn't sure she hadn't seen Ann, or if she was hiding something.

"Ms. Wall, this is very important. If you have some information on where I might find Ann Koehler, you need to give it to me."

"I . . . I don't know for sure where she is. I can try to find her, though. I may know something when you come this afternoon."

"All right. Give me your address."

An hour later, I was considering making a quick run to Gwen Tissot's Stop and Rob on Morgan Highway for a couple of slices of pizza, when Clark Ulrich and Sharon Counts walked under the yellow crime scene tape. Sharon headed straight for the CSI truck. Clark stopped at the meat wagon, said something to the attendants, and then walked over to my cruiser.

Reluctantly, I rolled down the window.

"Scorcher today," Clark said as he leaned against the car.

"And it's barely afternoon," I said.

"Every summer, right around mid-to-late July, we see a spike in violent crime. Go figure. Must be the heat that does it."

"Any new information you can share?"

He looked at his pad. "Ninety-nine percent probability that it's Steve Samples. We're running the prints now. Pythons have all kinds of information on file, and they're cooperating. We should know for certain in an hour or so. We found his clothes on a chair in the bedroom, with his wallet, keys, and some cash in his pants pocket. Want to hear something interesting?"

"Can you keep it short? All my cold air is getting out."

"Yeah, I know. That's why I'm standing here. Feels good. The interesting thing, first of all, is that the money is still there."

"Not a robbery," I noted.

"Most likely not. On the other hand, a couple of bills had

blood on them."

"That is interesting. Think it's Samples's blood?"

"Can't say for certain. There isn't any blood on the pants or any of the other clothes, and we didn't find any on the stairs or furniture upstairs. We'll try to run the DNA against Samples's blood, see if there's a match."

"Rage killing," I said.

Clark glanced back at the house, as we both recalled the grisly crime scene inside.

"You think? They chopped up that boy like they were making cornerback salad. Two, three dozen blows maybe. After a certain point, it's all kind of overkill."

"Could be drugs," I said. "There are drugs that will just make you lose all sense of perspective."

"True. Something about this killing, though, feels personal. Know what I mean?"

"Yes," I said. "I do."

FOURTEEN

The morgue boys loaded what was left of the body into the ambulance, and drove out to Morgan Highway. They didn't run the lights or the siren. Guess there wasn't much of a rush. I wondered whether they might even hit a burger drive-through on the way to Morgan.

I didn't think about it for long. The image was too grisly.

When I got back to the station, I found a man waiting for me. He was tall and broad, with a head of salt and pepper hair cut close to the scalp, and a handlebar moustache. He was dressed in slacks, sneakers, and a short-sleeved shirt with a Pooler Pythons logo. He stood as I walked in the door.

"This man has been waiting to see you," said Sherry, my civilian administrative assistant.

He extended his hand. "Harve Lucanian," he said. "I'm the defensive coordinator for the Pythons."

"I recognized you from the television," I said as I shook hands with him. "Let's step back to my office."

He followed me into the office and took a seat across from my desk. The wood creaked as he settled into it.

"Can you tell me anything?" he asked.

"Not really," I said as I leaned back in my chair. "Your wide receiver, Jermaine Coltes, found a body in Steve Samples's house around five this morning. They've taken the body to the medical examiner over in Morgan. They're running prints on it now, but we don't know for certain that it's Samples yet."

"But nobody's seen Samples."

"No. Which probably means the body is his, or he killed someone and ran."

"I can't see that. I . . . I guess the body was pretty bad off, then. I mean, if you can't identify it without fingerprints."

"It was bad off," I said. "I can't go into details right now."

Lucanian ran a meaty paw across his brow.

"This is just awful. Steve has . . . *had* a great future. We decided to bring him along slowly, give Ryan Kiper one more year in the Pro Bowl, maybe make the Hall of Fame, and then rotate Steve into the cornerback position. Ryan's looking at coaching down the line. He was looking forward to mentoring Steve Samples. Please let me know if you find out it was Steve got killed. I recruited that boy out of Oklahoma. Spent a lot of time talking with him and his parents. If someone needs to call his folks, break the bad news, I'd rather it be me."

"I appreciate it," I said. "It's a duty I really don't enjoy. From what I understand, Steve didn't stand much of a chance of going higher than third string this year."

"That's right, unless Ryan or Aidan Wyche gets hurt. Which is very possible, if you know the game."

"I know the game," I said. "Who's competing with Samples for the third-string spot?"

"Just one guy, really. Jake Tupper, a second-year guy out of Pitt . . . but, wait a minute, Chief. You don't suspect Jake."

"Sure I do. I suspect everyone. I suspect you. I suspect John Madden. Basically, I'm the only person I know who positively didn't commit this murder. Everyone else has to be cleared. I would like to know where Jake Tupper was between midnight and five o'clock this morning."

"That's easy enough. All the team members except for Steve and Jermaine stayed on the college campus last night. Practice starts pretty early in the morning, and everyone had a nine o'clock curfew."

"Do the players have private rooms in the dorms, or do they buddy up?"

"They have private rooms. The dorm they use is closed to students during the summer session, and there's plenty of space for each player to get his own room."

I didn't say anything. I waited for him to process what he had just said.

"No," he said. "I won't believe it. Besides, we sign the guys in each night when they come back to the dorm. There's a fine for being late for curfew. We'd have a sign-in sheet available that would say exactly when Jake checked in."

"What floor is he on?"

"Well, I'm not sure. I'll have to check. What are you saying? You think maybe Jake checked in, then climbed out a window, drove here, killed Steve Samples, and then drove back?"

"Is it possible?"

He thought about it for a moment.

"Well, if he's on the first floor of the dorm, I suppose."

"Where do the players park their cars when they're at training camp?"

"In a fenced lot. Some of these guys have high-priced wheels."

"Is the lot guarded?"

"Yes, in the daytime. At night it's patrolled every thirty minutes or so by the college security force."

"What about video monitoring? Any TV cameras?"

"Yeah."

"So, if Jake Tupper did leave the dorm, and if he took his car, it would be on a surveillance tape, right?"

"I guess."

"Okay," I told him. "I'm coming to the college sometime in the next day or so. I want to talk with Tupper. I also want to see that security tape. If you have any trouble getting it from college security, tell them to call me."

"You don't really think Jake Tupper killed Steve Samples, do you?"

"Can't say. I do know that I'd looked damned stupid if he did, and I didn't follow up on an obvious lead pointing to him."

FIFTEEN

After Lucanian left, I wrote up the report of my preliminary investigation into the murder, and then climbed into the cruiser to make a call on Tracy Wall in Morgan.

She lived in a Craftsman-style bungalow in one of the older parts of town, which probably would have been referred to as the historic district, if Morgan ever felt compelled to resort to pretense.

The house was well-kept, with a deep front porch and casement windows on each side of a massive mahogany cottage door. I rapped on the door a couple of times with a heavy brass knocker.

After a few moments, the door opened a few inches, and a teenage girl peered out through the crack.

"Tracy Wall?" I asked.

"Yes."

"I'm Chief Wheeler from Prosperity. I called you earlier today."

She unlatched the chain, opened the door wider, and said, "Come on in."

She looked eighteen or nineteen. She wore a tight knit shirt that stretched over her braless breasts and cutoff jeans. She was barefoot. Her toenails were painted copper. Her fingernails had been chewed to distraction.

"Are your parents home?" I asked.

"No. They work."

"When do you reckon they'll get in?"

"Dunno. Could be a couple of hours. Maybe more."

"How old are you?"

"Eighteen."

"Okay, then. I suppose it's all right to question you without them being present. You and a girl named Ann Koehler visited Steve Samples last night over in Prosperity."

I tried carefully not to phrase it as a question. She was more likely to tell me useful things if she thought I already knew them.

"Yeah."

"What time did you get there?"

"Sometime around midnight. This guy from Prosperity picked us up."

"Seth Kramer."

More sagacity. Before I was finished, this girl would think I knew her entire life history.

She nodded.

"And what time did you leave?"

"Around two, I think. I had a couple of beers."

She stopped. Drinking is illegal for people under twenty-one in North Carolina.

"Relax," I said. "This isn't about underage drinking."

Ironically, I realized that if Steve Samples hadn't been murdered, it would be about underage drinking. Providing minors with alcohol would have killed his pro career.

"Did Ann Koehler leave with you at two o'clock?"

"Yes. She and I rode back with Seth."

"How was Steve Samples when you last saw him?"

"Sleepy. He said he had to get up early. He had to go to training camp."

"What did you do at his house for the two hours you were there?"

She gnawed on one tortured nail then said, "Nothin' much. We watched a movie."

"Did Steve drink alcohol?"

"No."

"At any point, did you and Steve go upstairs?"

"No. Ann went upstairs with him, though."

"Did she say what they did?"

"Is Ann in some kind of trouble?"

I looked up from the legal pad on which I had been taking notes.

"Why? Is there some reason she might be?"

"No. I mean, she didn't do nothin' with that football player, if that's what you mean. She said they just talked for a few minutes. I was kind of surprised she went up there, to tell the truth, because she's kind of engaged."

"Engaged."

"Yeah. Well, not officially. Not with a ring or nothin'. But they've talked about it."

"Who is she supposed to be marrying?"

"Ricky Chasen."

"What can you tell me about Ricky?"

"Not a lot. He's been around for a while. I heard he went to jail a few years back, but he's all cleaned up now. He even works for some kind of church."

"I see," I said as I took notes. "You wouldn't happen to know how I can reach him, would you?"

"No. Ann would, though. I mean, of course she would, you know, bein' engaged to him and everything."

"Right," I said.

By that point, I'd pumped about all the information out of Tracy that she was likely to yield. I thanked her for her assistance without divulging that her host from the previous evening was now lying on a steel table at the morgue, and returned to my cruiser.

First, I turned the air on full blast. Then I toggled the button on my microphone and called Sherry at the station.

"Hey, Chief," she said.

"I need you to contact the Sheriff's Department in Morgan, and ask them to fax us a jacket on a kid named Ricky Chasen. Probably in his early twenties. Pulled a stretch within the last couple of years."

"Can do, Chief."

Then, I pulled out the cell phone and tried to call Ann Koehler. I got her stepmother again, who said that Ann still hadn't shown up. That bothered me a little. On the other hand, she was a teenage girl, a population from which consistency was rarely expected, so I just asked Missus Koehler to have Ann call me as soon as she came in. I included a veiled *or else* in my tone.

I didn't have an "or else," of course. Fortunately, she didn't need to know that.

Since I was already in Morgan, I drove over to the Bliss Regional Medical Center, and made my way to the basement, where Carla Powers served as the chief medical examiner for the county.

The waiting room at the morgue was empty, as was usually the case. I had tripped an electric eye when I entered, which alerted Carla that she had a visitor. I took a seat, and waited for a couple of minutes.

She chuckled a little as she came into the room.

"I was wondering how long it would take you to get here," she said.

"I was in the neighborhood. Have you had a chance to look at my dead guy yet?"

"You mean Steve Samples?"

"You've conclusively identified him?"

"The fingerprint info came in about a half hour ago. This is about as bad as I've ever seen someone worked over. What did they use, an axe?"

"Meat cleaver."

She winced then said, "He sure must have pissed off someone."

"That was my thought. I've already met with a representative from the Pythons, who's given me one or two names, and it turns out Samples spent some time last night with a Morgan girl who has an ex-con boyfriend."

"It's a start."

"That it is. The scene was pretty gory. I was wondering whether you'd been able to make an initial examination. Are there any defensive injuries?"

"Sorry. We're still processing the body. It will probably be tomorrow before we can really look him over head to toe . . . or *whatever* to toe, that is."

"You pathologists have a sick sense of humor."

"Now you know why I can't get any dates. Speaking of which, what's up with you and the teacher lady?"

Sixteen

I found the teacher lady lounging on the wicker chaise on the front porch of my house when I got there. She was reading a book and sipping a Pepsi from the bottle through a straw. The porch faces east, which means it's about the coolest part of the house in the late afternoon. I suppose she could have gone inside and enjoyed the air conditioning, but Donna is the outdoors type.

"Tough day?" she asked as I trudged up the steps.

"The toughest."

"I heard about it on the TV news. It sounds terrible."

"You kind of had to be there."

"Meaning you aren't going to spill any of the gory details."

"God, you are a perceptive woman."

I loosened my Sam Brown and hung it over the arm of the chair next to the chaise, and then unbuttoned and pulled off my sweat-stained blouse. I sat next to her on the chaise in my uniform trousers and T-shirt.

"It was a scorcher," she said, fanning herself with a magazine.

"Yep."

"Weather reports says it's going to be hotter tomorrow."

"So I hear."

"You need to put in a swimming pool, Chief."

I looked over at her. "A swimming pool!"

"You heard me."

"Now what in hell would I do with a swimming pool? We

have a perfectly good pond over the hill, back of the house."

"Well, hell, let's go swimming," she said.

She stood and grabbed my hand and tried to pull me from the chaise.

"I'm too tired to get a suit," I said.

"Shoot, Judd, there's fifty acres of nothing in every direction from that pond. Who's going to see us?"

After a cool dip and a rinse in the shower, I made dinner. It was too hot to turn on the stove or fire up the grill. Instead, I whipped up some tuna salad and stuffed it into a couple of hollowed-out beefsteak tomatoes. I sliced some cucumbers and onions, drizzled some oil and vinegar over them, and decided to call it dinner.

Donna and I ate at the kitchen table, under the feeble ministrations of an oscillating fan. I had the air conditioning turned on because it would have been foolhardy not to. Even so, the oppressive heat outside seemed to force its way through the walls and the ancient single-pane windows of my eighty-year-old farmhouse.

I drank a beer. Donna had iced tea. Being an athlete, she knew that alcohol and summer heat were a bad combination. Being a man, I didn't give a damn.

"Can you talk about it?" she asked.

"The murder? Sure. The question is, do you want to hear about it?"

"I'm worried. I remember what happened to you last year when Gypsy Camarena was murdered."

"Different set of circumstances. It wasn't Gypsy's murder that put me off kilter. It was where and how she was dumped."

A couple of kids had found Gypsy lying by the bank of Six Mile Creek, near Prosperity Glen High School. She was found in almost the exact same spot where my wife Susan had died six years before in an automobile accident. The coincidence had played a number on my head. After finding Gypsy's killer, and spending some time with my shrink, I had gotten past it.

Mostly.

"Somebody worked Steve Samples over with a meat cleaver," I told her. "I'm not a forensics expert, but it looked like the killer was pretty angry. I'd imagine Samples was dead after the first or second blow, but whoever whacked him just kept whacking."

She shuddered.

"Grisly," she said.

"Actually, it could have been worse. Tear a human up enough, he stops looking human. It provides a little distance. Makes it a little easier to tell yourself you're just looking at meat. The hard ones are the vics who still look like they might wake up in a minute or two. Kids, especially."

"Thank you. I think that will do nicely."

"See? You really didn't want to hear about it after all."

"Actually, I was a little more interested in your investigation."

"It's all preliminary. I guess I shouldn't be surprised that Seth is involved."

"Oh," she said.

"I don't think he had anything to do with the murder. He pimped a couple of girls to Samples's house last night. One of them went upstairs with Samples for a few minutes."

"Did she kill him?"

"Can't say. I don't think so. He was alive when she left. I haven't had a chance to talk with her yet, because she seems to have become a little scarce. According to the other girl, she has a boyfriend with a prison record."

"Which ignites your suspicions."

"Yeah. The other girl says the boyfriend's gone straight. I suppose I should give him the benefit of the doubt, talk to him a little before I shoot him."

"You're joking."

I stared at her.

"Right?" she asked.

"Yeah," I said. "I'm joking."

I knew I could tell Donna these things. We'd been together long enough that she knew the meaning of the word *confidential*. I'd told her things before that I would have otherwise taken to my grave. Partly, they were things I needed to talk about, to keep them from blowing up inside of me like a tire tube. I'd never heard a whiff of gossip come back to me afterward. What I told Donna about ongoing investigations had always stayed between us. I had no reason to believe this would be any different.

Besides, talking about things helped to organize them in my head.

"It's bad timing," I said.

"How so?"

"I have some other stuff that needs tending. Luther Steele has his first hearing coming up, and I just found out the guy who helped in that smashup next to the shopping center is a registered sex offender. I have to circulate some notices in his neighborhood."

"Get Slim and Stu to do it."

"Yeah," I said. "I can do that."

SEVENTEEN

The next morning, I copied Carl Sussman's picture from the state sex offender registry website, and pasted it to a form I'd developed a couple of years ago to create a flyer that could be distributed to Sussman's neighbors.

I called Slim Tackett on the radio as soon as I finished copying the notice.

"Yeah, Chief," he said, his voice tinny and distant.

"I have some Article 27 leaflets I need you to distribute over in Terry Heights and Blackstone," I said.

"Ten-four. I'll be around the station in about ten minutes."

"Ten minutes? There isn't a place in Prosperity that's more than five minutes away."

"Yeah, I know. I'm writing a ticket for some kid I caught doing seventy on Morgan Highway."

"Who is it?"

"Not a local. Some kid from Parker County."

"Okay. Come on by when you're finished."

I placed the thick stack of notices on Sherry's desk and told her to give them to Slim when he dropped by. Then I retreated to my office and tried to call Ann Koehler again. Her stepmother answered.

"This is Chief Wheeler over in Prosperity."

"Yes, Chief. Ann came in late last night. She's asleep. I was just about to wake her and tell her to call you."

"Go ahead and get her up. I'll come by in about a half hour.

Give me your address and some directions."

Ann Koehler lived in a neighborhood situated between Main
Street in Morgan and Highway 205 that led through the back
country to Mica Wells. The streets were lined with 1960s red
brick ranch houses with shallow roofs and open carports. Speed
bumps had been installed every hundred yards or so in the
streets, to keep people from using them as a cut-through. The
speed bumps were mostly useless, serving more as an annoy-
ance than a deterrent.

I parked the new cruiser in the Koehler driveway, locked it,
and strolled up the concrete walk to the front door.

A woman in her forties opened the door before I had a chance
to knock. She was artificially blond and thick around the middle,
her face laced with thin streaks of broken capillaries. Her lips
were thin, her nose broad, and her eyes sunken. She seemed
cheerful enough.

"Come on in, Chief," she said. "Ann's eating breakfast in the
kitchen."

She led me through the living room and a short hallway to a
kitchen that opened out onto the backyard through a sliding
glass patio door. A young girl who appeared to have inherited
her hair color from her mother's bathroom cabinet sat at a
round Formica dinette, spooning cereal and milk from a plastic
bowl.

She didn't get up when I came into the room, which was
fine. She was dressed in really short shorts that rode down the
small of her back, revealing one of those winged tattoos that
had become all the rage. Her tube top struggled to contain her
bosom, which jutted from her chest in the way that only youth
or implants can achieve. Her face was well proportioned, but
badly made up. Her scowl didn't help matters much.

"Ann?"

She nodded, chewing furiously on her cereal.

I pulled out the chair across from her and sat.

"You know who I am?" I asked.

"Cop," she said through a mouthful of chewed mush.

"I'm the head cop, over in Prosperity. Chief Wheeler. I need to ask you a few questions."

"What about?" she said just before she shoveled another load of oats into her mouth. She seemed neither intimidated nor suspicious that I was in her breakfast nook asking her questions. Experience has taught me that people do their damnedest to act nonchalant around cops mostly when they have something to hide.

"I spoke with Tracy yesterday," I said.

"Yeah," she said. "I know."

"Then you know what I want to ask you about."

"That football player guy?"

"Steve Samples. I know that Seth Kramer took you and Tracy over to his house night before last. I know from Tracy that you went upstairs with Samples for ten or fifteen minutes. I suppose you know by now that there was a murder in the house later that night."

"I didn't do it," she said. She tipped the bowl up and slurped the remaining milk.

"Don't disrespect the officer," her stepmother said from the kitchen. "Just answer his questions."

"Betty," Ann said, as she lowered the bowl to the table. "Go somewhere, okay?"

Her stepmother looked a little hurt, but didn't argue. She walked out of the kitchen. Moments later I heard a door slam in the back of the house.

"She thinks she's my real mom," Ann said. "My real mom lives in Myrtle Beach. Betty's just this bowling alley bimbo that Dad brought home after Mom moved out. I'll be damned if I'm

102

going to let her tell me what to do."

"I would suspect that you don't think much of letting anyone tell you what to do"

She didn't say anything. Her eyes, though, spoke volumes.

"Here's what I need to know," I continued. "I want you to tell me everything that happened between you and Steve Samples when you and he went upstairs to his bedroom."

"Everything?" she asked, her eyes gleaming. "You want a play-by-play, Chief?"

"Take it from the moment you were out of Seth Kramer's sight."

"I'd had a couple of beers. Seth and Steve weren't drinking, and there was this perfectly good six pack in the fridge, going to waste. I asked if I could have one. Steve said I could. So I drank that one, and then I drank another one."

"What about Tracy?"

"She drank a couple, too."

I made a mental note to check Samples's refrigerator. If she was telling the truth, which I somehow doubted, there should be two beers left.

"Steve excused himself, and said he had to go upstairs for a minute. I asked if I could go along."

"Why?"

"Why not? Have you seen that house of his? It's like a goddamn mansion. Swimming pool and everything. It's not like I get a lot of chances to see a place like that. Anyway, he said I could come, and I followed him upstairs."

"Tracy stayed downstairs with Seth Kramer."

"I guess. I didn't keep track of what she did. I was busy."

"Busy doing what?"

She smiled coquettishly, revealing a slight overbite, then said, "Blowing Steve."

She had intended to shock me. I decided not to let her.

"Which room?" I asked.

"His bathroom. He had gone upstairs to get a DVD Seth said he wanted to watch. While he was up there, he showed me around. When we got to the bathroom, he closed the door and gave me the look."

"What look?"

"That guy look. You know. The one that says 'get down on your knees.' I was like, what the hell, so I pulled down his pants and blew him."

"Just like that."

"Sure. It's no big deal. He looked a little desperate, so I tossed him a bone, you know? Seth had told me that he'd been shut up in training camp for a few weeks, and hadn't gotten any. That was one of the reasons Tracy and I went over. I suppose Tracy would have done it if I hadn't. That chick is wild."

"What happened then?"

"It didn't take long, that's for sure. Steve had a short fuse. After a minute or two he gasped a couple of times and spewed on my face. It got in my eyes. You ever get jizz in your eyes, Chief?"

I stared at her.

"It burns," she said. "I tried not to complain. You never know when you might get a chance for a repeat performance, and I could tell from what Seth said that Steve Samples was going to be rich. I figured if I showed him a good time he might invite me back over, maybe let me hang out at that sweet pool of his."

"Tracy and Seth told me that you were upstairs with him for about fifteen minutes."

"Yeah. Afterwards, he sat on the bathroom floor while I washed off my face at the sink. Then he said something funny."

"What was that?"

"He asked if I had change for a hundred."

"A hundred dollars?"

"Yeah. He said he only had a hundred dollar bill, and he needed change because he had to go back to training camp the next morning. Said he wanted to stop at a convenience store on the way, get something to eat, and the convenience stores don't take anything over a twenty. I told him I had about sixty dollars, but there was no way I could cover a hundred. He said that's fine and offered to give me the hundred for the sixty."

"Which you did," I said.

"Not at first. When he first said that, I was pissed, like he was making out in a back-handed way that I was some kind of ho', like this was his way of paying me for the hummer without, you know, really paying. Then he said that it was worth it to him, because he wouldn't get to training camp until after breakfast, and it was going to be a long time until lunch. I finally took the money."

"He gave you a hundred, and you gave him sixty."

"Sixty-three, really."

"What did you do with the hundred?"

She shrugged. "Spent it."

"Where?"

"At the beach. I went to see my mom."

"She can verify that."

"Of course. I'll give you her number."

She recited a telephone number with a Myrtle Beach area code, and I wrote it down on my pad.

"Do you recall what denominations the money you gave Steve Samples came in?"

"What?"

"Did you give him tens, twenties, fives, what?"

"I think it was a couple of twenties, some fives, and some ones."

"And Samples only had the hundred dollar bill."

"That's what he said."

"So, after you gave him sixty-three dollars, that was all the money he had?"

"I guess."

"Okay," I said. "I need you to think very carefully about this. I need you to try to recall where you got the money you gave Steve Samples."

"Why?"

"Just try to recall."

"That's easy," she said. "I got it from my boyfriend."

"Ricky Chasen?"

She blinked. "Yeah. How'd you know that?"

"Tracy told me about him. So Ricky gave you the money that you gave Steve Samples."

"Yeah."

"When did he do that?"

"Three days ago maybe. He didn't give me all of it. Just a couple of twenties."

"What for?"

She leaned back and cradled the back of her head with her hands. The leverage pushed her breasts out at me, as the tube top strained to contain them.

"I guess because he loves me," she said with a leer in her voice.

"That never crossed your mind while you were with Steve Samples?"

"Not really. It's not like I was cheating on Ricky. It was just a blowjob. I mean, *really.*"

I made a note to look up Ricky Chasen. Soon.

"How did you get to Myrtle Beach?" I asked. "You have a car?"

"No. Ricky took me."

"When?"

"We left early yesterday morning, before my dad and Betty got up."

"After Seth Kramer brought you home from Steve's house."

"Yeah. Ricky called me on my cell, maybe around five o'clock, and he asked if I wanted to go to the beach. I said sure."

"Just like that?"

"No, not really. We'd talked about it."

"When?"

"Earlier. Right after I got home."

"You talked with Ricky when you got home from Steve's house?"

"Yeah. He was waiting for me, on the front stoop."

"You told him where you'd been?"

"I told him that Seth had taken Tracy and me to see some hotshot football player. I told him about the house."

"You told him about the blowjob?"

"Sure. Ricky and me, we don't got any secrets from each other. We're in love."

I made another note, and clicked my pen a couple of times.

"They've identified the body found at Samples's house, Ann. It was Steve Samples."

"Yeah," she said, her eyes lifeless. "I figured."

"You know, when you told Ricky Chasen about giving Samples head, it provided Ricky with a motive for killing him."

"Not Ricky. He ain't like that."

"Everyone's like that, Ann. Do you know where Ricky was between the time he met you on the front stoop and when he called you to go to the beach?"

"No."

"Is it possible that he may have decided to have a talk with Steve Samples?"

"I don't think so."

"You don't think he did, or you don't think it's possible?"

"You're confusing me."

"Where can I find Ricky Chasen?" I asked.

EIGHTEEN

I pulled off Morgan Highway onto a gravel path that led past Nate Murray's tobacco-drying barn and a couple of falling-down equipment sheds, past a couple of weathered and moldering shacks that had, once, been a family's fine new home, past a quarter mile of rusting barbed wire fence, until I reached a gap between two cracked and rotting oaken posts. In the freshly mown field beyond the posts stood a large canvas tent.

Under the tent were rows of folding wooden chairs, set out with a wide aisle up the middle, facing a raised platform made from folding-leg partitions stitched together into a twenty-foot-square stage. In the center of the platform was a pulpit made of stained and polished red oak, looking regal and out of place amongst all the decay surrounding the tent.

To one side of the tent sat a ten-year-old excursion bus, the kind that musical groups use on tour. A window unit air conditioner set into one side of the bus struggled vainly against the outside heat. It was powered by a gasoline generator set up in front of the bus. Between them, they made a racket.

I walked up to the bus door and rapped on it twice.

"Over here," someone said, from my right. I turned toward the voice.

"Is there a problem, officer?" a man said as he wiped his face with a towel. He had been shaving at a porcelain washbasin set on a table behind the tent when I drove up. There was no way I could have surprised him, but he had allowed me to look over the place and approach his bus before talking.

"I'm Chief Wheeler. Prosperity Police Department."

"Prosperity," the man said as he slipped a short-sleeved white cotton shirt over the sleeveless tee he had been wearing while shaving. He was in his fifties, thin as a hard winter, his face a mass of canyon-like furrows. His eyes were almost black, as if they were permanently dilated, with just the hint of blue iris surrounding the pupils. His teeth sparkled with a gleam that could only be obtained by sitting in a glass at night. His hair was cropped short, in a GI flattop. He began to fasten the buttons. "That's the little town just north of here, right?"

"Wrong," I said. "It's the little town right here. You're inside the Prosperity city limits."

"Do tell. Right pretty place, I'd say."

"We like it."

The man strode up to me, his hand extended.

"Reverend Alvin Cross," he said.

I shook with him.

"You run this tent meeting?" I asked.

"This is my ministry. I have the privilege of bringing the Word to those who need its comfort the most."

"Uh huh. I see. You have permission to set up this tent on private property?"

"This is private property?"

"You know it is. Everything you can see from here to that hardwood forest way over there is Nate Murray's farm."

"Yes," Cross said. "Mr. Murray. Such a kind man. He gave me permission to bring my ministry here."

"That's easy enough to check."

"Yes. I suppose it is."

I looked over his setup again.

"You been pulling them in?" I asked.

"The Lord has smiled upon me. He has sent dozens of sheep

to my care during my ministry here."

"How long have you been here?"

"Five days."

"Planning on staying long?"

"No, sir. The nature of my ministry is more in the way of revival. I give my flock a spiritual jump charge, and then I move on."

"Where are you headed next?"

"Where the Lord points me, son. But you haven't told me why you're here."

"I'm looking for Ricky Chasen. I heard he works for you."

Cross stroked his newly shaven chin, which was shaped like a ski jump. Then he gestured toward the bus. "It's going to be a hellfire day," he said. "Why don't we step inside and talk about Ricky."

He grabbed a leather loop set into the folding bus door and yanked on it. The door opened, and cool air rushed out. He swept one sharply bony hand toward the opening.

"Don't want to let all the cold out," he said.

I stepped into the bus.

Inside, it had been set up as a sort of mobile home. Just behind the driver's chair was a small sitting area, with two captain's chairs and a vinyl sofa bolted to the floor and backed up to the left wall of the interior. Behind the sitting area was a galley made from veneered plywood, complete with a three-burner gas range, a microwave, and a sink. The left side was closed off behind the galley, leaving a narrow passageway, beyond which I could see a tiny bedroom with a neatly made double bed and a built-in dresser and closet.

"Nice motor home," I said.

"A gift. It used to be the property of a rock band in Florida. Three of its members attended my ministry one night, and were saved. In their gratitude, they offered me this bus."

"Mighty big of them."

"And it is such a comfort to me. I had been traveling in a converted school bus that didn't even have air conditioning. I didn't complain, though, because that was the Lord's plan for me."

Cross's righteousness was starting to make me itch.

"Ricky Chasen," I said. "I've been told he works for you."

"May I offer you something to drink? A soda, maybe?"

It was almost as if he hadn't heard me. Or maybe as if he was purposefully ignoring my inquiries. Cops don't like that.

"No, thank you."

"I hope you will not mind if I indulge," he said as he opened the refrigerator situated under the range and took out a bottle of spring water. "Such a hot summer."

"Yes."

He twisted the cap off the bottle and sat in one of the captain's chairs. He pointed toward the sofa, so I sat there.

"Ricky isn't here. Fact is, I haven't seen him since day before yesterday."

"Do you know where he is?"

"Can't say as I do. I wish I did. It isn't easy managing this ministry by myself."

"He didn't say where he was going?"

"No, but I can guess. I think it was that girl that drew him away."

"Ann Koehler."

"Yes. She is a trial for him."

"How so?"

"In the way that all women are a trial for men. You do know, of course, that Ricky was in prison."

"I'd heard."

"When he first came to me, he had been out for—what?— maybe three or four months. He was having a terrible time adjusting. Satan was just chucking opportunities at him right and left. I do believe that if our paths hadn't crossed he might have come to terrible harm, or perhaps inflicted it."

"He's dangerous?"

"Now? Hardly. When I met him though, I could sense the animal fury in him. I had to be very careful with him at first. There was always the potential that he might turn on me."

"How did you meet?"

"At one of my meetings."

"Your tent meetings."

"My AA meetings," he said.

I didn't know what to say to that.

"You shouldn't be shocked," Cross said, chuckling. "You'd be amazed how many men of the cloth have struggled with demon rum. As it happens, that's how I became an itinerant pastor. When I was Ricky's age, I was a reckless buck, full of piss and vinegar, always looking for a fight. Loved my drink. My special poison was tequila. You know the Twelve Steps?"

"Not really."

"One of them requires you to acknowledge your Higher Power. Well, Chief, let me tell you, when I was Ricky's age, I didn't have no higher power. I was top of the food chain. Except for Jose Cuervo, of course. He had a grip on me like a snapping turtle, only I didn't recognize it at the time.

"Then, my family kicked me out of the house. I had nowhere to go. I wandered the streets, getting into whatever trouble I could find. I rolled other drunks, robbed men in blind alleys, I did the most terrible things.

"Then, one night, it commenced to rain. It was a gullywasher, a frog strangler. Rivers ran in the city gutters, and I sought a place—any place—where I could take refuge from the deluge. I stumbled into an open doorway, which, as it happened, was a local mission. Inside, they were holding a meeting. I stayed for the cookies. The message crept up on me somewhat more slowly. I've been a three-meeting-a-week man ever since, a devoted follower of the teachings of Brother Bill."

I had sat quietly as he rambled. I recognized the rehearsed nature of his story. I was sure it went over great with the hicks and rubes who sweltered under his canvas tent each night.

"You met Ricky at one of these meetings," I said.

"About four months ago. He was required to attend as part of his parole, you see. I could tell the moment he walked in that he wasn't a true believer, that he was there at someone else's behest. Something about him reminded me of myself at his age, and my heart went out to him. I decided right there and then that I was going to make him my own personal long-term project."

"How did you go about that?"

"I walked up to him after the meeting and I asked him if he needed a job. Times being what they are, he accepted."

"Just like that."

"All the Lord has to do is open the door, Chief. Those who are meant to enter usually walk right through."

"I see. Well, according to Ann Koehler, your lost lamb was in Myrtle Beach between yesterday morning and this morning."

"That young girl is going to be his trial by fire."

"She's likely to be some kind of trial, anyway. I need to talk with Chasen at the earliest opportunity. If he should show up, I'd appreciate it if you would send him by the Prosperity Police Department for a chat."

"Is Ricky in some trouble?" Cross asked.

"I don't know. I do know that I need to talk with him. You might tell him that it's better for him to come to me than it is for me to run him to ground. Avoiding me might look suspicious."

"I shall be certain to pass the word along."

"You do that," I said.

Nineteen

Carl Sussman checked the edges of the two-by-four framing lumber wall he had laid out on the plywood floor of the first wing of his house, for square, and then began to pound nails into the wood.

It had taken the heavy equipment company half a day to level the site for his construction, and he had spent most of the rest of the day and half the night digging the footings. The next day he had poured the concrete for the footings and the day after that he had built the piers that would support the floor joists. He had spent most of the night before laying out the joists, and most of the morning placing the floor sheathing in place.

The end result was a flat raised surface that would someday become the foundation of his house.

Now, he was nailing together the wall sections.

While waiting for the concrete to set, he had begun to cut the individual two-by-fours for his walls on a chop saw he had set on a section of plywood suspended between two sawhorses. With his floor sheathing in place and nailed down, he was ready to begin assembling the frame for his house.

He had learned how to do this through a community college course while he had been in prison. At that time, though, it had been early spring, and he had been more concerned with possible frostbite than with heat exhaustion. He tended to become lost in his work, and had to remind himself to stop periodically to drink water and rest.

He finished nailing together the first wall frame, and dragged it around to the western edge of the first wing. There, he had already nailed a couple of two-by-fours to the outside edge of the floor sheathing. If he had been afforded the benefit of a work crew, he wouldn't have needed the stop blocks, but he was working alone and could use all the mechanical assistance he could get.

He hooked the rope from a block and tackle attached to a white oak tree near the edge of his house to the top of the wall frame. After assuring that the foot of the frame was solidly set against the stop blocks, he started pulling on the other end of the block and tackle rope.

Slowly, the wall section began to rise into place. Because of the number of pulleys needed to exert the force, it was slow going. After about fifteen minutes, and with yards and yards of rope piled around his feet, he decided to take a break.

He wrapped the pulling end of the rope around a cleat he had installed on the far edge of the flooring, peeled of his T-shirt, and wiped his dripping face with it.

"That would be easier if you didn't try to do it alone," someone said.

He jerked around, startled by the voice. He hadn't heard a car pull into his gravel drive.

A uniformed woman stood near the base of his foundation. She had the look he had seen in many of the corrections guards he'd known in the slam, what his father had once called a *rode hard and put up wet* look. She was sinewy and deeply tanned, and her face was all angles and tight skin. What he could see of her hair under her baseball cap looked sun-dried like wheat. Her eyes were a transparent blue, and seemed to cut through him like a buzz saw.

"Mr. Sussman?" she asked.

Her voice had an adrenaline edge to it, and echoed a

thousand regrets. He recalled voices like hers on the antique country-western records he had listened to with his father while he was growing up.

"Yes, ma'am."

"My name is Sharon Counts. I'm a CSI with the Bliss County Sheriff's Department over in Morgan."

"Welcome to my home, Deputy," he said. "I'd shake hands with you, but I'm all sweaty."

"I ain't no deputy. Just a crime scene investigator."

"Like on television?"

"Ain't much in law enforcement like the way it looks on the tube."

Sussman glanced around the construction site.

"I hope you'll pardon me, ma'am," he said, "But I'm not aware of any crime that's been committed here. Is there something I can do for you?"

"You can step down here and open your mouth."

"Beg pardon?"

"When you left the prison, they neglected to get a DNA sample from you. It's part of the registry law. They asked us to collect a sample and send it along for processing."

"Oh." He pulled the shirt back on and hopped off the first floor of the foundation, to within a couple of feet of her. His work boots kicked up a low-hanging cloud of red clay dust. He noted that she didn't flinch.

"Your mouth," she said.

He opened his mouth and she stuck a long wooden swab inside to take a scraping from the inside of his cheek. She secured it in a sterile test tube and placed the tube inside a plastic bag.

"Is that it?" he asked.

"That's all there is. We'll send this to Raleigh, and they'll do the DNA test. It will be added to your file there."

"Well, if there's nothing else, I need to get some water. Nice meeting you, Dep . . . uh, ma'am."

She started to turn toward the county car she had parked in front of his trailer, but stopped and looked back at the foundation. "You're trying to build this all by yourself?"

"It will mean more to me that way."

"You do this in your spare time?"

"All my time is spare time." He sat on the edge of the foundation. "I don't have a job. Don't really need one. Building this house keeps me busy, keeps my mind occupied. I figure I'll have it closed in and roofed by the time autumn gets here."

"Then what?"

"I'll start in on the workshop. I'm putting it over there." He pointed toward a cleared space back in the stand of longleaf pines at the far corner of the lot. "I'm thinking about making furniture."

"Thought you didn't need a job."

"I don't. I need to stay busy. Idle hands, you know."

"Yeah. I know. Well, have to run."

"Don't be a stranger," he said, swiping a sunburned hand across his forehead.

She didn't answer. She looked at him with those mournful x-ray eyes, and then returned to her car.

He noted that there was another person sitting in the front passenger seat as she slid behind the wheel and cranked the ignition.

She'd apparently needed the reassurance of backup to come out and collect his sample.

Sussman shrugged.

It was just something to which he was going to have to become accustomed.

TWENTY

I had told Sherry that I would be out of pocket for a few hours. I took the new cruiser across the South Carolina state line, and on to Columbia, where I turned west and drove another half hour to Newberry College.

The college was set in the middle of the town, which was set in the middle of Newberry County. It was kind of hard to give them points for originality, but the place itself was inviting. Much of South Carolina is in the Sandhills region, marked by flat course ground and scrubby trees or hardy pines that can survive the frequent droughts. West of Columbia, the land begins to roll, the trees become deciduous, and the landscape comes alive.

As towns go, Newberry had managed to avoid much of the urban invasion that troubled Prosperity. It was over a half hour from Columbia and nearly half again as far from Greenville-Spartanburg. As such, it retained much of its small-town charm, its streets lined with antebellum homes and centuries-old shade trees. Many of its families could visit members from five or six generations back by stepping outside their church sanctuaries into the denominational graveyards that had been tended by successions of rectors and pastors and even rabbis since before the Civil War.

Newberry College was a throwback, an Evangelical Lutheran institution that wasn't shy about teaching religion right alongside forensic science. It was a tiny school, by many standards, and lavished its students with personal attention. Even the football team was small potatoes, playing far out of the spotlight, in the NCAA Division II, against little-known schools.

I found the Pythons practicing inside Newberry's football stadium. The place looked smaller than the Prosperity Glen High School field, which was understandable considering that Prosperity had about two thousand students to Newberry's eight hundred or so. The field was flat, and there was no stadium to speak of. Each side of the pitch was lined by steel and wood bleachers maybe fifteen rows deep, with a frame and plywood announcers' booth set at the top center.

When I played football at Carolina, I had suited up for crowds measuring in the tens of thousands. I would have been shocked if any single game at Newberry drew more than twelve hundred spectators.

All of which, of course, made Newberry the perfect spot for the Pythons to hold their training camp each year. Far from the hustle of urban life, they could practice freely under the eyes of the coaching staff and the occasional stalwart fan who braved scorching temperatures to loiter in the uncovered stands.

I parked the cruiser just outside the field, and sat in the air conditioning as the day's training session wound down. I saw Harve Lucanian running the defensive line through some blocking drills, and tried to conjure up my own muscle memory of the sensation of slamming dummies in the searing July Carolina heat.

Lucanian drilled the players with an old-fashioned cone megaphone. He lined them up in groups of five and yelled for them to attack the sleds like their own worst enemy.

On the other end of the field, the offense ran passing patterns unopposed, lining up again and again to take signals from the rotation of underling quarterbacks. I could see the Python's star quarterback, Lennie Stockwell, sitting on the bench and watching the drills. A property like Stockwell, as much as he cost the team each year, you don't want to run into the ground before the season's even ticked over. On the other hand, Jermaine Coltes was on the field, running pass patterns with the second- and third-string QB hopefuls.

After about a half hour, Lucanian blew a whistle, and the team fell out on the sidelines. Trainers attended to some of the rougher-looking players while equipment boys and other support staff moved among the rest, distributing squeeze bottles of Gatorade and water.

I stepped out of the cruiser and was assaulted by sopping wet hundred-degree air.

Lucanian saw me and waved. I walked across the end zone toward the bench where he sat reviewing a legal pad sheet on a clipboard.

"Mr. Lucanian," I said.

"Chief Wheeler. I wish you'd called ahead. I could have had Jake Tupper a little more presentable."

"I don't mind a little sweat," I said. "Which one is he?"

Lucanian blew a short burst on the whistle, then put the megaphone to his mouth and yelled "Tupper!"

One of the players dragged himself off the turf, slowly regained his feet, and walked over to the bench. Like most good cornerbacks, he looked as if he had been stitched together from the better parts of two people. His legs were lean and long, perfect for making the highlight reel returns after drive-stopping interceptions. His upper body was all muscle and lots of it, right up to the neck that seemed like nothing more than an extension of his skull. Cornerbacks had to be fast on their feet, but they also had to have the bulk to bring down receivers the instant they caught the ball.

Tupper had a crew-cut head of very dark—almost black—

hair and a thick five-o'clock shadow. His nose had been broken at some point, or perhaps at several points, but his chin was firm and strong under thin, unsmiling lips. His eyes had the single-minded look I'd come to recognize as the athlete's stare.

"This is Chief Wheeler, of the Prosperity Police, up in North Carolina," Lucanian said.

"Is this about Steve?"

"Yes," I said.

"It's awful. I feel just terrible about it. I mean, I've only known Steve for a couple of weeks, but he seemed like an okay guy."

"An okay guy who just happened to be vying for your position on the team," I said.

His eyes seemed to focus suddenly, and his gaze drilled into mine. "Wait. No. You don't mean that."

"Right now I'm just asking questions. Motive, means, opportunity. I know how Steve was murdered. You're on a pretty long list of people who had a motive. I'm here to look into opportunity."

Tupper looked at Lucanian, his eyes pleading. Then he turned back to me. "Look, Chief Wheeler. I can come out right now and tell you I didn't kill Steve Samples. Fact is, I didn't, and I know that when you finally do solve this murder I won't be the guy you arrest. But you have to realize what those kinds of accusations can do to me, public relations–wise."

"Public relations?"

"Yeah. At best, I'm third string with the Pythons. If they cut me, my agent is going to be burning the phone lines trying to get me a shot at another team. If word gets out that I'm a suspect in a murder case, who's going to give me a chance? Hell, I could wind up playing arena ball in Slovenia!"

"Did Steve Samples present a threat to your place on the Pythons' roster?" I asked.

"Coach Lucanian's the only one who can tell you that. Steve was younger, stronger, and maybe faster than I am, but he was having a tough time learning the defensive playbook, and I've been with the team long enough to have it down cold. I'd say maybe, at least for this season, it was a draw."

I glanced over at Lucanian. He nodded.

"Sounds like motive," I said.

"Please," Tupper said. "How can I convince you I had nothing to do with this?"

"Where do you park your car?"

"Come on. I'll show you."

He handed his helmet and pads to an equipment boy and pointed toward a fenced area on the other side of a quadrangle of red brick buildings beyond the field.

"Those are our dorms. Right next to them is where we park our cars."

I followed him across the field and through the quadrangle toward the lot. Lucanian trailed us by a few feet. I wasn't crazy about having Tupper's handler in tow, but I was operating on their turf—technically, out of my legal jurisdiction, for that matter—so I decided not to make an issue of it.

We reached the fenced lot. Just as we did, a campus security golf cart trolled by, its battery-powered electric engine whining. The driver was a fat man in his sixties. By his side was a woman who looked as if she should have been taking summer classes instead of patrolling the campus in the blistering heat. I had a hard time imagining either of them protecting the campus from anyone tougher than an irate teenage skateboarder.

"Like I said," Lucanian told me, "they do that about every half hour during the day."

"Did you get the security tape?"

"Not yet. We've been kind of busy."

"I'll check it after we finish here."

Tupper walked through a chain-link door in the fenced lot, and pointed toward a BMW Z3 parked a couple of rows over. "That's my car."

I looked around. The fence wasn't terribly high, but it did have three strands of barbed wire around the top, angled toward the outside, to discourage interlopers. To leave the lot, drivers had to punch a code into a box at the exit gate, which would activate a chain-driven winch, sliding the gate open.

"So," I said, "if someone wanted to take one of these cars, they would have to know your exit code, right?"

"Right."

"I'm going to check the security tapes. If you drove your car off this lot the night before last, this would be a good time to tell me."

"I swear I parked in that space last Sunday when I got here, and I haven't moved the car an inch since then."

"No trips to town? No evening runs for ice cream or a restaurant?"

"No way. They feed us here like you wouldn't believe and— hot as it is—after a full day of practice all we want to do is eat and fall into bed."

I looked around the lot again. "Show me your room," I said.

"No problem. It's right there."

He pointed to a building next to the parking lot. It was newer than many of the other halls on campus, made of paler brick, and constructed in a fat L-shape.

"Brokaw Hall," Tupper said. "It's the only male dormitory on campus. I couldn't figure out why they put us in the building farthest from the football field, but someone told me it was because they didn't want a bunch of football players living in one of the girls' dorms. Hell, even during the summer sessions they only use one of them, but the school must have felt better confining us to the guys' dorm."

He was talking quickly as we walked, mostly about nothing. It was nervous patter, designed to fill the void in our conversation. He didn't know it, but I was staying quiet on purpose, and he was doing exactly what I wanted.

Maybe Tupper didn't kill Steve Samples, I had reasoned. If he had, letting him run off at the mouth like that might cause him to make a slip that I could jump on like a starving bear.

He led us into the dorm. As we opened the glass double doors at the front, a wave of cool air swept over us like an oasis breeze.

"Doesn't that feel good?" Tupper said. "I look forward to this all day long. My room's this way."

He led us through a lobby, and up a long hallway. At the end of the hall, he grasped a doorknob.

"Aw, hell," he said.

"What is it?"

"I forgot. The key's in my pants, back at the locker room. I didn't expect to have to come to my room."

His room was on the first floor, so I said, "Now's a good time to be honest with me, Jake. Let's say you wanted to sneak out after curfew, maybe run into town and grab a beer, or maybe some ice cream. You follow me?"

"No, Chief. I'd never do that. We sign in by nine o'clock, and Coach Lucanian would have our hides if we broke curfew."

"Let's just suppose, okay? If you were to decide to go out, how hard would it be for you to open your window and climb out that way?"

"I couldn't."

"Why not?"

"Come with me," he said.

He retreated up the hall we'd just walked, toward the front door. I followed him—reluctantly—back out to the inferno, as he led the coach and me around the building to the narrow side of the "L." When we reached the corner, he pointed at the window, about eight feet off the ground.

"See? It's fixed. The glass panel is set into a solid frame. There's no way to open it, short of throwing a chair or maybe a place kicker through the glass. If I wanted to leave the building after curfew, I'd have to go out the end door here, which is wired to an alarm, or I'd have to go through the lobby."

"And someone would see you go out that way?"

"Sure. The school has students on work study manning the front desk. They work up until one o'clock in the morning. After that, the front door is locked. Even if I did go out, I couldn't get back in."

"He's right," Lucanian said. "That's why we let Jermaine and Steve stay at home the other night after the banquet in Pooler. By the time they'd have gotten back, the doors would have been locked tight."

"And nobody else was out of pocket that night?"

"Nope. Just those two."

I looked up at the sealed window again. "I can see where it would be tough," I said. "Okay, Jake, you can go about your business. I'll get back with you."

"You don't think I killed him, then?"

"Let's just say the point spread is leaning in your favor. I'll check out the security tapes of the parking lot that night, and we'll talk about it later."

As it happened, the Security Office was also in Brokaw Hall. Since Brokaw was the men's dormitory during the regular school year, I suppose they decided to put the campus cops there on the supposition that boys would be rowdier than the girls. This particular notion ran counter to my memory of college girls back in my days at Chapel Hill, but this was a church-sponsored school and traditional gender roles meant a lot here.

I walked into the office and a young fellow dressed in a light blue work shirt and a blue college baseball cap stood and said, "Can I help you?"

I showed him my identification.

"I'm here investigating a murder," I said. "I need to know whether any cars left the fenced lot night before last. Can you show me the security tapes?"

"Gosh, no," the kid said. "I don't have access to them. You need to talk with Officer Head."

"Is he about?"

"I'll page him."

The kid picked up a UHF walkie-talkie and called out for Officer Head. A second later the unit crackled.

"Yeah, Wally. What's up?"

"There's a police officer here who says he's investigating a murder. He wants to see the security tapes from a couple of nights ago."

"Hold tight. I'll be right over."

"He's on patrol," the kid told me after setting down the radio. "Shouldn't take him more'n a couple of minutes. Have a seat, won't you?"

I took a seat on one of the vinyl-covered couches in the waiting area. The forced-air vent was right over my head. The frigid blast felt like heaven as it wrapped around me like a long-lost girlfriend. I fantasized retiring to that couch.

After a few moments, a totally bald man who looked like a temporarily displaced drill sergeant strode into the office. Wally nodded in my direction.

The man turned to me.

"I'm Corbin Head, Director of Security for the college."

"Judd Wheeler," I said, taking his hand. "Chief of Police, Prosperity, North Carolina."

"A little out of your jurisdiction, aren't you?"

128

"A mile or two."

"This about that Steve Samples business?"

I nodded. Head turned toward Wally.

"You didn't hear that, boy. Got it?"

Wally gulped and nodded.

"I need to see your security tapes from the Pythons' parking lot from night before last," I said.

"Why? Do you suspect one of the players?"

"I'm ruling out suspects. I need to know whether any of the cars left the lot after dark, or returned before daybreak."

Head scratched his scalp. It left a white comet trail in the pink skin.

"If it involved students, I'd tell you to go get a warrant," he said. "But I reckon it's okay, considering that lot is only used by the football team during the summer. Come on back to the electronics room."

Head led me back through a short hallway to an unmarked locked door. He fumbled with a ball of keys attached to a chained key at his waist, and finally found the right one. After unlocking the door, he held it open for me to walk through, then closed it behind us.

The room was almost as hot as the football field had been. One wall was lined with shelves of videotape machines. Perpendicular to the shelves was a desk with ten or twelve black and white monitors, each one showing a different area of the campus.

"This is the Pythons' lot," he said, as he thumped one screen with a gnarled index finger. "Number three."

He pulled a blank tape from a box under the desk, and pushed the eject button on the recorder labeled *THREE*. "These are long-play videotapes. They run on super slow motion recorders, so each one lasts about forty-eight hours."

He punched the rewind button, and the player whirred as the

tape reversed toward the beginning. Head didn't let it rewind all the way, since I wasn't really interested in the first several hours.

He stopped just as the last of the long afternoon shadows began to disappear from the lot, to be replaced by the stark glow of the mercury vapor lights. The tape jumped about five seconds for each frame. A time code raced along in the bottom right corner of the picture, through nine o'clock, ten o'clock, past midnight, and into the blue-black hours of the morning.

I told him to stop the tape when the time code reached four o'clock. I knew that Jermaine Coltes had arrived at Steve Samples's house around five, and it was an easy two-hour drive from Newberry to Prosperity. There was no point in watching the tape further.

"Thanks," I told him.

"Find what you wanted?"

"No," I said. "I appreciate your time."

"I'll walk you out."

"Tell me something," I said as we left the building and stepped down to the sidewalk. "If you wanted to leave in the middle of the night without being seen, how would you do it?"

"Leaving would be easy, once the front desk is unmanned. Getting back in would be impossible."

"What if you had someone waiting at the front door to open it when you got back?"

He dug in one ear with a thick forefinger, and thought about it.

"I suppose you could do that. You still think one of the players might have had something to do with this killing?"

"Probably not. I have to consider all the angles, though. Let's say it was two people working together—one to leave and go do the murder, and the other to let him back in once he got back to the dorm. The killer would still have to find some way to get to Prosperity and back, and no cars left the parking lot that night."

"I see your problem."

"And I see yours," I said as I pointed toward three television satellite vans that careened around a corner and parked in the street next to the field. "Looks like we kept the lid on this Steve Samples killing as long as we could. Now the whole damn world will be watching."

"I'll handle them," Head advised. "You go on and get your car. I'll ask around, see if any of the Pythons players are keeping their cars outside the locked lot."

I thanked him and jogged toward the new cruiser, just as the first of the newsies hopped from the cab of his roving studio and began casting about for someone to make famous.

TWENTY-ONE

Later that evening, as the sun set behind the rim of walnut and white oak and pecan and tulip poplar trees that ringed Nate Murray's farm, cars began to trickle down the dusty, rutted farm road toward Pastor Alvin Cross's tent revival. They drove through the opening in the fence, and parked in neat rows near the big top Cross had erected over his makeshift pulpit and his folding chair sanctuary.

They were farm people, sun-beaten, rough-handed folk who saw the world in starkly contrasting tones of black and white. Their entire spiritual existence was tied to the land they tilled and cultivated, and their God was a real deity on whom they depended for their very survival. These were people who believed, beyond any shred of doubt, that every single syllable of the Bible was divinely inspired and penned with the very touch of the Almighty guiding the writers' hands.

These were simple people, devoid of artifice and ripe for picking by people like Alvin Cross, who played on their child-like devotion and belief as a master musician plays on a fine violin.

They streamed under the stifling tent, where they found the hand-held fans Cross managed to cadge from local funeral homes wherever he traveled. Cross himself played an ancient, wheezing pedal organ on the modest stage he'd erected, expertly keying the notes to the oldest, most traditional of hymns, songs that his meager flock had known by heart from the time they had been little children.

There was desperation in this crowd. Most of them were older, well past fifty. Many came to the tent in walkers, or on crutches. They stood shoulder to shoulder in the smothering humidity, many of them clutching their fans with arthritis-gnarled fists; people with translucent, paper-thin skin, through which blue veins shown like neon cords.

They came looking for reassurance. Being farm folk, they were used to the vagaries of climatic whimsy. They were always a single failed harvest from destitution. Their symbiotic existence with disappointment urged them on to Alvin Cross's tent, where they yearned for words of comfort, where they craved a blessing that would steel their conviction in anticipation of a better life to come. They frantically sought the strength to muster on, day to day, season to season, in the sincere and sure belief that their devotion would be rewarded.

And Alvin Cross did not disappoint. He was tuned to their fears, and he knew how to play to them.

He jumped from the organ stool even before the congregation had finished the last trilling syllable of "Amen," and flung himself to the pulpit.

"I *know* why you are here!" he proclaimed, without so much as an introduction. "The Lord Almighty *Himself* came to me and spoke of the weakness of your flagging faith. He told me you would come, and here you are. *I am His messenger!*"

"Amen!" called someone from the back of the tent.

"Praise God!" recited some of the crowd.

Alvin Cross looked down on the first row of his audience, and smiled beneficently. As he spoke, his voice fell as faint as a stage whisper, then rose to a window-rattling crescendo.

"And I shall not disappoint," he said. "You have come to me as little children. You want to know that God himself has you in his heart and mind. Your faith is like that of children—simple in nature, but also prone to doubt. I will *remove* that doubt!"

He accented this by slamming his palm on the top of the pulpit lectern. The slap resounded through the tent like a rifle shot. Women on the front row jumped in their seats.

"Amen, Preacher!" someone shouted in the back.

"You haven't come to me for sermons," Cross continued. "You get sermons from the pastors of your own churches. You sit in the pews on Sunday, and your preachers tell you stories, and they remind you to be good to one another, and they are right. I shall *not* repeat their message. You did not come to me tonight to hear a message. Did you? *Did you?*"

"No, Preacher!" said a man in the back.

"No!" Cross yelled, as he strode back and forth across the stage. "There is no message that can fill the empty places in your hearts. You don't want messages. You want signs! You want portents! You want to see the love and devotion of God Almighty in *action!*"

This time the crowd needed no priming. They responded with a loud, enthusiastic *"Amen!"*

"Amen, indeed," Cross said. "I will give you signs. I will show you the power of God Almighty. You will leave here filled in the Spirit. I will make the lamest among you dance. I will make those without breath sing. I will drive the demons from your souls, and fill the spaces with the love and comfort of Almighty God Himself!"

The crowd was working its way toward frenzy now. They had no way of knowing, in their simple faith, that they were being manipulated. They had no concept of the intricacies of mass hypnosis. They had only want and the fears that kept them from sleep in the blackest hours of the night, when they dared to question their deepest convictions. They wanted to know they were right. Alvin Cross was ready to give them what they wanted most in the whole world, and they had not even a clue that all he was giving them was themselves.

Cross stepped off the stage, walked to the front row, and looked deeply into the eyes of an eighty-five-year-old woman who supported herself with a cane. Her back was stooped. One of her eyes was clouded with cataract. Her hands bent at strange and grotesque angles.

He reached out to those hands. He clasped them in his own strong palms. He locked his stare on her eyes, and she looked up into his face as a teenage girl gazes at her first love.

"Come, little mother," he said, not quite a whisper, just loudly enough that he could be heard in the back row. "Come with me to the altar. Let us make a miracle together."

It had been a good night. Alvin Cross's keen eye had yet again spotted those in the assembly whose afflictions were not truly crippling, and he had made them dance. He had whipped the congregation into such a tumult that when the time finally came to pass the silver-plated collection platters, the wallets opened and the meager wealth of his flock poured forth like spring water.

Cross sat in his bus, in the blast from the air conditioner, and carefully counted the take. He had long since removed his coat. His string tie hung loose beneath the open top two buttons of his formerly crisp starched white shirt, now soaked with perspiration.

A good night indeed. Cross loved the little towns, the dots that lined the blue highways of the road atlas. They were uniformly filled with the most trusting, most gullible of believers. His flock loved him. They showed that love by showering him with the riches he deserved for propping up their flagging faith.

There was a knock at the door to the bus.

Cross gathered the cash and deftly tied a rubber band around it. He stashed it in a secret cubby he'd constructed under his bed, and quickly fastened the top two buttons of his shirt.

When he opened the bus door, he found two people standing there. One was in his middle twenties, his hair dark red and tied back with a rubber band. He wore a long-sleeved white shirt and smartly pressed jeans. Cross could see the tail of a snake tattoo that sneaked out of the cuff of his shirt and ran across the top of his right hand.

The other was a young girl. She might have been eighteen, but it was difficult to tell through the road wear that etched her face like a filet knife. Her eyes were red, her makeup smudged. Her blond hair hung lifelessly across her narrow shoulders.

"What is it, child?" he asked.

She gestured to the man at her side. "He said I should talk with you."

"What's troubling you?"

She bit her lip, glanced at the young man, then back at Cross. "I heard what you said tonight. I listened to the revival. I saw what you did with that woman, the one who danced."

"Yes?"

"I . . ." she paused, as if trying to find the words. "I want to feel the way they did tonight. I want to rejoice."

Cross reached out and touched her hand. It was rough, the nails bitten back into the quick.

"You are far from home, child. Did you leave of your own free will?"

She nodded, her eyes widening.

"You believe they drove you away."

Tears started to well at the corners of her eyes.

"It's . . . it's as if you can read my mind," she said. "I knew it. I knew you were a miracle worker."

"Have you been baptized, child?"

"When I was a baby. My mama told me about it."

"Yes. But have you been cleansed in the Water of Life? Have you been born again in your heart and soul?"

Tears coursed down both cheeks. "No."

"The burden of your travels and your sins sit on your shoulders like a starving vulture, feeding on your immortal soul. You can only remove them by being cleansed of your sin."

She wiped at her cheek with one dirty hand.

"Can . . . can you cleanse me?" she asked.

"Are you ready to do whatever I tell you?"

She looked again at the man beside her. He closed his eyes, and nodded almost imperceptibly.

"Yes," she said as she clung to Cross's hands. "I'm ready."

"Step up into my home. I'll read to you from the Good Book. I'll minister to you. I shall lay on hands. I will reach into the depths of your soul. I will free you from your torment."

He tugged, ever so slightly, and she stepped up eagerly into the bus. He guided her to the sofa and bade her sit.

"Bear with me, for just a moment. I wish to speak with your companion," he said.

Cross stepped out of the bus, placed his arm around the man's shoulder, and walked away from the bus toward the tent.

"Where did you find her?"

"Myrtle Beach. She was panhandling on the Boardwalk. She was hungry."

"What do you know about her?"

"She's a runaway, from some town in Kentucky. I never heard of it."

"Surely her family is looking for her?"

"She tells me that they threw her out. Says they caught her dating a black boy, and they disowned her."

"Tragic. Such ignorance. And yet, it is part of the trail of events that has brought her to this place. The Lord does, indeed, work in mysterious ways."

"Amen, Preacher."

"You did well. Very well."

He patted the man on the shoulder and started to return to the bus.

"Is there anything else I can do?" the man said.

Cross stopped and thought for a moment.

"Yes," he said. "Take the shovel from behind the tent. Go over that hill there and dig a good, deep hole."

"Yes sir," Ricky Chasen told him.

"And, mind you, not too close to the other one, you hear?"

"No sir," Chasen said. Then he turned and strode toward the tent.

Alvin Cross licked his lips and started back toward the bus.

TWENTY-TWO

I was too tired to cook after returning from my unproductive trip to the Newberry College training camp, so I stopped by the Pizza Palace next to the Prosperity Police Department and ordered a takeout garbage pie. It would be hard to restrain myself from snarfing it down on the drive to my farm on the far side of town, beyond the blight of urban expansion housing developments.

As I pulled out of the parking lot, I saw a wagon train of television news vans parked across from the police station. Sherry would have left an hour or so earlier, so there was nobody to feed their obsession with new information.

That was fine with me. I drove past them, smiled and waved as one or two realized that I was the object of their attention, and kept trucking down the highway toward my farm.

I found Donna lying in the hammock I'd suspended between two oaks in my front yard. She was snoozing in the early evening summer doldrums, that period just near twilight when the wind stills before kicking up again after sunset. A book lay open on her chest. She raised her head when I slammed the door to the new cruiser.

"I want to be a teacher when I grow up," I said.

"How so?"

"Lying around all summer doing nothing sounds very much like paradise to me."

"Looks are deceiving," she said. "I actually spent the day re-

reading next year's senior honors English lit novel. That's sort of working."

"Think you can tear yourself away long enough for some pizza?"

She closed the book and swung her deliriously lovely legs around on the hammock, in a clumsy attempt at a dismount.

"I was at a good stopping place anyway."

I didn't feel like sharing my meal with mosquitoes and bluebottle flies, so I took the pizza inside. After hanging my Sam Brown on the hook next to the front door, I quickly changed clothes while Donna pulled a couple of beers from the fridge and placed some plates on the table.

"Productive trip?" she asked as I handed her the first slice.

"In the 'ruling out of suspects' sense? Yes. In terms of solving Steve Samples's murder, it was something of a bust, and not in the good way. It seems as if all of the Pythons except Samples and Jermaine Coltes were on lock-in after nine o'clock. Unless we're dealing with a very troubling conspiracy, I don't think this killing was about competition for the cornerback position—or any other position, for that matter."

I picked up a slice of the garbage pie and folded the crust at the middle, the way a cop from New York that I had known when I was on the Atlanta force had shown me. It made the wide slice a narrow sandwich, and it kept the goodies from falling off onto my plate.

"Narrows the field," she said as I took a bite.

I swallowed before I nodded because I didn't want to choke.

"Yeah. Before today, I had twenty million suspects. Now I have twenty million minus sixty."

"Sixty-two."

"Sixty-two?"

"Yes. We also know that you and I didn't do it."

"That's right. Twenty million minus sixty-two. I feel much

better now. Oh, and I had the most scintillating conversation with one of the girls Seth procured for his late-night party with Samples on the night he died."

"Finally tracked her down?"

"In a way. Found her eating breakfast. Lovely child. Asked me if I'd ever gotten jizz in my eyes."

"Ouch," Donna said. "It burns."

I stared at her.

"Don't ask me how I know that," she said. "May I ask in what context this question arose?"

"Seems Samples took her up to his room for a few minutes, gave her the come hither look, and she . . . um, came hither."

"Sounds like he came hither."

"Point taken. What's really interesting is that after she returned home, she told her ex-con boyfriend about her encounter. They seem to have this strange new definition of a monogamous relationship, in which she's free to hand out all the hummers she wants."

"I'm sure he's afforded some similar latitude."

"Yeah. What you said. I'd love to ask him about it, but he seems to have disappeared."

"After his girlfriend told him she'd snorkeled Steve Samples."

"Yes."

"And after Steve Samples was subsequently . . . that is, very subsequently murdered."

"Also correct. In my business, that makes him what we call a person of interest."

"Any idea where he is?"

"I know where he works. After his release from the slam, he hooked up with this traveling tent preacher, guy named Alvin Cross. I talked to Cross, who told me the kid hadn't been around for several days."

"You believe him?"

"About as far as I can throw him and his bus. Seemed the Christian thing to do was to give him the benefit of the doubt. I told him to contact me if the kid shows up."

"Why do I get the impression that you won't rest on your laurels waiting for him to call you?"

"Perhaps because your soul is so inextricably intertwined with my soul that you know my every thought?"

She snickered.

"You said *inextricably.*"

"I know big words," I protested.

"Yes, but they don't fit you well. You are right, though. Our souls are inextricably intertwined. Does that mean that you also know my every thought?"

"I do indeed."

"Do you know what I'm thinking now?" she said with a sly smile.

"Certainly. I would suggest, however, that we finish our dinner first."

The television vans were still encamped outside the police department when I arrived the next morning. I ignored them, parked in my space next to the front door, and hustled inside before they could descend on me like seventeen-year locusts.

Sherry, our civilian assistant, stopped me as I headed toward my office.

"Mornin' Judd. A Bliss County Sheriff's deputy dropped a package by for you this mornin'."

She held up a bulky manila envelope.

I took it and headed for the back storage room, where we kept the coffee machine. After preparing a cup, I strolled back to my office, ripped open the envelope, and examined the papers inside.

It contained a copy of Ricky Chasen's criminal record.

Ricky had been a very busy bad boy.

In North Carolina it used to be the custom to seal juvenile court records when a kid turned eighteen. Then, a few years ago, the legislature became weary of the dozens of complaints each month from district court judges that some perp came before the bench, charged with a truly heinous crime, and then was given a slap on the wrist because it was a first offense. Only later did the judges learn that the guy had committed the same crime—sometimes worse—as a juvenile.

The state legislature likes to stay in the good graces of the courts, mostly because so many of the legislators tended, eventually, to come before those judges. So the legislators passed a law that required only misdemeanor and minor felony records of juveniles to be sealed. Ever since, if a kid committed a Class A, B, or C felony as a juvenile, that record would be available to an adult court later on.

Ricky Chasen had a juvie file an inch thick, and it only reflected high-level felonies. Lord only knows how many minor felonies and misdemeanors he had committed in his wasted youth. He was a poster boy for bad genes and worse parenting.

When a kid is convicted in juvenile court, the judge usually requires a social history and a psychological evaluation before rendering a sentence, though they don't call it a *sentence* in juvenile court. Instead, it's called a *disposition*. Ricky Chasen's social history read like a bad soap opera.

His mother was Lumbee. The Lumbee Indian tribe is a strange racial subtype, found almost exclusively in a depressingly desolate section of the North Carolina Sandhills called Robeson County. They don't have a reservation, and they don't have casinos or federal protection, because the United States government refuses to recognize them as Native Americans. Even other Indian tribes don't want to have much to do with them.

Most Lumbees look more like the result of an illicit liaison between Scotsmen and blacks than traditional Indians. The larger majority have kinky red hair, blue eyes, and freckled reddish-brown skin. The government estimates that there may be sixty thousand of them, mostly with last names like Clark, Oxendine, and Locklear.

One popular theory of the origin of this self-proclaimed tribe is that they were at one time an offshoot of the Tuscaroras, called Croatoan. They lived in the area of North Carolina now called the Outer Banks. Sir Walter Raleigh attempted to establish a settlement there, which he dubbed the Roanoke Colony. He had to return to England, and when he finally made his way back to the Roanoke settlement he found that it was deserted, with only the cryptic word *Croatan* carved into a tree trunk.

The Lumbees hold that the Croatoan either assimilated the colony, or attacked it and killed the men before carrying off the women and children. They say that this explains their unusual physical characteristics. Some people say the resulting hybrids then intermarried with escaped black slaves, which finalized the commonly held triracial theory of the tribe's roots.

Whatever the case, very few people beyond the North Carolina state government and the Lumbees themselves seem to endorse their claim to Native American status. The area where they live in North Carolina is flat, sandy, unbearably hot in the summer—even more so than the rest of the state—and violent. The crime rate in Robeson County is the highest anywhere on the east coast, including New York and Washington, D.C., according to a report I read a few years back. Most of this is attributed to the soaring rates of illiteracy, poverty, and substance abuse. Robeson County is the only place I've ever been where a sign over the door of the local Waffle House declares that no automatic firearms are allowed inside the establishment. Apparently, you can bring in all the double-action revolvers you want.

Ricky Chasen's mother was an Oxendine named Naomi. She married a white man named Nathan Chasen, whom the social history reports indicate had a pretty impressive criminal record of his own. He would drift in and out of Ricky's life between jail stints, and whenever he did show up the reports indicate that Ricky's—and his mother's—quality of life deteriorated markedly.

Nate Chasen would arrive unannounced at the Chasen front stoop, and immediately assert his claim to what he considered his rights as head of the household—a household, one might add, to which he had not contributed in any real way for some time.

Nate also had some interesting ideas regarding the execution of his connubial rights with Ricky's mother. He was rough, foul-mouthed, loud, aggressive, and seemed to enjoy inflicting pain. On the rare occasions when Ricky's mother refused him, he settled for the inflicting pain part.

This went on until Ricky was fourteen, by which time he had already spent a night or two several times in the local juvenile detention center for assault and destruction of property. One night his father came home drunk, broke, and angry after losing whatever meager funds he had in a neighborhood craps game. His first target was his wife. She was in a foul mood of her own. She told him to ram it, and not the way he wanted.

Nate grabbed his wife by the front of her dress, whirled her around, and slammed her into the wall of her kitchen.

Ricky heard the commotion from the next room, and rushed to the kitchen to find Nate backhanding Naomi across her face, which was already swollen and bleeding. Enraged, Ricky grasped a heavy carving knife from the cluster in a ten-dollar wooden knife block sitting on the counter, and plunged the blade into Nate's back.

According to the notes from the detectives' interviews with Ricky and Naomi, Nate didn't die immediately. It took another four or five thrusts of the knife to hit something vital, during which Nate howled about the injustice and unfairness of it all, and vowed to rise from the grave to torment his wife and child.

When, at last, Nate fell silent and ceased breathing, the import of their act began to dawn on Ricky and Naomi. Being who they were, their first thoughts centered on how they might avoid being held responsible. After deliberating for a few moments, Naomi came up with the perfect solution.

The Chasen house was a tiny frame and masonite affair, which stood on concrete block piers, with the foundation surrounded by home center lattice board. To pass the time until night fell, Ricky and Naomi used an axe and a saw to cut a hole in the kitchen floor. Then Ricky climbed into the hole at dusk and began to dig.

Nate Chasen was deposited in a shallow grave underneath the kitchen floor where he had been murdered. Ricky temporarily covered the hole with a sheet of flimsy plywood, which Naomi in turn covered with an area rug she retrieved from the bedroom.

Naomi made Ricky promise never to talk about what had happened.

Their plan might have worked, had it not been for the natural process of putrefaction and the innate curiosity of the neighborhood dogs.

At his trial, Ricky's attorney attempted to make the case that Ricky had merely defended his mother from the vicious attack by his father. Ricky's own juvenile record weighed against him, however, and in the end the judge found him guilty of second-degree murder, and inflicted the harshest sentence he could under the North Carolina juvenile code. Ricky was sent to the Highrise Youth Facility in Morganton, for a period not to exceed his eighteenth birthday.

Released exactly the day he turned eighteen, Ricky at first attempted to make a go at the straight life. Within months, though, things began to fall apart for him.

He went to jail after a fight with another Lumbee, following a disagreement over the ownership of a dog. The economy in Robeson County, never robust, took an unexpected dive, and Ricky took to enhancing his unemployment check by boosting cars for a chop shop in Fayetteville. That lasted about three weeks before he was caught, tried, and sentenced to two years in a minimum detention facility.

There, Ricky made his first acquaintance with truly professional criminals, who made it their priority to indoctrinate him into the secrets of the underworld, along with the occasional prison gang rape.

Paroled a year into his sentence, Ricky did a quick U-turn back into the joint by burglarizing a house after ignoring the blatant sign in the front yard informing all would-be miscreants that the owners had installed a silent alarm.

The story went into something of a decline from there.

After reading the last of the documents in the file, I removed my reading glasses, tossed the folder onto my desktop, and rubbed the bridge of my nose to ward off a growing headache.

I felt as if I could use a stiff, hot shower.

It troubled me greatly that Ricky had gone to the juvie joint for killing his father with a kitchen knife. Modus operandi seldom changes much over time, especially in the dumber criminal population. It occurred to me that Ricky's history made him look very attractive for Steve Samples's murder. If I could figure out his motive—

My phone rang and I slapped at the loudspeaker.

"Chief Wheeler."

"Judd, this is Kent."

"Good morning, Mr. Mayor."

"Cut the crap, okay? Pick up the receiver."

Wearily, for so early in the morning, I picked up the handset.

"What is it, Kent?"

"You gonna do something about all those television trucks outside the office?"

"Are they speeding?"

"Hell, no. They're just sitting there."

"Then they aren't violating any town ordinances. Not much I can do."

"You could talk with them."

"About what? The case I haven't solved yet?"

"I'm coming over."

I held the receiver away from my face for a moment and stared at it.

"Suit yourself," I said and placed it back on the cradle.

Kent's mayoral office, along with the entire Prosperity City Government, was housed in the block of storefronts attached to the shopping center that constituted Prosperity's business district. According to the Town Charter, all commercial activity was restricted to five square acres at the junction of Morgan Highway and Highway 16.

It took him about fifteen seconds to stomp his way to my office.

"Want some coffee?" I asked when he appeared in my doorway.

"No. We need to do something about this, Judd."

"What's this *we* crap? You're the one who likes to talk to the media. Why don't you go out and fill them in?"

"I don't know anything. You've frozen me out of this case."

"I haven't frozen you out of anything. I've been busy running down leads. In addition, I would respectfully remind you that I work for the Town Council. I'm not obliged to keep you in the loop."

Although our friendship runs back almost a quarter century, forged in the fires of gridiron conflict and that certain understanding to which only leaders of men are privy, there is very little that Kent and I share in common, including political opinions, social beliefs, and such notions as honor, duty, and tradition.

Kent and I had gotten along much better before I became the top cop in Prosperity and he had become mayor. Our basic affection for one another was strong enough to weather most trials, but when he donned his cap of office he tended to become one royal pain in the ass.

I had a feeling he harbored similar feelings toward me.

He slumped in the chair across from mine, and crossed one ankle over his thigh. I could see the clockwork pattern of his manmade fiber socks.

"Would I be out of line if I were to ask you for an update?" he said.

"I guess not. You already know that the body found in your rental house was Steve Samples."

"Yes."

"It seems that your son—at Samples's request—brought a couple of girls around to Samples's house the night he died. One of them went upstairs with Samples and cleared his pipes for him."

"Cleared his pipes?"

I stuck my tongue in my cheek and pushed it back and forth a couple of times.

"Oh," he said. "I see."

"This particular young girl's boyfriend has a criminal history, which, I just discovered ten minutes ago, includes inflicting death on his father with a kitchen knife."

"Really?"

"If I'm lyin', I'm fryin'."

"That would make him the prime suspect, then."

"I thought so. On the other hand, I spent most of yesterday at the Pythons' training camp, ruling out suspects. While there is a very distant possibility that two or more Pythons could—and I wish to stress the word *could*—have worked together to pull off the murder, I think it's unlikely."

"Which leaves you with the boyfriend."

"Which leaves me, at least for the moment, with the boyfriend."

"So where is he?"

"Good question. He's been working for this traveling tent preacher who's running a sheep-shearing operation out on Nate Murray's farm. I've already been by there. The preacher, guy named Alvin Cross, told me he hasn't seen the boyfriend since the day before the murder. Cross seems confident that the boyfriend will show up sooner or later. He told me he'd call me when that happens."

"Does this boyfriend have a name?"

"Of course. Everyone has a name."

"What is it?"

I shook my head. "No way. There are eight news trucks parked across the street. People turn on television cameras, and you get diarrhea of the mouth. I have filled you in on the major aspects of my investigation. I don't want this kid's name going out over the airwaves. Might spook him into the next state, if he's stupid enough to still be hanging around—and I think he is."

"Stupid? Or hanging around?"

"Both," I said.

"So what are you going to do next?"

I drew a few small circles on my desktop with my index finger as I mulled over the question.

"I think," I said, "that I will return to the scene of the crime."

Twenty-Three

I suggested to Kent, since he was such a glutton for face time on the tube, that he might want to inform the hounds of the fourth estate that he would provide a brief update—on the other side of the shopping center. That would draw their attention away long enough for me to skulk out to the new cruiser and make my escape.

It worked like a charm. After the last of the trucks pulled up stakes and headed for the new venue, I slid behind the wheel and drove over to High Shoals.

I had hoped that there would be nobody there, but I was out of luck. As I turned onto Appaloosa, I saw a couple of satellite vans and several cars stationed across from the house.

I pulled into the driveway. Even before I switched off the car, video cameras and microphones were poked against my driver's side window.

I sighed, slipped on my hat, and opened the door.

I was pelted with questions immediately.

"What's the status . . . ?"

"Are there any developments . . . ?"

"What was the motive . . . ?"

I held up my hands.

"I have no information," I told them. "The investigation is ongoing."

One particularly persistent reporter pushed through the crowd and shoved a microphone under my nose.

"Is there any truth to the rumor that Steve Samples was part of a larger steroids conspiracy?"

"First I've heard of it. I suggest you ask the medical examiner. Then I'd suggest you ask her if she will remove that microphone from your ear."

That stopped him, just long enough for me to make a dash for the front door.

I ducked underneath the yellow crime scene tape and stepped inside the house.

The crime scene investigators, mercifully, had left the air conditioning running. The interior of the house was cool, dark, and still.

I slipped on a pair of nitrile gloves, and began flipping light switches. In a minute, the house went from dim to brightly illuminated.

Without Steve Samples's naked, bloody body splayed across the floor, the place seemed somewhat less intimidating, despite the massive brown stains on the carpet and the smears on the walls.

I wasn't certain why I had returned to the house. I suppose I had, for the moment, run out of things to investigate without retracing my leads. Sitting around my office and waiting for Alvin Cross to call seemed somehow counterproductive. At least, by taking a closer peek at the scene of the murder, I was doing something.

I took a few minutes to assemble my thoughts.

The first matter was to confirm part of the story told to me by Ann Koehler and Tracy Wall.

I entered the kitchen and pulled open the refrigerator. On the top shelf sat a cardboard carton of beer, with only two bottles remaining. Ann had told me that she drank two beers, and that Tracy had taken two. That part of their stories, at least, appeared to have been true.

I checked the rest of the refrigerator carefully. Maybe it was the question the reporter outside the house had asked regarding possible steroids. It seemed outlandish, given the NFL's hard-line stance against performance-enhancing drugs, but people are stupid, and athletes could be stupider than most other people.

I inspected the veggie crisper, the meat tray, the dairy rack, and I opened various containers. Samples hadn't spent a great deal of time in the house, so there wasn't much in the refrigerator to pick through.

I came up empty. I wasn't really surprised. Anabolics don't require refrigeration. It just seemed like a good place to hide drugs.

I looked through the freezer, mostly on general principles of thoroughness, and then closed the refrigerator door.

The meat cleaver intrigued me. I hadn't taken the time on the morning Samples was murdered to look closely at the kitchen. I figured the CSIs would do that. The handle of the cleaver had been made of black plastic. I knew that many people buy cutlery in sets, for convenience, so I rummaged through the kitchen drawers until I found a set of black-plastic-handled kitchen knives.

It wasn't conclusive, but this made it pretty likely that Samples had been killed with his own cleaver.

What did that tell me?

Using Samples's own kitchen implements implied that the crime was impulsive, and the weapon improvised. That increased the probability that his murderer hadn't come to the house with the specific intent to kill him. I couldn't speak for the average criminal, but if I were planning to punch some guy's ticket, I'd be certain to bring along some kind of weapon to do the punching.

So, why did the killer come to the house? Obviously, whatever the reason, it had led to some sort of conflict that enraged the murderer so intensely that he went after Samples with a fury bordering on passion. You didn't slice and dice some guy's head into gelatin unless you had a major grudge to exorcise.

I checked the cabinets and the appliances and found nothing. So I sidestepped the ochre stain on the carpet and went upstairs. There were two bedrooms at the top and two bathrooms and a long hall that led—I supposed—to a bonus room over the garage. One bathroom, actually a three-quarter bath with a standing shower rather than a bathtub/shower combination, opened out into the hall. The other bedroom—the master suite—had its own bathroom.

My guess was that the master bath was where Ann Koehler had afforded Samples his oral relief. I stepped into the master bath, and took a moment to ogle the appointments.

I've lived all my life, with the exception of my college days and a brief stint as an Atlanta cop, in the farmhouse my grand-father built from a kit he purchased from Sears and Roebuck in the 1920s. It's a craftsman bungalow, designed in the traditional style, which means that interior bathrooms—a relatively modern innovation in the second decade of the twentieth century, and a certain rarity in Bliss County at that time—tended to be considerably smaller than today's fashions dictate. The bathroom in my farmhouse is barely five feet wide, and maybe a dozen feet long, with a pedestal sink, a gravity-fed chain-operated toilet, and a clawfoot tub.

Five years before he died, my father had installed a modular fiberglass shower stall in one corner, as something of a nod to modern aesthetics. In the end, the primary effect had been to make an already cramped space almost claustrophobic.

In contrast, Steve Samples's master bathroom was almost as large as my bedroom. The floor was Mexican tile. The shower enclosure was curved, and as large as I had seen in some gymnasium locker rooms. One corner was dominated by a whirlpool tub, ostensibly designed for communal bathing. The opposite wall consisted of a six-foot-long cabinet with an Italian marble counter, framed in a counter-to-ceiling mirror rimmed with round frosted light bulbs. The sink hardware was highly polished gold-plated brass—compared to my own cast iron and porcelain—and the sink bowls themselves were ringed with inlaid turquoise.

It was magnificent, eye-popping, and utterly without soul. My first impression was one of cold, emotionless materialism. This room wasn't about getting clean. It was about being in style. This was a bathroom you left open to wow visitors. It was a showplace, and about as inviting as an abattoir.

While I never thought of my own bathroom as a vacation spot, I wasn't repulsed by it. This master bath would have made me uncomfortable, which probably was as much a reflection on my own provincial nature as it was a commentary on the room itself.

I pulled the maglite from my Sam Brown belt and flipped off the overhead lights. Training the high-intensity beam of the lamp on the floor, I swept it back and forth slowly, looking for any imperfections or stains.

I found it on the Mexican tile in front of the cabinet. Ann Koehler had told me that Samples ejaculated on her face, but I was betting there had to be some overflow. On the tile in front of the counter I found three small drops of dried, crusty, yellowish residue.

I took a marker from the pocket of my blouse, and drew circles around each droplet. I'd call Clark Ulrich, the CSI from the Sheriff's Department in Morgan, after leaving, and have him come by to collect a specimen.

Satisfied that Ann had told the truth about her interlude with my murder vic, I looked inside the bedroom.

The CSIs must have bagged the clothes they had found in the bedroom, because they were missing. I recalled that Clark had told me the twenty-dollar bills with the bloodstains on them had been located in Samples's pants pocket, so I figured Clark had taken all the clothes to the lab to be examined.

I slowly became aware of spiky, inconsistent thoughts and impressions. This, I realized, was why I had returned to the house. All of my impressions about this murder had been based on secondhand reports and the brief time I had spent inside the house before sealing it for the forensic guys. The more I examined the crime scene, the more I could begin to visualize the progression of the murder in my mind's eye.

What did I already know?

Samples was found on the floor just outside his kitchen, naked and chopped.

Why was he naked? I could understand if he had been found upstairs. People are naked in their bedrooms and baths all the time. Why, I wondered, would Samples have gone downstairs naked? I supposed, on one hand, that it wasn't all that unusual. With Craig out of town, Donna had walked out of my bath in the buff more than once. My bathroom, however, had only one door, and it opened to the hallway—a common design in early twentieth century craftsman homes.

In order to be in his living room in the altogether, Samples had to undress upstairs—obvious, since his clothes had been found there—and then walk downstairs. What was he doing in the living room without his clothes?

I looked at the bedroom again. Okay, he might have been in bed, sleeping naked, and had come downstairs to get a glass of water or maybe a soda. He lived alone. There was no particular reason for him to throw on a robe or a pair of shorts.

What was the chance that this was all a case of happenstance? I could imagine the scenario. Samples decides to come downstairs for a drink. What he doesn't know is that his house is being burgled. He surprises the intruder, who attacks him with the handiest weapon available, the meat cleaver.

That could fit, I thought. *Maybe it was an accident.*

Except for one thing.

The bed was immaculately made. Crime scene techs are meticulous, but they aren't going to make your bed for you after you've slipped this veil of tears. Steve Samples may have done many things on the night he died, but sleeping hadn't been one of them.

Backtrack, I thought. *Think it through again.*

I returned to the ornate bathroom and checked the shower. The soap was dry, as I probably should have expected, since Samples had been dead for more than two days. The bath mat, draped over the shower enclosure, was also dry. So, Samples might have been taking a shower when he was interrupted, but I had no way of knowing.

That didn't make sense, either. While an intruder might have entered while Samples was showering, he wouldn't have jumped out like Archimedes to dash downstairs stark naked.

Naked.

What in hell was he doing?

Whatever it was, he probably hadn't been doing it in the bedroom.

I checked the other bath quickly, so I could say I had if anyone asked later. This is the kind of thing you learn to do instinctively when you're a big-city beat cop, and I hadn't unlearned the lessons acquired during my patrol days in Atlanta.

Back downstairs, I stood and gazed at the giant bloodstain on the carpet, and its partners on the walls. Samples had fallen with his soon-to-be ruined head facing the stairs. Perhaps, I reasoned, he had been running toward them when he was at-tacked.

Attempting to escape?

That made sense. If someone came at me with a meat cleaver, I don't think I'd try to stand my ground. Escape would sound pretty damned smart.

I circled the living room, and wound up next to the French doors leading out to the patio and the pool.

I looked back, from this new vantage, at the stains. I tried to visualize the attack.

Samples was probably killed by one of the first strikes. I recalled that there had been defensive injuries to his hands, so he had tried to fend off the attacker. I reasoned that he faced down the killer with his back to the stairs. Killer swung once or twice with the cleaver, and Samples reflexively threw up his hands to ward off the blade. Slash, slash, and he realized that flesh against carbon steel was a bad bet.

So, he turned and tried to retreat up the stairs, perhaps hoping to lock a door, give himself time to think, or maybe to find a weapon of his own.

Before he got very far, the killer dropped him by burying the cleaver into the back of his skull. I know a thing or two about cranial anatomy, from my college days, and I know that we keep most of our more important master switches in that area. As soon as the cleaver penetrated the base of Samples's skull, the game was over. He'd only have time for a vague awareness of pressure or stinging before the blow dropped him like a bag of bones.

That didn't stop the killer, though. Driven by some kind of malevolent emotion, he'd pounded Samples's head over and over, until there was no resemblance to anything human.

That explained the spatters of blood on the ceiling and on the wall separating the living room and kitchen, but what about the broad coffee-colored swipes on the wall? They didn't look like hand prints.

Then it hit me.

I suppose the crime scene experts would have considered it immediately. I, on the other hand, had handled exactly one murder in the last decade. I was so overwhelmed by the damage the attacker had inflicted on Steve Samples that I had completely forgotten what should have happened to the killer.

You can't butcher someone on his own living room floor without getting his blood on you.

I replayed the murder again in my imagination. This time I tried to see it in all its gory Technicolor. As the killer made his first slashes with the cleaver, opening huge gashes on Samples's hands, the blood began to spray. Samples turned and tried to run. The cleaver arced down against the back of his head, and Samples began to fall, arterial spurt flying backward onto the murderer.

Each time the killer whacked with the cleaver, it would have been like slapping the water in a swimming pool, with sprays of fluid flying off the corpse. After ten or fifteen blows, the killer would have been soaked.

I tried to envision what happened next. Perhaps the enormity of what he had done had then caught up with the guy. He backed up, right into the wall. As he swiped against the wall, he'd transferred massive amounts of Steve Samples, leaving broad strokes.

I looked at the carpet, but didn't see any bloody footprints. That didn't seem to fit.

On the other hand, depending on where the killer had stood as he bludgeoned and hacked, he may not have gotten any significant spatter on his feet.

I backed up again, trying to absorb the scene, until my spine stopped against the French doors.

What had Jermaine Coltes told me? He'd walked into Samples's house, seen the body, and then bolted out the back, where he'd ralphed in the pool.

The pool.

I turned and tried the handle on the French doors. It turned easily, and the door swung open.

I checked the knob. There was no lock mechanism. Above the handle was a deadbolt, which appeared to be the only way to keep out intruders. Coltes had told me that he was so frightened that he'd flown out the French doors before blowing chunks.

That meant the deadbolt hadn't been thrown.

I stepped out onto the patio and looked around. Instantly, I was wrapped in smothering heat and humidity. A cloud of gnats swarmed over the deck table. The pool was flat and still.

I knew why Samples had been naked.

The scenario began to form in my head. After Seth Kramer left with the two girls, Samples couldn't sleep. Maybe he'd tried to sack out on the sofa, or maybe he'd just kept watching television.

Around four in the morning, he decided to take a cool dip in the pool. It was still hot. A swim would have felt great. He left his clothes on the chair in his bedroom and came downstairs, where he unlocked the deadbolt. It was, after all, four in the morning, and he had a decent redwood privacy fence surrounding the pool, so there was no reason to trouble with details like a swimsuit.

While he was in the pool, someone snuck into the house. Samples walked in from the deck and made it almost all the way to the stairs before he realized that he wasn't alone. He turned, there was a confrontation, maybe an argument, and then the killer pulled out the cleaver.

No. Wait. That didn't work. It didn't fit in with my original conclusion that the murderer hadn't come there intending to kill Samples. The decision to commit the crime hadn't come immediately.

That meant that there had to be a conversation—a damned embarrassing one for Samples, most likely, considering that he was standing in the middle of his living room with his dick hanging out.

That told me something more. He knew his visitor. In fact, he probably knew the killer fairly well, or he would have tried to cover himself. The killer might have been someone with whom he had been intimate, or was at the very least someone he trusted.

They talked. The conversation turned ugly. Threats, accusations, recriminations maybe. Angry words flew back and forth. The killer snapped, walked into the kitchen, ostensibly to retreat, get some distance between them, but the true motive was to find something to end the argument permanently.

Afterward, horrified at what he'd done, the killer backed away, swiped against the wall, leaving the smear, and . . . *then what?*

I tried to place myself in the murderer's shoes. I walked over to the broad stroke of dried blood on the drywall, looked down at the huge pool of Samples's blood, and thought.

"What now?" I said aloud. "What do I do next?"

I considered the problems. I had just killed a guy. I was covered with blood. I know a thing or two about evidence, because these days anyone who watches TV knows that blood can be traced.

I can't get into my car and just drive away, because then I might have to explain later why my seats and steering wheel are coated with body fluids.

"I can go upstairs," I said, again out loud. "I can use the shower, get cleaned up."

No good. There's still a problem with my clothes. Maybe I could strip down, take a shower, and clean my clothes in the washing machine, but that would take too long. The sun would be up in an hour or so.

What do I do?

I looked around the room the way the killer would have, desperately searching for some way to cover my tracks.

My eyes fell on the French doors.

The doors that led out to the patio.

The doors that led to the pool.

I pulled out my cell phone and hit the speed dial for the Sheriff's Department in Morgan.

"This is Chief Wheeler, over in Prosperity," I told Donald Webb's assistant when she answered the phone. "I need a CSI team back at the house where Steve Samples was murdered. I need them to gather some more evidence."

Twenty-Four

Carl Sussman finished loading three rolls of poly house wrap in the back of his pickup truck, and wiped his dripping face with a rag he'd stuffed in the back of his cutoff jeans.

He had finished the basic exterior framing on his house the day before. He still needed to construct the interior walls and install the roof trusses, but he could now begin to see the outline taking shape. After returning home, he'd begin the tedious process of stapling the moisture barrier house wrap to the frame, before nailing on the exterior sheathing.

He sat in the truck cab and allowed himself to do nothing for a few minutes as the air conditioner dried the sweat on his skin.

It occurred to him that he'd picked a hell of a time to dive into home construction, especially without any help. Because his work ethic tended to make him lose track of time, he had taken to placing an old wind-up alarm clock next to the house, set to go off every hour or so, to remind him to go inside and drink some water or juice.

He'd only been on the job for a couple of weeks, but he could feel the difference in his body. His shoulders, face, and arms had become sunburned. He had lost fifteen pounds, mostly around his waist, which had grown soft during the idleness of his incarceration. He could feel the strain in his arms and legs, which had been excruciatingly sore the morning after he'd begun the job, but which now had begun to acclimate to the exertion he forced on them.

His workday began at dawn, while the damp coolness of the night lingered in the air, and he worked through the day to dusk—almost nine o'clock in the evening—until the mosquitoes and night flies and no-see-ums drove him indoors, where he would eat a quick meal, shower until he could no longer feel the caked salt on his skin, and fall into bed exhausted until daybreak.

He felt invigorated. He felt stronger and happier than at any point he could recall in his adult life. He felt he had a purpose, as he watched his new home come together board by board, stick by stick, wall by wall. What had been conceived in his imagination as a tool to wile away the long lonely hours behind bars was now becoming a reality under his own hands, with no assistance from anyone. When it was finished, it would belong completely to him, in every sense.

For the first time in years, his life had begun to take on meaning.

He smiled as he dropped the truck into gear and turned to pull out of the building supply parking lot. It wouldn't do to waste time languishing in the cab of his truck. He was burning daylight.

It took him a quarter hour to make his way to Prosperity. He pulled into his driveway, felt the welcome crunch of gravel under his tires, slapped the gearshift into park, and saw the tail of the car parked behind his mobile home, near the stacks of stone he'd had delivered from the mason in Mica Wells.

"What in hell," he muttered to himself.

He was unaccustomed to visitors. He knew almost nobody in town.

It seemed, however, that a lot of the locals knew him.

He had first noticed it a day or so earlier, when he had stopped in at the grocery store. As he pushed his cart up and down the aisles, he had felt the glares that followed him, and had heard the whispers in his wake.

The cute girl at the checkout wouldn't look him directly in the face as she rung up his order. When he handed over the cash to pay for his food, she seemed unwilling to touch it.

It wasn't until he got back home, however, that he understood. Sitting on the railing of the front stoop of his trailer, held in place by a small rock, was a flyer with his picture on it. The words were familiar.

Second-degree sex offense.

Five-year sentence.

Registered sex offender.

Neighborhood notification.

He thought he had been prepared. When Chief Wheeler had told him that it would be necessary to notify the town that he had moved in, it was simply confirmation of what he had known would happen.

Perhaps, he thought, he had even imagined how the citizens of Prosperity would react to the news that he had come into their midst.

What a joke.

He had been completely unprepared for the stares and the suspicious looks in the grocery store. As he drove home, he had realized that it would be a long time before he could shop there again. Over time, given the limitation of memory and the tendency of priorities to shift to more current concerns, the people would likely forget that a monster walked among them. He would wait until tempers cooled and fears were abated, and he would live as quiet a life as he could manage. With time, he would try to become part of the community.

He inched out of his truck and walked around the mobile home.

The car sat in the midday sun, its engine ticking as it fought vainly to expel its mechanical heat. A person stood in the middle of his future living room, her hand shading her eyes as she examined the system of pulleys and ropes he had attached to the trees around his building site to use as makeshift cranes.

"Can I help you?" he called as he strode toward her.

She turned toward his voice, and he realized she was the CSI woman who had visited him several days earlier to collect the scrape from the inside of his cheek.

"Mr. Sussman," she said.

"Is there a problem, Deputy?"

She started to correct him again, but stopped when she saw the smirk begin at the corners of his mouth. She wagged a bony finger at him.

"You're making fun of me," she said.

"Only a little. Where's your bodyguard?"

"Who?"

"The guy who was in the car with you the other day."

She stuffed her hands in her pants pockets and crossed the plywood floor foundation in his direction.

"He's a coworker, another CSI, not a bodyguard. He's working. I'm off duty today. I was on the way home from the library, and I saw your house going up. I was curious."

"About the house?"

"About your progress. You said you were doing this all by yourself. I wondered how." She placed one hand on the stud wall that separated them. "It can't be easy. I've worked on a couple of Habitat projects. These wall frames are heavy. Then I saw your block and tackle system. Clever."

He noticed, for the first time, that she hadn't smiled once. It was as if her interest was entirely academic.

"I thought of it in prison," he said. "I had a lot of time on my hands to work out the details."

"Yes."

The air fell dead between them. In the copse behind the house, insects whirred at each other. Somewhere nearby a cowbird moaned mournfully.

"I didn't get your name," he said.

"Sharon Counts." She didn't offer her hand.

"You already know mine," he said.

"Yes."

"I reckon just about everyone in town knows it by now."

"You're the new sideshow attraction. Don't sweat it. They'll move on to something else in a few weeks."

She stepped down from the foundation and started to walk past him.

"Sorry to have trespassed," she said. "I'll leave you to your work."

She walked past him toward her car.

"Have you had lunch?" he asked.

She stopped and, without turning, said, "No."

"I was just going to have a bite. It's not much. Cold cuts, some potato salad. If you're not in a hurry . . ."

He let the unspoken invitation hang between them. He fully expected her to tell him to fuck off.

Instead, she turned back to him.

"Okay," she said.

He made sandwiches with beef bologna and ham and sweet hot mustard on fresh onion rolls, and spooned potato salad onto paper plates.

"The dishwasher is shot," he said as he slid a plate onto the table. "I have real plates, but I really hate to waste time washing them, time I could be using on the house."

"No problem."

"You don't smile much." He dropped his own plate on the table.

"No."

She had a fine talent for bringing a topic of conversation to a screeching halt. He decided to change the subject. "I have tea, spring water, some juice, and some Coke."

"Water's fine."

He pulled two bottles of water from the refrigerator and handed one to her.

"Why'd you pull your car behind the mobile home?" he asked.

"Because I work for the sheriff," she said as she speared a bit of potato salad. "People know my car. They know who you are. They know *what* you are. It wouldn't be good for me if people saw my car in front of your trailer. Might give them the wrong idea."

"What idea is that?"

"The *wrong* idea," she said again.

"I see."

She took another bite of the sandwich and swallowed.

"You don't look like a sex offender," she said.

"Thank you, I guess. You have a lot of experience with offenders?"

"I've run across one or two. So what's your story?"

He briefly recounted his previous life, and its unfortunate end.

"Let's just say I've had a long opportunity to reevaluate my priorities," he said.

"You don't talk like a sex offender, either."

"And yet, I am. I have the conviction and the prison sentence to prove it, and a lifetime to recover from it."

"Recover?"

"Sure. It's like anything else in life. I wasn't born a sex offender, but my personality helped pave the way for me to become one. Personality doesn't change. I'm still the same person I was when I raped that poor girl. If your personality makes it easy for you to become a drunk or a drug addict, you have to recover, and that recovery lasts a lifetime. I'll spend the rest of my life working on recovering from being a rapist, one day at time. I'll wake up on the morning of the day I die and say, *I won't rape anyone today.*"

"Sounds bleak."

"Hey, everyone needs a hobby," he said, smiling and hoping it would be infectious.

Her face didn't change expression. She shoveled a fork of potato salad into her mouth and chewed industriously.

"Tell me about your house," she said.

He cleared a space on the table and pulled out some printouts of the plans he'd drawn in prison. She looked over them and nodded.

"I see," she said. "Have you thought about this?" She took a pencil from her breast pocket and pointed at the main bedroom. "You're wasting space here with this closet. You could open up the room by placing your closet space off the master bath."

She drew in a sketch of a new closet with a door between the sink and the outside wall in the main bath. "Also, you have a wall here that could actually be an arch. The framing for the arch would be as sturdy as an actual wall, but it really doesn't matter because this wall isn't load bearing. If you put in the arch, it opens the entire main area and allows your natural light from the main window into both rooms." She demonstrated with the pencil, and then slid the paper back to him. "Otherwise, you did a pretty good job."

He studied the revisions. "Not bad. I can see it. Where'd you learn house design?"

"Like I said, I've worked on a couple of Habitat houses. You have to maximize space in them. I also watch a lot of home improvement shows on television."

"It's a good thing you showed me this before I started building the interior wall framing. I'll redraw the plans later tonight. I'm sure glad you dropped by."

"You are?"

"You bet."

She still didn't smile, but Sussman thought he could see a slight flush in her weather-beaten features.

"I have to go," she said after she'd finished the last of her potato salad.

"You'll drop back by? You know, to check on the progress?"

She wiped crumbs off her hands onto the paper plate and reached for her sunglasses.

"We'll see," she said.

Twenty-Five

The boy fidgeted on the wicker settee. The searing, humid air crushed in on him, making it hard to breathe. At least, under the protective shade of the front porch ceiling he didn't have to deal with the unrelenting sun that he knew was beating down on his father out in the fields.

His father had been worried all summer about something called a drought. The boy wasn't certain what that was, but the way his father said it made it clear that it was something really bad.

All he knew was that half the day was gone and there was still no sign of his mother.

Worse, the heat was lulling him to sleep. He tried to stay awake by watching the bumblebees that flitted from one set of plants to another in front of the porch, but after a while that became tedious.

He heard a footstep on the steps, and jerked up. Maybe his mother had arrived!

His father stepped onto the porch. He wore a pair of overalls and no shirt. His chest glistened with sweat. The brim of his wide-brimmed work hat was soaked through.

"Stay in school," he said. "Learn how to be anything but a farmer."

His father stepped off the porch, filled a bucket from the well-fed spigot at the side of the house, and splashed some of the cool, refreshing water on his face. Then he dipped a rag from his back pocket in the water and began to wipe at the back of his neck and across his shoulders and chest.

"No sign of her?" he asked needlessly.

The boy shook his head.

"Maybe she's lost," the boy said.

His father's eyes saddened.

"Yes. I think she probably is," he said. "I'm making lunch. You want some?"

A blue car rounded the far corner on the highway, a half mile away. The boy jumped from the settee.

"There!" he shouted. "There she is! I told you she'd show up!"

He ran down the steps into the front yard to greet his mother, so excited that he ignored the heat and hopped from one foot to the other.

The blue car passed the driveway without slowing.

The boy stopped hopping and watched the car fly by the farm and disappear in the distance.

His father watched it, too. He shook his head.

"It could have been her," the boy said without looking at his father. "Maybe she didn't see me out here and decided I'd gone somewhere else."

"Son . . ."

The boy turned to his father.

"Can I sit out at the highway?" he asked. "Can a take a chair and sit out next to the mailbox? That way there's no way she'd miss me."

"It's so hot," his father said.

"I could take an umbrella. I'll sit back from the highway. I just want her to see me when she comes."

His father dipped the rag in the bucket again, balled it in his fist, then placed it on top of his head and squeezed. The cold well water flowed down across his brow and cheeks, and then cascaded down his shoulders and chest.

"What about lunch first?" he said.

"Can you bring it out to me, at the mailbox? I don't want to be inside when she comes. She might think I'm not here."

"*You're sure?*"

The boy nodded.

The father wanted to pick him up, take him inside, and tell him everything. He wanted his son to understand, the way he understood, the mother's nature. He wanted so much for his son to have things he could never provide, not in a million years. More than anything, he wanted his son to be happy. He feared, almost more than anything else in all of existence, that this was the day the boy would learn an awful truth.

"Okay, then," he said. "Take one of the folding lawn chairs. I'll bring you a sandwich, and a pitcher of lemonade. Don't want you to dry up and fly away, sitting out there next to the highway."

TWENTY-SIX

"Where's your partner?" I asked, as Clark Ulrich climbed from the cab of the Chevy SUV the Bliss County Sheriff's CSIs used as a rolling crime lab.

"Partner?"

"Sharon."

"Oh. She's not my partner, not really. We get paired up on shift rotations from time to time. She's off today. Whatcha' got, Chief? Dispatch said you needed some new evidence samples collected."

I glanced over at the collection of news trucks and assembled reporters who watched hungrily from across the street, where I'd banished them.

"Come on inside before we roast to a cinder or get famous."

I led him under the crime scene tape at the front door and into the foyer.

"Here's the deal," I told him. "It turns out that Samples had some visitors the night he died. One of them, a girl from Morgan, gave him a blowjob upstairs in his bathroom. I've circled some semen stains on the floor that I need tested for DNA, just to be sure they're his."

"Why? We know he was here."

"Yes, but if these stains aren't from him, I want to know who they belong to. It might mean that someone else was here, someone I don't know about."

"I see. Okay."

"There's more. Come over here."

I led him across the living room, again carefully avoiding the huge blood pool on the carpet near the kitchen, to the smear of blood on the wall.

"I couldn't figure out why Samples was naked," I said. "Then I found out the French doors to the pool were unlocked. I reconstructed the murder in my mind, and I think I know what happened. It looks as if Samples went for a moonlight skinny-dip. When he came back in, he had a visitor. I think they argued, and then the visitor attacked him with the meat cleaver."

"Speaking of which, we finished all the tests on the cleaver. Whoever killed Samples was very careful. There weren't any prints."

"Any other stuff you could test? Skin, maybe?"

"The cleaver was spotless. Considering how short a time Samples had lived here, it's possible the very first time it was used was to kill him."

"Okay," I said, as I thought it through. "No prints means that either the killer wore gloves, or he improvised some kind of barrier between his hand and the cleaver handle, or he wiped the cleaver clean before digging it into the hardwood floor."

"Your theory about the killer not intending to kill Samples when he arrived seems to argue against gloves," Ulrich said.

"Yes. And yet, after Samples was dead, the murderer backed up and swiped against this wall here, smearing blood on it."

"Probably true. Then what?"

"I don't think he left immediately. I think he realized that he couldn't get far if he was covered in blood. I think maybe he jumped in the pool, clothes and all, to clean up."

"It's a stretch," Ulrich said.

"But worth checking. The pool filter system would have cleaned the water, but all those blood cells might still be trapped in the filter."

"I don't know. I'll remove the filter and take it to the lab, but you have to remember that this pool is chlorinated, and the water has been bombarded with UV radiation from the sun for the last two days. More than likely, even if we do have some residual blood cells in the filter, the sunlight might have destroyed any DNA evidence in them a long time ago."

"What about hair?"

"What about it?"

"I've cleaned a few pool filters in my time, and there's always a wad of trapped hair in them. We lose hundreds of strands each day. If this guy jumped in the pool and cleaned himself off, maybe he lost some hair. Is it possible the DNA in hair could survive longer than blood cells?"

"Sure. The keratin in hair is a lot sturdier stuff than the cytoplasm in blood cells. It might have stood up. But do you have any idea how many people could have gone swimming in this pool since the last time the filter was cleaned?"

"No. On the other hand, Samples lived here alone. He moved in a few weeks ago and has spent most of his time at training camp down in Newberry. For all I know, the other night was the first time he's had a chance to get in the water. You can separate hair by textures, length, color, that kind of thing, can't you?"

"In the lab, sure."

"So here's what I'd like you to do. Collect the semen stains in the bathroom upstairs. Get the filter from the pool. Carla already collected tissue from Samples's autopsy, so you have some baseline DNA to work from. I want to know if the semen upstairs is from Samples, and whether someone else's hair is in that pool filter. I want to know how many different people's hair is in the filter, and I want DNA tests run on each of them."

"That could get pricey."

"Don't worry about it. The mayor owns this house. I'm sure

he'll approve the testing costs. Can you put a rush on it?"

"It will still probably take a couple of days to separate out the different hairs—if there are any—and longer to run the PCR."

"Then you better get started."

After Clark finished collecting his specimens, I glowered at the reporters while he backed the crime scene van out of the driveway.

A few minutes later I parked the new cruiser in front of the Prosperity Police Department.

A man and a woman sat in the waiting area. He was a tall, portly gentleman with carefully-arranged hair, graying at the temples and sideburns. She was short, thin, and nervous, with reddened eyes and smeared mascara. The man looked cowed.

"I'm Chief Wheeler," I said as I approached them. "Can I help you?"

"Pete Samples," the man said as he shook my hand. "My wife, Darla. We're Steve's parents."

"Why don't you come back to my office?"

They followed me down the hall and sat across from my desk.

"I'm sorry for your loss," I said.

"Thank you. We just got to town this morning. We live in Ames, Iowa."

"Pete is the assistant football coach at Iowa State," Darla said. "We flew into Pooler this morning. We would have been here sooner, but . . ." She pulled a plastic pouch of tissues from her handbag, snatched one out, and dabbed at her eyes. "It's just so hard . . ."

Pete cleared his throat. "Steve went to Oklahoma. The Sooners. Damn near broke my heart. I'd always hoped he'd go to Iowa State. He was a starter, though. Free safety."

"He was drafted as a cornerback with the Pythons," I said.

"That's what he played in high school. He had a little experience. The Sooners didn't need a corner. They needed a free safety, so they moved him. I gotta tell you, Chief Wheeler, it was one of the proudest days of my life when he got drafted for the NFL. Is there anything you can tell us about what happened to him?"

"It's all just supposition at this point. We know that he was killed in his home, and we're pretty sure the weapon was . . . one of his own kitchen implements."

I hesitated to use the term meat cleaver.

"The medical examiner is still working on the postmortem," I continued. "I hope to get a report from her today. I should know a little more then."

"Did you ever meet Steve?" Darla asked.

"Yes, I did. Our mayor here in Prosperity owns the house where your son was killed. He had us over for a cookout a few days ago. I met Steve there."

"Did he seem," she started to say, but her voice broke. She stopped, took a deep breath. "Was he happy?"

"He was competing for a spot on the Pythons' roster. I don't think he believed he was a lock, so there was some obvious tension. On the whole, though, I'd say he was pretty content with the way things were going."

Pete stroked his chin. I could see his eyes glistening, as if it took everything he had to keep from bawling in front of me.

"Is there any chance at all that his murder was related to the Pythons?"

"I don't think so. I've been to the training camp. If someone on the team did kill him, they would have needed a lot of help. A thing like that is hard to arrange, and harder to keep a secret afterward. As far as I can tell, all his competitors for the cornerback slot were asleep when he was killed."

"I guess I didn't really think so, either," Pete said.

He looked at his wife, who looked down at the floor. Something passed between them. I had a feeling they had talked about a lot of things on their trip from Iowa.

Pete Samples coughed lightly and swept a meaty palm across his brow.

"Hot as hell here," he said.

"Yes," I said.

"Always like this?"

"No. August is usually hotter."

"How do you stand it?"

"You adjust."

He took his wife's hand. He seemed to be playing for time, trying to figure out how to move on to his next agenda item. He took a deep breath. "By any chance, has Steve's brother been around town?"

"His brother?"

"Rusty . . . Russell, that is. We call him Rusty. We haven't seen him for a few weeks, but that isn't unusual. On the other hand, when we got the call about Steve, we thought Rusty might have come here to . . . to see him, I guess."

"I'm not aware of any brother," I said. "Is he younger or older?"

"Older," they both said at once. Mrs. Samples fell silent and squeezed Pete's hand twice.

"Older," Pete replied again. "By about a minute and a half."

"Twins?"

"Yes. Uh, fraternal twins."

"Those are the ones who don't have the same DNA, right?"

"Correct. However, Steve and Rusty are very similar, in many ways. Same height, same basic build, at least at one time."

"How do you mean, at least at one time?"

"Steve kept working out after high school. Rusty . . . didn't."

I steepled my fingers and tried to sort it all out.

"What has Rusty been doing for the last four years?"

Pete glanced over at the top of his wife's head. She wouldn't take her gaze off the floor.

"Not much," Pete said. "Rusty is the older of the twins, but I suppose that's just the luck of the draw. I figure whoever was first in line would be the oldest. Somehow, you expect the older brother to be more responsible, don't you? I mean, isn't that the whole basis of the birthright in the Bible?"

"I don't think responsibility has anything to do with it," I said. "Sometimes people just need a pecking order."

"Yes. You may be right. Rusty has taken a sort of different path from Steve. Until they graduated high school, they were virtually identical. Steve was taken by OSU. Rusty signed a letter of intent with Purdue, but dropped out in his first semester, before the football season even started. Had some kind of . . . breakdown, I guess. Folded under the stress.

"Maybe it was because, for the first time in his life, he was faced with a challenge he had to beat alone. He'd had Steve to lean on all his life. Now Steve was at Oklahoma and Rusty was in Indiana. Steve did great. Rusty . . . didn't, I guess."

"What happened to him?" I asked, though I had a feeling I already knew the answer.

Pete looked up at me. His eyes were moist.

"Nothing, Chief. Nothing happened to him. Not a goddamned thing. He came home, laid around on the couch, watched a lot of TV, stopped training. I tried to get him to go to the college. He has a free ride, since I'm on the faculty. He didn't seem interested. He'd take a class here, another one there, but he never put a lot of effort into them. It was like, after he dropped out of Purdue, he just—I don't know—gave up."

I could see it. I'd known guys like Rusty Samples, a lot of them. Some people spend almost their entire lives as big fish in little ponds, artificially propped up by the hopes and dreams of people who can never aspire to half their talent. Everyone tells them how great they're going to be, how they're going to set the world on fire someday.

Then they hit the real world the way a watermelon hits the sidewalk from ten stories. They were the hot shit in their own little towns, but then they enter a realm where everyone was the hot shit in their own little towns, and some were a lot hotter shit. Maybe most.

Life has a way of kicking the props out from underneath us and, if we can't stand on our own, we crumple. Steve Samples went to Oklahoma and excelled. Rusty Samples went to Purdue and slammed the wall.

"Why do you think he might be here?" I asked.

"I couldn't think of anywhere else he might go," Pete said. "He's left home a few times over the last several years, never for more than a few weeks at a time. He'd call, tell us he was at this friend's or that friend's house, leave a number where he could be reached. Sooner or later they'd toss him out, and he'd come on back to our house for a while. Then he left a few weeks ago and we didn't hear from him. Still haven't heard from him. We knew Steve had moved into a house here in Prosperity, and we thought maybe Rusty had come here to be with him. Seems Rusty's never been complete without Steve."

He looked again at his wife, who sniffled as she stared at the floor.

"Don't know what in hell's gonna happen to Rusty now," Pete said.

"You have a picture of Rusty?"

Pete pulled out his wallet, and slipped a two-by-three photo from a plastic sleeve. He slid it across my desk. I picked it up.

"It's a couple of years old," Pete said.

I could see the resemblance to Steve Samples. Rusty had the

same cheekbones, same strong jaw line, same piercing eyes. There was something missing though, something I'd seen in Steve that Rusty lacked. Steve Samples had known what he wanted and where he was headed. Rusty looked confused.

"I'd like to copy this, if you don't mind," I said.

Pete nodded. I took the picture out to the copier and made some blow-ups. Then I returned to my office and handed the picture back.

"I need Rusty's full name," I said. "And I'll need some other information."

A half hour later, I took the picture and a report I'd written out to Sherry's desk, and handed them to her.

"I need you to put out a BOLO on this guy," I said.

"Wow," she said. "Is he the dead guy's brother?"

"Yeah. Chances are he's a thousand miles from here. On the other hand, if he's in Bliss County, I want to have a chat with him."

"He's kind of cute."

"I'm no judge. I wouldn't get too attached to him, though. About thirty minutes ago, he became a person of interest in this case."

"What a shame. All the good ones are married, gay, or murderers. I received a call from the courthouse while you were in with the parents. Luther Steele's trial is tomorrow morning at nine. They want to set up a transport order to have a couple of deputies taxi him to Morgan."

"No way," I told her. "I promised Luther I'd keep him out of the sheriff's hands until his trial is over. Call Don Webb and let him know that I'll have one of my men transport Luther to the hearing."

"Can do. Sheriff's not going to be happy about that."

183

"He'll survive. He's a tough guy. He understands promises."

I returned to my desk and tried to catch up with some overdue administrative garbage. The Piggly Wiggly had to be paid for the meals it had supplied to Luther, and to a guy named Jake Wiley who lives over off Morris Quick Road. Wiley, a nearly toothless, wheelchair-ridden old guy who lived in a one-bedroom shack, had provided me with the key information that helped me solve the Gypsy Camarena murder the previous year. In return, I had seen to it that the Piggly Wiggly delivered two meals a day to his house.

I cut a purchase order for the store, and was just about to deliver it to Sherry for processing when my telephone rang.

"Chief, this is Carla Powers," said the medical examiner when I picked up the handset.

"Doctor."

"I've finished the post on Steve Samples."

"Did you talk with Clark Ulrich?"

"He called about twenty minutes ago. Said you wanted to be certain I captured some DNA. What's up?"

I told her what I'd discovered at Samples's house.

"That's interesting. You realize, of course, that even if we do find DNA other than his in the pool filter, it probably won't match anything on record."

"On the other hand, if we should come across a likely suspect, we would be able to prove that he was in the pool."

"Or she."

"You saw the way Samples was hacked, Carla. You think a woman would be capable of doing that?"

There was a pause.

"Yes. If she was sufficiently riled."

"Seems to me it would take a lot to make a woman that angry."

She chuckled into the receiver.

"You might be surprised, Chief," she said.

"I might at that. So, what did you find in your examination of Samples?"

Through the receiver, I heard her rustle some papers as she opened a report folder.

"Based on the examination, I'd say that Samples had been dead for less than two hours at the time he was discovered. Cause of death was a combination of two factors. First, a severing of the posterior cerebral artery, which would have caused brain death relatively quickly if, in fact, another blow to the base of the skull with the murder weapon had not ablated a significant portion of the medulla."

"Meaning he died very quickly."

"Once the medulla was cut, it would have been like snuffing out a candle flame. He might have felt the first blow, the one that cut the artery, but he probably never knew what hit him with the second."

"I suppose his family will find some comfort in that. What about the defensive injuries?"

"Two large lacerations on the heel of each palm."

"He was trying to protect his face, the way a boxer does."

"That makes sense. The killer came at him with the cleaver, and he raised his hands in front of his face with the heels out. The murderer took two quick swipes, slicing Samples's hands, and Samples probably turned to run."

"That's exactly the way I reconstructed it at his house earlier today. What I can't figure out is why he was butchered the way he was."

"Rage. Whoever did Samples nurtured one hell of a grudge. I figure they hit him more than a dozen times. After a while, it was like chopping barbecue. If you can compile a list of people who Samples pissed off, I bet your killer will be on it."

"Well, I suppose it's a start."

"One more thing you should know," Carla said. "Samples had an STD. Chlamydia."

"A venereal disease?"

"Yes. We found it on the standard blood tests. It's hard to say how long he'd had it. As you may be aware, chlamydia can be present with absolutely no symptoms."

"Now, what makes you think I'd know a thing like that, Carla?"

She ignored me. "In both males and females, fifty percent of patients are nonsymptomatic. They call it the 'silent STD.' "

"Interesting."

"How so?"

"Could provide a hell of a motive for murder, if he passed it along to the wrong person."

There was a pregnant pause on the other end.

"Yes," she said. "It would, wouldn't it?"

Twenty-Seven

Marla Kennedy had just finished cleaning her kitchen after lunch when the front doorbell rang.

She folded the drying towel and looped it though a drawer handle and rushed to the door. She peered quickly through the fisheye peephole.

The man standing on her front porch was tall, bone-thin, and sharp-featured, with a prominent chin and a military buzz cut. She wasn't worried. Her husband worked nights, and at that moment was relaxing in the den reading the newspaper.

She opened the door.

"Mrs. Kennedy?" the man asked.

"I'm Marla Kennedy. What can I do for you?"

"My name is Alvin Cross. I am a Servant of the Lord, an itinerant shepherd. I've come to your lovely county to spread the Good Word at a tent revival a couple of miles from here."

"Well," Marla said. "I'm afraid we don't contribute to people who go door-to-door."

"Please," Cross said. "I think you may have gotten the wrong idea. My humble flock provides for all my needs, as the Lord wills. My mission here, today, is somewhat more personal."

"I don't understand."

"By chance, is your husband at home?"

"Yes," she said. "He's just inside, in the den."

"Would it be possible to speak with the two of you? In private?"

Marla glanced back into the house.

"Charlie!" she called.

"What is it, Marla?"

"There's a man at the door. He says he would like to talk with us."

Seconds later, Charlie Kennedy joined his wife at the door.

"Can I help you?"

"Quite the contrary," Cross said. "I think perhaps I may be able to help you. It concerns . . . well, it concerns Dena."

Marla's hand flew to her mouth. Tears immediately filled her eyes.

"What in hell are you peddling, mister?" Charlie demanded. "Dena disappeared almost two years ago."

"So I understand. That's why I was hoping to speak with you today. You see, I ran across her a few months ago and told her I'd stop by to talk with you if I happened to visit the area."

Marla grasped Charlie's arm.

"Just a few moments of your time," Cross said.

Charlie could read the plea in Marla's eyes. He suspected that the gaunt figure at the front door was running some kind of scam. On the other hand, he was half a foot taller than Cross, and weighed twice as much. He decided that if any trouble broke out, he could handle it.

"Maybe you should come inside," he said.

He unlatched the screen door, and swung it open to admit Cross, who stepped inside the foyer and stopped, looking around the house.

"You have a lovely home," he observed. "Perhaps we could have a seat somewhere?"

Marla pointed toward the living room.

"Yes," Cross said. "This will be fine."

They followed him into the living room, not even realizing that he had taken control of the interaction. Cross sat in one of the wingback chairs facing a sofa.

"Can we get you something to drink?" Marla asked.

"That can wait." Charlie turned to Cross. "What do you know about Dena?"

"Please," Cross urged. "Have a seat. Both of you. This may take a few minutes."

Charlie took Marla's hand and led her to the sofa.

"I travel all across the southern states," Cross said. "I never stay in one place for more than a couple of weeks. So much suffering on the Lord's behalf, you see. So many souls to reach.

"Sometime last year—oh, I think it was in April, or perhaps May—I was holding a revival in Dorgan, Georgia. Do you know the place?"

"No," Marla said.

"It's a small town, somewhat like Prosperity, I can tell you that. One of the men attending the revival brought me a young woman. She seemed distressed. I'd say she was about seventeen. Came up to my chin, as I recall. She had short red hair. Her eyes, as memory serves—and it serves less and less reliably these days—seem to have been blue-green."

"That sounds like Dena," Charlie said.

"She told me her name, and she said she had left home after a series of arguments. She didn't say what they were about."

"School," Marla said. "Dena wanted to quit high school and get a GED at the community college over in Morgan."

"It was foolish," Charlie said. "Anyone in their right mind knows that a high school degree beats a GED any day. I'd have let her do it, though, if I had known she was going to leave home over it."

"How fortunate that she has, at least occasionally, encountered the kind assistance of strangers," Cross said. "She was hungry. She said she had been working a number of low-paid temporary jobs, most of them off the books, to get by.

"I took her in, fed her, and gave her some clothes I keep on hand from donations I receive along the road. She was very relieved. I suspect that she had become somewhat . . . desperate."

"Why didn't she call us?" Marla asked.

"She was afraid. She thought she had burned her bridges. I encouraged her to telephone you, but then she became ill."

"Oh, no!" Marla gasped. "What was the matter?"

Cross waved a hand in the air.

"Fatigue, poor food, who knows? Her resistance was very low by that point, I would imagine. It began with a respiratory infection, but quickly spread to her lungs. By the time I got her to a hospital, she had developed pneumonia."

Charlie looked deeply concerned, as Marla wept openly. She reached again for Charlie's hand. He grasped it and placed a comforting arm around her shoulder.

"What . . . what happened?" he asked. His worst fears floated on his words like dandelion petals on the wind.

"It was touch and go," Cross said. "It was a small regional hospital, nowhere near state-of-the-art. She gave them a phony name and address. I urged her to tell the truth, so that you could be summoned, but she refused. As she had taken me into her confidence, I felt obligated to maintain her secret. For that, I am deeply aggrieved.

"She did recover. I'm happy to tell you that. A week of close care and antibiotics, with good food and rest, and she was able to leave the hospital. While she was in the doctors' care, I tried to find a place for her to light. It wouldn't do, you see, for her to travel with me. I am a man of the cloth, but I am—after all—a man. What might people think, me traveling from one random town to another with a young girl walking in my footsteps? It wasn't fitting. I'm sure you understand."

His lilting voice and the rhythmic drone of his words had

lulled them into something like a trance. They both nodded that they did, indeed, understand.

"In the end, I left her at a boarding house, with enough money for a couple of weeks. I again strongly urged her to contact you. When I left her, she gave me this."

He pulled an envelope from the back pocket of his trousers and handed it to them.

Marla held it as if it were some dread contagion. Charlie gazed at the envelope fearfully.

"Open it," he said.

Marla slid a finger along the seal of the envelope, and pulled out a single sheet of paper.

"It's her writing," she said, almost a sob. "Charlie, this is from our little girl!"

"I know," Charlie said, pulling her closer. "Read it, dear."

"Dear Mom and Dad," Marla recited, "I am so sorry that I have upset you so badly. If I had known how hard life would be on my own, I never would have left. Now I am afraid I can never return. I have done things that I am not proud of, and I still haven't found what I'm looking for out here in the world. Someday, perhaps, I will be able to return home. For the moment, I depend on the kindness of men like Reverend Cross, who took me in when I was in a very terrible situation. I can assure you that he has been a perfect gentleman, and that he took very good care of me."

Marla paused to take a breath before she continued. "I have asked Reverend Cross to bring you this letter if he is ever in the area of Bliss County. I hope that I will be able to come home someday. Until then, I will think of you often and I will try to get word to you to let you know how I am doing, when I am able. I'm so sorry that I have disappointed you. I hope to do better. I love you both so much. Dena."

Marla carefully folded the letter, placed it back into the

envelope, and turned a tear-streaked face to Cross. "All this time," she said. "We contacted the police. We put notices on the Internet. Her picture was on a milk carton. We feared the worst, the absolute worst. Mr. Cross, you have no idea how much this letter means to us."

"You don't know what's become of her?" Charlie asked.

"Sadly, no. I have no permanent address, being an itinerant servant of the Lord. She would have no way to contact me. She did tell me, before I left her, that she intended to try to change her life and to begin working her way back to you. In all honesty, I had dearly hoped as I came to your home today that I would find her here, happy and healthy. I can't tell you how it breaks my heart to find that she hasn't returned."

He slowly stood and wiped his hands together. "I must be going. I have a sermon to deliver this evening and I need time to prepare it. It is a load off my mind, having delivered this letter. I feel that I have fulfilled my promise to your daughter."

He started toward the door. Charlie stopped him with a gentle hand on his elbow.

"Reverend," Charlie said. "I feel as if we . . . owe you something. We had almost given up hope of hearing from Dena."

"The satisfaction of having brought you joy is all I need."

"But you must be out a lot of money, what with paying for Dena's food and her doctor bills."

"The money came to me from my flock, as an offering to God's work. The way I see it, that was exactly where it went. Thank you for the opportunity to bring a little joy into your lives. Now, I really must be going."

He turned toward the door.

"Wait!" Marla Kennedy said.

Cross stopped again and looked back at her.

"Yes, ma'am."

"Just stay here for a moment."

She stood and ran into the kitchen. Cross watched as she rounded the corner. "Dena took strongly after her mother," he told Charlie. "I can see the resemblance."

"Yes," Charlie said.

Marla returned moments later with a checkbook and a pen. She glanced quickly at Charlie, who nodded.

"It would be wrong," she said, "to let you leave empty-handed, after what you have done for us today. You went to great expense to help Dena. If you won't allow us to pay you back for that, could we at least contribute to your ministry?"

A shadow seemed to fall across the preacher's face for a second, as if he were mentally wrestling with a moral dilemma.

"I'm not sure it would be right," he said, shaking his head. "What I did, I did out of Christian charity."

"Then allow us to offer a little of our own," Marla pleaded. "You know, so that you can keep helping people like our Dena."

"May I pray on it?"

"Of course," Marla and Charlie said at the same time.

"Pray with me, then."

He fell to his knees on the soft pile carpet of the living room floor, and gestured for them to join him. All three knelt in a quiet circle, as Cross clasped his hands in front of him and nodded silently, as if seeking some spiritual guidance.

"Amen," he said at last. "I can see your point. The life of a traveling shepherd is not an easy one, what with prices being what they are and all. I can only see a minor problem with accepting your warm offering."

"What's that?" Marla asked.

"It's a little embarrassing. As I said, I travel from town to town, state to state. I'm never in one place long enough to establish a residence. As a result, I have no bank account. The money flows in, the money flows back out."

"Well, that's no problem," Charlie said. "We can make it out to *cash.* You can drop by our bank and cash it there."

"I suppose that would be all right," Cross said. "There are some repairs I would like to make to my tent."

"Would a thousand be enough?" Marla asked.

Cross summoned all his powers of self-control to stanch the slightest glimmer of avarice in his eyes.

"Why, yes," he said. "That would be most generous."

TWENTY-EIGHT

I dropped a bag of groceries on my kitchen table and started to put them away. Donna had gone into Morgan to browse a used book store. With my son, Craig, off in South Carolina working to raise college money, the house seemed unusually spacious with just me filling it.

This was just the beginning, I mused. In only a year, Craig would be off at college. He'd come home every other weekend for the first couple of months, and then it would be once a month, and after that only at the semester breaks. I was quickly becoming an empty-nester with a badge.

After folding the grocery bags and storing them in the pantry, I grabbed a legal pad and a pen, settled on the couch, and began assembling everything I knew.

The timeline, thankfully, was pretty short. Eight to midnight, Samples and Jermaine Coltes were in Pooler for the sports banquet, or en route home. From midnight to two-ish, Samples played host to Seth Kramer and his two girls from Morgan, during which Samples got a humjob from Ann Koehler.

Seth delivered Ann Koehler and Tracy Wall back to their homes in Morgan. Ann Koehler was met there around three o'clock by her boyfriend—and Alvin Cross's right-hand man—Ricky Chasen. She told him about her interlude with Steve Samples.

Sometime around four o'clock, Samples decided to take a skinny-dip in his pool. Shortly after, he was hacked to death in his living room.

Ricky Chasen showed up at Ann Koehler's house between four-thirty and five, and took her to Myrtle Beach to see her mother. I made a note to call Ann's mother and confirm the visit, a detail I'd neglected.

Jermaine Coltes showed up at Samples's house around five o'clock to take him to Newberry for training camp, and blew chunks in the swimming pool after finding the body.

I arrived at the house about fifteen minutes later.

There was only one big hole in the timeline, between two-thirty, when Ricky Chasen talked with Ann Koehler, and four o'clock, when Samples was supposedly murdered.

Plenty of time for Chasen to build up a head of steam, make his way over to High Shoals, confront Samples, and kill him, then wash off the evidence in the pool, get back to Morgan, and pick up Ann Koehler to go to Myrtle Beach by four-thirty.

It was tight, but it made sense.

Then there was the Rusty Samples factor. Steve's brother had gone missing two weeks before the murder, and hadn't been heard from since. Maybe he was off on some kind of vision quest, trying to figure out why his brother seemed to get all the goodies. Surely, though, by now he had seen a report of the murder on the television, or heard about it on the radio. Still, he hadn't surfaced.

I wrote "Guilty Conscience?" on the notepad next to his name.

Without knowing Rusty's whereabouts, I had to make Ricky Chasen my number one suspect.

I heard tires on the gravel of my driveway, and thought it might be Donna returning. I pulled a Corona from the refrigerator and walked out on the front porch to greet her.

Cory True, the reporter from the *Morgan Ledger-Telegraph,* turned off his car and opened the front door.

"Afternoon, Chief!" he called. "Ain't it a scorcher?"

"This isn't my birthday, Cory."

"No? Well, I don't reckon it can be every day, right?"

"You know what I mean. This is no-man's land, so far as the press is concerned. Unless you're bringing me a cake, a present, or a confession, you're out of bounds."

"Maybe I'm bringing you some interesting information."

"Now, why would you do that?"

"One hand washes the other, know what I mean?"

"I know what the saying means. What it has to do with you and me is a little fuzzy."

He pointed toward the beer in my hand.

"Got another one of those?"

"Yes."

The air between us hung heavy and charged for a few silent moments.

"Can you spare one?" he asked, at last.

"Are you old enough to drink?"

"As many times as you've made me show you my ID? You know I am."

"I reckon you are at that. Be right back out."

I walked back into the house, grabbed another Corona from the refrigerator, and took it out to him. He had climbed the five stone steps to my front porch and had taken the opportunity of my absence to impose himself upon one of the wicker porch chairs underneath the ceiling fan.

"That's my seat," I told him.

He jumped and moved over to the wicker loveseat.

"This better?"

"We'll see."

I handed the beer to him.

"You were saying," I said.

"Remember Dena Kennedy?"

197

"Runaway. About two years ago, as I recall. What about her?"

"I got a call from one of her parents' neighbors earlier today, woman named Esther Hoyt. Miz Hoyt sometimes does a little stringing for the paper. We're a small daily, you know. We can't afford to place a reporter in every little town in Bliss County—"

"Get on with it."

"Okay. Miz Hoyt talked with Dena's momma earlier today. Said the momma was almost hysterical. She'd heard from Dena. Miz Hoyt, she thought maybe it would make a nice human interest story."

"I'm with you so far."

"So, I called the momma, Marla Kennedy. She told me she'd had a visit from some tent preacher earlier in the day."

"Alvin Cross?"

Cory took a long swig from the beer bottle.

"Now that you mention it, Chief, it was precisely that individual. Anything you can tell me about him?"

"No."

"All right, then. According to Missus Kennedy, this Alvin Cross brought her a letter from Dena. She recognized the handwriting immediately. Cross told her that he'd come across Dena in a bad way down in Georgia, some little wide place in the road called Dorgan. Said she'd gotten sick, had to go to the hospital down there. Said he'd paid the medical bills."

"What became of her?"

"Who knows? Cross told the Kennedys that he found a flop for her in some boarding house before he pulled up stakes and moved on. She wrote the note and asked him to deliver it to her folks if he ever ran across Bliss County."

"And when was this?"

"April or May, last year."

"About nine months after she lit out."

"Roughly."

I took a drag from the bottle of Corona and scratched my head.

"Makes sense she'd head south," I said. "Once fall came and it started getting cold, she'd want to be somewhere warm. Maybe she wintered in Florida, and was working her way back north the time she ran into Cross."

"Interesting story."

"Did the Kennedys give Cross any money?"

Cory looked across the porch at me.

"You know, it never occurred to me to ask. Maybe I'll drop by this guy's tent meeting, ask a couple of questions."

"I'd ask the Kennedys first."

"Why, Chief? You want me to steer clear of Cross?"

"Not exactly. The Kennedys are more likely to cooperate. I've had a word or two with Mr. Cross already. Sometimes it's hard to draw the facts out of him. Tell you what, Cory. You dig into this story a little deeper, maybe find out what boarding house he left Dena Kennedy in down in Georgia, locate the doctor who treated her. I'd like to know a little more about what really happened down there."

"What are you saying? You think there's more here than a simple human interest story?"

"I think it's interesting that Cross seems to have his fingers in a lot of pies around Prosperity right now. You get this information for me, and if it leads to anything nefarious I'll cut you in on an exclusive to the story."

"Maybe I'll be ahead of you," Cory said. "Maybe I'll figure everything out and cut you in on an exclusive."

I watched a pair of bluejays chase a squirrel around the branches of white oak between my porch and Morgan Highway.

"Could be," I said. "I reckon there's a first time for everything."

★   ★   ★   ★   ★

Donna arrived a half hour later, just as I was boiling a pot of water on the stove. I poured some apple cider vinegar into the water and dropped in a couple of bay leaves as she walked in the front door, kicked off her shoes, and plopped on the couch.

"What's that smell?"

"Vinegar. I'm boiling some peel and eat shrimp for supper."

"Yum."

"Find any intriguing books?"

"A couple."

I cut a lemon, squeezed half of it into a small bowl, and spooned in some freshly prepared horseradish. After mixing it thoroughly into a paste, I squeezed in some catsup and mixed it, adding more catsup until it reached the consistency I wanted. Making good shrimp cocktail sauce was an art handed down to me from my father, along with the secrets of grilling the perfect steak.

I had learned to take pride in the things I did well, however meager they might be.

"Catch any murderers today, Chief?"

"Nope."

"Getting any closer?"

"Hard to tell. I have a couple of names that look promising, but they haven't bothered to drop by the station, turn themselves in."

"Hate it when that happens. It's just plain impolite that these miscreants make you go out and find them."

"Miscreants? Now who's using big words?"

"I am an English teacher, dear," she said as she stood and walked into the kitchen. "I have a big word license."

The water had reached a rolling boil, so I dropped the shrimp in and stirred them with a wooden spoon to keep them from clumping so they would boil evenly.

She draped her arms around my chest and clasped her hands in front of my breastbone. "Does this take long?"

"About five minutes, maybe six."

Her voice became small and high-pitched, like a moll in a 1930s gangster movie.

"That's a long time to make little me wait."

Her face was in my back, but I could hear the pout anyway.

"On the other hand, after they come out I have to ice them down for an hour before we can eat," I said.

"Oh, goodie," she said.

A couple of hours later, we sat at the kitchen table, smelling clean and fresh after our shower. We took turns peeling shrimp and dipping them into the sauce between bites of the salad I'd made.

Donna popped a shrimp in her mouth and chewed languorously.

"I think I'd love you even if you weren't good in bed if you made this for me every night," she said.

"Would get boring after a while."

"I said I'd love you. Didn't say I'd stay with you."

"Ah, it is my fate to be yoked with a fickle and capricious woman."

She almost choked.

"You quoted Virgil?"

I smiled and peeled another shrimp.

"I went to college," I said. "I know things."

"What do you know about this murder?"

"Not much more than I did last night, I'm afraid. I'm still waiting for all the pieces to land so that I can pick through them."

"But you have a suspect."

I held up two fingers.

"Two suspects," she said. "You've had worse."

"Unfortunately, I can't seem to find either one of them, not that I've tried that hard. I figure I'll need to put a lot of effort into running Ricky Chasen to ground tomorrow."

"And the other?"

"He's been missing for two weeks. For all I know he's not even within a thousand miles of here. If he surfaces, I'll talk with him."

She took a sip from the Corona I'd placed in front of her and attacked another shrimp.

"What if you find out neither one of your suspects had anything to do with it?"

"Damned if I know. I'm just a small-town cop. I hand out speeding tickets and direct traffic at the main intersection when the light shuts down. Once in a long while I have to arrest a redneck when he goes after another redneck with a tire iron. The only way I know to do this thing is take one step at a time, work through it logically, eliminate everyone who couldn't have killed Samples, and then shoot the rest and let God sort it out."

She dipped a shrimp in the sauce and chewed on it.

"You had me right up to the shooting part," she said.

"Thought it sounded macho."

She shook her head.

"Damn," I said. "Blew right through macho straight to stupid."

"But you recognize it. That counts for something. What do we do after dinner?"

"You've already seen my big finale," I said. "While the shrimp were cooling."

"Guess we'll have to improvise."

"Reckon so," I said.

TWENTY-NINE

I arrived at the station a little early the next morning, since court in Morgan would be called into session at nine-thirty, and I had to get Luther to the courthouse.

He was just finishing his breakfast when I arrived. I handed him his basket of toiletries through the opening in the cell door, and he washed his face, brushed his teeth, and shaved while I watched.

"Sorry I can't let you have a suit or some street clothes," I said. "I know you want to look good for the judge, but the best I can do is give you a fresh set of jailhouse orange jumpers."

"That's all right, Chief," he said as he pulled his shirt off. "You gotta do what you gotta do. Whatta ya think they gonna do to me today?"

"That's between you and your attorney. Given that everyone knows you shot that deputy while he was in the course of executing his legal authority, I'd recommend you plead guilty as sin and throw yourself on the mercy of the court. What you do is up to you."

"If I plead guilty, they gonna send me away again."

"Luther, you think there's a chance in hell you're going to walk on this thing? I hope your lawyer hasn't been filling your head with fool ideas. You know you shot the man. He knows you shot him. Everyone who watched Channel Nine that day knows you shot him. Best thing to do is own up to it and take what's coming. If you're genuinely sorry about it, maybe the

203

judge will go light on you, send you to some minimum-security facility. You might get off with short time."

Luther had wriggled into the fresh jumpsuit. He sat heavily on the bunk in his cell and put his head in his hands.

"Swear to God, Chief, I don't know why I did it. They was gonna throw me out of my house."

"You hadn't paid rent in four months."

"It was a rough patch. I admit that. But I was good for it. Soon's I got some work, I was gonna catch up."

"Tell it to the court, Luther. The judge will listen. I'm going to unlock the door now. I need to cuff you before we go out to the cruiser."

"Yes, sir," Luther said as I reached for the cell door keys. "What kind of day is it out there?"

"Same as the last two weeks. Hot and humid. They say we might get a thunderstorm toward dark."

I opened the door and gestured for him to turn around. I wrapped the cuffs on as gently as I could.

"You done treated me all right," Luther said. "You coulda gone back on your word and handed me over to the sheriff's deputies, but you didn't. I appreciate that."

"A promise is a promise, Luther. Those too tight?"

"No, sir. I reckon they're just about right. I don't suppose they'd allow me to come back here after the trial."

"I don't see that happening," I said.

"That's what I thought. If I don't get to tell you before they take me off, I want you to know you got the nicest jail I ever got locked up in."

"Thank you," I said. "We aim to please."

I arrived at the Bliss County Courthouse in Morgan about fifteen minutes early, and walked Luther into the holding area for processing. While he waited for his hearing, he would be placed in a holding cell about the size of a decent closet. It would be equipped with a steel bunk and a toilet and not much of anything else.

I signed custody over to the bailiff's deputies and watched as they escorted Luther off to his cell. Then I took the elevator to the third floor where they kept the courtrooms.

I saw Luther's attorney, Taylor Noble, as I stepped into the hallway. He looked up, saw me walk toward him, and shook his head.

"We are gonna get reamed today, Chief."

"Speak for yourself."

"Yeah. Guess you're right. We're in Courtroom Five. Jejo's sitting."

"Tough break," I said.

Jejo was Judge Jubal Early. He was a cantankerous jurist of the oldest school—that is, the school that likely spawned the ilk of Roy Bean and Isaac Parker. The reference "Jejo" came from the first initials of his real behind-the-back nickname, "Judge Early, Judge Often." Nobody dared call him either to his face, though it was certain that he had heard the terms at least once. Most people figured he secretly reveled in his reputation. None felt tempted to poke that stick in the lion's cage.

If Luther had drawn Jejo's courtroom, it was as unlucky as drawing aces and eights.

"I had a little talk with Luther while he got ready for court this morning," I said. "I wouldn't pretend to second-guess an attorney, but I hope you aren't planning any fancy maneuvers on his behalf."

"I'm just the mouthpiece," Noble said. "I do what my client asks me to do."

"If he fights these charges, Jejo's gonna have him making little rocks out of big rocks, and that'll just be on Sundays. You know that, don't you?"

Richard Helms

"What are you saying, Chief? You think I should advise Luther to prostrate himself before the bench?"

"Seems like good advice, all things considered. I figure a little contrition would be good strategy. Luther's already been down twice. There's no third strike law in this state, but that's never stopped Jejo. If he doesn't talk a little about how sorry he is, Judge Early's gonna lock him away and melt the key."

"Maybe I need to have a little talk with my client before his case is called."

"Holding cells are that way," I said, pointing toward a locked door at the end of the hall.

A couple of hours later, I paid a courtesy call to Sheriff Donald Webb's office in the Law Enforcement Center next to the courthouse.

I had known Don Webb for almost thirty years, ever since he had been a teacher at Prosperity Glen High School when I was a pup. As a fifty-year resident of Bliss County, he had pretty much watched me grow from boy to man, and had graciously offered more than a little helpful advice after I'd pinned on the badge as police chief.

His administrative assistant smiled as I walked into the outer office and jerked a thumb toward Sheriff Webb's office door.

"Go on in, Judd. He's alone."

I knocked once and opened the door. Webb sat at his desk, peering out the window toward the center of Morgan's five-square-block downtown.

"Judd," he said as I walked in. He stood and extended his hand. "How'd it go with Steele?"

"Jejo went a little light on him. Seems Luther was just ate up with remorse in the courtroom. Apologized directly to the deputy he shot and everything. He's going to the minimum-security unit over in Pooler for a year. With good behavior he might get parole in six months."

"Not a lot for aggravated assault."

"The boy he shot seemed satisfied."

"Well, I suppose that's good enough for me."

I took a seat across from Webb and said, "I thought I'd drop by and tell you personally. I know you didn't like me keeping him in the Prosperity lockup."

Webb waved his hand in the air. "Over and done with. I got bigger fish to fry. There's a new gang war brewing in town."

"More bikers?"

"Vulcans and Outlaws are having a falling-out. Seems one of the Vulcans got smoked in a parking lot over off Eisenhower."

"I think I read about that in the *Ledger-Telegraph*. Small article. Third page. Under the fold."

"Vulcan gets snuffed, that's about all it deserves. Allegedly it happened right after a big powwow at Racker's pool hall over next to the mall. Dead guy's name was Steger. The back channel intelligence from our undercover guy with the gangs says he had just brokered a major deal with the Outlaws, something to do with drawing new lines for meth distribution."

"I seem to recall he wasn't killed in the usual . . . uh, flamboyant style."

"It's troubling. Someone stuck an ice pick in his neck, fucked up his brain with it. Killed him almost instantly."

"Doesn't sound like the Outlaws' style."

"No, but they're getting the blame. Several of the less intellectually endowed Vulcans were ready to ride on the Outlaws soon's it happened, but the interim management talked them out of it, wanted to give the Outlaws time to prove they didn't have Steger killed. The Outlaws deny everything, of course, but the clock's ticking on them."

"Sucks to be you right now."

"Tell me about it. Election's coming up this fall. I'm on the ballot, but I'm kind of hoping I don't win."

"This gang war thing will flash off long before the election".

"Yeah," he said. "The only person I'd like to be less than me right now is you."

"You mean the Samples thing."

"Exactly. Are you anywhere close to solving it?"

"Don't you start in. I'm getting that from everyone else. Thanks for sending me Ricky Chasen's jacket. I don't suppose he's shown his face around the courthouse in the last day or so."

"Fat chance. Odds are, if he did kill Samples, he's three states away by now."

"Naw. That would be the smart thing to do, and I don't get the impression that Chasen was in line for any Rhodes Scholarships. He's still around. I have a feeling I'd run across him if I hung around that tent preacher's site over in Prosperity."

"Sounds like you're hatching a plan."

"Gotta do something. All this waiting's gonna put me to sleep."

I had just slid back behind the wheel of the cruiser when the radio chirped. Sherry's tinny voice crackled over the speaker.

"Chief, Prosperity Station. Over."

I picked up the microphone.

"This is Prosperity One. Over."

"Got a call from the morgue over in Morgan. You still there?"

"I was just about to head for the shed."

"Well, stop by the hospital first. The ME has some information for you."

"Ten-four. Out."

I started the cruiser and sat for a moment while the compressor sludged coolant around the AC system. It was only eleven o'clock and already in triple digits on the asphalt of the courthouse parking lot. For some reason, it always seemed five degrees hotter in Morgan than it did in Prosperity.

Ten minutes later I pulled into the Bliss Regional Medical Center lot and reluctantly switched off the engine.

Fortunately, the bubbletop on my cruiser and the badge on my blouse allowed me to park in a cop slot right next to the ER entrance. I walked in, nodded at the charge nurse, and told her I had to make a quick trip to the morgue. This was clearly something she didn't hear much, and she just pointed in the direction of the exit to the waiting area.

I made my way to the basement, where Carla kept her offices. She was sitting at the front desk of the morgue, reading a dog-eared copy of an old Harold Robbins novel and eating a ham and cheese sandwich.

"You read Harold Robbins?" I asked.

"You don't?"

"I find that the intricate symbolism interferes with all the sex. Sherry says you wanted to talk with me. We don't have to go to the back with all the dead guys, do we?"

"No," she said as she put down the sandwich and the book. "I probably could have phoned you with this, but it's so good I had to do it in person."

"Jesus, Carla, it's a hundred and fifty in the damn shade outside. You made me trot across the parking lot for your personal amusement?"

"That and the look on your face I'm going to enjoy when I drop this one on you. I got the initial results back on the blood from the bills that were found in Samples's pants pocket."

"And?"

"It didn't come from Samples."

I sat in the nearest waiting room chair.

"Really," I said.

"Absolutely. The DNA test is still a couple of days off, but the blood on the bills typed out to AB positive. Samples was O neg."

"That's a new twist," I said. "Any way to tell how old the blood was on the bills?"

"I'm glad you asked. It seems there's some interesting work being done by the Russians and Germans on that very question. One of them, a Russian fellow named Logvinenko, has been working on a process for determining the age of blood using the colorimetric method."

"Spare me the details."

"I'm a science geek, Chief. I love the details."

"They'd be wasted on me. Get to the point."

"No more than two days," she said, disappointment etched on her features.

"What? Two days? You mean the blood came to be on the money only two days before Steve Samples was murdered?"

"According to Logvinenko, whom—to my knowledge—has never given me reason to doubt him."

"Damn," I said, settling back in the chair. "It barely had time to dry."

"Actually, it had plenty of time. If the prothrombin count is high enough, blood can dry completely in only—"

"I know. I was making a point. You say the DNA results on the money blood can be back in a couple of days?"

"At the outside. It's amazing how throwing money at something speeds it up. Your mayor has urged us to make this case a priority. The independent lab asked me to express its gratitude for the incentive. I should have the results from Samples's . . . uh, samples back by then too."

"I'd appreciate any information you can give me about the source of the blood on the money. Gender, age, race, anything would be helpful."

"Why?"

"Because it's just possible I'm dealing with more than one murder here."

THIRTY

Nate Murray's farm looked like a lot of the land in Prosperity after four solid weeks without any more rain than fell in an average thunderboomer. The acres of corn were stunted and brown. Another twenty acres that Nate had planted with soybeans looked depressed. The sun had wilted everything in sight.

Even the closely cropped grass around Alvin Cross's canvas mission tent had turned brown and crispy. I heard it crunch under my brogans as I strode across it toward Cross's motor home.

He opened the door several seconds after I banged on it with my fist. His face was slack and his eyes rheumy, as if I'd interrupted his nap. It was a little past noon. Perhaps I had.

"Mr. Cross," I said.

"Ah, the police chief. Please forgive me, but I can't retrieve the name."

"Chief Wheeler."

"Yes, of course."

I thought that he was going to ask me inside the bus, but then he stepped down to the ground.

"Warm," he said.

"Yes. I wanted to know whether you'd run across Ricky Chasen since we last talked."

"Not even his shadow. It's as if the boy has disappeared. I sincerely hope he isn't hanging out in some bar somewhere, indulging in the devil's brew."

"Is it possible that he's gone back to Robeson County, maybe staying with his mother?"

"You know about that, eh?"

"I had a look at his police record."

"I reckon it hasn't been updated lately, at least since he got out of prison. Ricky's mom died about eight months ago. Lung cancer."

"Tough break," I said.

"What do you expect in a state that raises tobacco on a pedestal? Never took it up myself. I'll keep an eye out for Ricky, Chief, I sure will. If he shows up, I'll call you first thing."

"You drawing some crowds?" I asked, turning and looking over his tent.

"The Lord has blessed me. It seems there is no end of hearts seeking solace in your county."

"Uh huh. So I guess you're raking it in, collections-wise."

"I'd suspect that nobody is giving more than the Lord asks. The tithing has been pretty average."

"How much do you pull in on an average night?"

"Why do you ask?"

"Curiosity. I never had much time to talk with a traveling tent preacher before."

Cross hawked and spit a wad of mucus away from us. It landed in the dirt and raised a small cloud of dust.

"You want to ask me what you really want to know?" he said.

"Didn't mean to strike a nerve."

"Yeah, you did. I done set up missions in fourteen states and Lord only knows how many towns up and down the Atlantic coast. I've preached in ankle-deep snow in Virginia and in places that make this sunburned little hick town look like a polar paradise. I've met dozens of law officers over the years and not many of them liked me worth a tinker's dam. Some of them come right out and accused me of ripping off my flock. Some of them were right artful about it. I reckon you fall somewhere in between. You ain't gonna hurt me with words, Chief. Ask your questions."

"You paid a visit to Charlie and Marla Kennedy yesterday," I said.

"That's right. Figured you'd hear about it sooner or later."

"Tell me about the letter Dena wrote to them."

"Well, to tell you the truth, I ain't never read it. I saw the way Miz Kennedy teared up after she saw it, though. I suppose it contained Dena's real feelings."

"Did you take any money from them?"

"I didn't ask for any. In fact, when they offered, I told them it wouldn't be right to accept money for doing a kindness. They insisted, however. In the end they made a donation to the ministry."

"Big donation?"

"Compared to my meager needs? I'd say it was right generous. I didn't ask for a penny of it, though."

"Sure you didn't."

"You have something to say, Chief?"

"Turning them down was the classic stall. It's part of the game. Taking their money the first time they offer makes you look like you were playing them. Refusing it leaves them in the position of forcing it on you."

"Nobody forced nothin' on me."

"No, I don't reckon they did. I'd imagine they only needed to offer it two or three times before you buckled."

"They were insistent."

"Of course they were. You'd provided them with the first decent shred of evidence they'd seen in over a year that their daughter was still alive."

He hawked and spit again.

"It was the Christian thing to do," he said.

"So which boarding house was it, exactly? The one in Georgia where you placed Dena before rolling up the highway?"

"It was almost a year ago," he protested. "That was mebbe fifteen towns ago. You can't expect a poor itinerant preacher to recall details that fine."

"Dorgan, wasn't it? The town where you left her?"

"As I recall."

"That's what you told the Kennedys."

"You've been very busy, Chief. Seems you have most of the story already."

"I'm working on it."

"Then let me fill you in with a few details I didn't give Mister and Miz Kennedy. Ricky Chasen brought Dena to me after he found her peddling sawbuck blowjobs behind a biker bar south of Dorgan. She didn't have pneumonia, but she sure looked like it when she went into withdrawal from all the drugs she'd pumped into herself. She was cleaned up when I found that boarding house for her. I'll bet a shiny new silver dollar that she didn't stay that way.

"Now, I could have shared all that information with the Kennedys, but it would only have destroyed the last shred of hope they harbored of ever seeing their little girl breathing again. I am in the business of instilling hope. It is my calling to stand between my flock and their deepest fears, to offer them a glimpse of salvation and to alleviate their desperation. You tell me, Chief Wheeler, would it have been charitable and kind to tell Miz Kennedy that her whore daughter was probably lying dead in a pauper's grave somewhere? Where is the charity in that?"

"Why bother them at all?"

"Because their daughter asked me to. She gave me a letter, perhaps the very last tangible part of her that her parents will ever receive. I promised to deliver it. I kept my promise. I don't particularly enjoy standing in my own front yard and being accused of running some kind of con, just because I was true to my sacred word. Is there anything else? It's damned hot out here, and I'd just as soon be inside relaxing."

"I don't suppose," I said.

"All right then. I commence preaching at eight o'clock tonight. You are, of course, welcome to visit and see how I carry out the Lord's desires for me. I'd be happy to have you as my guest tonight. Maybe a taste of the Gospel will rid you of some of that cynical suspicion that seems to ride around over your head like a circling carrion bird."

"I think I have other plans."

"Then let me leave you with another thought, before you drive off. You're not the first peace officer to accuse me of evil. I don't imagine you'll be the last. There was one, a boy down in Alabama, who tried to run me out of town. The good people who'd spent night after night under my tent, in the worst of conditions, decided they didn't care for the way he'd treated me. They made life very rough for him. One night, a well-meaning but deluded young man in a pickup truck ran this officer's police cruiser off a country dirt road. The cruiser rolled three of four times before it came to rest on its roof. Last I heard, the poor officer still breathes through a tube and steers his wheelchair with a gadget that reads his eye movements."

"Why does that sound like a threat to me?"

"I'd never threaten a man of law," he said, his flinty eyes never leaving mine. "But one must be careful. The flock doesn't take kindly to the wolf that stands between it and the shepherd. People have minds of their own, Chief. I can't be held responsible if they exercise God-given free will, however misdirected their intentions might become. You have a fine day. I'm going inside so I can get back to my afternoon nap."

He turned and walked toward the motor home. Somewhere off in the distance, I heard the lonesome cry of a hawk that circled listlessly in the updrafts high over Nate Murray's farm, searching for some hapless rodent among the desiccated fields.

"You got a problem," the County Building Inspector, a man named Newton Slipe, told Carl Sussman as they walked around the inside of the frame of Sussman's house project.

"Hope it's not a big one," Sussman said.

"It'll do. Bliss County passed a new tornado ordinance about two, three years ago. Seems we had a storm come through that pulled a couple of new-built houses over in Golf Acres clear off their foundations. So, the County Commission rewrote the building codes."

He knelt next to a wall frame and pointed to the bolts that held it fast to the cinderblock foundation wall. "Now, you've done all right for normal circumstances, bolting these walls down the way you did. In the old days, they'd just nail them down. Code calls for metal straps around the top of the bottom plate, at least twelve-gauge thick, and at least eighteen inches long, lag-bolted into the foundation wall on six-inch centers. They need to be set no farther apart than every two feet all around the perimeter of the first floor."

"But I've already nailed down the floor sheathing," Sussman protested.

"You're gonna have to un-nail it. Until the tornado straps are installed, I gotta put a stop-work order on the house."

He finished filling out a sheet of paper, tore it from his clipboard, and stapled it to one of the cripple studs near a window frame at the front of the house.

"This piece of paper says you can't do any more structural work on the house until the tornado strap deficiency is corrected," he said. "You can call me when the straps are installed,

217

and I'll re-inspect your frame."

Slipe started to turn and step down from the structure, but Sussman stopped him.

"Just a second. Is there some place I can buy these straps?"

"Not that I know of. Most boys just go out and buy some eight-foot lengths of twelve-gauge steel flat and make their own."

"Is there anything else you see that I should work on? I don't want to finish this fix and then find out there's something else wrong."

Slipe sighed and started walking around the structure again. He stared carefully at several of the interior wall frames. "This a bathroom?" he asked as he pointed to a small enclosed area.

"That's the plan."

"You shoulda framed it with two-by-six instead of two-by-four."

"Why?"

"Practicality sake. You're gonna have all kinda pipes running through that hall—water pipes, vent pipes, that kind of thing—and you gotta drill holes in the frame to run 'em through. Drill enough holes, and you begin to compromise the structural integrity of the studs. It ain't code, exactly, but you'll be sorry if you don't redo this section of the interior wall with two-by-six."

"Anything else?"

Slipe scratched his head and looked around again. "You plan on living here?"

"I'm building this house for myself, yes."

"How much are you subbing out?"

"None of it. I'm doing the whole thing myself."

"Can't say I approve. There's a lot of craft work in tossing up a home, and a lot of it benefits from experience."

"I have experience. I had a lot of training in . . ."

"In prison," Slipe said.

"I didn't say that."

"Didn't have to. I know who you are. Fact is, I guess just about everyone in a two-mile circle knows who you are. Every house for three neighborhoods in each direction got a flyer about you."

"Including you?"

Slipe nodded.

"Tell me something. You're a local. You know what's what around here. Let's say I go about a mile down the road and take a look at that development they're building off Morris Quick Road. Am I going to find these tornado straps, twelve-gauge thickness, bolted on six-inch centers, spaced every two feet on each and every house they're building there?"

Slipe reddened. "Maybe you will, and maybe you won't, but I can guaran-damn-tee you that you'll find them on *this* house, or this frame is about as much structure as you're ever going to be permitted to finish. Do we hear each other clear?"

Sussman wiped the sweat that streamed from his matted hair with an orange work cloth and stuffed the rag back into his back pocket. "You'd rather I just move on."

"I'd rather you'd never showed up. You're here, though. Can't do much about that. This house is going to be built to the absolute letter of the code. I'm going to see to it."

Sussman leaned against the framed door opening. "I bet you have a whole ream of those stop work orders over in your car."

"I have enough."

"Then I guess we do hear each other clear."

THIRTY-ONE

One of my officers, Slim Tackett, had started dating a woman named Jennifer Ryser, who lived on the other side of Mica Wells in a small unincorporated community most people just referred to as Oak Hollow.

Jennifer was a rock-ribbed, born-again Christian, water-dunked and doubled-christened. She went to church on Sunday mornings and Wednesday nights, like a lot of folk in Bliss County, and she taught Sunday school to boot. There was a lot of grace in Jennifer Ryser, which may have been one of the attractions for a straight arrow like Slim.

Despite my own personal doubts regarding religion in general, I was happy for Slim. He was a young man looking for roots, and I figured he could do a lot worse than Jennifer.

Jennifer had given Slim a flyer she'd picked up at her own Primitive Baptist Church in Oak Hollow the previous Sunday. She said it would be nice to spend an evening in the presence of the Lord. Slim, being basically girl-stupid, probably would have agreed to ritual fingernail extraction to be close enough to Jennifer to breathe her air. He said he'd be delighted to accompany her to Reverend Cross's tent service, and maybe they could even go out for some ice cream afterward.

Slim arrived at Nate Murray's farm in a small parade of aged cars and farm trucks. He parked in the close-cropped field next to the big canvas tent, and he and Jennifer made their way to a couple of folding wooden chairs. Jennifer had insisted that they sit up front. She didn't want to miss a word of the divinely inspired lesson.

"Sin!" Cross began after the last strains of the hymn "Amazing Grace" died away. "God *hates* sin. Won't have nothin' to do with it. There's not a man, woman, or child in this holy congregation tonight that's fit to enter the Kingdom of Heaven and mingle with the blessed throngs therein. We are ate up with sin, my gentle brethren. Sin is in all of us. We may think we live a holy life, and that we're right with the Lord, but the Almighty, he knows better. He sees everything, right into the core of our hearts, and He knows that, deep down, we are all irretrievably wicked, unworthy of the bountiful blessings He has bestowed upon us!"

A red-headed young man in the back of the tent shouted, "Amen, Brother!"

"Amen!" the crowd responded.

Slim turned around to see who had prompted the outburst, but all he saw was a sea of nodding heads in the rows of folding chairs.

"Not a one of us!" Cross exhorted. "Without the blood of Christ, we are as detestable to the Lord as the foulest muck in a cesspool. Even I, your humble messenger, am not fit to wash the feet of my Lord. You see, God can see everything. He knows that we covet. He knows that we lie. He knows that we lust in our hearts for that which we know we cannot have. There is no place in his Kingdom for the sins we all harbor."

Slim felt uncomfortable, sitting close enough to Cross's stage to catch the occasional drop of spittle that flew through the air as Cross made a particularly juicy point. After all, he hadn't come out of a heartfelt desire for cleansing and revival. He was mostly there to be with Jennifer, and for some reason he felt as if the ranting of the preacher was somehow directed toward him.

He squirmed in his seat as Cross continued.

"We all know, beloveds, that there is salvation, though. We know that we are not condemned to wallow in sin, as a sow wallows in the mud. We have a door through which we can pass, and that door's name is *Jesus!*"

As he yelled the last word, Cross slammed his Bible down onto the lectern, and the sound reverberated through the tent like a cannon.

"Praise God!" a man in the back exclaimed.

"Praise Jesus!" another yelled.

Slim felt the crowd begin to sway to the rhythm of Cross's voice, the cadence of his words, and fall into the passion of his fervor.

Then, just as it seemed that Cross could yell no louder, or rail more vehemently against sin, his voice fell almost to a whisper.

"And, yet," he said, and paused several seconds for effect. "And yet, dear brethren, can we live for Christ, and still allow sin?"

"No, Preacher!" a man in the back yelled.

"No!" echoed the crowd.

"No-sir-ee Bob!" Cross shouted. "Because, as I've said time and again, the Lord hates sin. He hates those who commit it, and He hates those who condone it."

Cross pulled a slip of paper from the lectern and held it over his head. "I have come into possession of this flyer, dear friends. Some of you may have seen it on your own doorstep, delivered by an agent of the local law enforcement agencies. It is a dreadful warning. It portends terrible things for our children. Sin has come to live amongst us, with the consent and the sanction of the police and our so-called enlightened courts. Shall I read to you from this disgusting flyer? Shall I describe in all its despicable detail the acts of Satan's minion who now resides among us? Would you be frightened and outraged to learn that a man who lives by sin itself is walking alongside you as you go about your daily lives?"

Slim could only watch as Cross waved the flyer he had himself delivered to the neighborhoods surrounding Carl Sussman's property only a few days before.

"A *sex* offender!" Cross expounded. "A man who rejects all that is good and holy in man and woman, who desecrates the greatest gift the Lord has given us. This man lives in your fair community, and nobody does a thing to stop it! This man, Sussman, only scant weeks ago was a prisoner. He was remanded to the state penitentiary system for a vile and depraved act on a young woman, and they let him go free!

"Do you hear me, brothers and sisters? Free! Do we see this man Sussman under our tent tonight? Has he come to prostrate himself before the Lord and ask divine forgiveness for his horrible sins?"

"No, Preacher!" the man in the back yelled.

"No, indeed!" Cross shouted. "He is unrepentant! He lacks remorse! He flaunts his depravity and his sin in our faces, and denies the very salvation that he so desperately needs.

"We can renounce sin, dear souls. We can cleanse our own souls of iniquity. We can open our hearts and accept Jesus Lord as our savior, and vow to live our lives by the very Commandments that our Lord has given to us. And, yet, if we allow sin to move in next door, have we done our duty by the Lord? I say no! *No!* The soldier of Christ cannot allow sin to flourish in any place, no matter what the law and the courts and the misdirected prison systems claim. The soldier of Christ is bound by the blood of Christ and the waters of salvation to march forth and burn out the demon of sin! Do you hear me, dear souls? Sin must be *burned* out our lives! It is only by extinguishing sin in the purifying flames of our holy faith that we can hope to be worthy of walking the golden streets of Heaven.

"I don't know about you, brothers and sisters, but I live in terrible trepidation of standing before my Lord and Savior at the great accounting. I do not wish to enter into the presence of the Lord and have to explain why I allowed sin and iniquity to exist when I could have done something to stop it. Do you hear me, beloved?"

"Amen!" the man in the back shouted.

"Amen!" the crowd responded.

"Do you *hear* me?" Cross cried again.

"We hear you!" the congregation replied. "Amen, Preacher!"

"Then let us pray," Cross said. "Let us raise a joyful noise unto the Lord. Let us see miracles! Let us see healing! Almighty God in Heaven, this is going to be a joyful night!"

As he watched Cross step down from the platform and wade into the adoring crowd that he had worked up into a fervent lather of righteous adoration, Slim couldn't help but feel that something had been let loose under the steaming canvas tent that evening—something that was going to be terribly hard to corral and cage up again.

I sat on the sofa in my Craftsman farmhouse, Donna curled up and cradled underneath my arm. Something was playing on the television, but I wasn't certain what it was. I was too content to pay much attention to the tube.

I had met Donna only a few months after my wife Susan had died in a tragic car–truck accident at the place where Morgan Highway crosses over Six Mile Creek, in the middle of Prosperity. Part of my job as police chief includes putting in a few hours each week at the high school, and Donna was a fresh new teacher there.

We met in September. At first I denied the attraction, felt that it was a betrayal of my marriage. Despite my college education, I tend to still have a rather simplistic cop's view of the world. Right is right, and you can't do right by doing wrong. In my mind, I had married for life, and that included *my* life, even after Susan was long dead and buried.

Over the course of months I slowly warmed to the idea of spending time with Donna. New teachers tended to be assigned the most dreaded committees, and Donna had been directed to take part in a school committee to reduce gang violence—a preemptive move at best, since there isn't much gang violence to speak of in Prosperity.

As the occasional School Resource Officer at Prosperity Glen High School, I was also a member of this committee, which required me to be in contact with Donna every two weeks, whether I liked it or not.

I liked it. True, I felt pretty bad about liking it for the first ten or twelve meetings, but as time went on I realized that living the next forty or fifty years in some kind of perpetual state of mourning for Susan seemed too ascetic and monastic for my tastes. I was still almost a young man, with a young man's juices, and it just seemed, somehow, a waste to let those juices simmer down to nothing.

A night does not pass now that I don't revel in the wisdom of my decision to pursue a relationship with Donna, a relationship that had nothing to do with gangs or committees or school.

She stirred a little under my arm.

"What is this show about, anyway?" she asked, nodding her chin toward the television.

"Damned if I know."

"Then why are we watching it?"

"I'm not. Thought you were."

"Hell, no. I was dozing off. I thought you wanted to watch it."

"Not me," I said.

"Well, aren't we silly?"

"The silliest."

"Did you find your killer yet?"

"No."

"Did you get closer to him today?"

"Or her."

"Him or her."

"I heard some interesting news from Carla Powers at the morgue."

"Isn't she that tarty little doctor who keeps coming on to you?"

"It's sad. I hate to disillusion the woman, though. She seems to enjoy her vain hopes of being with me."

Donna pinched my side. It stung.

"So what did Dr. Powers tell you?"

"Some blood tests came back. Seems there was blood on the money inside Steve Samples's pockets the night he died."

She shuddered. "From what you said, there was blood all over the place the night he died."

"Well, yes. But this particular blood seems to have been on this particular money before Samples was murdered. More interesting stuff: it does not appear to belong to Samples."

"That is interesting," she said as she cuddled closer. "What does it mean?"

"I don't know."

"But you will."

"Yes," I said. "I will."

"What do you think it *might* mean?"

"Blood on the money could mean any number of things. I know that the twenties in Samples's pockets came from a girl in

Morgan. I know the girl from Morgan is involved with Ricky Chasen."

"One of your suspects."

"My prime suspect. I know that Chasen likes knives and other pointy things, because he killed his father with one and went to prison for assault with another."

"See? You know more than you thought."

"I also know that, in my timeline, Chasen had time to get from Morgan to Samples's house on the night of the murder, and then back to Morgan in time to take the girl to Myrtle Beach."

"Means and opportunity."

"That's exactly what I was about to say. Stop reading my mind."

"That leaves motive, right?"

"So they say. How did you know that?"

"I'm an English teacher. I read books. I also sleep with the chief of police. After a while, you learn things."

"I teach you things while I'm asleep?"

She turned around and kissed me. It was long, deep, and wet.

I liked that, too.

"No, darling," she said. "You teach me things *before* you go to sleep."

"Well, you know what they say."

"What's that?"

"When the pupil is ready, the master will appear."

This time, when she pinched my side, it really stung.

THIRTY-TWO

Slim sat across from me in my office. His face was drawn. He looked worried.

"I tell you, Chief, this Cross fella's up to no good."

"You think?"

"You should've heard him last night. He just as good as told the folks at his tent meeting that they'd be doing the Lord's work if they went out and lynched that guy, Sussman."

"That's troubling," I said.

"You shoulda been there is all I have to say. It was scary. This man, Cross, he can whip up a crowd like nobody I ever saw. It's like he can tap into something deep inside of 'em, poke at 'em with the things that scare 'em the most. Before he finished last night, I think most every person under that tent would've took a bullet for him."

"That's the way these tent revivalists work, Slim. If they could color inside the lines, they'd be preachers at some tiny country church somewhere, doing real good work."

"I reckon. I gotta tell you, it was like bring-your-own-snake night. This guy danced around the stage like some kinda circus freak, and then he brought people up and he healed them, right in front of everyone."

"I've seen it before. It's part of their shakedown. Sooner or later the money will dry out, and Cross will pack up his tent and move on. Maybe, once he does, I can get a break in this Samples murder case."

"How's that?"

"I think Cross is protecting my number one suspect. If he pulls up tent stakes, I can find out where he lights next, and maybe Chasen will be there."

"I'll be happy to see him go," Slim said. "There's something very troubling about that man. Once he does go, I'll be happy to track him down for you, if it will help solve this murder."

"I may take you up on that, Slim. Tell me—your cousin, Ray, does he still ride with the Tarheel Outlaws?"

"Can't say for certain. We don't exactly invite him to the family barbecues. Ray's burned a lot of bridges with our family."

"Maybe it's time to mend them."

"How come?"

"I owe Sheriff Webb a favor for sending me the Ricky Chasen jacket. Word's out that there's some bad blood between the Outlaws and the Vulcans. Seems one of the Vulcans' top dogs got put down over in Morgan a few days ago."

"No great loss."

"No, but if war breaks out between the gangs, some innocent civilians could get caught in the crossfire. Think you could cozy up to Ray a little, get him to talk about what's going down with the Outlaws?"

"Pour enough beer into him, Ray'll tell you whatever you want to know."

"I don't want to cause any conflicts between you and Jennifer. I know how the Baptists over in Oak Hollow feel about alcohol."

"I don't think it would be a problem. The kind of places Ray likes to drink, you don't find many Baptists."

"You'd have my gratitude, and I'm sure Sheriff Webb would appreciate it too."

I stood and grabbed my hat and aluminum duty folder.

"You heading out?" Slim asked.

"Yeah. I thought I might drop by Carl Sussman's place, see how he's coming with that house of his."

The traveling carnival of news vans had dwindled over the previous couple of days as the attention deficit of the viewing public was diverted by some other, newer crisis. That was fine by me, as long as the new crisis was outside my district.

A lone cameraman hoisted a camera to his shoulder as I stepped through the front door of the station. I flashed him the peace sign and slid into the new cruiser. In the rearview mirror, I saw him ease the camera off his shoulder and turn back to the van. I had a feeling his heart wasn't completely into his attempt to catch me on videotape.

It was just past eleven in the morning. It felt like storm weather. The air was hot and wet and oppressive, and it clung to me like molasses, even in the blast of the air conditioner. It would only take a small cold front to coalesce all the moisture in the air into a convection system that would keep the night sky alight with a show of electric fury.

I had driven by Carl Sussman's house project once or twice in the course of patrolling in Prosperity, but it had been several days since I'd stopped in to check on his progress. He was standing next to the house when I pulled into the gravel drive. I pulled on my hat and half-heartedly stepped out of the cruiser.

He had several eight-foot lengths of flat steel on a work table. Next to the steel was a cutoff miter saw, in which the usual toothed wood blade had been replaced by a compound metal cutting wheel. He had also attached a heavy iron vise to the table. When I stepped out of the car, he revved up the cutoff saw and lowered it to a piece of the flat steel. A shower of sparks rooster-tailed off the metal, accompanied by the screeching sound of the blade biting through the flat.

As soon as the piece was cut, he was careful to shut down the saw, but he didn't let go of it until it stopped spinning. It said something that he put such emphasis on workplace safety. Mostly, it said that he realized he was pretty much on his own. A bad accident could put him in a really tough place, if nobody knew he was injured.

He slipped the two-foot-long length of metal into the vise and closed the jaws down on it, then hammered at the protruding six inches with a small mallet he'd placed on the table for that purpose.

"Taking up blacksmithing?" I asked.

He whirled to face me, the hammer raised defensively. Almost immediately, he relaxed.

"Damn, Chief, give a guy a little warning," he said, trying to regain his breath.

"Didn't mean to startle you. I figured you'd heard the car when I pulled up."

Sussman pointed to one of his ears. "I've been cutting metal straps all morning. I stopped hearing stuff about an hour ago."

"What's all this?"

"Building code. This jerkoff Napoleon wannabe with the Building Inspector's office told me I had to install tornado straps all around the foundation of my house or he wouldn't sign off on the framing. I have to comply, so I'm cutting straps."

"Tough deal."

"The worst part is that I got the distinct impression he was yanking my chain. He admitted that he lives in one of the neighborhoods nearby, and that he got one of those notification flyers you guys passed around. You think every new house in the county has to put these straps in?"

"Probably not," I said. "The major developers can probably slip by the regs with a little well-placed juice. There is a downside, though."

"What's that?"

"If a tornado does come through, their houses may become airplanes."

"Bet they don't care. Once they finish the houses and sell them, their responsibility ends."

"No," I said. "Just their accountability. You do what the inspectors say and you'll have yourself a good safe house in the end. It's a chore now, but you'll be grateful later."

"You sound like my father."

"I might be. What was your mother's name?"

He chuckled and dropped the hammer on the table. "Good one. You thirsty? It's just about time for a break."

"Nothing for me. I just wanted to drop by, see how the house is going. Also wanted to give you a heads-up."

"About what?"

"One of my patrolmen attended this tent meeting a couple of miles from here last night. It seems you were the focus of the sermon."

Sussman sat on the edge of his house foundation and mopped at his face with a rag.

"People who go to these tent meetings tend to see things pretty simply," I continued. "The preacher said a lot of nasty things about you. Don't suppose you two have ever met."

"I don't know any preachers, Chief."

"Didn't think so. This preacher seems to think you represent some kind of plague that needs eradicating. People around here are pretty peaceful, for the most part, but if they get riled they sometimes act before they think."

"What are you saying?"

"Watch your back. I'd hate to see you get hurt because some redneck went off half-cocked."

Sussman tossed the rag on the plywood sheathing of his floor. "Do you think this is ever going to end?"

"Hell," I replied. "I don't think it's even gotten good and started yet. I don't want to stand here and lay heavies on you, Carl, but you probably could have chosen a better place to settle. This is Republican country, one of the reddest counties in a very red state. People have a strong sense of law and order in these parts. They're not likely to readily understand concepts like debts being paid to society. Far as they're concerned, you're nothing but a pervert and a pederast."

"But my victim was an adult."

"Doesn't matter. 'Sex offender' to them means 'child molester.' People in this community, by and large, aren't big on distinctions."

"So I'm in for a tough time."

"Most likely. I'll keep an eye on things. So long as you keep things in the road, you're fine by me. If you start getting hassled—in an illegal manner, that is—I'll try to put a lid on it."

Sussman stared off into the woods for several moments, as if digesting what I'd said. Then he ran both hands through his hair and twisted it back off his neck.

"And you might consider a haircut," I added.

He laughed. I guess we both laughed.

"Thanks for coming by, Chief," he said. "And thanks for keeping an eye on things."

"Just doing my job," I said as I shook his hand. "I'm here to keep the peace."

I walked back to the cruiser and started it up. As I backed out the gravel drive past Sussman's trailer, just before I hit the main road, I saw the front door of the trailer open and Sharon Counts stepped out on the wooden deck.

I hesitated at the end of the drive and our eyes locked for an instant. It was as if she had wanted me to know she was there.

I backed on out and turned toward Morgan Highway. Half a mile down the road I chuckled and shook my head.

"There's just no figuring people," I said to nobody in particular.

THIRTY-THREE

The *seven-year-old boy had found that if he raised and lowered the umbrella quickly every once in a while, it created a brief cooling breeze.*

He sat in a folding lawn chair with multicolored nylon webbing, which prickled at his skin as he squirmed to find a comfortable position. He held the umbrella close over his head, to ward off the worst of the midday sun that beat down on him mercilessly. The crisp, clean shirt he'd donned that morning had long since soaked through. His bottom itched from sitting for too long.

A half-empty plastic pitcher of lemonade sat next to him on a folding porch table his father had brought out with his lunch. The ice in the pitcher had melted. Every several minutes the boy's mouth became parched again and he'd pour a little more of the lemonade into the anodized aluminum cup and wash out his mouth.

He glanced at his watch, for the fifth time in the last fifteen minutes. Three-seventeen. Each minute that passed reduced the amount of time he would have with his mother once she arrived. That disappointed him. It had been weeks—maybe months—since he had last seen her, so whatever time they had together would be welcome.

He swatted at a bluebottle fly that flitted at his face, attracted by the salt in his sweat and the sugar from the lemonade and the crumbs of the bologna sandwich on the paper plate, left over from lunch.

Every several minutes a car would appear on the horizon, shimmering like a desert mirage in the heat risers emanating from the

235

asphalt. He could hear the cars before he saw them, and each time the sound of a distant engine reached his ears, he'd stare down the road, waiting for an image to fade into view.

Some of the cars were blue. None of them brought his mother.

Each one that whizzed by on the highway raised a quick wind, which felt nice.

The father took a break around four o'clock and sat on the front porch. He sipped a glass of iced tea and mopped at his face and neck with a wet towel. He couldn't take his eyes off the boy, sitting in the lawn chair down next to the highway, warding off the heat with an umbrella, waiting faithfully for his mother the way a dog waits all day for its master to return home.

The father's heart broke as he watched. As a younger man, he had thought his life was perfectly laid out for him. In the certainty of youth he had believed that whatever he wanted could be attained, simply by working hard and believing in himself. He had cherished the vision of working the land and making it fruitful, and watching his children grow, with this loving wife by his side, and of growing old together gracefully, of loving the lines that would gradually crease their faces as a symbol of their devotion and shared memories.

Time had a way of dashing your hopes. Life had a way of taking you down roads you'd never imagined to exist. The father couldn't have conceived as a young man of trying to be both mother and father to a young boy. The very thought would have been overwhelming.

And yet, he seemed to manage.

Barely.

The father wondered whether there might have been another way. He had prayed on it repeatedly, examined every facet of what had happened, tried to understand why things had gone the way they did, and it still made about as much sense to him as quantum mechanics.

What she had done was unforgivable. It was a violation of her sacred vows, a complete rejection of everything the father held to be holy and right. Worse, she had divulged everything to him without a shred of contrition.

"A thing is what it is," she had said. 'It can't be something else.'

If a thing was only what it was, and if that thing was intolerable, then it had to be rejected. In the end, the father's beliefs and standards had become intolerable to the mother, and she had decided she couldn't stay.

He had pleaded with her, for the sake of the boy, to remain. She had refused. She had promised to visit the boy, and even intimated that someday she might be able to take him.

This was what the father feared most. The woman he had loved so deeply, with such a committed fervor, had proven to have no more values than a stray cat. It was unthinkable that he might ever turn over his wonderful son to her.

The boy didn't understand a bit of this, he realized. A dreadful mother is still a mother. The boy didn't know the difference. The father couldn't hurt the boy by telling him who and what his mother really was.

The father sat on the front porch and drained the rest of the glass of iced tea. He walked back to the kitchen, washed out the glass, and set it upside down in the plastic wire drying rack next to the sink. Then he pulled on his broad-brimmed straw hat and walked out the back door, so he wouldn't have to see his son roasting under an umbrella, in a plastic lawn chair next to the highway, waiting faithfully for the mother who would probably never come.

THIRTY-FOUR

I eased the new cruiser into the Koehler driveway in Morgan, pulled on my hat, and walked up to the front door.

Ann Koehler's stepmother answered the door on the first knock.

"Sorry to visit without calling first," I said. "I was wondering if I could have a word with Ann."

"Ann's not here."

"Do you know when she might be back?"

She twisted the dishrag in her hand as if trying to wring some desperate truth from it.

"Fact is, Chief, I don't know where Ann is. Haven't seen her for a couple of days. I'm getting a little worried."

Something like an icy worm seemed to crawl around the inside of my chest.

"She didn't go off with Ricky Chasen, did she?" I asked.

"I can't say. I came home from shopping a couple of days ago and she was gone. I haven't heard a word from her since then."

"May I come in?"

She looked up and down the street and then nodded tentatively. She opened the screen door and I walked inside.

The house looked little different than it had during my last visit. Maybe it was a little cleaner. Nervous energy has to be expended. For Betty Koehler, it was apparently channeled into housework.

"Please, sit down," she said, pointing toward a rumpled sofa.

I sat and opened my duty folder to take notes. Betty Koehler sat in a glider rocker next to the fireplace.

"I had considered calling the local police," she said.

"But you didn't."

"Not yet. Ann does this, sometimes. She's very strong-willed. Almost bull-headed. She goes off for days at a time, doesn't tell me where she's going, and then shows up again out of the blue without an explanation."

"What's different this time?"

"Well," she said, worrying the dishrag. "We have good times and bad times, you see. Some days we get on very nicely. Others, she treats me like some kind of hired housekeeper. She resents me, I know that. I didn't try to replace her mother, but she often sees me as some kind of interloper. We were getting along very well a couple of days ago, and I told her I'd like to take her to the mall to shop for some clothes. She seemed very excited about it. Then I came home and . . . well, nothing."

"This isn't like her?"

"Not when there's something she's looking forward to doing. At the worst, she leaves me a note or calls me from her cell phone to let me know that she's not going to be home. When there's something she looks forward to doing, that is."

"Yes. So you said. This time, though, no call, no message?"

"Not a word."

"Did you try calling her cell phone?"

"Oh, yes. The first night she wasn't home for dinner. I wanted to know whether to keep her food ready for her. She didn't answer."

"And she hasn't called or answered her cell phone since then?"

"Not a peep. I'm very worried."

"What does Ann's father say?"

"He's off in Louisiana, on another business trip. He said I should give her some time and she'll show up. I don't know. This time is different. I don't like it."

"Do you have a way to contact Ricky Chasen?"

She shook her head. "Ann's father doesn't like that boy. I can't say I do either. I think it's the tattoos."

"Or maybe his prison record?"

I watched all the color drain from her face. For a moment I thought she might faint.

"He's been to prison?" she asked.

"You didn't know?"

"Ann never told me. Oh, this is just awful. When her father finds out. . . . What did he do?"

"You don't want to know. It would worry you more. Is it possible that Ann went to Myrtle Beach again? Maybe to see her mother?"

"I haven't checked."

"I have her number. I need to speak with her anyway about Ann's trip down there last week. Have you seen Ricky Chasen here since I visited the other day?"

She shook her head. "He did call, but if he's been by the house, it would have been while I was out. You're going to call Ann's mother?"

"Yes."

"If you hear anything, you'll let me know, won't you? Katy and me, we don't get on well at all. If I call her, she'll just slam the phone down in my ear. If Ann's with her, please call and let me know."

I assured her that I would and let myself out. It occurred to me that Betty Koehler, for a woman who probably started out as a trophy wife about fifty pounds back, seemed to genuinely care for her stepdaughter, despite their differences. I figured that Ann could do a lot worse.

I just hoped she hadn't done a whole lot worse.

As soon as I returned to the station, I went directly to my office and, after checking the number in my records, placed a call to Myrtle Beach. Katy Koehler answered on the third ring.

I identified myself, and could feel her stress level jump about five points even over the long-distance lines.

"What's happened?" she asked.

"Nothing that I know of, ma'am. I interviewed your daughter Ann a couple of days ago in connection with a murder we had here in Prosperity, and I need to ask you a few questions."

"A murder!"

"Please, ma'am, don't be alarmed. Ann may be a material witness, but I don't think she was directly involved in the killing. I need to talk to her, and I wondered whether she was in Myrtle Beach with you."

"No. Why? Isn't she in Morgan?"

"No, ma'am. I talked with her stepmother, who said she hadn't seen Ann for a couple of days."

"That bitch."

"Ma'am?"

"Betty. Betty the Bitch, I call her. You knew she was the reason for my divorce."

"No, ma'am, I didn't."

I had suspected it. I was just too polite to say so.

"She seduced my husband. It was no better than theft. She's a whore and a thief, far as I'm concerned."

"I understand you're upset—"

"You have no idea. I'd love to get my hands around her scrawny chicken neck, I can tell you that."

During a moment of silence, I imagined her remembering who was on the other end of the phone.

"You understand, of course, that I'd never actually . . . I

mean, it's a figure of speech."

"Of course," I said. "If you don't mind, ma'am, when was the last time you saw Ann?"

"A week ago. She came down for a visit. Stayed a day or so."

"Did she come alone?"

"No. She was with that boy, Ricky."

"Ricky Chasen."

"Yes. I'm not sure I like him."

I stifled the impulse to tell her that there was a lot about Ricky Chasen not to like. "How was Ann when you saw her last week?"

"I don't understand."

"Did she seem different in any way? Maybe more nervous than usual?"

"I don't think so. Fact is, I only saw her for a few hours. She came in with that Ricky boy, they visited for a while, had some breakfast, watched a little TV, and then they were out the door again. Said they wanted to go to the beach. They came back around dinnertime and we went out to a fish place."

"They stayed overnight?"

"Yes. Not in the same room. I know Ann's grown up in the eye of the law, but I'm not one of those permissive parents who'll let her daughter sleep with some boy under my roof without being married. Ann slept in the guest room. Ricky stayed on the couch."

I made a couple of notes on my pad.

"And you haven't seen Ann since that visit?"

"No. Why? Is she missing?"

"Not exactly, ma'am. Nobody's filed a missing person report. I just need to talk with her, and her stepmother hasn't seen her for a day or so. Like you said, she is an adult in the eyes of the law. She can pretty much up and go wherever she pleases whenever she pleases."

"That's disturbing. It's hard to let go, you know."

"Yes I do, ma'am."

"You have children?"

"One. A boy."

"It's different with boys."

"I wouldn't know, ma'am. I do know it's hard with them. Can't say whether it's harder with girls. To tell you the truth, I'm kind of glad I don't have to find out."

"Could you do me a favor, Chief?"

"You want me to call you if Ann shows up?"

"That's exactly what I was going to ask."

"I'll be happy to," I said.

After we finished the conversation, I walked down to the Piggly Wiggly, bought a pork chop lunch from the hot bar, then returned to my office to eat.

As I worked on my meal, I reviewed the facts as I knew them. Maybe Ricky Chasen had killed Steve Samples, and maybe he hadn't. If he had killed Samples, it was possible that Ann Koehler didn't know. Her mother had said that Ann didn't seem at all different on her visit, after the murder. I had only met Ann once, and had found her to be a cool customer—maybe even a little disrespectful—but I also know that there are some things you can't just slam to the back of your head and forget.

Maybe Ricky killed Samples, but didn't tell Ann what he'd done. Ricky had a lifetime of experience at holding back on the truth. For certain, even if he had done the killing, Ann's natural mother might not have noticed any difference. Maybe, for people like Ricky Chasen, killing didn't carry the emotional impact that it did for other people. Killing another person can etch some mighty graffiti on your soul, but with some people you can't read it by looking in their eyes.

Then there was the possibility I really didn't want to face—

that Ricky Chasen, despite how good he looked for this thing, wasn't involved in the murder at all. Maybe all the stuff I'd picked up over the last week was circumstantial. Maybe I'd been barking up the wrong tree all along. Maybe I was going to have to backtrack and start sniffing down a different trail.

There was a knock at my door.

"Come in," I said between bites of pork chop.

Kent Kramer opened the door and stuck his head inside my office.

"You busy?"

"Just wolfing down some lunch between interrogating suspects. Come on in."

Kent closed the door behind him and sat across from me. I didn't stop eating. In the cop business, you eat when you can. Besides, Kent and I had known each other for so long that we could do just about anything in each other's presence.

"What's up?" I asked.

"Seth left this morning for Atlanta. Training camp, you know."

"I know."

"You know he left?"

"I know about training camp."

"I guess what I wanted to ask . . . well, what I mean is . . . Judd, is Seth in trouble?"

"You mean in this Steve Samples thing?"

"Yes."

I wiped my mouth with a napkin, and thought as I chewed the last of a bite of fried squash drenched in catsup.

"Hard to say," I said at last. "Legally, I think he's in the clear. On the other hand, if it does turn out that Samples was murdered by the boyfriend of the girl Seth brought to his house, it could be bad for his karma."

"Karma."

"Yes."

"What in hell does that mean?"

"Your boy was basically procuring for Samples. Samples said he wanted to get his ashes hauled, and Seth rounded up a couple of fillies to do the job. Now, if Ricky Chasen killed Samples because he got a hummer from one of the girls, that kind of places Seth squarely in the chain of events leading up to the murder."

"But he couldn't go to jail."

"It's a tricky question. You see, Samples asked this Koehler girl to break a hundred, but she only had sixty-two dollars. He gave her the hundred and took the sixty-two. That means she came out thirty-eight dollars to the good."

"So?"

"After she rocked his boat, he gave her almost forty dollars. Maybe it's all innocent, but there are people who would consider that a transaction. That makes it prostitution, and Seth set it up. People might say he pimped that girl."

"Even if he didn't get any money?"

"He wasn't looking for money. He wanted to get on Samples's good side. He was fishing for a recommendation down the line when he turns pro. There was some serious *quid pro quo* going on in that house the night Samples died."

"You don't really think Seth could be charged with prostitution, do you?"

I speared another piece of fried squash and dredged it in the catsup.

"I don't think it's a question of prosecution," I said. "We're talking moral obligations here. What goes around comes around. If Seth contributed to Samples's death, there could be some serious karmic cleansing called for down the line."

Kent crossed his arms and leaned back in the chair. "Why do I get the impression that you're fucking with me?"

"Probably because, for you, morality is subjective. It isn't the kind of thing you place a high priority on and, genetically speaking, the fruit most often don't fall too far from the tree."

Kent rubbed his face with the palm of his hand and grinned. "You know, Judd, half the time I don't understand a damn word you're saying."

I sipped some iced tea.

"Yeah," I said. "Don't worry about it. It's okay. We're still friends."

And that, I realized, was what he really wanted to know.

Carl Sussman sat in the cool air of Dr. Kronenfeld's office and stared at the floor.

Jerome Kronenfeld sat across from him, waiting patiently. Everything about Kronenfeld was soft—his body, his voice, and his demeanor. He made his living by listening to people and trying to clarify their lives without making judgments. Sometimes he actually managed to pull it off.

He was thick through the body, with a mustache flecked with gray, which sat on his sallow face above prominent jowls. He had allowed his hair to thin on top without any attempt to disguise it by pretentious comb-overs, but he had decided long ago that the shaggy strands he allowed to fall about his ears and the collar of the sport shirts he preferred to wear was just compensation. When he did speak—almost never without something significant to say—his voice remained calm and soothing. It was his belief that his job was to reflect and analyze, not to provoke.

This was his fourth session with Carl Sussman. Kronenfeld already knew most of what there was to know about Sussman's history. They had reached a point in his treatment where the focus was on processing.

"Sometimes, it just seems unfair," Sussman said.

"What seems unfair?"

"I did my time. I paid my price. I admitted my crime, and I didn't ask for early parole. What I did was awful. I know that. I regret it every day. I'm trying to live a good life. Even so, it's like I walk into a shitstorm every time I leave my house. People look at me as if I'm some kind of monster."

"You frighten them."

"No. What I did frightens them."

"They can't separate the two things. You aren't Carl Sussman to them. You are 'that sex offender.' That's your identity."

"But it isn't. It really isn't."

"It is to them. That's their perception. Perception is reality."

"I can't buy that," Sussman said.

"You already have. Remember when you described your crime to me? You said that the drugs made you think you could do anything. Could you really do anything?"

"No."

"And yet, you believed that you could. Your perception, at least for that moment, became your reality, and you acted on it. The people in your community aren't any different. They've been conditioned to think in a certain way. The media have done an exemplary job of indoctrinating them."

"But if they only knew me . . ."

"They would still be wary. A thing is what it is, Carl."

Sussman gave out something between a laugh and a sob, a barking sort of noise that represented his frustration. "What is that, some kind of zen thing? The sound of one hand clapping?"

"It's an observation of the way things are," Kronenfeld said. "And you have three choices."

"Sure doesn't seem like I have any choices at all."

"But you do." Kronenfeld held up three fingers. As he enumerated each choice he pinched a finger with his other hand. "You can accept things the way they are—however unpleasant they might be—and learn to live with them. You can escape. Or, you can make changes."

"Escape sounds pretty good right now."

"But that option ignores a fairly important fact."

"Which is?"

"Wherever you go, there you are."

"Another quote."

"But a realistic one. You are going to remain on the sex offender registry for ten more years. Anyplace you go, you will be on that list. Anyplace you go, your neighbors will have to be notified of your status."

"So there is no real escape."

"No. Only temporary reprieves. If you don't register, you go to prison. If you do register, people will find out about your past."

"All right. That leaves options A and C."

"Accepting or changing."

"The way things are sucks."

"Yes. You find it intolerable."

"I think I just said that."

"But is it completely unacceptable? Is there no way to adjust to the way things are?"

"I can't see how."

"Then that leaves you with a single option."

"Change?"

"Of course."

"Change what? I can't change the fact that I'm on the offender registry. I can't change the way people look at me when I go to the store, or hit the pizzeria for lunch."

"You could change their perceptions."

"How? You said it just a couple of minutes ago. A thing is what it is."

"Yes. On the other hand, the perceptions of the people you meet aren't based on you as a person, but you as a sex offender.

Slowly—perhaps even imperceptibly at first—as they get to know Carl Sussman, the person, they may start to lower their defenses."

"Sounds like a tall order."

"It is. And I see that our time is up. Would you like to reschedule for, say, two weeks from today?"

Sussman made arrangements to see Dr. Kronenfeld again and let himself out.

I parked the new cruiser in front of Dr. Kronenfeld's office building and walked inside. As I took the elevator to his floor, hearing but not hearing the Melachrino Strings' rendition of "Like A Virgin," I thought about how I could phrase the questions I had for him. The concepts I had mulled over on my drive into Morgan had seemed muddled. I felt as if I was losing control of the events in Prosperity. I thought I might benefit from a different perspective.

I opened the office door and almost walked right into Carl Sussman.

He stopped dead in his tracks.

"Chief Wheeler," he said.

"Mr. Sussman. I didn't know you were coming to . . . that is, well, this is something of a surprise."

"I'll say."

Sussman held out his hand. "Good to see you."

I thought it an odd thing to say. On the other hand, Sussman had always been civil to me, and I had no reason, yet, to be concerned about his risk to the community. I shook his hand.

"Take care," I said.

As Sussman left, Dr. Kronenfeld stepped into the outer office.

"Chief Wheeler," he said. "I didn't know we had scheduled a session today."

"We haven't." I pointed toward the outer door to the hallway. "Kind of a surprise to see Carl Sussman here."

"I can imagine. What can I do for you?"

"Do you have a few moments?"

"Is anything wrong? You haven't been having posttraumatic symptoms again, have you?"

The previous year I had experienced a recurrence of nightmares and flashbacks surrounding the death of my wife Susan, when Gypsy Camarena's body had been found on the banks of Six Mile Creek at almost the same spot where Susan had died six years earlier. Dr. Kronenfeld had told me that I wouldn't rid myself of the symptoms until I found Gypsy's killer. He had been right.

"No, thank goodness. What I need today falls more under the category of . . . well, of a consult."

"A consult regarding . . ."

"A case I'm working on."

"Ah, I see. I think I have a few minutes. My four o'clock canceled earlier today. Why don't you come on back to my office?"

I followed him to the inside office and sat in my usual seat. Kronenfeld checked a schedule book on his desk, and then sat in the chair across from me. I had always liked the way he never sat at his desk when I was in the office. I suppose it was part of the therapy process, some kind of procedure that was drilled into him at psychology school, but it did put me at ease.

Most of the time.

"I'm working this murder case," I said.

"The football player."

"I didn't realize you kept up with Prosperity news so closely."

"I keep up with football. I have a season pass to the Pythons games."

"Good seats?"

"Second level. Thirty yard line."

"Doc! You've been holding out on me. I'd sure be interested in buying any tickets you can't use."

He shook his head. "Sorry. I can't sell them to clients. Ethics. Tell me about the murder."

"Well, it's not so much about the murder that I'm here. It's more like a side issue."

"Really?" he said, leaning back in his chair.

"I don't want to go into too much detail, but I've run up across this preacher, and things about him don't feel . . . right, I guess."

"What kind of preacher?"

"He's a tent revival guy."

"Oh."

"What?"

"Nothing. Just . . . oh."

I paused to see if he might break tradition and expound a little. I needn't have wasted my time. There were some things Kronenfeld didn't do. Expounding needlessly was one of them.

"There's something about him that bothers me. I confronted him the other day and he seemed to make vague threats."

"He tried to intimidate you?"

"Exactly. It's as if he was trying to scare me away from him."

"And that made you suspicious."

"Yes. But that's not why I want to talk about him. Actually, this kind of concerns Carl Sussman."

Kronenfeld didn't say anything. He sat and waited for me to explain. For some reason, that tactic worked for him, even if he never responded to it from others.

"You know about Sussman, of course," I said.

"I can't talk about any person who may or may not be another client," Kronenfeld said.

It was like some kind of litany. It was the first time I'd ever heard him say a word that sounded even remotely rehearsed.

"Confidentiality," I said.

"Yes. I also don't talk about you with other people. I'm sure you'd appreciate that."

"Sure. Of course. I can talk about Sussman all I want, though, can't I?"

"Is there some way to discuss your preacher without bringing Mr. Sussman into it?"

"I don't think so."

"All right. I'll try to direct all my comments to the preacher. What's his name?"

"Alvin Cross."

"Cross. Interesting name for a revivalist."

"I hadn't thought about it, but you're right."

"Do you think it's his real name?"

I considered the question for a moment. "I don't know. Sounds like something I should check."

"Yes," Kronenfeld said.

"Anyway, one of my patrolmen happened to be at Cross's tent meeting last night, and he says things got really strange."

"In what way?"

"In a snake-handling, miracle cures, speaking in tongues kind of way."

"Ah," Kronenfeld said. "A charismatic. Very interesting subset of Christianity. There have been a number of studies on it."

"What about the healing?"

Kronenfeld shrugged. "Maybe half con, half mass hypnosis. You took college psychology, right?"

"Yes."

"Then you know about Sigmund Freud's claims to have cured hysterical blindness and paralysis through therapy, by removing the underlying conflicts and anxiety that caused them."

"You believe that?"

"I believe the brain is capable of the most astounding deceits. I think people like your Reverend Cross draw the type of congregations who are looking for miracles. That makes them highly susceptible to suggestion. I've seen some of these guys at work. Their speech is rhythmic, the cadence is uniform, and it's filled with suggestions. Not a great deal unlike the way that Milton Erickson used to be able to hypnotize people who claimed they were incapable of being put under. I'd guess that Cross doesn't start out with the cures, but gets to them late in the service."

"My patrolman said something about that. Yes."

"By then, he has them under his spell. That, and a little selective discrimination of the people he chooses to 'heal,' and he can have the flock emptying their pockets in no time, so that they can share in the divine providence."

"So it's a scam?"

"I wouldn't go that far. Remember, some of these people he cures have very real disorders. They're just not physical disorders. Like Dr. Freud and Dr. Jung, Cross has found a way to reach inside their minds and remove the blocks that are causing the physical symptoms."

"But Freud and Jung did therapy. Cross is a huckster."

"The Taoists say that there are many paths to God," Kronenfeld said. "What they mean, of course, is that enlightenment can be attained through any number of ways. Therapy might be one way—often a long, protracted way. What Cross does might be another. Consider a woman with horrible arthritis. Cross lays on the hands, does some of his speaking in tongues mumbo-jumbo, and the arthritic lady is convinced that she's full of the spirit. She was ready to receive it, because Cross has spent an hour already 'putting her under' with his hypnotic speech.

"Now, because the woman believes that God is inside her,

her anxiety is relieved. Her brain stimulates the production of endorphins—natural morphine—and the pain in her hands and joints disappear. She can dance, she can turn cartwheels, because there's no pain. The crowd sees what they expect, a miracle. It reinforces their mass hypnosis, and they think Cross can do anything. Is it fraud? Hell, I don't know. The woman feels better, so maybe it isn't."

"What you're telling me is that Cross is an expert at manipulating people's emotions."

"Sure he is. It's a gift for him. Give him five minutes, and he can have you believing anything."

"Does that make him a psychopath?"

"Who can say? Maybe he's a very convincing person who has found his calling in life."

"You wouldn't say that if you met him. He's kind of creepy."

"In his business that isn't necessarily a liability. It sets him apart. Makes him look more other-worldly. The faithful like that sort of thing. They are drawn to mysticism."

"So people leave his services poorer but inspired."

"Of course. That's precisely why they went in the first place. The people who attend these tent revivals feel as if there's an empty place in their hearts that isn't being filled by their own churches. Or, perhaps they've reached a crucial point in their lives and feel that they need some sort of heavenly intervention, a sort of bonding with their perception of the Almighty. They come to Cross's tent hopeless, and leave hopeful, because they see evidence of the power of their God through Cross's miracles."

I thought about this. "But what if it's false hope?"

Kronenfeld leaned forward. "I'll tell you a secret, Judd," he said. "For most people, false hope beats hell out of no hope at all."

THIRTY-FIVE

Around five-thirty that afternoon, the clouds began to roil to the west, the sky darkened, and flashes of lightning began to crackle on the horizon. The wind kicked up, with gusts that broke small twigs from the trees outside my office.

I closed up the station at five, hit the store quickly for some supper supplies, then hauled ass down Morgan Highway to my farm, trying to outrace the storm that bore down on me like an overtaking tidal wave.

I realized on the way home that I had been so fascinated with Dr. Kronenfeld's explanation of what Alvin Cross did under his big canvas tent each night that I had completely forgotten to ask him about the potential threat to Carl Sussman. I also noted that he hadn't brought the subject back up.

It didn't take a Freud to figure out the connection. Kronenfeld had implied that a lot of what Cross did involved some sort of mass hypnosis, an attempt to implant suggestions into the heads of his admittedly simple congregation. Cross wanted them to believe in him as a conduit to their own personal salvations. Every story needs a hero and a villain. Cross had used Sussman as the symbol of evil in their community, in order to bond them to him, to make them believe he had special powers endowed to him by God Himself, to protect them from that evil.

At least, I hoped that was his motive. I didn't like to think what might happen if the crowd huddling in the stifling heat of his revival tent began to take his message literally.

I pulled up in front of the house to find Donna sitting on the front porch in a halter top and a pair of shorts that gave me lascivious and lustful thoughts.

"Coolest it's been in a week," she said, as I climbed from the cruiser and stepped up to the porch. "I love sitting out here and watching the storm blow up."

I hung my Sam Brown on the rack just inside the front door, and sat next to her on the wicker loveseat.

As I settled in, there was a bright white flash in the not-too-distant western sky, and I swore I could hear the sizzle as it ionized the air around it. The explosion of thunder that followed only seconds later seemed to come from everywhere around us, and it shook the house as it reverberated like a living thing, rattling the dishes in the kitchen and the tin roof over the porch. Even the bedrock beneath our feet seemed to retract and vibrate under the shock wave.

"Okay," Donna said. "That was great. Let's go inside."

We watched the weather radar on the cable TV while I made dinner. I mixed some mesclun greens, some grape tomatoes, and some thinly sliced onions and cucumbers, and placed the salad on plates. Then I sliced two ripe avocados into quarters, and lined the edges of the plates with the slices. I finished the salad with strips of grilled chicken I'd picked up in the deli section of the store.

It was quick, easy, effortless, and energy efficient—everything I was looking for in a summer meal.

I placed the plates on the table while Donna opened a bottle of white zinfandel and poured part of it into a glass.

As she filled her glass, another peal of thunder rattled the house.

"Okay," she said. "Fun's fun, but . . ."

"It seems to have settled right on top of the farm," I said. "What kind of dressing do you want?"

"Russian. Wow, look at the radar picture on the TV. It's moving like crazy."

"Probably blow through in a half hour, leave everything muggy, and won't drop a quarter inch of rain for the farmers."

She sat across from me at the table and poured some of the dressing on her salad.

"Anything interesting today?" she asked.

"Well, it seems that one of my witnesses has vanished."

"Nice trick, if you can pull it off."

"She's probably shacked up somewhere with her boyfriend the axe murderer."

"Cozy thought."

"Oh, and Kent dropped by my office. He was very strange."

"How so?"

"He seemed concerned about Seth. Wanted to know whether the boy might be in some kind of trouble."

"Guilty conscience?"

"Could be. Maybe Seth put him up to it. Who knows? I tried to reassure him, but I don't think he bought it."

"Is Seth in trouble?"

"Constantly. For better or worse, though, his trouble is mostly moral and ethical. He seems to have some kind of sixth sense when it comes to keeping one toe inside the bounds of legality."

"That could be his special talent."

The house shook again under the onslaught of a monstrous thunderclap, and I heard the first solid thump of a raindrop on the metal roof. Like the sound of popcorn in a kettle, it only took a few moments before individual plops became a constant roar of water hitting the house.

"A quarter inch, you said?" Donna noted.

"Wait. In a minute or two it'll cut off like a water spigot."

She nibbled at her salad and waited. I speared a slice of avocado. The weather radar on the TV screen showed a huge blob of dark green situated right over the center of Bliss County. This was one time I wouldn't mind being wrong. Despite the fact that half of Prosperity had been turned under the earth to make way for some kind of yuppie paradise carpet bombed with starter castles, everything east of Six Mile Creek still consisted mostly of farm land—land that had suffered horribly over the past month from the blistering heat and lack of rain. I hoped the rain would last for hours, and then settle into a slow, soil-drenching shower that would answer the prayers of the farmers whom I called my neighbors, and those to whom I had rented the larger portion of my own property to plant their own crops.

It wasn't to be. As I had predicted, the roar on the rooftop fell to a staccato string of watery firecrackers and then ceased altogether. I looked out the front door and saw the steamy risers of fog drifting up from the asphalt of Morgan Highway.

"Damn," I said.

"Don't you just hate always being right?"

"About this? You bet."

Sharon Counts finished her shift with the sheriff's CSI department, changed clothes in the Law Enforcement Center locker room, and walked to her car.

She thought about getting in a bite to eat. The last thing she'd had was a fast-food burrito on the way back to the station after collecting evidence at a hit-and-run, and her stomach had started to protest.

That wasn't unusual. Everyone presumed she ate almost nothing at all, because she remained bone-thin and the skin of her face hugged her skull the way her latex gloves encased her hands on the job. She didn't bother to talk about her rampant metabolism, and the fact that her body temperature had settled in at a steady hundred degrees years before, never to fall again. She didn't dwell on the fact that she, in fact, ate prodigious amounts of food without ever having to worry about it affecting her weight or girth.

She didn't, for that matter, talk about most things in her life. She had learned through sad experience that opening up to people, at least for her, had almost always ended in tears. Thirty-six years old, and she felt she had never really tasted the life her peers knew. There had been lovers, but none who reached into her heart. After a succession of unsatisfying sexual gymnasts with all the affection and understanding of a garden implement, she had decided that it wasn't her fortune in life to meet Prince Charming. She had given up on Mister Right, and was content every several months to settle for Mister Right Now.

Sometimes, when she allowed herself the liberty of too much alcohol or an excess of self-examination, she wondered whether the problem might not be her. Maybe she was missing some fundamental emotional nerve cluster in her brain, which prevented her from really connecting with anyone.

She was chronically aware that, like her lovers, her entire life seemed to be an unending series of "now's," with no connection to the past or the future. Jobs were temporal. Lovers came and went with barely a flutter of her heart. One house, she had determined, was pretty much like another, and she never felt a particular attachment to any single dwelling.

She was flotsam. That was the only explanation. Some people put down roots. She rolled with the wind, like tumbleweeds and thistledown. Sooner or later, she'd tire of Bliss County, or the Department, or her partners, or simply the unending dreariness of day in and day out, and she'd tender her resignation, pack her car, and hit the blue highways until some place or another tugged at her long enough to keep her attention. That was the way she was. It wasn't pleasant and it wasn't tragic. It was her condition.

Sharon hit the drive-through at a burger joint and left with a double cheeseburger and a barrel of fries. She drove aimlessly, munching potatoes and sipping from a huge cup of soda. She could have gone home, but she wasn't ready, just yet, to face the empty walls and the silence of her four rooms. She knew herself well enough to realize that enough of that was sufficient cause for fantasies; visions of stuffing the loud end of her service automatic deep into the back of her mouth and squeezing the trigger.

She'd even tried it once or twice, to see what it would be like, though each time she had been careful to remove the magazine and the single bullet that no good cop left unchambered, before dry-firing her weapon and imagining the instant of pressure and sensate redness before darkness overwhelmed her.

Nothing made sense. Life, she decided, was a string of unrelated snippets of sensation, separated by the searing pangs of regret.

"And then you die," she said over the drone of her tires against the asphalt. "Some fucking payoff."

Almost without thinking of it, she found herself on Morgan Highway, headed west toward Prosperity. She turned onto Bostian Road, as if her hands cranked the wheel of their own volition.

She knew where she was going. It was like watching a television screen, a show that you've seen before, a plot you know like an old friend. A mile ahead was Carl Sussman's trailer, and the house he was building by himself. Sussman would have sacked out hours earlier, practically the moment the sun blinked out over the horizon, exhausted from the day of work that stretched from can't see to can't see.

She was drawn to that place. When she had been there earlier in the day, before heading into Morgan to walk through her work shift, Chief Wheeler had dropped by. She could have remained in the trailer, out of sight, but she had willed herself to step out on the front porch as he was leaving. It wasn't necessary to speak with him. All he had to do was see her. Whatever he made of her presence was his business, but at least she wouldn't allow herself to slink around in secrecy. She had damned little self-respect, in general, but she cared enough about herself for that.

In all likelihood, there was nothing in Carl Sussman for her. He was as damaged as she was, as hardened and impervious to intimacies of the heart. Whatever sympathies and emotional vulnerabilities he might have carried before his crime had been burned out of him in prison. Now all he wanted was peace and solitude and an opportunity to live without being hassled. His capacity for even the most casual of physical relationships, however, seemed to have been ablated during his five-year stretch. It was like some kind of phobia, as if he was afraid that if he allowed himself any form of intimacy, he might lose control and commit another rape.

So, she realized, he channeled all his energies and passions into his house.

Perhaps that was why she felt the attraction toward him. She, disillusioned with sex, and he, unable to allow himself to engage in it, made a perfect match. What they had in common, beyond their lack of physical desire, was an interest in the house.

She topped a small rise between two pastures, and saw a glow a half mile ahead, in the direction of Sussman's home. He had talked about being worried that he was falling behind as he tried to meet the demands of that rat bastard building inspector, and had said he might get some halogen lamps so that he could work into the night. She hadn't planned to go near his trailer, let alone check on his progress. Now, though, she was curious.

As she got closer to the site, concern grew inside her like a malignant bubble. The light looked wrong, somehow. Halogen lamps gave off a yellowish-white glow. This light was orange, with hints of yellow and red. Not only that, but the closer she got, the more animated it became—not at all like worklights, but more like—

Fire.

She knew it even before she saw it clearly. Something terrible was happening at Carl Sussman's place. She buried her foot in the accelerator and her car leapt forward.

As she neared the trailer, the smell of wood smoke began to filter into the car through the air conditioning vents. The glow had turned into a tableau of dancing light, with sparks flying skyward over the pine trees ringing the home site.

She nearly spun the car as she turned into his driveway, and the true horror of the fire dawned on her.

The entire frame of the house was in flames. Tendrils of fire rose fifty feet in the air, amid rolling plumes of smoke and flying burning ash. Several of the trees nearest the structure had begun to smolder. She could see Sussman's tools, or at least their incinerated carcasses, sitting in the middle of the plywood floor sheathing, which sagged under their weight as the fire eroded the structure. Sharon had seen a few home fires in her time, and she knew what would happen next. As the flames finally burned through the floor, the rest of the structure would fall inward, to be consumed in an inferno pit, which had at one time been the crawlspace beneath.

She grabbed her cell phone, dialed 9-1-1, and as calmly as her leaping heart allowed, informed the dispatcher of the blaze. As she spoke, she jumped from the car and ran around the back of the trailer, expecting to find Sussman struggling vainly to quench the fire with the water hose fed by his artesian well.

Instead, even more terribly, she saw that the back of the trailer had begun to burn, torched by flying cinders and burning branches from the overhanging pines and oaks.

Sussman was nowhere in sight.

She screamed into the phone that she needed an ambulance, and then dashed around to the front of the doublewide. Through the front window, she could see that the flames had breached the back wall of the trailer. The door was locked. She kicked at it once, twice, and on the third try the flimsy lock gave way. She waded into the solid wall of smoke that filled the living room.

Working mostly on memory, she sprinted across the living room into the short hall leading to Sussman's bedroom, where she found him sleeping in his underwear on top of the covers of the double bed. She grabbed him by the shoulders and shook him forcefully.

"Carl!" she screamed. "Wake up! The goddamn trailer's on fire!"

He didn't respond, and she realized that he had probably been overcome by smoke and carbon monoxide. She rolled him over and slapped him across his cheek, twice, trying to rouse him. He moaned a little, but didn't wake.

Sharon stood just under five and a half feet tall and weighed only a little over a hundred pounds. Even so, she surprised herself when she reached under Sussman's arms, locked her hands across his chest, yanked, and he came off the bed. Slowly, tortuously, she dragged him across the tiny bedroom, and then into the hallway, and from there to the living room.

Her lungs burned from the smoke and her body ached from the exertion of trying to lug his dead weight to safety. Her head began to pound. Her vision grew dim and she felt dizzy. Lights danced around the living room as the flames began to consume the furniture, and the heat rolled over her like a lava flow.

She tried to curse, but the words wouldn't come as her chest heaved and she coughed, trying to clear her lungs of the smoke that—even then—she knew was killing her.

She tried one more time to drag Sussman to the door, where fresh, lifesaving air awaited. As she lifted him, something seemed to explode in her head, the room whirled around crazily, and before she could stop herself she was lying on her back, on the floor, next to Sussman's prostrate body, and she knew that this was the way that her life was going to end—first suffocated by the smoke and gasses, and then immolated in the flames that would shortly consume the trailer.

She felt a sudden fatigue, and wanted nothing more than to close her eyes and sleep.

But before she slipped out of consciousness, she became aware of a sudden cold breeze and a stirring of brown and yellow and red as the front door flew open. She felt herself dropping into a deep, cold well that grew darker and darker, until there was only the pinpoint of light at the top, and then that blinked out, after which there was nothing at all.

Thirty-Six

I usually take Saturdays off, and I almost never visit the site of fires. We have a perfectly good volunteer fire department in Prosperity, and anything suspicious is investigated by a fellow with the County Fire Marshal's office in Morgan.

In this case, though, I had made an exception.

Since the fire at Carl Sussman's property had been called in shortly before midnight, patrol duties in Prosperity had been handed over to the State Troopers. Somehow word had filtered down to Don Webb's office in Morgan, and he had put in a courtesy call to me around six in the morning.

I had told him I'd drop by in a while, and then I rolled over and went back to sleep for about a half hour.

I was troubled by dreams, though. Mental images of flames and smoke kept creeping into my head, and somewhere, down deep in the depths of my psyche, a voice reminded me that Carl Sussman, a man whom I knew to be brave and was trying to be decent, had run into a very bad night.

Finally, around six-thirty, I gave up on sleep. Without rousing Donna, I rolled out of bed, hit the shower, and dressed in my civvies. I did pin my badge onto the front of my sport shirt, just in case I ran into anyone officious who might question why I was traipsing around the smoldering corpse of what would have been a damned fine house.

I drove the Jeep, since I wasn't actually visiting Sussman's home site in an official capacity. When I turned off Bostian

Road onto his gravel drive, I nearly didn't recognize the place.

The house had been reduced to ashes, right down to the brick foundation. Charred cinderblock piers rose from the ground and a blackened brick wall no higher than my knee outlined the former structure, but everything else was gone.

Worse, Sussman's mobile home, where I had discovered the body of Donnie Clift the previous year, had been virtually destroyed. The center portion was gone from the floorboards up, with the kitchen on one end and the sleeping area on the other in smoky tatters. I suppose the VFD had some intention in putting out the fire, but it was clear that there was nothing left of the doublewide worth salvaging.

Sussman's truck, which had been parked behind the trailer, had been damaged. Bubbled paint and cracked glass on the side that had faced the house stood witness to the heat of the flames.

Sharon Counts's car was still parked in front of the trailer, and looked no worse for wear.

There was a red Bliss County Fire Marshal's car parked in front of me when I climbed from the Jeep. Nobody jumped from the fire-ravaged pines to stop me, so I walked around back to the construction site.

A man stood in the middle of the foundation, holding a clipboard and a tape measure. He had a canvas tote bag hanging from one shoulder. He wrote furiously as I walked up.

"Find anything?" I asked.

The man's head jerked up.

"Jesus," he said. "I didn't hear you drive up."

"Chief Wheeler," I said. "Prosperity PD."

"Gallo, Fire Marshal's office," he said as he walked over to the perimeter and offered his free hand. He was dressed in a white shirt and black khakis, and a badge on his chest read "S. Gallo." I wondered what the S stood for.

"What's it look like?"

"It was set," he said. "The firemen thought maybe it got hit by lightning during the storm last night. I wasn't here five minutes before I knew better."

"What tipped you off?"

He sniffed the air. "Smell that? The insecticide scent?"

"Now that you mention it."

"Diesel fuel. Someone poured a bunch of it around the floor perimeter, and set it aflame."

"I've heard that diesel fuel is hard to light," I said.

"It is. You could pour a cupful of it on your campfire, and all it's likely to do is put out the fire. The guy who did this was cagey, though."

Gallo pulled a baggie from the canvas tote and showed it to me. Inside was a piece of heavy-gauge wire with burned residue on it.

"Fireworks sparkler," he said. "Made of aluminum and magnesium. Once you get this thing burning, you can put it underwater and it will remain lit. It makes its own oxygen as it burns. Hot, too. Maybe eighteen hundred degrees. I found it lying on the ground next to the foundation, just over there."

He pointed toward the eastern side of the house.

"A fuse," I said.

"That's the way I see it. Whoever torched this property doused the frame with fuel oil, lit the sparkler, and then laid it on the side of the frame. He had time to drive away before the sparkler flame reached the fuel oil. The oil probably smoldered for a moment or two, and then it caught. You're right, Chief. Diesel is hard to light, but once you get it to flame up it's also very hard to put out. Once that oil caught fire, this house was toast."

"I don't get it," I said. "Whoever burned this place must have known you'd find the evidence proving it wasn't accidental."

"You know something, Chief? I don't think this little firebug gave a damn."

I asked Gallo to send me a copy of his report. He assured me he would. Then I climbed back into the Jeep and headed back out Bostian Road toward Morgan Highway.

I stopped at Gwen Tissot's Stop and Rob, and grabbed a couple of sausage and egg biscuits and a soda. If Donna had caught me eating that stuff for breakfast, she'd have boxed my ears. She kept telling me that I was a candidate for a first-class coronary.

Don Webb had told me that the ambulance crew had taken Carl Sussman and Sharon Counts to Bliss Regional Medical Center in Morgan. According to the early reports, Sharon was going to be fine, but Sussman was in a bad way. He'd inhaled a lot of smoke and fumes before Sharon had reached him. When the firemen made it into the doublewide, they had found both Sharon and Carl lying in the middle of the living room. Sharon was all but unconscious. They couldn't rouse Sussman at all.

I pulled up in front of the ER, parked in a cop space, then walked in through the automatic double doors used for ambulance crews. The charge nurse recognized me immediately.

"You're out of uniform, Chief," she said as she whisked by me toward one of the examining rooms.

"It's Saturday. I'm not really here."

"Whatever. I'm kind of busy. Something I can help you with?"

"A couple of people were brought in late last night from Prosperity. House fire."

"Both got sent upstairs," she said. "The man's in the ICU. The woman they put on the med floor. If you want to hold on a minute, I'll get you the admitting doctors' names."

Fifteen minutes later, I found my way to the ICU, on the fifth floor. Visiting times were still a couple of hours off, but my badge got me in the door. I waited at the nursing station until one of the health techs noticed me standing around looking big and stupid.

"Can I help you . . . Officer?"

"Chief Wheeler, Prosperity PD," I said. "I'm here to check on Carl Sussman."

"I'll get his nurse."

The ICU was arranged like a big octagon, with a horseshoe-shaped nurses' station in the center, and the patient rooms ringing the outer edge. From the station, you could see every patient room, though many were darkened or had shades drawn to keep out intruding eyes. Most of the people in the ICU lingered between life and death, and modesty tended to take a back seat to pragmatism. The curtains were there to remind everyone that no matter how many tubes they had coming out them, the residents of each room were still people.

A woman in surgical scrubs tapped me on the shoulder.

"You wanted to know about Mr. Sussman?"

She was short and overweight, with florid features.

"Yes."

"Are you family?"

I tapped my badge. "Police. Prosperity. I'm investigating the fire that put him in here."

"I see. All right then. Mr. Sussman is in critical but stable condition," she said, wheezing between sentences. "We're giving him corticosteroids to help prevent long-term lung damage or pneumonia. Inhaling smoke and gases can really irritate the lungs. I'd expect that he'll be upgraded to serious before the end of the day. He should be moved to a med floor by tomorrow. Is there anything else I can do for you?"

"Has he said anything about the fire?"

"Mr. Sussman hasn't said anything about anything. He's

been unconscious since he arrived. He should wake up later today, unless he's sustained brain damage from lack of oxygen."

"That could happen?"

"It's hard to tell. We really won't know until he regains consciousness."

"I've heard there are tests. MRIs, that sort of thing."

"Yes," she said, with the first tinge of humanity I'd heard in her voice. "And they're expensive. Mr. Sussman doesn't have insurance. The hospital won't approve the test without assurances of being paid."

"He's wealthy," I said. "He has money."

She glanced toward the rooms, and then toward me.

"On him?" she asked.

Sharon Counts was awake when I knocked on her open door. She had cranked the mechanical bed so that she could sit up and look out the window. Her face was even more drawn and haggard than usual. She clutched the sheet that covered her up to her waist. Her eyes were red.

"Chief," she croaked. "Sorry I'm so hoarse. The smoke."

"That's okay," I said. "I just dropped by to look in on you. Word has it that you tried to get Carl out of the trailer."

"Tried. Yeah, that's about it."

"You may have saved his life. The reports say the entire back of his trailer was on fire by the time the fire department arrived. If you hadn't dragged him to the living room, he would have burned to death before they got to him."

She sipped though an articulated straw from a six-ounce can of ginger ale. "What about the house?"

I shook my head. "Nothing but the foundation's left. The heat was so intense, I'd imagine the mortar is weakened. Probably a total loss."

"Damned lightning!"

I pulled up a chair and sat next to her bed.

"About that," I said. "It wasn't lightning."

Her eyes opened wide for a moment, and then she settled back in the pillows.

"Makes sense," she said. "Someone torched it."

"That's how it looks. It wasn't sophisticated. Some fuel oil and a fireworks sparkler fuse, the fire investigator thinks."

"Carl wouldn't . . ." she started to say, as her eyes filled with tears.

"I don't think he did."

"Who, then?"

I shrugged. "There are a lot of people in Prosperity who don't like the idea that Carl's moved in. He frightens them."

"They don't know him."

"And they don't want to. People get crazy when they're threatened. Sometimes they do things they could never imagine doing otherwise."

She turned her head toward me, her eyes flashing through the wetness. "You're excusing them?"

"Explaining. I didn't say I approved."

The accusing fire in her eyes raged on until, finally, it died a little and gave way for her tears.

"What about Carl. They won't tell me anything."

"Critical but stable, the ICU nurse said. She thinks he might wake up later today, maybe make it to this floor by tonight."

She dabbed at her eyes with a tissue she'd yanked from a dispenser on her table. "That's good."

"About you two. You mind me asking?"

"Yes. I do."

"All right, then," I said as I stood. "You might want to take a nap or something. All this chatter is likely to wear you out."

For the first time ever, I saw her smile.

"You come back," she said. "Don't be a stranger."

I decided to stop by the station before heading back to the house. It occurred to me that I might want to write some kind of report about the fire, since it was in my district and appeared to have originated in an act of malice.

When I walked into the station, Cory True was sitting in the waiting area.

"Where in hell have you been?" he asked. "It's ten-thirty."

"Duty calls. You're lucky I showed at all. I'm usually off on Saturday."

"Any comment on the fire at that sex offender's house last night?"

"No. Want some coffee?"

"Sure. The back channel chatter says it was arson."

"Whose back channel chatter?" I asked as I led him to the back of the station, where we kept the coffeemaker. "You know I don't take well to people withholding evidence, Cory."

"I know a guy with the Fire Marshal's office over in Morgan."

"Does this guy have a name?"

"Not one I'm interested in divulging," he said as I handed him a foam cup. "Besides, that's not why I'm really here."

I filled my own cup, dumped in some artificial sweetener and some artificial creamer, mused for a moment on whether my cup of coffee actually existed with all this fake stuff in it, and then walked back to my office with Cory in tow.

After we'd both taken our seats, I took a sip of my coffee and nodded in his direction.

"All right," I said after swallowing. "Shoot."

"I checked out this place, Dorgan, in Georgia. There are a total of seven licensed rooming houses in town. I called each and every one."

"None of them ever heard of Dena Kennedy," I said.

"How'd you know?"

"Lucky guess. What about the hospitals?"

"Well, as you know, there are all these pesky federal rules about divulging medical information."

"But you know a guy . . ."

"I do know a guy. I won't get specific because what he did was sort of illegal, but let's just say he's a guy the hospital wouldn't mind releasing information to."

"Insurance guy."

"Discretion and journalistic principles forbid me saying more. In any case, the hospitals in the Dorgan area needn't fear about getting the feds up in their face . . . faces."

"Because none of them ever heard of Dena Kennedy either."

"Well . . . yes. If you knew all of this, why'd you ask me to look into it?"

"I didn't know it. I suspected it. Getting you to look into it saved me a lot of legwork."

He pulled a folded sheet of paper from his pocket and slid it across the desk to me.

"Bet you didn't know this," he said.

I opened the paper, looked at it, and said, "Hmmm."

"I ran a Lexis search on tent preachers," Cory explained. "Tossed in a couple of terms like *letter* and *runaway*. This was one of the hits."

It was a copy of a story from a small-town paper in east Tennessee, from two years ago. According to the reporter, a couple in town had received a surprise visit from a traveling revivalist bearing news of their daughter, who had been missing for twenty-seven months.

The parents had told the reporter that the daughter, a girl named Ashley Prine, had run away from home after a series of run-ins with the local juvenile court over small-time beefs like skipping school and driving without a license. Her parents stated that Ashley had always been a "problem child," headstrong and impulsive, but they hadn't expected her to run off without ever again calling them.

Then, according to the story, this preacher appeared at the door with a tale of running across Ashley in Goose Creek, South Carolina. The girl had appeared at his tent meeting, tired and hungry, begging for food. The preacher had sheltered her for a few days and had attempted to get her to phone home, but she had refused, saying that she was too ashamed.

Finally, the preacher said he had convinced her to write a letter to her parents and give him their address. He promised to deliver the letter if he ever passed through their town.

The parents, understandably, were relieved to know that their wandering darling was alive, and they rewarded the preacher with a "contribution" to keep his good work going.

The story said the preacher's name was Shelton Boyd. The picture of Boyd and the Prines, however, clearly revealed him to be none other than Alvin Cross.

"So, what do you think?" Cory asked.

"What I've thought all along. Cross is a huckster. He's found a nice way to shake the trees wherever he lands, and enhance his take from the collection plates. I wouldn't be surprised to find that he chooses the small towns he visits just because he has a letter to some distraught parent there."

"What can you do about it?"

"Do? Not much."

"Isn't this fraud?"

"No. Can't see that it is. Cross doesn't demand anything from these parents when he visits. He's the bearer of glad tidings, a messenger from the prodigal daughter. Parents are so overjoyed to finally get some kind of news of their missing kids that they volunteer to open their pocketbooks."

"He lies, though. He lied about taking Dena to the hospital and setting her up in a boarding house."

"I know, Cory. I talked with him about that. The real story—and this is deep background that I would be very unhappy to see in print—is that Dena had been whoring around Georgia and had developed a nasty familiarity with needle drugs. If you were the Kennedys, would you rather hear that, or some lie that she had been placed in a comfy rooming house overseen by Aunt Bee, with a couple of cats lounging in the windows."

"But . . ."

"This is the way it is. Cross tells some of the truth, holds some of it back, and fills in the gaps with happy fables that make the parents feel good. If he didn't take money from them, he'd probably be seen as some kind of saintly nomad. As it is, he's really not much more than a creepy old con man."

"Isn't that illegal?"

"Sure. What Cross is running is a particularly distasteful version of the Spanish Prisoner con."

"Never heard of it."

"It used to be fairly common, back before split-second communications. Guys played it on high-society bleeding-heart types who were impressed by royalty and titles. The way it worked was that the con man would work his way into a social situation, identify his mark, and then tell a story about being in the states to help a relative who was unjustly placed in prison in some far-off country. Spain was popular. The hook was that the guy was placed in prison because he was born into a family of nobility, and some rival wanted him out of the way. Then the con man would explain that he had an in with the prison administrator, and if he could produce 'X' amount of money, he could get the Spanish Prisoner out of jail to claim his rightful place in society."

"And people fell for this?"

"It was romantic. They were bored. Money, for them, was a means to an end, and the end was entertainment. It amused them to think they were interfering in the politics of some distant land. Hell, Cory, for the con man it was like printing money.

"And in Cross's case, he's thrown a twist into the story, claiming that he's already paid to 'save' a girl months ago."

"You've got it. Now, what decent parent wouldn't volunteer to reimburse such a kindness?"

"But, like you said, it's a con. Isn't it illegal?"

"Sure. It's a misdemeanor. You'd probably get more time shoplifting than you would for bunko. Odds are that Dena Kennedy is dead, or worse. It's sad and tragic, but there isn't much we can do about it, even if we wanted to. Not every story has a happy ending. You of all people should know that. On the other hand, when Cross hits the asphalt he'll leave behind a couple of parents who've found a shred of hope. In their shoes, how much would that be worth to you?"

He thought about it, wringing his hands. "This is troubling," he said. "You're supposed to uphold the law, no matter what your personal feelings are."

"Let me tell you something about the law. It's written on paper, not in stone. Law changes from one generation to the next. If we lived by the laws of our fathers, we'd still be stringing up horse thieves. Hell, I don't know if anyone nowadays would know what to do with a horse if he stole one. What I do know is that sometimes justice has nothing to do with the law. And sometimes, the law has very little to do with justice."

"You're saying there's no story here."

"No, Cory. That's not what I'm saying. There's a story. Probably a damn fine one. You could write it up, maybe use it to do an investigative series, some kind of exposé on cheats and cons who pose as real men of the cloth. Might pull down a couple of regional journalism awards, make your bones with the brass down at the *Ledger-Tribune*. You might even get noticed by one of the big-city rags, get an opportunity to shake the dust of this hick rural county off your boots. Could be a big opportunity for you."

"Yeah," he said. "But it would kill Charlie and Marla Kennedy."

"Collateral damage," I said. "Small price to pay for journalistic greatness and the pursuit of truth."

"You think?"

"No. I'd be ashamed to consider it."

"Yeah. I was thinking the same thing."

"Good for you," I said as I drained the last of my coffee. "Good for you."

THIRTY-SEVEN

I got back to the house around noon. The grass cracked under my feet as I walked up to the front porch. The rain from the all-too-brief thunderstorm the night before had been sucked up by the dry ground, bypassing the roots of my lawn almost entirely. What remained, trapped in the leaves of the trees and on hard surfaces, had evaporated hours earlier, leaving the air heavy and damp. The temperature was climbing quickly. It would be above a hundred again by one or two in the afternoon.

This drought was beginning to piss me off.

I found a note on the kitchen table from Donna. It read, simply, "At the pool."

I grabbed a couple of sodas from the fridge and hiked across the field behind my house, over the hill, to the pond.

I saw her from a distance, floating on her back, treading slightly to keep from sinking. A large beach towel lay baking on the bank of the pond, her clothes neatly folded at one corner.

I sat on the towel and opened my drink. The sound of the pull-tab startled her and she submerged herself up to her neck.

"Don't let me stop you, teacher," I said.

"Jesus, Judd. You took a year off my life."

"Want a drink?" I asked, holding up the second can.

"Sure."

She swam to the shore of the pond with smooth, athletic, self-assured strokes, and stepped from the water like some kind of mythic nymph. Without a shred of self-consciousness, she

278

walked naked up the bank to the towel and sat. She ran her hands through her hair, slicking it back on her scalp, and then reached for the drink.

I sipped and admired the view. "Well, ain't we just like a Manet painting?" I asked.

"I'm not going to give you the satisfaction of my surprise," she said. "Where'd you run off to so early this morning?"

"I had a cop thing. Someone burned down Carl Sussman's house last night."

The can stopped halfway to her mouth and she turned to me. "The one he was building?"

"Yes."

"You think it was set?"

"I know it was. The fire investigator was there when I dropped by. Somebody snuck onto the site after Sussman hit the sack and set it on fire with fuel oil. The fire got into some trees and jumped over to Sussman's trailer."

"Is he all right?"

"He's in pretty bad shape. Remember me telling you about that woman who works as a CSI for the Sheriff's Department? Sharon Counts? Seems she's been hanging out with Sussman some lately. She drove over to his place after getting off work last night, got there just in time to call the VFD. She tried to drag him out of the trailer."

"Tried?"

"They were both overcome by smoke. They'd both be dead today if the fire guys had been a minute or two slower. Sussman's been unconscious since he got to the hospital. Sharon's in better shape."

"What did the doctors say about Sussman?"

"I didn't talk to any doctors. A nurse told me she thinks he's going to be all right. Time will tell."

Donna took a sip of her Coke, then slid down on her side,

propped up on one elbow, facing me.

"Sometimes I don't get it," she said.

"What?"

"Small-town attitudes. Prejudices."

"I have a feeling that what happened at Sussman's place started with Alvin Cross. Slim's girlfriend took him to Cross's tent meeting the other night. Cross held up one of the flyers we'd circulated as part of the neighborhood notification on Sussman. He claimed that Sussman was some kind of embodiment of evil in Prosperity. It isn't much of a stretch to imagine that one of his congregation decided to burn Sussman out of town."

"Cross again. Can't you do something about him?"

"He's here legally, even if some of the things he's doing are shady. Fact is, I need him around until we figure out this Steve Samples murder. His boy Ricky Chasen is a prime suspect, and I think Cross is protecting him. And it's not just small towns."

"What?"

"The attitudes. The prejudices. They're everywhere. When I was a cop in Atlanta, I pissed off some lieutenant and got myself assigned to Techwood."

"What's Techwood?"

"The most dangerous part of the city, at that time. They've cleaned it up since, but ten years ago it was a human septic tank. I was assigned to a squad of cars that patrolled the streets in groups of two or more. We got a call on an assault or a shooting or a rape about once an hour. Kids couldn't play outside. The stores in the area couldn't sell food, because the people who lived there would steal it. You could knock on doors all day long and never find a single apartment where someone hadn't been convicted of a serious crime, or was the victim of one. The drug gangs had a hold on the neighborhood like it was their balls and someone was swinging a baseball bat at them.

"So, one day word got out that this guy in the neighborhood

had been inviting kids to his apartment to watch television and eat cookies. People talked, the way people do, and folks started saying the guy was a molester.

"Then, one night, one of the kids who had been to his apartment told her mother that the guy had her sit on his lap. She didn't say he'd touched her inappropriately or raped her or exposed himself or anything like that. He just had her sit on his lap.

"Now, Techwood was the same area where Wayne Williams abducted a bunch of young boys during the eighties before killing them and dumping them in the Chattahoochee River. Folks in Techwood were still a little sensitive about the concept of a child molester living in their midst.

"We got a call from the guy's neighbor later that night, said there was a rumble going on next door and she'd heard screaming. We rolled on it, got there maybe three or four minutes later. We found the guy tied to a chair with cable wraps. Someone had caved in his ribcage and broken his knees with an aluminum baseball bat, burned the letters TWBP on his chest with a soldering iron, and his dick had been cut off and stuffed in his mouth. TWBP stood for Techwood Bat Patrol. That's what vigilante groups in Techwood called themselves when Williams was doing his thing."

Donna started to get dressed.

"This isn't the kind of thing you tell a girl when she's lying naked next to you, Judd," she said.

"I'm sorry," I said as I handed her shirt to her. "But I haven't gotten to the bad part yet."

"Spare me."

"I can't do that. The bad part was that the guy wasn't a molester. He was a preacher, sent into Techwood by some outfit in Chicago to help find a solution to all the violence. He had kids come up to his place to give them something to do besides hang around on the playground, dodging stray bullets. The guy was clean, but the gangs in Techwood were too ready to believe the worst about him, so they didn't get their facts straight before they tortured and killed him. It's not just small towns, Donna. The kind of people who torched Carl Sussman's house happen everywhere."

After my story, Donna decided she'd had enough time outside. We walked back over the hill to the house, where she showered while I made lunch. When she stepped back into the living room from the hallway, I had a couple of pastrami sandwiches and some homemade potato salad on the table.

She walked to me and put her arms around my neck. It was a stretch for her since I stand a good head and a half taller. She leaned her head against my chest, as if listening to my heart.

"I'm not from here," she said. "I grew up in cities. I know they're violent. Somehow, I thought—I hoped—that coming to Prosperity would be like . . . like moving to Mayberry."

"What? I'm Andy Taylor and you're Helen Crump?"

She chuckled, but it was a sad sound. "I never thought about it, but she was a teacher, wasn't she?"

"An English teacher, as I recall."

"Does that make Slim Barney Fife?"

It was my turn to laugh. "No way. Slim's probably a better cop than I am. I'd trust Slim with my life. Hell, I'd trust him with *your* life."

"I came here to make a fresh start. I'd seen too much desperation and fear and ugliness in my life. I was up to my neck in ugly, and I had to get away, find some beauty and peace, a place where I could settle and feel safe."

"Burning Sussman's house to the ground doesn't fit in with your peace and beauty," I said.

"That, and Gypsy's murder last year, now Steve Samples get-

ting hacked . . . it just seems out of place, like the town is falling apart."

I led her to the couch. We sat and I stroked her arm as I tried
to find the words.

"Ugly is everywhere," I said. "I've never gone anywhere that
it didn't seem to show up and try to spoil the party. People are
people wherever you go. If they weren't, Prosperity wouldn't
need a police force, and they wouldn't need me to be the chief.
I guess my job is to keep all the ugly down to a bare minimum,
and stop it where I find it."

She buried her head in my shoulder. I could smell the sweet
lemon verbena in her soap, and the green apple scent of her
shampoo. "Are you're going to stop it this time?" she asked.

"You bet," I said.

After lunch, we decided to wait out the hottest part of the day
with a nap. I was lying in bed, staring at the ceiling, trying to
figure out how I'd go about finding the guy who torched Sussman's house, when the telephone rang.

"Damn," Donna muttered from her side of the bed. She
didn't bother to turn over.

I picked up the phone. Sheriff Webb was on the other end.

"You put out a BOLO on a kid named Russell Samples the
other day?" he asked.

"Yes sir."

"Well, he's shown up. Seems he spent the last several days in
a hospital over in Laurinburg."

"Is he hurt?"

"No. He was in a rehab program. Checked himself in Monday
night."

That got my attention. Steve Samples had been murdered on
Monday morning.

"How did you find out about him?" I asked.

"Seems he was in a therapy session this morning, and had some kind of emotional breakdown. His therapist says he confessed to killing his brother, and he demanded to be sent to the jail here in Morgan, so he could give himself up."

"Has he been transported?"

"He arrived about ten minutes ago. Since the killing was in your district and you put the BOLO out on him, I thought I'd make a courtesy call to see if you want to be in on the interrogation."

"I'll be there in twenty minutes," I said.

I hung up the phone and started to dress.

"What is it?" Donna asked.

"Steve Samples's brother has confessed to the murder. I have to go to Morgan to interview him."

She rolled over and sat up in bed. "It can't be that easy," she said.

"Sometimes it's exactly that easy. In this case, the kid was in a rehab hospital down east. Apparently he finally sobered up enough to realize what he'd done and he wants to clear the air. Damn it, where are my socks?"

THIRTY-EIGHT

With the lights whirling and my siren blaring, I made it to Morgan in twelve minutes. I parked in the visiting law enforcement officers' space in front of the jail, and made my way to the fifth floor, where Don Webb kept his office.

I found him standing outside his office, talking with a couple of deputies from Scotland County. Apparently, they'd just finished signing off on the transfer and custody orders.

"Come with me, Judd," Sheriff Webb said after sending the deputies back to Laurinburg.

We took an elevator to the sixth floor, where new prisoners were in-processed.

"The deputies say the kid is in a pretty unstable state," he explained on the way up. "They had to shut him up three or four times on the way over, to keep him from incriminating himself before he could be properly *Miranda*ized."

"Does he have a lawyer yet?"

"No. I have a court reporter here from the on-call service to take his statement. What do you think? Could he have done it?"

"Sure. Steve Samples was murdered around four in the morning. Laurinburg's only two and a half hours away. If Rusty checked himself in to the hospital there on Monday night, that left him all day to get his load on. What was he rehabbing for?"

Webb held out his arm and slapped the inside of his elbow.

"Shit," I said. "He's a junkie?"

"That's what the hospital said. They said he was almost

285

incoherent when he checked himself in, and that he's been in withdrawal for four days. This morning was his first therapy session after drying out. According to the doctor who called me— with Rusty's permission—the kid broke down about two minutes after he walked in the door."

We left the elevator car and walked down the hall to a series of steel doors set into concrete block walls. The doors were controlled by extremely powerful electromagnets set into the frame. Once activated, the rooms could contain a bull elephant. No ordinary skell was likely to break out.

At the end of the hall, two Bliss County deputies stood by one of the doors, facing each other so that they could see inside the interview room.

"I'm not taking any chances," Webb said. "I say this kid is a suicide risk, and I'm going to see to it that he's under direct observation as long as he's in the jail."

"Good idea. How long until the court recorder gets here?"

The recorder arrived ten minutes later. Webb ordered the deputies to open the door to Rusty Samples's room. They relayed an order to the control room, and a second later there was a buzz as the magnetic field in the door frame collapsed.

Webb led me in, with the recorder following closely behind.

There was a table with several chairs bolted to the floor in the middle of the room, but Rusty Samples sat in the corner, his knees curled up to his chest, his hands covering his face.

Webb nodded to the deputies, who stepped into the room and helped Samples stand and walk to the table. He sat in one of the chairs, his face slack, his eyes red. Under the fluorescent lamps, his skin looked greenish-yellow. He looked like every junkie I'd ever encountered. He smelled scared.

Webb read Samples his rights, very carefully. He made the kid acknowledge each one as he finished it. The Supreme Court might have eased up on Miranda over the last several years, but no self-respecting cop wanted his ass handed to him in court by some punk twenty-something public defender because he didn't attend to the details while reading the rights.

Finally, satisfied that Samples understood the entire spiel, Webb turned to me.

"Rusty, my name is Judd Wheeler," I began. "I'm the chief of police over in Prosperity, where your brother lives."

"Lived," Rusty muttered.

"Lived," I said, taking the path of least resistance. "Sheriff Webb here tells me that you have something you need to say."

"I killed him," Rusty said.

"Okay. We'll get to that in just a minute. First, I want to know how you got down here from Iowa."

He pulled his hands from his face and looked up at me. "How'd you know that?"

"Your parents visited me a few days ago. They said that you had been living with them until a few weeks before your brother died."

"That's right. I hopped a bus in Ames, rode it most of the way. Got off in Knoxville, fell asleep in the station, and missed getting back on. I kicked around Knoxville for a while, thought I might find a job or something. I was out of money."

"Why were you coming to Prosperity?"

"Stevie was in the show, man. He had connections. I thought he might be able to find me a job somewhere, maybe an assistant trainer, or maybe a spot on the practice squad. I don't know."

"How'd you get strung out?"

He sighed and sat back in the chair. "Sometimes I feel like I was born strung out. I picked it up in high school. I had a sports hernia, which is a polite way of saying a groin pull. They put me in the hospital. Around midnight, I started hurting something awful, so I called the nurses' station. They sent someone in with a needle full of Demerol. The needle hurt like hell, but five minutes later I didn't give a damn. It was sweet, more relaxed than I'd ever felt. It was like I didn't have a bit of pressure anywhere in my body or my head.

"I guess I've spent the better part of the last five years trying to get back to that point. I kept it a secret for a while, but it's hard. People talk, you know? I had to start going out of town to score. Finally, I couldn't find any Demerol anywhere, but it was easy to score heroin. Hell, you can do that on any big-city street corner.

"I picked up a few bucks panhandling the first night in Knoxville. I bought a burger and a shake with part of it, and then I scored some smack and a cheap set of fresh works— some diabetic needles, still in the paper. The next week is all a little fuzzy."

"How'd you wind up in Prosperity?"

He held up his thumb. "Caught a ride with an over-the-road trucker. He let me off in Pooler. I took a bus to the shopping center near the county line. Walked the rest of the way."

"When?"

"When what, man?"

"When did you get to my town?"

He thought about it for a moment. "Two weeks ago? Maybe. I can't recall for certain. The truck driver hooked me up with some oxy, and I did some of that until it ran out. Steve didn't know—at least, I don't think he knew—until I told him when I got to his place. I just showed up on his doorstep, dirty, hungry, looking like shit. He took me inside. I begged him not to tell Mom and Dad I was there until I could get myself straightened out."

"You were living in the house with Steve?"

"Yeah, but he was hardly ever there. Training camp, you know.

I asked him to take me with him to the camp, to see if I could land some kind of job with the team, but I kept fuckin' up."

"What do you mean?"

"I couldn't get straight. I tried, really. I tried lying by the pool, I tried locking myself in the bedroom and daring myself to stay there, I tried anything I could think of to get off the shit. Every time I thought I was there, I'd go out, get some fresh air, and run across some guy who had some junk for sale. I was never in shape to go to camp."

His eyes were drooping. The stress of withdrawal, the trip from Laurinburg, and baring his soul was getting to him.

"I'm sleepy, man," he said.

"Just a few more questions," I said.

"Whatever," he said, his voice slurring.

"What happened last Monday morning? I know part of it. I know about Seth Kramer bringing the two girls over to the house, and Steve taking one of them up to the bedroom. I know he went skinny-dipping in the pool."

"Both of us," he said, sleepily.

"What?"

"We were both swimming. I wasn't at the house when the girls were there. I got home around three."

"Where were you?"

"Walkin'. That's all. Just taking a long stroll in the moonlight."

"You were high?"

"Hell, yeah."

"And you came back to Steve's house around three."

"Uh huh."

"You two went swimming in the pool."

"It felt nice. The water was a bit cool. It was still hot outside."

"You were skinny-dipping together?"

Rusty held up two fingers, tight together. "We . . . were . . . like . . . this," he said. "We're twins, man. Born within minutes

289

of each other. I'm the older one, you know. I should have gotten the goodies. But we were tight. We used to have our own language when we were little. It's true, man. Skinny-dipping with each other, it was nothing. It was like skinny-dipping with yourself. We didn't get shy around each other. Besides, the water felt so good."

"What happened next?"

"Maybe after I take a . . . little . . . nap," he said, his head nodding.

Another several seconds, and I'd have lost him for the duration. I raised my hand, and slammed it down on the tabletop. The report echoed around the cinderblock walls like a cannon shot. His head jerked up, his bloodshot eyes wide.

"What in hell!" he said.

"I need you alert for five more minutes," I said. "What happened, Rusty? What did you and Steve fight about?"

"What do you think?" he said, tears coming to his eyes. "The same old shit. I wanted him to help. He wanted me to take charge, get my shit together. I begged him to take me to the camp, hook me up with a job with the team. I just wanted to be part of the show, man."

"He refused to take you to Newberry with him."

"Shut me down, man. It was cold. He was my twin. He should have taken care of me. It could have been me, you know. If I hadn't pulled my groin in high school, I never would have had trouble with drugs. I was as good as Steve back then. We were like this . . ."

He held up the fingers again. "I asked him to take me to Newberry with him. I was going stone crazy lying around the house, only going out at night so people wouldn't see Steve Samples's strung-out brother. I wanted to be part of the team. He told me he couldn't. I begged him. He shut me down again. He said he had to go upstairs, get some sleep, because Coltes was coming by to pick him up at five.

"I grabbed him by the arm. He shook me off like I was dirt. I couldn't handle it. The cleaver was lying on the counter. I grabbed it, and before I knew what I was doing I hit him with it.

"He turned around, and he gave me this . . . this look. It was awful. It was like betrayal and shock and horror all mixed together. I raised the cleaver again and I swiped at him. He tried to stop it with his hands, but it was like cutting through a soap bubble. His hands were sliced to fuckin' ribbons, man. He turned and tried to run up the stairs. I hit him again and he went down. Everything went red in front of my eyes. I hit him and hit him and hit him, until I couldn't raise the cleaver one more time."

He had both hands on the table now, palms up. He stared at them as if he couldn't believe they had wielded the cleaver.

"You realized what you had done," I said. "You backed away, into the wall. You were covered with blood. When you hit the wall, you wiped the blood from your body onto it. You couldn't figure out what to do because the drugs were confusing you."

"What? Were you there, man?" he asked. "How do you know this shit?"

"You decided that you needed to cover your tracks," I continued. "You couldn't just walk away, all covered with blood and gore."

"I'm going to be sick," he said.

"So you ran back out through the sliding door, to the pool, and you threw yourself in. You washed off all the blood."

"Yes."

"You washed off the cleaver in the pool, and you wiped it down with a towel, to remove your prints, and you buried it in the hardwood floor next to your brother. Then you went upstairs, got dressed, and left."

"Oh, my God," he said. "It's true, every word. It didn't have to happen. All he had to do was help, don't you see? All I wanted was a chance to be in the show. Was that too much to ask?"

"I don't know," I said.

"That's all I wanted," he said, his face green, tears rolling down his cheeks. "He was my twin. He should have helped me. I was the oldest. He owed me. Didn't he?"

He looked back and forth, between me and Webb.

"Didn't he?" he asked again. Then his stomach heaved and he vomited all over the desktop.

"What do you think will happen to him?" I asked Sheriff Webb when we got back to his office.

"The DA will charge him with murder first, of course. They always go for the hardest time. Capital cases draw the better legal talent, and from what I hear his parents can probably pay for it. When all is said and done, I reckon he'll plead guilty to voluntary manslaughter. With diminished capacity, he might draw five years, get out in three."

"For killing his brother?"

"Under the influence. He's dried out now and doesn't seem all that well hung together. Can you imagine what he was like when he was flyin'? I'm amazed Steve Samples would let him in the door, let alone allow him to live in the house."

There was a knock and Clark Ulrich stepped into the office.

"Afternoon, Sheriff. Afternoon, Chief. The folks downstairs told me you were here, so I thought I'd bring this right up." He held up a manila envelope.

"What is that?" Webb asked.

"The DNA results Chief Wheeler asked for at Samples's house the other day. From the detritus in the pool filter. I ran a rush on it, like he asked."

"Have a seat," Webb said, pointing toward the chair next to mine.

Clark sat and opened the envelope. "This is really strange," he said. "We were able to extract several dozen hairs from the filter. A couple of them were completely intact, including the follicular structure and some of the sebaceous bulb."

"Say again?" I said.

"The follicle is the part of the hair that's under the skin. The sebaceous bulb provides the oil in hair. Anyway, there was lots of material to collect DNA from. We found two distinct DNA patterns, which means the hair came from two different people. It's really strange, though. The patterns on some of the alleles are so similar, I'd say they must have come from first-degree family members."

"Like, say, fraternal twins?" I said, winking covertly at Webb.

"Yeah! Or brothers. Could be father and son, I guess. The DNA indicates that the hairs came from male donors."

"By gosh," I said to Webb. "Clark here may have solved the case!"

"You think?" Webb said, trying to suppress a grin.

"Sure. Steve Samples's parents told us he had a fraternal twin brother. What if—and I'm just supposing here, you understand—what if Samples's brother showed up at the house in Prosperity? That would explain how his hair got into the pool filter. You know what else? Samples's parents told me that Steve's brother . . ." I snapped my fingers, as if trying to recall his name.

"Rusty?" Webb suggested.

"Yeah. Rusty. They said this kid Rusty was an athlete, too. You know what I think? I think maybe the dead guy in the house wasn't Steve Samples at all, but his brother Rusty. I think maybe Steve killed Rusty, and tried to make it look like he had been killed himself."

"Wow!" Clark said. "You really think it could have happened that way?"

Webb and I glanced at each other, and then back at Clark.

"Damn," Webb said. "Now I'm going to have to tear up a perfectly good confession."

"What confession?" Clark asked.

"The one Rusty Samples just gave us up in the holding cells," I said. "The Scotland County sheriff's deputies delivered him here about an hour ago. He confessed to killing Steve Samples."

"Oh, so you guys were just shittin' me."

"Yeah," I said. "We were shittin' you. That report's still useful, though. This evidence tends to corroborate the confession, so I'm sure it will be presented in court as part of the DA's case."

"If it gets that far," Webb said.

"Of course," I said. "On the other hand, this kind of lets Ricky Chasen off the hook. I guess I'm not looking for him anymore."

I glanced at my watch and picked my hat up from Sheriff Webb's desk.

"It's been fun," I said. "But I have one more errand to take care of on my day off."

"What's up?" Webb asked.

I pulled my sunglasses from my blouse pocket. "I have a tent preacher to meet with," I said.

THIRTY-NINE

It was almost five in the afternoon when I pulled off the oiled dirt road on Nate Murray's farm into the closely mown field where Alvin Cross had erected his canvas tent. The motor home was still where I had last seen it, set on jacks to level it, with the drone of the electrical generator moaning quietly over near the tent.

I knocked on the door of the motor home. Seconds later, Cross opened it.

"Chief Wheeler," he said as he stepped down from the coach. "To what do I owe this unexpected pleasure?"

"I need to have a word with you."

"Of course. Would you like to step inside the bus?"

"I won't be here that long. What I have to say is short and sweet. I want you out of Prosperity. Tonight."

Cross looked hurt. His face collapsed into a mass of sun-dried wrinkles. His eyes went dark.

"I'm sure I don't understand."

"It's not very hard. You. Gone. Tonight. I want you to take down your tent, pull up stakes, and hit the highway. I want you out of Prosperity, and I don't want you to come back. Preferably, I want you out of North Carolina, but I can only control my little part of it."

"I think you owe me an explanation."

"Not really, but I'm in a charitable mood. Several nights ago you made an example out of Carl Sussman during your sermon.

According to one of my officers, who attended that meeting, you called him a sinner, and you told every person under your tent that they needed to burn that sin. As I recall, he heard you say that it had to be purified in flames."

"It's a terrible thing to allow sin to flourish right under your nose," Cross said.

"Well, someone seems to have taken what you said as marching orders. Last night, the house Sussman was building was burned to the ground."

"Surely you don't think—"

"What I think doesn't matter. You told them to do it, and someone did. Maybe the two things aren't related. Maybe tossing you out of town is a cruel injustice for which I will have to answer when I stand to accounts in a higher court down the line. All I know right now is that, in my opinion, your presence in Prosperity constitutes a nuisance, and I am ordering you to bug out. Tonight."

"But . . . but tomorrow is the Sabbath day," Cross protested. "It's the Lord's day. Surely you wouldn't keep me from ministering to my flock on the Lord's day."

"What you mean is that you'd be out a bundle if you can't fleece the flock on the day they feel most guilty."

Cross straightened, and I could see the fire in his eyes.

"You are talking to a man of God, sir," he said, his voice icy and condescending.

"I'm talking to a huckster and a con man. Do you want to deny it, Shelton?"

He started to say something, but stopped. "What did you call me?"

"Shelton Boyd. Isn't that the name you used in Tennessee when you paid a visit to Ashley Prine's family with a letter she'd written them while you were 'caring' for her? Sounds a lot like the story you handed the Kennedys here in Prosperity a few days ago. So, tell me, is your name Shelton Boyd, or Alvin Cross? Or is it something entirely different? If I get a search warrant, how many letters am I going to find stashed away in this motor home? Tell you what, Alvin, or Shelton, or whatever your real name is. Why don't you hand them on over to me now, and I'll see that they're mailed to the families you intended to shake down with your shuck and jive."

"I am doing the Lord's work!" he exclaimed. "You, sir, if you attempt to interfere with this ministry, are conducting Satan's mission. The Lord will not condone such blasphemy!"

"Sell it to the hayseeds, Alvin. I've given you fair warning. Ricky Chasen is off my radar screen. Someone else has confessed to killing Steve Samples, so I no longer have any interest in him. You, on the other hand, are a burr under my saddle. I want you out of here tonight, or I'll run you in for inciting your flock to commit arson. Have I made myself clear?"

"You're protecting that sodomite, Sussman? You take the side of a rapist and a libertine against the people of the Lord?"

"He's a citizen of Prosperity and a taxpayer. He gets the same protection from me that anyone else living in my town would."

"The Lord will have his day with you, don't you doubt it," Cross said. "He does not take kindly to people interfering with his work. I will obey, of course, for as our Lord and Savior said, we should render unto Caesar what is Caesar's. I warn you, however, that we will come face to face again in that heavenly court and you will be held to account for your sins and your protection of sinners."

"Tonight, Alvin," I said. Then I turned and walked back to my cruiser.

FORTY

The press had a field day.

By sundown on Saturday, word leaked out that Rusty Samples had been arrested in the murder of his brother, Steve. Once again, news trucks descended on Prosperity, and on the courthouse in Morgan.

Stu Marbury, my other officer, dropped by the station in the middle of his shift to hit the bathroom, and was nearly mobbed by reporters who demanded some shred of information about the case.

He called me as soon as he could lock the front door and reach a phone.

"Hell, Chief, we got CNN, Fox, ABC, NBC, CBS. We even got ESPN out there. What in hell am I supposed to tell them?"

"Nothing," I said. "When you leave the station, walk to your car, get in, lock the door, and drive away. They won't follow you. They think someone's going to come out of the station and give a press briefing."

"Are they?"

"No. I don't plan to get anywhere near the station, and Kent Kramer is out of town until Wednesday, fishing at the Outer Banks. They'll give up after a few hours and go home."

"If you say so, Chief."

After he hung up, I pulled out my cell phone and called Cory True at the *Ledger-Telegraph*.

"I promised you an exclusive," I said. "I guess I owe you for running down that information on Cross."

"They say Samples's brother has been arrested for the murder," Cory said.

"This is off the record," I said. "You got that, Cory? If I see any of this attributed to me in the *Ledger-Telegraph* tomorrow, you won't be able to get into or out of Prosperity without catching a traffic ticket. Are we clear on this?"

"Crystal, Chief. What's the story?"

"The kid's name is Russell Samples. He's Steve's twin brother. He says he killed Steve early on Monday morning. The evidence supports his story. You might want to call this hospital in Laurinburg for some background information."

I gave him the number for the hospital, and some not-too-delicate details.

"It's not much," he said.

"It's more than the other reporters are getting. I'm sure you can corroborate all of this with some of your contacts down at the jail. If you hurry, you can make the front page of the Sunday paper, above the fold. Scoot now, Cory."

I hung up the phone and opened my duty folder. It took me a moment to find another number I had stashed in there.

Pete Samples picked up on the second ring.

"Mr. Samples, this is Chief Wheeler over in Prosperity."

"Thank you for calling, Chief. Can you tell us anything? We haven't been able to get anyone at the jail in Morgan to return our calls. The television news people say that Rusty's been arrested."

"I am truly sorry to have to tell you this, sir. Rusty confessed to the murder earlier today."

"Please hold on for just a moment."

The phone was muffled on his end, as if he had placed his palm over the mouthpiece. I heard a mumble and then what sounded like a scream. Even with the mouthpiece muted, I could hear Darla Samples's desperate "Oh, my God! Not Rusty!"

It was a sad duty, and one of the worst parts of my job. Every once in a while, some poor kid would plow off Morgan Highway into an oak tree while hotdogging the overpowered sports car his parents had stupidly given him for his sixteenth birthday, and I'd have to give those parents the bad news. It's a grim thing to walk up to a front door, your hat in hand, and tell some couple that all their hopes and dreams came to an end on a wet curve on some goddamned country road. Most of the fathers tried to be brave. Most of the mothers crumbled.

I figured, as soon as I could let him off the phone, Pete Samples would break down as badly as his wife. For the moment, though, the compact between men forced him to put on his game face and remain stoic.

The sound from his end cleared suddenly. I could hear Darla crying in the background.

"When . . . when can we see him?" Pete asked.

"I'm going to give you a direct phone number to Sheriff Don Webb's office. You call him Monday morning and he'll get you in before lunch. I promise. If you can't reach him, call me and I'll take you up there personally."

"Did he look . . . was he all right?"

"He's pretty rough," I said. "He's been in a hospital for the last several days. It hasn't been easy for him."

"A hospital. Was it . . . was it the drugs?"

"You knew about that?"

"We didn't want to admit it. We knew, yeah."

"You call Sheriff Webb on Monday morning. He'll set everything up for you. In the meantime, you might want to start shopping around for an attorney."

We talked for another couple of minutes, mostly about how he had been overwhelmed with funeral arrangements for Steve, and now had to go about making legal arrangements for his other son. I had a feeling that Pete Samples was getting a sneak peek at a special corner of Hell that few people experience between the cradle and the grave. I hoped, for his sake, that this was the worst moment he would have to face, because that would mean that everything from here on would be an improvement.

I hung up the phone, and took a long drag from a Killian's Red I had brought out to the front porch. Donna reached across the small table between our two wicker chairs and stroked my hand.

"It's the worst part of the job," I said. "I'm glad it's over."

She nodded and stroked again.

"I'm running that preacher out of town," I said. "High point of my day, so far."

"How about I take you out to dinner?"

"I could eat."

"Then, maybe we'll have to think of something that will be an even better part of your day than kicking that preacher out of town."

"I'm game," I said.

Carl Sussman was moved out of the ICU into a regular room on Sunday morning.

Around noon on Sunday, the hospital decided they needed Sharon Counts's bed more than she did, and they sent her home. Her lungs still burned when she breathed deeply, but she took a long shower, changed into a fresh set of clothes, and drove back to the hospital. She went directly to Carl's room and sat with him until the nurses ran her out of the building.

Monday morning, as soon as visiting hours began, she was back again.

By that point, Carl had improved markedly. No longer pallid, he could take three breaths without nearly horking up a lung. Even better, there didn't seem to be any long-term neurological effects of his smoke inhalation. The worst symptom he exhibited was a tendency toward rapid fatigue.

Sharon sat with him throughout the day. She didn't say much, since she never did, but she wanted to be close by in case he needed anything. She wasn't exactly certain why. It wasn't as if she felt that she owed Sussman anything. She'd saved his life, after all, not the other way around. Even so, she wanted to be there, and she was on administrative leave from the sheriff's department until she was medically cleared to return to work, and she really had no other place to go, so—she reasoned—she might as well spend her time keeping Carl company.

Sussman, for the most part, slept. He awoke every several hours, expressed mild surprise that she was still there and, for that matter, that he was still there, and then lapsed back into somnolence after taking a drink of ginger ale or a bite of food.

On Monday night the nurses had to order her out of the unit.

When she arrived Tuesday morning, she was surprised to see him sitting in her chair, eating breakfast and watching the morning news on the TV.

"I need you to do something," he said.

"All right," she said.

"You don't even know what it is."

"It's still all right."

He stared at her for a moment the way a cat stares at a doorknob. "Okay, then," he said. "I need a new place to live. From what I hear, my doublewide is now a couple of small open-air duplexes. I need you to find someone to drag that son of a bitch off to the scrap yard, and then I need you to find me a new trailer."

"Another doublewide."

"Hell no. Nothing fancy. I won't be living in it that long. If you can find someone out there who rents the damn things, that would be even better."

"You aren't staying?"

Carl smiled at her. For a moment, she looked panic-stricken. He hated playing with her emotions, but he enjoyed watching her show anything other than her usual stony reticence.

"Hell, yes, I'm staying," he said. "I'm going to get someone to clear out all that burned sheathing and those charred stud walls, and I'm going to get that goddamn building inspector out there again to certify the foundation. If I can't build on the foundation, I'm plowing the thing under and starting fresh."

"You're building the house?"

"Of course I'm building the house. I own that land. It belongs to me. I'll be damned if I'm going to let anyone run me off of it. I need your help, though. I need you to find me a trailer, locate someone to clean up the site, and call the inspector for me. The rest I'll tend to after I get out of this place."

"I'll check in later," she said.

As he watched her leave, he thought that she was the strangest woman he had ever met.

Then she walked back into the room, crossed to his chair, leaned over, and kissed him on the cheek. She straightened up, her cheeks red with embarrassment, and she fumbled with her hands.

"I . . . I'm glad you aren't dead," she said.

By the time I got back to the station on Monday morning, the press had pretty much given up on Prosperity and had moved on to Morgan to set up encampment at the jail there. I figured they'd move on again after a day or two. Rusty Samples wouldn't be arraigned until Wednesday—the next day that Administrative Court was scheduled—and by then some other more pressing world crisis would intervene.

By August, nobody but the most avid sports fans would recall the murder of Steve Samples.

I wrote up the report of the interrogation of Rusty Samples, stapled it into the file I'd developed on the murder, and then wrote *Case Closed By Arrest* across the front of the folder. I dropped it off on Sherry's desk for filing, then decided that it was time to get back to the job I'd been hired to do.

I climbed into the new cruiser and headed off for my weekday patrol. It was nice to get back onto the back roads, listen to the snick of the high-speed radials on the road seams, and relax into a normal rhythm. I'd had to deal with two murders in Prosperity in less than a year. I hoped that I wouldn't have to cope with another.

I didn't need an exterior thermometer to tell me that we were going to hit a new record temperature before the day was out. It seemed that this summer had been nothing but a string of progressively hotter days, hung together by the occasional noisy but not-terribly-dampening thunderstorm.

I could tell there was no chance for a storm today. The sky was steely and transparent, and the sun bore down on the fields like an old debt. I saw the occasional hawk circling lazily in the sky, but mostly I saw turkey buzzards, carrion eaters, lying in their aerial wait to uncover the carcass of a rabbit or deer felled by the unyielding and incessant heat.

It was a regular summer day in Prosperity again. I could live with that.

They released Carl Sussman from the hospital on Wednesday morning, with an advisory to see his own doctor as soon as possible. They gave him a prescription for expectorants, and another for steroids to build back up his tortured lungs, and packed him on his way.

Sharon walked out of the hospital at his side, since nobody else seemed interested in giving him a ride home. He fell into the passenger seat of her car, and she drove him back down Morgan Highway toward his home site.

When they pulled into his long, winding drive off of Bostian Road, he had expected to see charred husks of his trailer and the remains of his house.

Instead, there was a slightly worn singlewide mobile home blocking his view of the building site.

"You did this yesterday?" he asked.

She nodded. "It wasn't hard. There's a place just off the Eisenhower Highway."

"And they hauled off the old one?"

"I had that done first."

"Well, I'll be damned."

"It's furnished," she said. "I went to one of those places that sell furniture by the room. I had to guess about your taste."

She parked the car next to the singlewide. He was out before she could dart around the back of the car to help him. She seemed a little disappointed to find him standing by the side of the car. She held out a key ring with a plastic tag.

"Your house key," she said and followed him to the mobile home.

The delivery folks had rigged a temporary set of wooden steps up to the front door. He realized he missed the makeshift front porch that Donnie Clift had built and nailed to the front of the old doublewide. He thought he could build a substitute in a day or so, but came to the conclusion that it would be wasted effort. He didn't plan to spend a substantial portion of his future in this trailer.

He opened the door and stepped inside. Sharon followed closely behind him. He had a feeling she was trying to gauge his reaction through the back of his head.

He stopped in the middle of the living room and looked around. The place was a lot more cramped than his old double-wide had been, but that was to be expected. He could cross the front room in five steps before coming to a new microfiber sofa with cherry-veneered end tables and matching lamps. Perpendicular to one end of the sofa sat a cozy recliner chair.

To the far side of the living room was a small dinette set—a round table and three chairs—off the tiniest kitchen he had ever seen outside of a camper.

"The bedroom's back this way," Sharon said, pointing in the other direction.

He cocked his head as he looked at her, and swallowed a smile at her obvious embarrassment.

"I mean . . . you might want to see the furniture in there," she said.

"Of course."

He walked past her, into the T-shaped alcove that housed the bedroom and bath.

The furniture in the bedroom was functional but, like everything else in the singlewide, that seemed to be its primary purpose. The dresser was veneered, the double bed not much more than a mattress and box springs on a metal frame, and a four-legged plastic parsons table sat next to one side of the bed to hold up a blinking digital alarm clock.

"You did all right, Sharon," he said.

"I figured you'd want stuff you'd have a hard time getting attached to."

"Good reasoning."

"Plus, it's leased. Once the house is done, you can send it all back."

"Even better. Let's take a look at the house, shall we?"

She followed him out the front door and down the meager steps. He paused at the bottom to get his breath, and coughed several times to clear his lungs.

"Pollen," he said.

"Sure."

Then he walked around to the back of the trailer.

Again he was surprised.

The fire had been devastating. There was nothing left above the brick foundation wall, except the tornado braces he had installed after the inspector's last visit.

"They concentrated on trying to save the trailer," she explained. "Once it was a loss, they turned to the house. By then . . ." She shrugged.

"Where's the debris?" he asked as he peered over the foundation wall.

"There wasn't much but ashes," she said. "The rest I had hauled away."

He turned to her, and then back to the foundation. "When?"

"Yesterday."

"Well, I'll be damned. You have been busy."

He pulled a rag from his back pocket and wiped his forehead with it. Then he turned and sat on the foundation wall.

"I . . . I don't recall a lot over the last several days," he said. "I don't remember whether I ever thanked you."

"For what?"

"For saving my life."

"The firemen did that. They saved mine, too."

"I hear you dragged me from the bedroom into the living room. If you hadn't done that, they wouldn't have gotten to me in time."

"Luck of the draw," she said. "I wasn't even going to be there."

"That's another thing. What were you doing here?"

"Bored. Just got off work. Driving around. You know."

"That's it, huh?"

She nodded, avoiding his inquisitive stare.

"Well, thank you," he said.

"You're welcome. There's food in the refrigerator. I'll make you something to eat, and then I can drive you into Morgan to the building supply."

He shook his head. "Got a problem with that. My plans were burned up in the fire. I need to redraw them."

"Oh."

"I seem to recall that you had some interesting ideas about the layout of the floor plan. Think you could recall all of them?"

"Sure."

"Tell you what. Instead of the building supply, let's hit a discount store and buy a decent computer and some drafting software. I can redraw most of the original house in no time. I did it twenty or thirty times in the lockup. Then we'll make some changes, and make sure all my materials meet code so that damned building inspector won't have a reason to shut me down. What do you say?"

"I can do that," she said.

Forty-One

Wednesday afternoon I pulled up stakes on a traffic watch and drove back in to the station for a late lunch. I stopped off at Gwen Tissot's Stop and Rob and grabbed a couple of fresh ham sandwiches with swiss, lettuce, tomatoes, and hot mustard.

I walked into my office with the food and a large cola and found Slim there, sitting at my desk, waiting for me. He jumped up when I walked in the door and moved to a chair.

"You the acting chief today?" I said as I sat at my desk.

"You could bribe me to do a lot of things, Chief, if'n you had enough money, but you couldn't bribe me to take your job."

"Disquietingly comforting. Have you eaten?"

"I had some Chinese a couple of hours ago."

"Mind if I eat while we talk?"

"Don't make me no never-mind."

"Good. I'll chew. You start."

I unwrapped my sandwich and took a bite. He dug one cowboy-booted foot into the rug and pushed the chair back until it lodged against the wall behind him.

"This preacher business is still botherin' me," he said.

"I ran him off," I said between bites.

"Maybe you shouldn'ta ought to have done that, Chief."

"Why?"

"I ran my cousin Ray to ground last night. Found him in a biker bar over to Tudorville."

"Tudorville's in South Carolina, Slim."

"I know."

"You weren't in uniform, were you? South Carolina is out of our jurisdiction."

"I seem to recall you doing a little investigative work down there last week."

"Point taken. So what's up with Ray?"

Slim scratched his head and then slid both hands behind his neck. "You know Ray. Shoot him in the head and his brain'll drop out and roll across the floor. I could tell he's been doing crystal again, from the way his eyes lit up. He's a sad case."

"Did he know anything about this Clay Steger killing over in Morgan?"

"He was there."

"Do tell? When Steger was murdered?"

"No, but earlier in the evening. Sheriff Webb seems to have good intel on this one. It was a summit meeting between the Outlaws and the Vulcans. Seems they've been stepping on each others' toes lately, crossing boundaries to sell meth and brown tar heroin. Things were getting a little tense among the tribes, know what I mean?"

"I do."

"So they decided to meet at this pool hall out on Eisenhower, pump back a few brewskis, maybe figure out a way to relieve the tension. Clay Steger had risen to a position of some importance after Trigger Chaney got put away last year for nailin' that Mexican kid to a white oak, so he led the contingent for the Vulcans.

"Anyway, according to Ray, some money changed hands, a sort of peace gesture to show that the incursions were unintentional and there was no ill will."

"Incursions," I said.

"Am I not talking loud enough for you, Chief?"

"No, you're fine. I just never expected to hear you use a word like 'incursions.' "

"*Readers Digest,*" he said. "*Improve Your Word Power.* Like I was sayin', Steger repped for the Vulcans, and the Outlaws sent one of their toughest, and Steger walked out of the bar with a wad of bills that would choke a porn star."

"A tribute."

"That's the word Ray used. The Outlaws laid this cash on Steger like it was his cut of the business they'd knocked off on his turf. Steger sucked back another Bud, and then said he had to go see his ol' lady. Half an hour later the rest of the bikers decided to call it a night. When they left the bar, they found Steger in his car, his head leaned back on the front seat, doin' the thousand-yard stare."

"What about the money?"

"Ray says they checked. It was gone."

"So it was a robbery."

"Mebbe it was, and mebbe it warn't. Ray and me, we got to talkin' about this and that, and suddenly, outa the blue, he says 'It's a shame Clay got killed instead of that fuckin' preacher.' Just like that."

"You don't say."

"I tell ya, Chief, it got my attention. So I asked him what he was talkin' about. He said that when Clay got to the pool hall, there was this holy roller in the parking lot tryin' to convert the whole lot of 'em. Steger told him to blow, but he kept at it, so Steger jacked him up and tossed him on the trunk of a beater Buick parked next to the pool hall entrance. This preacher jumped off the car and started screechin' hellfire and damnation, until Steger and his boys got bored and went into the building."

"Where was the preacher when they came back out and found Steger?"

"Nowhere to be seen. He was gone, and the cash was gone,

and Steger was sitting in his front seat dead. Now, what do you make of that?"

"I find it very interesting."

"Well, that ain't all. I asked Ray to describe this preacher in the parking lot, and he said the guy looked like a scarecrow, with a buzz cut and a big ol' silver cross hangin' around his neck on a heavy chain. Said he had a nose like an eagle and a chin like a backhoe rake. I'd say that's a pretty good description of Cross, wouldn't you?"

I nodded as I took the last bite of my sandwich.

"That's good information, Slim," I said after swallowing. "Good police work."

"There's more. You wanted me to find out what's shakin' between the Vulcans and the Outlaws. The answer is plenty. The Vulcans, they're a little short of brain power since Chaney got sent to Central Prison and Steger got his eggs scrambled. They figure the whole meet out on Eisenhower was a setup, that while the Outlaws were inside the pool hall makin' peace with Steger and the Vulcans, some more of their guys were outside waitin' for Steger to leave, so they could jump him when he left and get their money back. Ray says the Outlaws wanted to have their cake and eat it too, and the Vulcans aren't gonna stand for it. They're stockpiling weapons and lookin' around for decent deals on bulk war paint."

"Did Ray say anything about when they plan to hit the Vulcans?"

"He didn't say nothin' about a hit. He says they're gettin' their shit together in case a war breaks out."

"All right," I said. "Guess I need to pay Don Webb a visit over in Morgan, tell him to hunker down. Maybe he can arrest some of the key members of the gangs, give them some time to cool off."

"What are you gonna do about that preacher?"

312

"Nothing. By now, Cross is probably somewhere over the state line. He's some other jurisdiction's problem."

"But if he icepicked that Steger fella . . ."

"You know something?" I said. "If he did, it might be the only worthwhile thing he accomplished the whole time he was in Bliss County. Good work, Slim. I'll see there's a note in your folder."

Sheriff Webb fiddled with a rubber band and a paper clip while I told him what Slim had learned from his cousin Ray. Every once in a while, he'd nod, and then he'd grunt "uh-huh" to let me know he was still listening.

"This is interesting," he said when I finished. "Interesting and troubling. Is this Ray fellow reliable?"

"He's a low-life shit-for-brains," I said. "But Slim and Ray have been close for almost thirty years. I don't reckon the uniform shuts Ray up much. If he told Slim there's a rumble coming, I'd say there's a rumble coming. What's going on with Rusty Samples?"

"He's on suicide watch over in the jail. The more his head clears of the drugs, the more despondent he becomes. Sooner or later, he's gonna do something nasty to himself."

"Have his parents gotten here?"

"Saw them Monday morning. They told me you called them. That was pretty nice of you. It's gonna take a lot of effort to keep that boy alive until his trial. Once he gets to prison . . ." Webb shrugged, acknowledging a sad inevitability.

We jawed for a few minutes, mostly making mental wagers on whether the Vulcans could beat the Outlaws, or vice versa, and I excused myself to head home. I figured, after all the overtime I'd put in the previous week, I was due an afternoon off.

I hadn't mentioned Alvin Cross and Slim's speculation that

he might have had something to do with Clay Steger's murder. I don't know why. Maybe, hindsight being twenty-twenty but foresight being blind, I didn't think it was that important.

The thing that surprised Sussman most was how quickly he got tired.

He and Sharon had spent most of Wednesday buying and setting up the new computer.

She was able to return to work on Thursday, after visiting the doctor contracted by the sheriff's department to conduct fitness reviews.

While she worked, Sussman alternated taking naps on his new couch and redrawing the basic house plans he kept securely in his own head. He'd gone over them so many times mentally, it was like doing transcription in the CAD program he'd bought for the computer. He was careful to include modifications to meet all the corrective suggestions the county building inspector had mentioned, and he even downloaded as much information as he could from the guy's office to assure that he didn't make any more potentially disastrous mistakes on the second try at building his house.

Sharon left the trailer, only to come back around dinnertime, with a bucket of chicken, some mashed potatoes, some slaw and biscuits. She looked over the plans as they ate, made a few comments, and together they moved things around on the screen.

The end product didn't look much like the plans he had developed while in prison, but he realized that the new plans were more functional, with improved flow from room to room. In the end, he agreed that this would be a better house than the one he had intended to build.

The best part was that the footprint was identical to the one he had already built. If the fire hadn't ruined his foundation, he ought to be able to build the new house on the ruins of the old one.

That seemed appropriate, somehow. It symbolized the way he saw his life, flying high before being dashed to the ground, and then rising again from the ashes to become something wholly different—maybe even better.

He arose on Thursday morning with the intent of starting in on the house. He ate, washed his face, shaved, and brushed his teeth, then threw on his work clothes for a hard day's work.

He spent the first hour walking the perimeter of the foundation. He couldn't see any clearly defined breaches in the brick and cinderblock wall surrounding the crawlspace. It looked intact, if a bit sooty in some sections. There was a heavy creosote smell about the project that hung in the air and burned his sinuses. He figured that it would be washed away in the first heavy rain.

He wasn't fool enough to actually begin any construction without having the place inspected first and issued an approval for building, so he went back inside the mobile home and called the inspector's office from the cell phone he'd borrowed from Sharon.

"Newton Slipe, please?" he said when the secretary answered.

"I'm sorry, Mr. Slipe is in the field."

"This is Carl Sussman. Mr. Slipe inspected my house under construction last week and made some recommendations. It burned over the weekend, and I was hoping to schedule a time for him to drop by and inspect the remaining foundation to see if it is still usable."

"Did you say Carl Sussman?"

"That's right."

"Mr. Sussman, there must be some confusion. Mr. Slipe has you on his schedule for this afternoon. Did you already call once to set up an appointment?"

"No. I have a friend who's been helping me since the fire. Maybe she did it. Thanks. I'll keep an eye out for him."

He hung up and printed out a set of the plans he and Sharon had drawn up the night before. If Slipe was planning to come by later, he'd want to take a look at the new layout.

While he waited, Sussman opened the architectural program and ran a quick materials estimate for the new house. Then he called the building supply house and ordered new fir studs— including some in two-by-six for those interior walls that would have plumbing running through them—and several dozen sheets of plywood sheathing for the floors.

His larger power tools had all been destroyed in the fire, so he took his heat-blistered truck into Morgan to the home supply, and bought a chop saw and a new compressor and nail gun and a new supply of nails.

By the time he got back to the mobile home, he was exhausted. He hadn't imagined how difficult it would be to do simple things, and he realized just how far he had to go in his recovery. As he sat at the table and chewed unenthusiastically on a ham sandwich, he thought about how close he had come to dying, and the thought provoked a shiver that ran up his spine like a treed squirrel.

After lunch, he made certain that all of his papers were together for Slipe, and then he lay on the sofa for a short nap to regain his strength.

A knock on the door woke him around two o'clock. Thinking it was Slipe, he rose, pulled his hair back into a ponytail, and tied it in place with an elastic band. He grabbed his papers from the table and opened the door.

A girl stood on the front steps. She was willowy and blond and her arm was in a sling. She searched his eyes for any hint of recognition.

"Can I help you?" he asked.

"Are you Carl Sussman?"

He nodded.

"My name is Allison Petrie."

She extended her un-slung hand. He shook it automatically.

"Is there something I can do for you, Allison?"

"You don't know who I am, do you?"

He was certain he would remember if they had met before. "I'm sorry," he said. "I can't place you."

"You saved my life."

Then he recognized her. She was the girl in the auto accident at the intersection in Prosperity.

"You sure look a lot better," he said. "How are you healing?"

"It still hurts a lot when I roll over in bed, or try to sit up, and when I laugh. Otherwise, I can tell it's getting better. The ambulance driver told me that if you hadn't been there, I might have punctured a lung right on the spot. They said I could have died."

Sussman's sense of courtesy suddenly took hold. "Would you like to come inside, out of the heat?"

"No, thanks. Actually, I wanted to get a look at this house you're building."

"Now, how on earth do you know about that?"

"My uncle told me. Could you show me where it is?"

"Sure. Just a moment."

He dropped the plans on the table and stepped down from the front door to lead her around the mobile home.

It was only as he rounded the corner that he saw the four or five cars parked there. A small group of men huddled around the nose of Sussman's pickup truck. One of them was Newton Slipe. Sharon was sitting on the brick foundation of the house, watching the scene with the barest hint of amusement in her eyes.

Sussman stopped short as he saw the crowd.

"What's this?" he asked.

Slipe stepped forward. "Ms. Counts told me what you did for Allison," he said. "Allison is my niece, my sister's girl. They live over in Mica Wells. We knew someone had come to her aid when she was in the traffic accident the other week, but we never could find out who it was. We figured it was just some good Samaritan. Sharon and I—well, all of us, really—work on Habitat for Humanity houses. She came to me yesterday and told me that you were the one who saved Allison's life. I just wanted to take an opportunity to . . . well, to thank you."

He extended his hand. Sussman looked at it warily, as if he expected it to turn into a fist. He glanced over at Sharon, who was smiling, if only a little. Then he took Slipe's hand.

"You're welcome, I guess," he said.

"I called some of the guys last night, after Sharon told me, and I asked them if they were up to throwing together a house frame the right way this time, according to code. When they heard you were the one who took care of Allison, they all agreed to toss in with me."

Sussman was momentarily dumbfounded. He looked over at Sharon again, and she nodded.

"I'll tell you the truth, Mr. Slipe, I really wanted to build this house myself, to prove that I could do it, but ever since the fire I get weak as a kitten after a few minutes' work. I figure it's going to be a couple of weeks before I get all my strength back, so I could use all the help I can get. Thank you, you and all your friends. I'd welcome the help. As a matter of fact I've just ordered the studs and flooring, and they should arrive Saturday morning—if that's not too soon."

"Hell," Slipe said. "Saturday's when we do our best work. We all got jobs, you know."

"That would be terrific. Sharon and I redrew the plans last night, I'd like to show them to you, get approval for some of the items. And, if it's not asking too much, I was wondering if you could take a look at the foundation to see if it can still be used."

"Let's start with the plans," Slipe said. "The boys will clear away the rest of the fire debris, and I'll look over the foundation."

"The plans are in the trailer."

He started to lead Slipe around the mobile home, but Allison grabbed his arm. He turned to her, and she threw her one good arm around his neck and kissed his cheek.

"I want to thank you, too," she said. "My momma told me what you did, and why people don't like you so much, but I think maybe you're a good man. I owe you more than I can ever repay."

"It's just nice to know you're going to be all right. I figure the help your uncle and his friends are going to give will be repayment plenty."

She hugged him again, and thanked him again and again, until his embarrassment forced him to untangle himself from her. She walked over to the foundation and sat next to Sharon.

He started to lead Slipe around the trailer, but first looked back at Sharon. She gave him a thumbs-up. Her face, seemingly frozen forever in a stoic cast, seemed to light up a little as their eyes met.

Thanks, he mouthed.

FORTY-TWO

The war began with a bang, early on Sunday morning.

The Carolina Outlaws kept a chapter house just west of Pooler. At one time, maybe fifty years ago, it had been a damned fine house, but now it was little more than a shack, with rotting exterior wood siding and windows dotted with cardboard to replace broken panes. The front porch arced down precipitously, which also canted the gambreled roof on one side and gave the whole structure a lopsided, stricken appearance.

The Vulcans snuck up under cover of darkness, after hiking through the trees that surrounded the shack. They had parked their bikes half a mile away, arriving one by one to reduce the noise and cover their advance.

An Outlaw named Vin Abbott had been assigned to keep guard in front of the shack that night. His interpretation of the assignment was that he should sleep on the sofa parked on the front porch and check the perimeter every couple of hours when he got up to take a piss.

Lulled to sleep by whiskey and marijuana, he never heard the band of Vulcans march on the shack. He might have awakened for a brief instant while one Vulcan clamped a palm over his mouth and rammed the hunting knife into his chest, but if so he didn't stay awake for long.

From that point on, it was wholesale slaughter. Everyone in the house was either asleep or passed out. The Vulcans simply walked in the front door, positioned one of their members at every room, and—at a prearranged signal—kicked in the room doors and started shooting pump shotguns loaded with double-ought buck.

The entire attack took about half a minute. A minute later, the Vulcans had melded back into the woods. Slowly, the wildlife that had been startled into silence began to come back to life, and ten minutes after the guns fell silent, nightsong resumed around the charnel house that had been an Outlaws stronghold.

An Outlaw named Darrell Souter returned from the beach around noon, and rode directly to the chapter house with his girlfriend on the back of his bike. He had ridden straight through and couldn't wait for a cold beer, a toke of White Widow, and a session of hide the salami with his new old lady.

He knew something was wrong as soon as he reached the front of the house.

"Stay with the bike," he said as he propped the kickstand and rolled off the saddle.

"What's wrong?"

"Shut your hole and stay with the fuckin' bike!"

The Vulcans had rolled Vin Abbott over, with his back toward the yard. Darrell grabbed his shoulder and yanked. Abbott rolled off the sofa onto the splintered boards of the porch, a splotch of ugly matted brown the size of a steering wheel on the front of his shirt.

Darrell's girl screamed. He held up a hand to silence her, grabbed the rifle Abbott had left next to the sofa, threw the bolt to check the chamber, then walked into the house.

A half minute later he stumbled out, dropped the rifle on the porch, fell to his knees in the dust at the bottom of the steps, and spewed his breakfast onto the ground.

He shook his head to clear it, took one more look through the front door as if he needed to reassure himself that he had really seen the carnage inside, and unsteadily got to his feet.

"We have to go," he said. "We have to tell the others."

Trey Scott had been a Vulcan for five years, ever since he had flunked out of the community college and his parents had tossed him out of the house, thinking that if they forced responsibility on him he might accept it.

They couldn't have been more wrong. With the Vulcans, he found people who accepted him no matter how bad a fuck-up he was, and he was a pretty awful one.

The Vulcans had put Trey in charge of one of their mobile meth labs—old school buses with blacked-out windows and stock car paint jobs that housed cabinets loaded with laboratory equipment and the raw stuff of drug-making. The buses parked in a different, relatively inaccessible prearranged spot each night, and the Vulcans' chemists would arrive after dark, to work through the black hours manufacturing enough crank to keep all of Pooler bouncing off the ceiling for a month.

They assigned Trey to drive the bus because each mobile lab contained tanks of hydrogen and acetylene and other combustibles, and because Trey was completely expendable. If he got busted, he wouldn't be missed. If he got killed, he'd be forgotten in a week.

They didn't tell Trey this, of course. The senior Vulcans filled him with visions of advancement and riches, and convinced him that he was a key player in their master plan. Trey, having more or less the intelligence of a vinyl wallet, bought the lies and attached himself to his job the way a tick attaches itself to a fat dog.

On Monday afternoon he pulled himself off of the cot he had placed in the back of the bus, ignored his own stink, and climbed behind the steering wheel with a couple of packs of Twinkies, a fried apple pie wrapped in wax paper, and a

Mountain Dew. The largest part of his job, since he knew almost as much about chemistry as he did about personal hygiene, was to drive the bus around for most of the day, which allowed the multiple generators attached to pulleys under the hood to charge the banks of batteries used by the chemists at night to light their work and power their electronic equipment.

Trey pulled the bus out from behind an empty big-box discount store on Eisenhower Boulevard in Morgan, where he had parked it the previous night, and pointed it toward the South Carolina state line. He knew a girl down in a small town twenty or thirty miles south of the border who wasn't particularly scrupulous about things like cleanliness or intelligence, and whose primary attributes seemed to be her almost nymphomaniacal desire for frequent and athletic sex and her total disregard for protection. Trey didn't care that she possessed all the beauty of a bulldog. He had learned how easy it was to keep his eyes closed, and she didn't demand much in the way of attention afterwards.

He had cleared the Morgan city limits when he saw the pair of cycles pull in behind him on the highway. Being a minor functionary, Trey had not been told about the Vulcans' plans to raid the Outlaws' chapter house two nights before, so he wasn't wary when he saw the Outlaw patches on their vests. Bikes were bikes, as far as Trey was concerned. He liked bikes, especially hardtail choppers, and the bikes these guys were riding had been very nicely tricked out.

Half the time he watched the road, and the other half he kept his gaze on the huge side mirrors, watching the bikes behind him.

As he hit a long, straight stretch of blacktop, with no traffic coming in the opposite direction, the bikes pulled into the left lane, alongside the bus. Trey thought that they meant to pass, so he stuck one arm out the window to wave them by.

Seconds later he heard the crash of breaking glass behind him and saw the bikes skid to a stop. He glanced in the rear-view mirror and saw light streaming into the bus through a broken side window.

It occurred to him that those boys had tossed a rock through the window. He felt a flash of anger because he knew that the Vulcans wanted the windows to stay closed and painted over. There would be hell to pay when the top dogs found out what those Outlaws had done to his bus.

That was about all he had time to think, before the grenade that had been tossed into the bus lit off. Shrapnel flew in every direction, blowing out windows and scattering safety glass all over the highway. One piece of shrapnel penetrated the back of Trey's seat, under and to the left of his right shoulder blade. It sliced two major arteries and would have hurt like hell if all his sensation hadn't already been stanched by the piece of metal that had flown into the back of his head, severing his spinal cord. Either piece of metal probably would have killed him. Together, they made it a certainty.

Trey's head slumped over and his hands fell from the steering wheel at the same instant that the gas from the hydrogen and acetylene tanks ignited on residual flames from the grenade blast. The flames flew back along the gas trails to the tanks, which exploded.

The very last thought that crept through Trey Scott's head wasn't words at all, but more an image of regret that probably would have translated into something like *I sure wish I had gotten to fuck that bulldog-faced girl one last time.*

There wasn't time for that, of course, because in the blink of an eye the entire bus was consumed in a miniature mushroom cloud that rose two hundred feet above the surface of the highway, scorching trees on each side of the asphalt, blowing shards of metal and glass and wood hundreds of yards, and melting the very surface of the roadway underneath into a pool of misshapen black goo.

They had to close the highway for two days to clear the debris and repair the blacktop.

Nobody ever found a bone, or a tooth, or a piece of skin from Trey Scott's body.

He was completely forgotten by the end of the week.

The Vulcans didn't stop with their raid on the Outlaws' chapter house, and they didn't wait for their rivals to retaliate before striking again. Even as Trey Scott was in the process of being immolated on the highway south of Morgan, a raiding party of five Vulcans walked into a cycle repair shop in Pooler, locked the door behind them, and emptied illegally modified automatic rifles into every Outlaw in sight.

They spread gasoline around, and the last Vulcan out the door tossed a match into the fumes.

By the time the fire department was alerted, the attackers were several miles away. They watched the helicopter television reports of the firemen fighting the three-alarm blaze from a bar in Morgan, as they hoisted beers and saluted their triumph.

I watched the reports of the escalating war between the rival gangs with a sort of detached fascination. Prosperity had been spared any association with the conflict, since the gangs tended to focus all their attentions on Pooler and Morgan.

On the other hand, I couldn't escape my suspicions that the entire gang war was the result of an essentially random act of violence that had involved neither Vulcans nor Outlaws.

On Tuesday morning I drove into Morgan, sat under the cool blast of an air conditioner vent in Don Webb's office, and recounted Ray Tackett's story about the murder of Clay Steger in the pool hall parking lot. I included the part about how Steger had tossed a street preacher who sounded a lot like Alvin Cross onto the trunk of a dilapidated Buick.

"God damn, Judd, I wish you'd told me about this earlier."

"I can't say why I didn't," I told him. "I guess it just didn't seem significant at the time."

"It makes sense. I suppose I haven't been totally straight with you, either. Been too damned busy with this gang mess."

He picked up his telephone, dialed four numbers, and said, "This is Sheriff Webb. Can you come up for a minute?"

When Clark Ulrich stepped inside, he nodded toward me.

"Clark, I need some technical information from you," Webb said.

"I'll do what I can."

Clark took a seat next to mine and glanced over at me the way I recalled my partners in crime stealing nervous glances, in my childhood, as we sat in the principal's office awaiting summary judgment for some schoolyard scrape.

Webb pulled a report from his desk and opened the folder. "Judd, I could use some help explaining something. Can you think of some way that money with Clay Steger's blood on it might have found its way into the pocket of your murder suspect down in Prosperity?"

It took a moment for the words to work their way into my thick skull. "You want to say that again, Sheriff, in little pieces?"

"Clark here got the results back from that DNA test you requested on the money that was found in Steve Samples's pocket the night he died."

"Right. I couldn't figure out how his blood could have gotten on the bills in his pants upstairs, if he was killed naked downstairs."

"The short answer is that the blood on that money wasn't from Samples. Clark?"

Ulrich cleared his throat and gestured for the file. Webb

handed it across the desk to him. He flipped to the test results.

"When this came back, I knew right away it wasn't from Samples," he said. "You recall that I did the tests on the hair from the pool drain, which connected Steve and Rusty, so I was already familiar with most of the allele patterns."

"I'm with you so far," I said.

"It's common procedure to run a cross-match on unidentified DNA patterns. As it happens, we took blood from Clay Steger during the autopsy, and I'd already received the results of that test and entered them in the state database."

"All right."

"So, when I ran a search for matching DNA patterns to the blood on the money from Samples's pocket, the program made a match pretty quickly."

I rocked the seat back and forth as I worked through all the connections.

"Ann Koehler told me that Samples asked her to break a hundred dollar bill, but she only had sixty-two dollars," I said. "She gave him the money she had and he gave her the hundred. I asked her where she got the money in the first place and she told me that it came from Ricky Chasen."

"And Chasen works for Alvin Cross," Webb said.

"Who fits the description of a man who was in the parking lot preaching to the unwashed the night Clay Steger was murdered," I added.

"Clay Steger tossed Alvin Cross onto the trunk of a beater Buick."

"And Clay was killed with an ice pick an hour or so later. Yeah. It fits. Either Alvin Cross killed Steger, or he had Ricky Chasen do it for him."

Webb squeezed his nose, then massaged his temples. "Some days this job really sucks," he said. "Judd, you got any idea where Alvin Cross might be right about now?"

"I ran him out of town last Saturday. I have a feeling he was involved in an arson case down in Prosperity. So far as I know, he's in the next state by now."

"What kind of vehicle was he driving?"

"Some sort of motor home, like a converted bus."

"A school bus?"

"No, one of those used by charter services. The sides were skinned in where the windows usually are, and what windows there were had been covered with dark film so you couldn't see inside."

"Got any idea which state the plates were registered?"

"Never wrote it down. It didn't seem important. I didn't plan on dealing with him once he blew town. The bus was brown and white with some red striping."

"Okay," Webb said. "We can deal with Cross later. Right now I have a war to put down. I'm going to call Sheriff Gates up in Pooler and have him round up every high-ranking Outlaw he can find. I'm going to do the same here in Bliss County. We're going to get them together and explain how we think Steger was killed. Maybe we can get them to call a truce long enough to work things out, before some innocent civilians get hurt."

"I wouldn't count on it," I said. "Maybe Cross lit things off by killing Steger, and maybe he didn't. I have a feeling this thing is like those feuds way back in the Appalachians. After a while, people forget who stole whose pig, but they sure remember who killed who last week."

"I hope you're wrong," Webb said. "You could do me a huge favor if you'd start the process of finding Cross and Chasen. If we can get them back to Bliss County and charge one or the other with the murder—"

"I'm way ahead of you. I'll have a BOLO put out on that bus later today, and I'll send a message to every county in North and South Carolina, asking local law enforcement to keep any eye out for any traveling tent revivals."

"There are going to be a lot of pissed-off preachers out there this weekend," Webb observed.

"I only care about one of them," I said. "And, at this point, I don't give a damn if he blows his top."

FORTY-THREE

After we firmed up our plans, and each person's role for the next day or so, I begged off to head back to Prosperity.

The AC had barely cooled off the car before I hit Morgan Highway and headed toward home base. Soon I crossed the Prosperity town limit. About a mile ahead was the oiled dirt path leading back to Nate Murray's farm.

I'm not sure why I turned down that road. Instinct, maybe, or curiosity, or maybe I simply wanted to see for myself that Preacher Cross really had bugged out.

We hadn't seen a lick of rain since the night Carl Sussman's house had burned. The grass beyond the weathered timber gate to Murray's pastureland was brown and withered. The heat surrounded me like a physical presence as I stepped out of the cruiser. I left the motor running so the car wouldn't heat up again, and surveyed the site of Cross's revival meeting.

The tent was gone. I could see the bare dirt outline in the trampled, defeated grass where it had stood, where the lack of sunlight and incessant tromping of work boots and Sunday-go-to-meeting shoes had beat it down to the roots in cadence to Cross's invocations and exhortations, as he whipped his congregations into a frenzy each evening before raping their pocketbooks.

The air was heavy and damp and still, hot as the hell with which Cross had threatened the faithful under that sweltering tent. The farm was silent, save for the distant barking of a pack of dogs chasing after some vermin prey in the fields.

Late July was a time I had come to associate with violent crime and irrational tempers. There was something about the heat that did it. Run the thermometers into three figures day after day after day, and sooner or later people were bound to snap. Resentments long kept under wraps tended to surface with the smallest provocation. Long-simmering feuds erupted into fury and shooting. Sullen youths took out their boredom and stupidity on the innocent, preying on the weak or trusting. It was in the broiling month of the Thunder Moon that I expected the very worst of mankind. To my regret, mankind seldom failed to meet those expectations.

I climbed back into the cruiser and drove farther up the access road until I reached Nate Murray's farmhouse. Nate was a solid citizen in Prosperity, a dependable neighbor, and I knew him to be as troubled about the influx of bedroom communities from Parker County as I was. Most of the farm people in Bliss County, people whose families had tilled the soil of this bucolic patch of southern earth for almost three centuries, dreaded the approaching end to a way of life that was like religion.

It would have been like Nate to offer his land to a man like Alvin Cross. I'm sure Cross represented a different time to Nate Murray, a period of history populated by raw-boned, leather-skinned, hard-working men who toiled from the pink-hued skies of sunup to the first twinkle of the eastern star, confident of only one certainty in life—that they would do it all again the next day, if the Lord didn't take them in their sleep. Cross was part of a more reverent, more conforming time, when it was easy for a man to know his place in the world, and his worth was defined by the product of his sweat and muscle and effort.

It would have been comforting for Nate Murray to have a tent revival in his pasture. He would have seen it as a sort of omen, a sacrifice of one small patch of his land to appease an angry, Old Testament sort of God whom he perceived as granting or not granting him fertile and fecund fields from one year to the next, based on what sometimes seemed little more than divine whimsy.

I stepped up to the gray-weathered front porch of Nate Murray's farmhouse and knocked on the front door.

There was no answer. I could see through the glass, straight down the shotgun hallway that bisected the house like a spine. The rooms were dim, the curtains in the windows still. There was no sign of life.

I figured that Nate was out in the fields, or had driven into Morgan to pick up supplies at the FCX. I made a mental note to call him later in the day, to see whether Cross might have mentioned before leaving where he planned on landing next.

I drove back out to the site of Cross's tent meeting and reluctantly pulled myself from the cool environs of the cruiser one more time to take a last look around the area. The sun pounded down on me like a relentless drumbeat.

I wasn't certain what I hoped to find. If Cross—or his minion Ricky Chasen—had been responsible for the murder of Clay Steger, it wasn't likely they'd leave much behind in the way of evidence. Years of running the short and long con would have left Cross with a keen, perhaps compulsive, desire to break camp with barely a trace that he'd ever been there, save for the expanse of dead earth left in the shadow of his canvas tent.

I walked around the dusty perimeter with my eyes focused in the distance, looking for anything out of the ordinary, any scrap of paper or shred of detritus. In the distance, the dogs continued their frenzied howling. I couldn't believe that any creature could muster that kind of energy in this midsummer blast oven.

Curious to see what had riled them, I walked toward the hill over which I heard their growls and barks. Dogs were a fact of

life on farms, as were cats. They weren't pets. They were working animals, charged with controlling the destructive vermin
that could ruin root crops and tender leaf vegetables. Right-
thinking dogs, however, hardly ever ventured abroad in the heat
of the day. They were more typically found languishing in the
shade, panting heavily to stay cool, waiting until the sun hit the
horizon to begin their nightly hunts.

As I approached the crest of the hill, I had a sense that
something was out of kilter. Borne of my own years roaming
the hills and pastures of my father's farm, I knew damn well
that dogs exerting energy during the hottest part of the day was
out of place.

Cops are drawn to things that are out of place.

I stood on the top of the hill and looked down on a pack of
five or six blue-tick hound dogs, scraping at the dirt and shov-
ing around one another. Suddenly, one of them broke from the
mob and sprinted toward me, carrying some prize in his maw.
He ran right up to me and stopped, his head lowered, his eyes
canted upward toward me, as if half-expecting me to rob him of
his take.

It occurred to me that the dogs must have come across some
dead animal in the hollow, maybe a deer or a large raccoon, and
they were engaged in parting the carcass out. Dogs never seem
to care much how decomposed meat is, and they never seem to
learn from their sad experience with eating carrion. I guess
that's why my dad always referred to simple people as being
"dog-dumb."

The matter in this hound's teeth, however, didn't look right.
There was no fur, which should have been present if it had
been ripped from a dead animal. As the dog regained his cour-
age and sprinted past me, I thought I saw the pattern of printed
cloth embedded in the hunk of meat between his jaws.

I rushed down the hill toward the pack, my pistol drawn,

ready to shoot them if necessary to keep them from any more destruction, even as my stomach twisted in anticipation of the grisly scene I knew I would encounter.

The dogs had been digging, perhaps for some time from the looks of the ground. As they scattered in all directions, I saw four depressions, each cratered around the exposed carcasses that protruded from the centers of the excavations like shipwrecks reaching from ocean sand.

As I backed up the hill to escape the stink that emanated from the cratered holes, I reached to my shoulder and toggled the microphone of my two-way radio.

"Prosperity Chief to Prosperity Station!" I rasped.

"Prosperity Station," Sherry responded. "What's up, Chief?"

"I'm at Nate Murray's farm," I said. "I need Stu Marbury to meet me here. Then call Sheriff Webb's office in Morgan and have them send a CSI team out here."

FORTY-FOUR

I had become something of a master at controlling a crime scene during the past several weeks.

In this case, Stu and I had been able—mostly—to keep a lid on my find at Nate Murray's farm. It was reasonably far off Morgan Highway, and reasonably isolated from the surrounding farms. The arrival of a couple of ambulances and the crime scene team from Morgan had elicited very little alarm from the neighbors. Without the efficient network of party-line telephones to spread the word, the discovery of four bodies in a lonely pasture went practically unnoticed.

The only reporter who drove up the dusty oiled path to Nate's farm was Cory True. He skidded to a stop just short of the old cruiser that Stu had parked across the road, and jumped from his car with a steno pad and a tape recorder in hand.

"Hold it right there, Cory," I said.

"The police radio says you have a crime scene here."

I didn't say anything, simply looked at him menacingly, trying to impart the fact that he would get no closer to whatever he imagined to be over the hill, beyond the emergency vehicles that had congregated to collect the remains.

"Can't you tell me anything?" he asked after a moment.

"No."

"That's it? Just no?"

"Yeah. That's it. Just no."

"Isn't this the farm where that con man preacher was set up?

Does whatever's over that hill have anything to do with Cross?"

I stared at him through my sunglasses, hoping that the barrier of smoked glass prevented him from reading any emotion.

"C'mon, Chief," he said. "Give me something."

"Later, Cory. If you take one more step toward that hill, I'll arrest you for interfering with police business, and obstruction of justice. Do you understand?"

"Chief!"

"Do you understand?" I asked again. "I'd sure as hell hate to have to drive you over to the station and lock you up. You go back to Morgan, and I promise I'll call you the first chance I get. Right now, though, I have other things to do besides babysit you."

He looked hurt.

I didn't care.

Didn't have to.

"You'll call me first?" he said, a plea.

"Before I talk with any other reporter. But to get that exclusive, you have to turn around and go away."

He lowered the tape recorder.

"And if you've been recording me, I want the tape," I said.

"I wasn't, Chief. Honest."

I nodded, but I didn't let my gaze leave his, even as I knew he couldn't tell I was staring him down. All he could see was his reflection in my lenses.

"I'll be at the paper," he said.

He stepped back without turning, and then climbed into his car and put it in reverse. I watched him until he reached the highway.

Then I trekked back up the hill.

I had hated the smell of wintergreen since I was a little boy, when my parents had spread Vap-O-Rub on my chest when I had a cold. As I watched Clark Ulrich and Sharon Counts direct the teams of crime scene specialists to disinter the bodies, though, I was grateful to have a smear of the stuff under my nose.

Clark took a break and trudged up the hill.

"Dogs," he said. "Amazing animals. They can smell decomp through two or three feet of Carolina red clay."

"Is that a fact?"

"I heard about this one cadaver dog, down in Florida, who located a body that had been buried under a concrete carport for fourteen years. Sniffed out the decomp and told the police exactly where to dig. Is that something, or what?"

I pointed toward the holes. "What does it look like, Clark?"

"Three females. One male. They weren't all buried at the same time. I'd say there's about a two-week spread from the first to the last, based on the differences in deterioration. We have three of them out of the ground already. The last should be up in another fifteen minutes or so. It may be hard to determine the exact cause of death on all of them. The dogs made a mess of whatever they could expose. Pretty grisly. Any idea how they wound up there?"

"Yes."

He waited for a more complete response that I wasn't ready to give him.

"Is it okay for me to go down there yet?" I asked.

"Sure. We've already done most of our surveying of the site, but you don't want to tramp around a lot. Straight in and straight out would be best."

"All right."

I followed him down the hill. Where the dogs had left four shallow concave holes, the crime scene analysts had produced excavations almost eight feet across in every direction. They had tried to dig around the bodies without disturbing them, for fear of damaging whatever evidence might remain after days in the ground.

"You think that's all of them?" I asked as we approached the scene.

"We checked the perimeter and didn't find any signs of disturbed ground, but it's a big farm. Who knows how many places there might be to stash a body? Who owns this place, anyway?"

"Local farmer, guy named Nate Murray."

"Does he have a family?"

"No. He's a widower. His kids left the farm years ago. Took off for better opportunities, over in Pooler."

"Any farmhands live on the property?"

"Nope. Nate hires some Mexican boys to help during the busy season, but otherwise he tends to the place by himself."

"Sounds like a setup for a serial killer. This guy, Ed Gein, was a farmer, up in Minnesota. Lived by himself. Started killing local women and stuffing them, like that guy in *Psycho*—what was his name?"

"Norman Bates," I said absently.

"That's it. Norman Bates. It isn't good to isolate yourself the way your friend Murray did. Too much time alone puts weird thoughts in people's heads."

"Nate Murray isn't a serial killer," I said as we reached the first body.

"How can you be so sure?"

I pointed to the body at our feet.

"Because that's Nate Murray."

By the time they got around to raising the last body out of the ground, dark had begun to set in. With twilight came the predators of the night—mosquitoes, black flies, no-see-ums—that tormented us as the work continued. Swarms congregated around the halogen lamps that had been erected to light the scene. Nobody dared to stand closer than three feet to any single light pole.

The technicians didn't attempt to move the bodies much after pulling them from the ground, for fear of ruining any potential forensic evidence. Instead, they laid the bodies onto stretchers and trekked them over the hill to the waiting ambulances.

I stood far enough back to avoid becoming a nuisance. I had a right to be there, as the bodies had been found within the Prosperity town limits, and I am the law in Prosperity. On the other hand, Clark and Sharon and their crews were exceptionally well trained at what they did, and they didn't need me to supervise them.

The last body came up like a loose mass of bones in a leather bag. The team carefully placed it face down on the stretcher.

"Shit," I said as I looked at the remains. This one was a woman, no more than twenty. That wasn't what caught my eye, though.

"Wait a minute," I said as I walked over to the stretcher.

With each step, the spoiled hamburger smell became stronger, blasting through the Vap-O-Rub barrier like a bunker buster through a box of doughnuts. I tried to ignore it.

"Look at this," I said, pointing to the exposed small of her back. "The tattoo."

"What about it?" Clark asked. Sharon Counts joined us at his side but, as was her custom, remained silent.

"I've seen it before. Recently. When you start with the IDs, she goes first. Unless that tattoo is some kind of mass-produced design, this girl is Ann Koehler."

"Who?"

"She was Ricky Chasen's girlfriend, one of the last people to see Steve Samples alive. She was the one who gave him the money with Clay Steger's blood on it."

"No shit," Clark said. "Why do you reckon they killed her?"

"She became inconvenient. She was book-dumb but street-smart. She figured out from the questions I asked her that I suspected Ricky in the Samples killing. Maybe she got curious, asked the wrong questions about the wrong murder and Chasen decided she was a liability. Worse, maybe she knew about the other three bodies out here. Whatever happened, I'll bet a month's salary that either Chasen or Alvin Cross killed her and buried her in that hole, which means that either Chasen or Cross—or maybe both—did all of these."

"But why? And who are the other two women?"

"Runaways," I said. "Remember that article in the *Ledger-Telegraph* the other day? The one about Cross visiting Dena Kennedy's folks with a letter from her? That was one of the reasons I ran him out of town. I figured he was running some kind of scam. I never imagined that it involved murder."

I leaned down, despite the overwhelming stench of death, and tried to get a look at Ann Koehler's face.

"It makes sense, though, now that I think about it," I said. "The Spanish Prisoner con depends on the mark believing there's a prisoner when there really isn't. Cross's scam could only work if he really did meet up with the runaways who wrote the letters. It wouldn't do for him to show up at Charlie and Marla Kennedy's place with a letter from their daughter, only to find that she had made her way back home already. If he was going to get anything out of the parents, he had to make sure the girls were out of the way after he got them to write their letters."

"But that's . . . that's monstrous."

"It's what monsters do. We find Alvin Cross and his motor home, and I'll bet we find the letters those other two girls wrote, maybe a lot more. It might help you identify them, so we can get word to their families."

"How many?" Sharon whispered.

"What?"

She turned to me, her eyes glazed over. "How many did he do over the years?"

"No way of telling," I said. "My job now is to see he doesn't do any more."

I drove straight to the station, where I issued notices on as many intrastate and interstate police networks I could find, describing Alvin Cross and Ricky Chasen and the motor home.

By the time I finished, it was after ten o'clock. I grabbed some takeout Chinese from the restaurant at the shopping center behind the station and headed for the farm.

Donna was waiting for me in the living room. I had called her before sending out the BOLO notices, to let her know I'd be late. Because she's Donna, and because I trust her more than any other person on earth, I told her why.

I placed the food on the table, and without saying a word I went into the bathroom, dropped my uniform on the floor, and took a long, hot shower. I scrubbed and scrubbed, but I couldn't get rid of the stench of human decay that I imagined came from my clothes and my skin and my hair and my pores.

When I turned off the shower, Donna was there with a towel and a robe.

"You ready to talk, Chief?" she said.

"Let's eat first."

I dried myself and slipped on the robe. We sat at the table and divvyed up the shao mai and the fried rice and the mu-shu shrimp. The woman who worked the counter at the Chinese place knew me, and she always included extra pancakes and hoisin sauce.

I ate largely in silence, except for an occasional heavy sigh.

Donna ignored it. She knew I'd tell her everything as soon as I felt ready. She talked a little about some shopping she had done earlier in the day, and the phone call from my son Craig she had received shortly before I got home. I heard some of it. Most of it flew over my head.

We finished eating. I picked up the silverware and the plates and rinsed them in the sink before placing them in the dishwasher. Donna disposed of the containers. I refilled my glass of iced tea and sat on the couch. She sat next to me.

"I blew it," I said.

"Bullshit."

"You talk to all cops that way?"

"No, just ones spouting bullshit."

"I knew that Cross was dirty. Instead of building a bunko case against him and slamming him in jail for fleecing innocent parents, I decided he was a nuisance and ran him out of town. For all I know, Nate Murray was still alive. Maybe if I'd chucked that preacher's sorry ass in the can for a spell, Nate would be alive right now."

"Or maybe Nate and the girl—what's her name?"

"Ann."

"Maybe Nate and Ann were already dead, and by running Cross out of town you prevented him from killing someone else."

"No," I said.

"No?"

"All I did was prevent him from killing someone else in *Prosperity*. I remember the day I told him to hit the pavement. I patted myself on the back and told myself that he was somebody else's problem now. Well, he sure as hell is. Some poor girl's going to meet up with Cross and have the worst day of her entire miserable life."

"Unless you stop him."

"Right. Unless I stop him."

"And you're going to do that, right?"

"You seem pretty certain. You know something I don't?"

She grabbed my hand closest to her, lifted it up, and wriggled underneath it. Then she pressed herself against my side and wrapped my arm around her like a protective shroud.

"I know all I need to know," she said. "I know you."

FORTY-FIVE

Karen Craighead had just gotten off her job as a waitress at an upscale restaurant in Mica Wells, the sort of place that had sprung up to accommodate the more discerning and sophisticated tastes of the folk who had immigrated into Bliss County from Pooler. While claiming to yearn for the simplicity and quiet of the countryside, the vanguards of suburban sprawl wasted little time trying to remake their new pastoral surroundings in the image of the city they'd only recently escaped.

One of the accommodations they'd sought was longer hours at the local groceries, and Prosperity's lone supermarket, situated in the strip mall behind the police station, was only too happy to provide them. For once, Karen realized as she stepped out of her car around midnight, the big-city folk had done something right. Since she worked until eleven-thirty most nights, buying groceries had always been a problem. Now, with this store open around the clock, she didn't have to make an extra trip during the day to pick up her foodstuffs.

She blinked as her eyes grew accustomed to the brilliant fluorescent lamps inside. Then she grabbed a cart and set about gathering the items on her list.

As she rounded the corner from canned meats to sauces and spices, her cart collided with one that came from the opposite direction. Her purse fell from the child carrier, where she had perched it on top of several boxes of macaroni and cheese.

The person who had commandeered the other cart, a tall,

sun-bronzed man with long, blond hair in a ponytail, bent over and picked up the purse.

"I'm so sorry," he said. "I worked all day and I'm asleep at the wheel."

He flashed an engaging grin, handed her the purse, apologized again, and pushed his cart up the next aisle.

Something about the man was familiar, Karen realized. She wondered whether she had seen him in the store before, or maybe he was a patron at her restaurant.

Several times over the next moments, she thought she had it, that she had remembered exactly where she had seen the tall blond man before, but each time the snippet of a memory popped into her head, it was gone just as quickly.

He's cute, she thought. *I wonder if he's single.*

When she reached the checkout lane, the man was paying for his groceries. The clerk handed his change over the counter, and he carefully folded it and placed it in his pocket. As he did, he turned and saw her standing behind him.

"Sorry again," he said. "Hope you have a nice evening."

"You, too," she said as she wheeled her cart up to the clerk.

She watched as he left the store, still confounded as to where she had seen his face. She wondered whether trying to recall would keep her up all night. It was the sort of thing she did and it had cost her more than one night's sleep.

Finally, she decided that the memory would come more quickly if she didn't prod it so much. She paid for her order and wheeled the cart out through the automatic doors into the parking lot.

She arrived at her car and noted that the lights on the tall pole next to it were out. She was certain they had been lighted when she pulled in. She was always careful to park in well-illuminated spaces. After all, a girl couldn't be too careful.

She was loading the groceries into the trunk of her car when she heard quiet footsteps come up behind her. Before she could turn, a hand slipped around her cheek and sealed against her mouth. She felt the tight band of panic seize her chest. Without thinking, she tried to turn and retaliate, but all she managed to do was throw one arm back. She grabbed at anything she could reach to gain leverage, but all she grasped was hair, tied back with an elastic band.

The image of the man in the grocery store flooded back to her. Even as it did, her attacker pulled a coarse canvas bag over her head and she was dragged backward, the crepe heels of her work shoes scraping along the asphalt of the parking lot. She felt herself lifted and tossed down onto a hard surface. Almost immediately, she heard an engine start and realized she was in a truck or a van of some sort, and that she was being abducted.

Stories she had heard for years flashed through her head, of women who had simply disappeared one night, never to be seen again. She wondered whether they had felt the way she did.

The inside of the canvas bag smelled of dank and decay. It began to sicken her. Then it was joined by another smell, like brackish water, and she realized that, in her panic, she had peed herself. She reached up to grab the bag away, but strong hands gripped her wrists.

"You don't want to take that off," a man said. "Long as you don't see my face, you might live through this night. Lie back and try to relax. I'm gonna take good care of you. I got a pocketful of rubbers. They're part for your protection and part for mine. They got my DNA on file over in Raleigh. So, you ain't gonna catch anything and you ain't gonna get knocked up. You got nothing to worry about."

She cringed as she felt rough, tight hands reach for the buttons of her uniform.

Then she screamed.

★　★　★　★　★

Slim Tackett had rotated over to the night shift the previous weekend, and he was just about to call it an evening and hand the patrol duties over to the Highway Patrol boys.

Ever since he and Jennifer Ryser had attended Alvin Cross's tent meeting, things had started to sour. Slim knew he came across as some sort of hayseed shit-kicker, but he considered himself a sharp, intuitive cop, and he knew bull-hockey when he heard it. He saw right through Cross and tried to tell Jennifer that the preacher was a con man, but all she saw was the miracles. She truly believed in her deepest heart that Cross was a genuine prophet, sent by the Lord to do heavenly things on earth.

Slim thought the world of Jennifer, but he couldn't see shackling himself to someone who would eventually condemn him by confusing realistic appraisals with cynicism.

This was the train of thought that occupied Slim's mind as he drove Morgan Highway toward the Prosperity Police Station. He was so internally conflicted, in fact, that he almost missed seeing the lumpy, pale form lying by the side of the road.

He was beside it before he realized it wasn't a white plastic garbage bag discarded illegally, or bounced inadvertently off the back of a pickup truck. As he passed it, he realized that it was alive and—worse—it was human.

He slammed on the brakes. The tires screamed in protest as he slid to a stop a hundred feet or so past the collapsed figure. He flipped on the flasher lights and slowly backed up the highway.

After grabbing his shotgun, he stepped carefully from the car, checking in both directions to make certain nobody was coming.

He pulled a small flashlight from his belt and turned the beam on the form.

"Dear God Jesus holy shit!" he said, the words falling dully into the night on each side of the highway.

It was a woman, naked save for socks and a pair of crepe-soled shoes. She was curled into a ball, shaking like an epileptic and sobbing between moans.

I caught up with Karen Craighead at the hospital in Morgan. She was still in the emergency room, lying in a fetal position on a bed in a closed room, covered with a sheet and a couple of blankets. She stared at the wall as I walked into the treatment room, and she didn't acknowledge me when I introduced myself.

Her gaze slowly rotated in my direction as I tried to find out what had happened.

"I know what you've been through has been terrible," I said. "The last thing I want to do right now is put a lot of pressure on you. But I need to make sure you understand that our best chance of catching the man who did this to you is early on, within the first day or so after the attack."

Her mouth opened and I saw the gap where her front top incisors had been, before her attacker had elbowed her in the mouth to keep her quiet. One eye was swollen shut. The other had patches of blood in the sclera. As hard as it was to look at her, I knew that didn't hold a candle to how things looked from her side of the conversation.

"Dark," she said, as if that one word took every ounce of her strength. "Parking lot . . . grocery store . . . tall man . . . tan . . . ponytail . . . seen him before . . . don't know . . . where."

"You saw him when he attacked you?"

She shook her head. "In . . . store . . . went to car . . . grabbed me . . . I grabbed ponytail. Very tired . . . very tired." Her eyes closed and I thought maybe she had gone to sleep. I made a couple of notes on my pad.

Her eyes shot open. "Rubber . . . wore rubber . . . said his

DNA was in Raleigh."

I suddenly felt very cold. Tall. Tanned. Ponytail. DNA in Raleigh. Reluctantly, I pulled a copy of the Article 27A notification on Carl Sussman from my aluminum portable desk.

"I'm going to show you a picture," I said. "I want you to tell me if it's the man you saw at the store." I held up the notice.

She let out a wet gasp. Two pink tears escaped her good eye before she shut it tight.

"It's him," she said with a sob. "That's the bastard."

I called the dispatcher at the Bliss County Sheriff's Department and told her that I needed some backup. The deputy met me at the intersection of Morgan Highway and Bostian Road. I stepped out of the new cruiser and walked over to his side window.

"We had a woman raped in Prosperity," I told him. "She's identified a known sex offender who lives up this road. I'm going to arrest him now."

"You gonna have to break into the house or anything?"

"I know this guy. He'll probably come peacefully, but I need your help if he doesn't. Understand?"

"This is your town. You're the boss. I'll follow you in."

"Keep your flashers off. I don't want to scare him."

A couple of minutes later we pulled into the gravel drive and left our engines running. I peeked around the side of the trailer and was glad to see that Sharon Counts's car wasn't there. I couldn't figure out her relationship with Sussman, but it wouldn't have helped her any to be on the scene when I arrested him.

I walked back around to the front and rapped on the front door of the trailer.

A moment later the door opened. Sussman stood there in a T-shirt and a pair of shorts.

"Chief? What's the matter?"

"May I come in, Carl?"

"Sure."

I turned and gestured to the deputy to stay at the base of the steps, then followed Sussman inside.

"Are you alone?" I asked.

"Just me and my demons," he said, trying to make a joke.

"All right then. I have to take you down to the station. I'll follow you into your bedroom and let you pull on a pair of pants and a nicer shirt, if you like."

"What's this all about?"

"We can talk about it at the station. You want to get dressed?"

A couple of minutes later, he locked the front door of the trailer and trailed me to the cruiser. I asked the deputy to follow me to the station.

Once we got there, I walked Sussman back to the holding cells. He didn't argue when I escorted him into one of them, but he became a little agitated when I closed and locked the door.

"You want to explain any of this now, Chief?" he said. "Why in hell are you putting me in jail?"

"Protective custody and suspicion, for the moment."

"What in hell does that mean?"

"Were you at the Prosperity supermarket around eleven-thirty last night?"

"Yeah. I worked late on the house and I needed to pick up a few things for lunch and dinner tomorrow."

I pulled a chair from against the wall and sat near his door. "Have a seat, Carl."

He lowered himself to the steel bunk bolted to the concrete floor.

I took off my hat and placed it on a filing cabinet next to my chair. Space in the station was so tight, we'd taken to storing documents in the holding area. Seemed appropriate, if unconventional.

"Okay," I said. "The protective custody is to keep you from getting hurt when people in this town hear the news tomorrow. The suspicion comes from a woman who was abducted from the supermarket parking lot around eleven-thirty. She was raped, and abandoned along Morgan Highway. She identified your picture. We're going to have to wait for some forensic tests to come back before filing formal charges, but for the time being I'd say that both you and the community are probably safer with you behind these bars."

I thought Sussman might go nuts when I told him he had been accused of rape again. Instead, he clasped his hands, leaned forward, and stared at the floor for a long time.

"It's bullshit," he said finally. "I didn't do it."

"If I were you, I'd stay quiet until we figure out what happened. I haven't formally read you your rights."

"And whatever I say could be used against me, right?"

"That's about the size of it."

"Do I get a phone call?"

"You haven't been arrested yet. Being held on suspicion means that you don't have the rights of someone who's formally charged. I don't want you talking to anyone out there who might make things worse for you, whether they mean to or not. Let's hold off on phone calls for a while. You get some rest. I'll see that they bring you a good breakfast after sunup, and we'll see where things stand then."

I rose early the next morning, and arrived at the station by seven-thirty. I called the ER in Morgan and was told that Karen Craighead had been admitted for observation. I was glad to hear that they hadn't sent her home. I had a feeling she was in line for a ton of seat time with rape counselors. Leaving her alone so early after her attack wouldn't have been a very good idea.

I walked down to the grocery store and spoke with the manager there. He agreed to show me the security tapes from the previous evening. We walked to the back of the store, where he extracted the long-running tape from the recorder, replaced it with a fresh blank, and then popped the recorded tape into a player.

"Around eleven o'clock," I said.

He fast-forwarded the tape until the time slug read 11:00 P.M. Then he ran it at normal speed, about fifteen frames per minute. Figures darted about the aisles at quadruple time, jerking forward in jump-shots like bad animation.

"There," I said, pointing at the screen. "That's the rape victim."

We watched as she rounded a corner and her cart rammed another cart, piloted by my suspect.

"He was there," I said. "And he had contact with the victim. Do you make security tapes of the parking lot?"

The manager shook his head. "Too expensive. We tried at a couple of stores, but kids kept stealing the cameras or plinking them with pellet guns. We gave up on it."

On my way back I picked up a couple of take-out breakfasts—scrambled eggs, grits, biscuits, and fried bologna—and a couple of foam cups of coffee. Making Carl Sussman drink the toxic waste we brewed in the station coffee pot might be construed as cruel and unusual punishment, if not a violation of the Geneva Conventions.

Carl was awake when I returned. He sat on the steel bunk, propped against the wall behind him with his hands behind his head, staring off into space. He didn't look at me when I opened the door to the holding cells.

"Hope you weren't too uncomfortable last night," I said.

"Nice and firm," he said as he patted the rubber-covered mattress on the bunk. "Great lumbar support. I got used to steel beds in prison. Can I make a phone call now?"

"Not quite yet."

I slid the box with his breakfast through the rectangular opening at the bottom of the cell and handed him the coffee through the bars.

"Need sugar or creamer?" I asked.

"Sugar would be nice," he said.

I grabbed a couple of packets of sweetener from the back room and handed them to him.

As I fixed my own coffee, I said, "You're still under suspicion. If I were you, I'd be careful about talking. I, of course, can say anything I please. You follow?"

He nodded, opened the box, and speared the eggs with a plastic fork.

"Here's what I know, as of this moment. Last night, you were in the supermarket next door around eleven-fifteen. Your buggy ran into another buggy. The buggy you ran into belonged to the victim. I have this on the store surveillance tape.

"This same tape shows that you paid for your groceries and left about three minutes before the victim. Moments after she checked out, she was abducted in the parking lot by a man she said had a ponytail, like yours. She didn't see his face. He did tell her, however, that he was going to use a condom when he raped her because his DNA was—and I quote—'on file in Raleigh.' Based on her description, the tape showing you in contact with her moments before the assault, the attacker's admission that his DNA is on file, and your record as a convicted rapist, I thought it might be a good idea to get you off the streets while I figure out exactly what happened."

"Can I say something?"

"I'd recommend against it. If you insist, let me read you your rights first."

"Go ahead."

I *Mirand*ized him and then started in on my own eggs and grits.

"How's your breakfast?" I asked.

"Really tasty. Thanks."

"Nothing but the best for our guests."

"I need to make a phone call," he said. "I can prove I wasn't the person who raped that girl, but I don't want to say anything before I talk with someone."

"Sharon Counts?"

He lowered his gaze and stabbed at the bologna and eggs.

"What is it with you two?" I asked. "She must know that hanging with you isn't helping her career."

"She doesn't care about that. Nothing is permanent for her, Chief. She operates in a world wholly separate from the one you and I occupy. I can't say for certain I understand it myself. She showed up one day while I was working on the house and stayed like a stray cat."

"She's living with you?"

"No. Nothing like that. It's more like she gets something out of being around. I can't explain it. It's not what you're thinking. I haven't touched her, not like that. I have a feeling that if I did, it would spook her and she wouldn't stop running until she hit Texas. There's a lot of bad road in Sharon's past."

"That other boy who was at your place when I picked you up last night was a Morgan Sheriff's deputy. He knows why I rousted you. I figure Sharon will hear about it before the morning's out. If she can vouch for your whereabouts, I'd prefer that she come forward of her own volition."

He took a bite of his biscuit and nodded as he chewed.

"I can see why that would be better," he said. "You have to believe me, Chief. I didn't do anything to that girl. I recall running into her with my cart, but that was an accident. I was bone-tired from working on the house all day. I couldn't tell you right this moment whether I was pushing the cart, or it was pulling me. I ran into her while coming around an aisle in the store, and I picked up her handbag for her. I apologized. That was it. I seem to recall that she was behind me in the checkout line."

"She grabbed at the man who raped her," I said. "He had a ponytail. She remembers yanking it."

"It wasn't me."

I finished my eggs and grits and started in on the biscuit. I thought things through as I chewed and swallowed.

"Here's what I'm going to do," I said. "Word's going to get out if it hasn't already, and people are going to want to see you decorating the end of a short rope in a high tree. Staying in this cell is your best option right now, and I have another—" I glanced at my watch "—eighteen hours or so before I have to charge you or cut you loose. I'll have Stu run by your house every hour or so to make sure people aren't burning it in effigy. Maybe by nightfall we'll know better how this thing is going to play."

Sussman agreed to the plan, and told me he had nothing to fear because he hadn't done anything wrong. I allowed him to languish in his own naiveté, dumped my empty breakfast box in the trash, and walked back to my office.

Sherry, my civilian police assistant, wasn't scheduled to arrive until nine, and it was only eight-thirty. I shuffled some papers on my desk and generally wasted time until I heard the front door open and shut. Moments later, Cory True knocked on my door.

"May I come in?" he asked.

"Could I stop you?"

He stepped into my office and sat in the chair across the desk from me. "A guy who strings for me in the Law Enforcement Building over in Morgan says a woman was raped here in Prosperity last night."

"Slim found her by the side of the road out on Morgan Highway. She's in Bliss Regional Medical Center. We're waiting for the results of the rape kit tests."

"What's going on down here, Chief? This used to be a quiet little town. Now you got police standoffs, five murders in one year, people getting grabbed out of the grocery store and raped, Mexican kids nailed to trees—I gotta tell you, the *Ledger-Telegraph*'s getting sick of paying me gas money to drive down here. They're talking about opening a satellite office."

I spread my hands. "What can I tell you? Things were fine until developers started buying farms out from under their owners. More people means more crime."

"Any leads in this rape?"

"No comment."

"Any leads on the four murders out on Nate Murray's farm?"

"No comment."

"I smell breakfast in here."

"No comment. Is there anything else I can do for you, Cory?"

He folded the steno pad and slipped his pen back in his breast pocket. "Use your bathroom?"

"Be my guest. Flush when you're done."

I allowed myself exactly fifteen seconds to be smug, self-satisfied that I had successfully blown him off before I realized that I had actually screwed up in a big way.

I jumped to my feet and dashed to the office door in time to see Cory walk back toward me with a shit-eating grin on his face. The door to the holding cells stood wide open, exactly as I had left it after my breakfast with Carl Sussman.

Cory waggled a finger at me.

"You can't write about this," I said.

"The hell I can't, Chief. The man in that cell is a convicted rapist. You can't tell me it's a coincidence he's locked up the day after you had a brutal rape in Prosperity."

"I could, but I won't. Step into my office."

"Sorry, got a story to file."

"Step in or get dragged in."

Reluctantly, he walked past me into my office.

"You want an exclusive?" I asked after he sat down.

"Of course."

"Then give me some time. I have a feeling that Mr. Sussman in there is going to be cleared by lunchtime. Putting him in holding was a precaution I took for his own safety."

"Then why's he locked up?"

"Until he's cleared, he's a suspect. The exclusive isn't about him. It's about those four bodies out at Nate Murray's."

I thought I could hear Cory salivate. He pulled out the pad and his pen.

"What do you have?" he asked.

"Nothing. Not yet. I need you to do some research for me. You found that story from Tennessee about Alvin Cross. I need you to find out exactly where he had his tent pitched there."

"Now, how in hell am I supposed to find that out?"

"You're an investigative reporter. Investigate. Check with the local charismatic churches. Hell, it's Tennessee. They're probably all charismatic churches. Someone at one of those churches should recall going to Cross's tent revival. Find out where it was held. You do that, and I promise you that when we catch the people who left those bodies behind, you'll get the whole story first."

"Straight from you?"

"My word on it. But, if you want this deal, you have to keep

Carl Sussman's name out of this thing until I say you can release it."

"What if I hear about him from some other source?"

"If you can verify it, I can't stop you from going with the story. You'd better be able to verify, though, because if you print a claim that Carl is in jail for raping that girl, and it turns out he didn't, and if any bad comes to him because of it, I'm coming looking for you personally. Is there anything about that you don't understand?"

"Grammatically? All of it. I get the idea. I should tell you that I'm going to try to interview the victim at Bliss Regional. If she fingers Sussman, I will sort of have to follow up on it."

"You gotta do what you gotta do."

FORTY-SIX

I was just about to break for lunch when Sharon Counts walked through the front door of the station. Sherry tried to intercept her at the front desk, but she blew by Sherry and stomped straight to my office.

"Hi, Sharon," I said as she stood, glowering, at the edge of my desk.

"Is Carl in your jail?"

"Carl Sussman? Why, yes. Yes, he is."

"You arrested him for that rape in Prosperity last night."

It wasn't a question so I didn't treat it like one. I waited for her to make her point.

"Carl was with me," she said after an uncomfortable pause.

"If that's true, then it would be a great help for him. Tell me more."

"I got off work around ten last night. I drove over to his place. He was working on the house. When I checked the refrigerator, I saw that he was running low on food and bottled water, so I convinced him to make a run to the store."

"So you were at the supermarket, too?"

"Yes."

"What time?"

"Between eleven and eleven-thirty. I waited in the truck, in the parking lot."

"Why?"

She blushed, the color rippling along the striations of her

Richard Helms

"Carl is reluctantly famous," she said. She didn't say more. I think she knew that she didn't have to. Besides, I had a feeling that Sharon had a running tally of words she'd used in her head. She seemed to think she had only so many, and when they had been used she would run out forever. I decided not to force her to waste any.

"What time did Carl come out to the truck?"

"I don't know. I had no reason to check my watch. Around eleven-thirty, maybe."

"And what happened then?"

"What do you mean?" She sounded irritated.

"Sharon, if this case goes to court, and you have to testify that you were with Carl, the DA is going to want a second-by-second account of what happened that night."

"But Carl didn't do anything. I already told you, I was with him from at least ten-thirty until after one in the morning."

"You can prove this?"

"No. Look, we drove to the grocery store. He went in, he came back out. We drove to his trailer, had a bite to eat, talked until about one o'clock, and he fell asleep. I let myself out and went home. End of story."

"You'll testify to this in court if called?"

"Yes! Of course."

I looked over my report of the rape from the night before, over Slim's notes that documented how he found Karen Craighead by the side of Morgan Highway around one o'clock, and over the statement Karen had given me at the hospital.

Without a doubt, Sharon had heard about Carl's detention because the deputy who had accompanied me to the trailer had talked about it when he returned to the Law Enforcement Center. I hadn't told the deputy anything about the timelines for the rape, though. For that matter, I hadn't discussed the

360

details with anyone. Despite that, Sharon had provided Carl Sussman with an alibi—however tenuous and shaky it might be—for the entire period during which Karen Craighead had been beaten, raped, and abandoned.

She didn't leave me much choice.

I stood, walked to the back of the station to the holding cells, and unlocked Sussman's door.

"You've been listening?" I said as he stood from the bunk.

"Kind of hard to miss," he said. "You believe me now?"

"Let's say the case against you just became somewhat more flimsy. Do I have to tell you not to leave the county for a few days?"

He rubbed his forearms and pulled his hair back to put an elastic band around it.

"Where in hell would I go, Chief?"

They found Alvin Cross's motor home around three that afternoon.

I had returned from the hospital in Morgan, where I told Karen Craighead that Carl Sussman had an alibi for the times of her attack and that she had mistaken her rapist for the man she'd run into in the store. She denied it at first, insisting that Sussman had been the man who assaulted her. That lasted about five minutes, until she broke down in sobs and agreed that, based on the new information, it probably had been a coincidence. I promised to keep looking for the guy who had abducted her.

Between the time I released Carl Sussman and my visit to Karen Craighead, I had been informed by the CSI unit in Morgan that they had found hairs on Karen that were not hers, and that they had taken scrapings from under her fingernails that appeared to be from the rapist. I told her that—if we could catch the guy—we could probably make a case against him

361

based on the DNA from the scrapings and the hairs.

On the drive back from Morgan, I couldn't get the image of her broken, toothless face out of my mind. I began to feel an old, familiar rage build deep inside me, something feral and ancient that begged to be loosed to ravage the countryside in search of the vermin who had preyed on an unsuspecting woman, robbing her of her dignity and her trust in her fellow humans.

I had concluded long ago that there are souls walking the earth that seem to have sprung fully formed from some alien genetic strain. They move quietly among us, but their perceptions of the world are not like ours. They respond only to those most primeval emotions and drives, every facet of their interactions impelled by the reptilian vestiges of the brain. Their limbic motivations divide the world into predators and prey. They are not confused into which camp they fall. These proto-humans don't respond to values or morals or ideals—they count their victories in scalps and skins.

I recalled, back in college, reading about Maslow's *heirarchy of needs,* which, in my way of trying to reduce all complex concepts to their simplest parts, seemed to say you can't contemplate the wonders of the universe on an empty belly. For the subhumans who wander in our midst, violence fills the void in their souls where compassion should reside. Asking one of these people for mercy only fuels their lust for fear.

I was aware, of course, of all the sociological rationalizations for the existence of the most criminal in our number. Parental abandonment, physical and sexual abuse in childhood, exposure to violent role models—I had heard all of them in my two decades as a cop. I had sat in on an interview with a man in Georgia who was mere ticks of the clock from his long walk to suck the green gas who had told the well-meaning priest who had come with hopes of administering absolution that if he really wanted to do the condemned a favor he'd drop to his knees and administer a final blowjob. I puzzled over this for years after, trying to get my head around how this man, minutes from his own demise, could still engage in wanton emotional cruelty. In the end, I came to the conclusion that trying to understand what went on in some people's heads was about as useful as sticking your hand in a wood chipper.

So, I realized, it would probably be once I found the man who had brutalized Karen Craighead. If I expected revelations and explanations from him, I was sorely bound for disappointment. In the end, he'd probably claim that she had been raped because "she was there."

When I arrived back at the station, I found that my friends from the Fourth Estate had returned. Despite my best efforts to keep a lid on it, news of the discovery of the four bodies the day before had flowed over the county line. The streets outside the police station were crammed with satellite trucks, their microwave antennae extended like phallic spires, rising above the crests of the maples and oaks lining the sidewalks near the station.

I parked the cruiser at the door and hustled inside before they could descend on me.

"When did they get here?" I asked Sherry.

"About half an hour after you left. One or two tried to muscle their way through the door. I told them you'd put them in holding if they didn't get their asses back across the street."

"You know I can't do that."

"They don't know it, though. It worked. There's a message for you on your desk, from Perry Mabry up in Pooler. He said it's important."

Perry Mabry is the chief of police in Pooler. He's a rock-solid cop who worked his way up from squad car patrol to detective, and finally to the penthouse suite. I had learned long ago that he was a man who could be trusted.

The number turned out to be Perry's direct office line. That told me something.

"Glad you called, Judd," he said. "You put out a BOLO on a motor home belonging to one Alvin Cross yesterday?"

"Sure did."

"Looks like we've found it. Someone drove it into a camp-ground, jacked it up level, rolled out the awning, and put some chairs and camp tables around the front door to make it look like they were vacationers. The camp director noticed that they hadn't hooked up the electricity and became suspicious. He's been knocking on the door every hour on the hour for the last couple of days, but nobody answers. Finally, he called it in."

"Got an address?"

Perry gave me the name of a public campground near the huge man-made lake just north of the city.

I called Sheriff Webb in Morgan to see if he could arrange for a super-fast search warrant.

He was happy to comply.

"Someone took off the license tags," Mabry said as we walked around the all-too-familiar motor home. "The officer who responded to the call from the campground manager was going to ticket it for no plates, but needed some way to know who to write the ticket to. He checked the VIN number. When he ran it, the ID triggered the BOLO alert."

Mabry was built like a hockey goalie, thick and tight. He wore a blue suit with a white shirt and a red tie. His face was pockmarked with ancient acne scars, and deeply lined and tanned. His eyes, perched above a flat, bent nose, seemed to take in everything around him.

"I love technology," I said, reaching for the door handle. It didn't give. "You wouldn't have a pry bar in your cruiser, would you?"

"I think I can scare one up."

He popped the trunk on the Pooler police squad car and pulled out a foot-long crowbar. "You want to do the honors? He's your skell."

I wedged the blade end in the door log and put some weight behind it. I heard a metallic pop and the door swung open.

"So far, so good," I said. "I heard about this guy once who rigged the door of his motor home to the trigger of a hard-mounted shotgun. When some poor bastard opened the door, he got a gut full of deer slug."

"You might have mentioned that before opening the door."

"I stood off to the side."

"I didn't."

I tapped the side of my head. " 'The best offense is a good defense.' Knute Rockne. Want to take a look inside?"

We stepped carefully up into the motor home. The air conditioning was off, and the interior heat pressed against us like a giant hand. It smelled musty and sharp, like hot metal and mold and human disuse. I didn't smell any decomp.

That sort of made things better.

"It was Jack Dempsey," Mabry said.

"What?"

"It wasn't Knute Rockne. It was Jack Dempsey. And he didn't say 'The best offense is a good defense.' He said 'The best defense is a good offense.' "

"I don't believe you."

"Look it up, you hayseed flatfoot."

I had opened some drawers in the miniature kitchen, which seemed as good a place to start as any. I used my asp baton to push items around in a drawer full of knives and spatulas and wooden spoons. I didn't know what I was looking for, or what it would look like when I found it. I suppose I was looking for anything out of place.

"So what's the story on the guy who owns this bus?" Mabry asked.

"Itinerant tent preacher and possible mass murderer."

"Oh, yeah," he said. "Saw that on TV."

"He's a con man. My concern is that he takes in runaway girls, gets them to write to their parents, and then kills them. A few months later he shows up on the distraught parents' doorstep, gives them a little false hope, claims to have nursed his victims back to health, and allows the parents to bestow gifts upon him."

"Sounds like the kind of guy I'd like to get my hands on."

"You gotta stand in line for that one. Flushing this guy's stuff is gonna be an E-ticket ride."

I rummaged about lightly for a few moments, and then stepped back into the middle of the living room.

"This is no good," I said. "We could turn this place upside down and only succeed in ruining any evidence that might be here. You want some of the credit when we run this creep to ground?"

"Sure."

"I'd be obliged if you'd tow this can to your garage in Pooler and have your crime scene guys disassemble it."

"What are you looking for?"

"Letters, first of all. If we locate letters to girls' parents, we might be able to identify a couple of bodies we dug up in Prosperity the other day. That would prove a link between Cross and the victims. Also, I'd be very thankful if you'd dust this place for fingerprints and run them through AFIS. I'd kind of like to know exactly who this Alvin Cross fellow really is. We've already found a reference to him using at least one other name."

Mabry toggled a transceiver he carried on his belt, and gave the order to have the motor home towed.

"You know what?" he said, looking around and sniffing.

"What?"

"The fact that we found this tub parked bothers me."

"How so?"

"Makes me wonder whether this guy really is on the run, or if he's gone to ground somewhere nearby."

"I think he has an accomplice, a half-Lumbee ex-con named Ricky Chasen. Maybe Chasen picked him up and they hit the blue highways, trying to disappear."

"Or maybe he's still walking in our own backyard. Maybe Cross was holed up here in the campground, licking his wounds after you tossed him out of Bliss County, when he saw the news bulletins that you'd dug up his bodies. That backed him into a hard corner. Want a tip?"

"Any time."

"You might want to keep your doors and windows locked tight. This Cross fellow, or whatever his name is, sounds like the type to hold a grudge."

FORTY-SEVEN

By the time I got away from Pooler it was after six in the evening. I stopped off at the Prosperity supermarket on the way home, and bought four salmon steaks, some ginger marinade, and a bag of pre-cut stir-fry vegetables.

I got back to the farmhouse and lit the fire on the stone grill before going inside to change clothes.

Donna had left a note saying that she was heading into Morgan to do some shopping for school clothes for the upcoming academic year. The house was still, save for the incessant ticking of the grandfather clock that stood in the living room. I placed the groceries on the counter, and had just turned to go to my bedroom to change when I heard a knock on the door.

Carl Sussman and Sharon Counts stood on my front porch.

"We tried to reach you at the station," Sussman said.

I have a curious insistence on separating my professional and personal life. Instead of inviting them in, I stepped out onto the porch.

"We've been talking," Sussman continued. Sharon looked as if she would echo every word if she felt she could spare them. Her eyes urged me to listen to Sussman.

"About the rape?"

"Maybe. Can we sit?" he said, gesturing toward the wicker chairs.

"Sure."

They took the loveseat. I sat in one of the chairs, on their left.

"I don't like coincidences," Sussman started.

"Me, either."

"Well, what with the fire, and this poor woman getting raped right after I spoke with her last night, I'm thinking maybe someone is focusing on making my life miserable."

"You don't think that's a little paranoid?"

"Sure it is. But what if I'm right? Sharon and I were talking about it over lunch. Maybe the rape last night was intended to be some kind of diversion."

My first thought was how difficult it must be to carry on any kind of lengthy conversation with Sharon Counts. Then I chewed on Sussman's assertion.

"Tell me more."

"Look at it this way, Chief. The television is full of reports about those bodies you found. That preacher who had his tent on the land where you found them told his congregation to burn me out. Then last night someone tried to make it look as if I had kidnapped and raped some woman. If Sharon hadn't been in the truck waiting for me, I'd probably still be sitting in your jail. Maybe whoever burned down my house and tried to pin that rape on me is trying to keep you from looking in the right direction."

"With the murders, you mean?"

"Yes! They want you to concentrate on this rape, and on me as the rapist, so that they can slip away while you're looking somewhere else."

"I have an APB and BOLO notices out on Cross and his buddy Chasen," I said. "Every cop in North and South Carolina is going to be looking for them. We've already found their motor home, up in Pooler. I have a hard time seeing the percentage in staying around here, setting you up for a rape charge, when they could be running for the Mexican border."

"Evil," Sharon said. "Their mission."

"Right," Sussman said. "Somehow, even before the murders, they had focused on me as being some kind of demon. They're obsessed with getting rid of me."

"To the point of ignoring their own personal well-being? I just don't see it, Carl. Maybe this time, a coincidence is just a coincidence."

"Then tell me what this character Ricky Chasen looks like."

"Right now? I don't know. I've never met him. He's been on the run ever since Steve Samples was murdered last week."

"Do you have a picture?"

I stepped off the porch to the cruiser sitting in the gravel drive. I retrieved my aluminum duty folder and brought it back up to the porch.

I handed them the picture of Chasen that I had copied from his conviction jacket.

"I don't recognize him," Sussman said. He handed the picture to Sharon Counts. She looked at it and shook her head.

He handed the photo back to me and said, "What if Chasen has a ponytail? Maybe he's grown his hair out since this picture was taken."

"There's a lot of *if* in this whole line of conjecture."

"You said that the woman who was raped last night grabbed at the rapist's ponytail. If Chasen has grown his hair long, doesn't that make him look a little suspicious?"

"I'll be honest with you, Carl. At this point I'd be happy to hang just about any charge on Chasen or Cross, up to and including the Lindbergh baby kidnapping."

"That's why we came to see you tonight," Sussman said. "I have a criminal record. I'm not allowed to own a firearm, not even for protection. Sharon has to secure her weapon in a trunk safe when she visits. If Cross and Chasen decided to say fuck it and pay me a late-night visit to finish the job, I'd be hard pressed to stop them."

"What is it you want?"

"I'd say protection, but I know your department is already stretched thin. Maybe I want you to be aware of what we've been discussing. If Chasen and Cross are still around, and if they still have me in the crosshairs, you might stand a pretty good chance of nailing them by hanging around my place."

"Concentrate the Prosperity police patrols in your neighborhood?"

"That's it. Look, Chief. I spent five years in prison as a sex offender. That's like walking around with a target on your ass. After a year or two of that kind of attention, you develop a sixth sense about when you're at risk. Right now, that sixth sense is sending off air raid sirens in my head."

In the end, as a gesture of southern hospitality, I invited Carl and Sharon to stay for dinner. In a reciprocal gesture of southern manners, they had the good taste to decline. It was a ritual in this part of the country, born out of the pioneer days and later propagated in the Great Depression, that if people showed up at your doorstep at the dinner hour, you offered to feed them. It was also considered a violation of the social contract to accept that offer.

About twenty minutes after Carl and Sharon left, Donna returned from Morgan, staggering under the weight of five paper bags full of clothes.

I pointed at the bags. "Girl stuff. Goes to your house."

"Shut up and help me."

I grabbed the bags from her, amazed at just how much cloth could weigh, and hoisted them up the steps and into the house.

"You have the grill going," she said.

"I picked up some salmon. It's marinating in the refrigerator."

I nodded toward the paper bags. "Did you leave some for the other ladies?"

"I'm not keeping all of it. I'll probably return about half. Maybe more."

"If you're going to return it, why'd you buy it?"

"I needed to bring it home, see how it looked on me."

"Don't they have fitting rooms for that sort of thing?"

She smiled. "Of course they do. But I have to bring them home to see how they'll look on me here."

I scratched my head and tried to figure out her answer. It was like trying to wrangle bees.

"I give up," I said.

"That's because you're a man. Men are different."

"I've heard that."

"Men only shop when they know what they want. They go into the store, they grab what they want, they pay for it, and they leave. And they never, never take it back."

"If I thought I'd have to go to the trouble of taking it back, I wouldn't buy it."

"Man."

"You say that like it's a bad thing."

She sidled over and placed her arms around my chest.

"No, darling. It's not a bad thing. I didn't hear on the radio that you'd found that preacher."

"No. However, we found his motor home. Chief Mabry's crime techs up in Pooler are tearing it apart for me."

"Neighborly of him."

"He gets a cut of the collar, if it leads to Cross. Perry has political aspirations. He's looking for feathers to line his cap. Are you ready to eat?"

"Will the fish take long to grill?"

"Ten minutes. Maybe twelve."

"I thought I'd freshen up a little. Maybe take a shower."

"You have time. I can stir-fry the vegetables."

"Oh, let me do that when I get out. I know how to use a stove, but I could never get the hang of grilling."

"Man like fire," I said. "Man like stone. Man like wood."

"Yes, yes, I know. And you are the quintessential man. I imagine that's why I love you so much."

She stood on her toes, and I leaned down and kissed her. We stayed like that for a long time.

FORTY-EIGHT

Chief Mabry had done a great job of keeping our discovery of Alvin Cross's motor home a secret, so when I arrived at the Prosperity Police Station the next morning, many of the television trucks were still in place, waiting for some scrap of a story.

I wasn't going to give it to them.

I hustled into the station before they could descend on me, grabbed a cup of coffee from the back, and settled in at my desk.

Over breakfast, I had watched the morning news on the local channels. Most of them gave the murders in our quiet town about a minute and a half, since there wasn't much to say that hadn't already been chewed over for a day and a half.

More important were the reports about an abrupt change in the weather headed our way. A hurricane had brushed the Bahamas a couple of days earlier, bringing with it a huge bubble of low pressure that was sucking out to sea the high pressure system that had kept our temperatures in triple digits for weeks. This had goosed the jet stream from the Canadian provinces, which was arcing lower and lower over the country, bringing with it massive storms that had caused monstrous tornadoes in Illinois, Indiana, and Kentucky.

The weathercasters said that the front could hit North Carolina by early evening, bringing with it the sort of climatic tumult normally associated with Wagnerian operas.

The upside was that within twenty-four hours, and if we weren't flattened by F5 tornadoes, our month-long drought and heat wave would be broken.

My telephone rang.

"Chief Wheeler," I said after hitting the speaker button.

"Cory True."

"How's it hanging, Cory?"

"To the left. I got that information you wanted."

I straightened in my chair and picked up the receiver. "On Cross?"

"Yeah, only he called himself Shelton Boyd then, remember?"

I remembered.

"Anyway, I checked the local phone book for Tryson, Tennessee, and figured that the Pentecostal churches in the area might be a good place to start. I hit pay dirt on the second call."

"Tell me."

"Spoke with a preacher named . . . hold on, got to check my notes . . . Fry. Alton Fry. He didn't attend Cross's tent meeting down there, but his daughter did, and she happened to be at the dinner table with him when I called. She said that Cross, or Boyd, had set up his tent just outside the town limits, on a farm owned by a guy named Able Johnson. I got the address right here."

He read off the address and I wrote it on my desk calendar, along with the county.

"Good work, Cory," I said. "Here's a tidbit for you that the television folks don't know, but you can't write about it until tomorrow. We've found Cross's motor home, up in Parker County. The Pooler Police Department is searching it now."

"Cool. Nobody has this, you say?"

"Nobody but you. Also, I've cleared Carl Sussman on that rape case. He didn't do it. You understand me?"

"Who did?"

"We don't know yet, but Sussman has an alibi. He's cleared. I don't want to read anything in the *Ledger-Telegraph* saying he was ever a suspect, you got that?"

"Loud and clear. Why can't I run with the motor home story?"

"Because we don't know yet what it's going to tell us. Cross may still be hanging around the area. I don't want to spook him off. You hang on to the story for one more day, and I promise you'll still be the only one with it."

After Cory rang off, I looked up Tryson, Tennessee. Alton Fry's daughter had said that the farm on which Cross had pitched his fleecing tent was just over the city limits, which meant that it probably fell into unincorporated land. That made it the sheriff's jurisdiction. I checked the phone number on the Internet and dialed it.

The woman who answered the phone put me through to Sheriff Rufus LaFollette.

"Where in creation is Prosperity?" he asked.

"Bliss County, Sheriff. North Carolina."

"That's Don Webb's territory, ain't it?"

"It sure is."

"Good man, Webb. Met him at a conference up to Appalachian State a year or so ago. So Prosperity is in Bliss, is it? I'd have thought it the other way around."

I thought I could hear him spit a wad of tobacco juice into a cola can. I tried very, very hard not to visualize the scene.

"I'm calling for assistance with a murder case down here," I said.

"Think I saw something about it on the television set. Got some bodies buried on a farm down there or some sort of thing, right?"

"That's right. There's a traveling tent preacher who goes by the name of Alvin Cross, but I don't know whether that's his real name. He called himself Shelton Boyd when he ran a revival in your county a couple of years back."

"That name sounds familiar."

"He made the local papers. There was a girl from Tryson, a runaway. He brought her parents a letter from her."

"Yeah, I vaguely recall that. You think he's the guy who buried all those people in your town?"

"He's a very strong suspect. I need a favor. I found out that he pitched his tent on a farm just outside the Tryson town limits, a place belonging to a man named Able Johnson. That would be your jurisdiction, right?"

"Sure is. There are only three incorporated towns in this county. The rest of it is my territory."

"Here's what worries me, Sheriff—"

"Call me Rufus."

"All right, Rufus. What worries me is that he might have been doing this for a very long time. I'm concerned that he might have come across some runaway girl while he was set up for business in your county. It occurred to me—"

"I'm with you. Tell ya what, Chief; why don't I get my K-9 deputy to take his blue-tick out to the farm and have a little sniff? If his dick gets hard, we'll dig ourselves a hole. How's that sound?"

"Like you took the words right out of my mouth. Just one thing, Sher . . . Rufus. We're working a pretty tight schedule here. We've located a motor home used by the preacher. We're hoping it will give us some idea where we can locate him. The quicker we know whether he buried some poor girl in your county, the better."

"Don't have to ask me twice. We'll get right on it. I'll have my K-9 guy out there in about a half-hour. I'll keep you posted."

I thanked him and broke the connection. He sounded like a hillbilly, but I knew that a lot of those mountain county sheriffs got their jobs through shrewd manipulation of the voters, and kept their jobs by doing exactly what they said they'd do.

A former Speaker of the House had intoned that *All politics are local.* What he hadn't said was that local politics can be the nastiest of all.

Only a couple of months earlier, I had been forced to back my friend of over a quarter century, Kent Kramer, up against a wall in his office, flashing papers in his face detailing years of illegal kickbacks in his real estate business, in order to keep him from condemning my farm for a city park. The papers had been a last bequest from his predecessor. It was just how politics worked in a small town.

Small-town politics. Tougher than bare-assed naked tackle football.

And nowhere near as fun.

I had grown weary of watching the phone and waiting for the ring, so I decided to shut my office and take the new cruiser out for patrol.

As soon as I left the station I could tell that there had been a change in the air. Formerly hot and oppressive, it was now downright soul-smashing. Breathing came with difficulty, as my lungs fought to force the saturated oxygen into my system. Clouds had gathered overhead, dark as pig-iron and rolling across the sky like giant bags of sodden dough. A storm was coming.

The stratosphere was so dramatic that the news teams almost didn't notice me walk to the cruiser and climb behind the wheel. By the time they gathered their forces, I had peeled rubber out of the parking lot and was a thousand yards down Morgan Highway.

I stared back and forth between the road and the clouds, watching for any tell-tale rotation or unusual puckering. Unlike the cinematically dramatic tornadoes of the Midwest, those in my part of the country tended to conceal themselves deep inside thunderstorms. More often than not, North Carolina victims of tornadoes reported absolutely no warning that they were about to be struck because the weather outside their homes had already been fouled by wind and heavy rain. Sometimes the only way the storms telegraphed their destructive intent was in their formation. By the time the rain started to fall, it was too late to know whether it would end with a pretty rainbow or the complete demolition of your house.

I set up a figure-eight racetrack pattern for my patrol. With each lap, I made a point of driving down Bostian Road, past Carl Sussman's building site. Taking this route left very few decisions to make, unless I came across some speed demon determined to make my day, and I had time to think again through all the permutations of this Alvin Cross case.

I had known very few people who had spent so little time in my peaceful town and yet had wreaked so much havoc.

Halfway through my fourth tour, the radio crackled, and Sherry said, "Chief, I have a call from Chief Mabry up in Pooler. He says he needs to talk with you right away, but he doesn't want to do it on the airwaves."

"Roger that. I'll return to the station in about six minutes."

I broke off my racetrack pattern and cut across the back roads toward my office. The wind had kicked up and the clouds overhead whipped and rolled all over each other. In the western distance I could see flickers of electricity dance from one bank to another. By nightfall we were in for one hell of a blow.

I went straight to my office and dialed Mabry's direct number. He picked up on the first ring.

"Judd Wheeler here," I said. "I hear you have some news for me."

"Yes. We've found something in the motor home. I think you

should see it yourself."

"What's the news?"

"The kind of shit I'm going to have a hard time keeping out of my nightmares. Can you get down here?"

"Give me an hour."

It actually took only forty-five minutes. I arrived at the Parker County Law Enforcement Center, parked the cruiser in a visiting cops' space, and made my way to Perry Mabry's office.

"He's waiting for you, Chief Wheeler," his secretary said as I walked into the waiting room.

Big-city police chiefs like Mabry, contrary to the stylistic portrayals in the movies, don't keep their offices in some glass fishbowl in the middle of a squad room. They're executives, like any other civil service supervisor, and they get the perks that go with it. Mabry's office was on the top floor of the center, with fancy wallpaper above oak wainscoting. His secretary sat behind an ornate walnut desk.

Mabry sat behind a desk made of highly polished mahogany, twice the size of his secretary's desk in the outer office. There were piles of paper on each side of his desk blotter. For the first time in quite a while, I was glad to be a small-town police chief. I couldn't imagine the personnel and management headaches Mabry must face each day.

"Have a seat, Judd," he said.

"What did you find?" I asked.

"We were taking apart the bedroom in the motor home and found a hidey-hole. We haven't contacted the manufacturer, but the fit and finish made it look like a factory-installed feature. Inside, we found these."

He handed over a sheaf of envelopes, bound with a thick rubber band. I sorted through the stack. Each one had been carefully addressed. Each one was sealed.

"Got a letter-opener?" I asked.

"That's evidence," Mabry said.

"Seems to me that there's evidence to spare. Opening one isn't going to hurt."

Reluctantly, Mabry handed me a brass letter opener with a rosewood handle. I slid it along the top seam of the envelope, slitting the paper with a whispered hiss. I handed the opener back to Mabry and pulled out the paper.

It was, as I had expected, a letter. From someone named Glenda. The envelope was addressed to Tom and Barbara Markey, in Gainesville, Florida.

The letter was full of regrets and teenage angst. It reflected Glenda Markey's fears of parental rejection, and suggested that since she had left home she had engaged in any number of sordid activities, before being found by Reverend Sidney Clement, who had urged her to write the letter. Glenda gushed about Clement and said that she might have been dead if he hadn't saved her. She begged her parents not to worry about her, because Reverend Clement was helping her to find a job and a place to live, and she would contact them again once she got her life in order.

Knowing what I already did about Alvin Cross, a.k.a. Sidney Clement, I found the note pathetic and foreboding. I had no doubts that poor Glenda Markey had long since been murdered, and now lay in an unmarked grave in some forlorn, poorly traveled country tract.

I handed the note to Mabry. He read it, then he placed it gingerly on his desk.

"Five minutes," he said. "That's all I want. Five minutes with this bastard in a locked room without witnesses."

"I'll watch the door for you. Did you find anything else?"

"Plenty. First of all, we lifted a bunch of prints from the inside of the motor home. We ran them through AFIS."

"I love it when you big-city cops toss jargon around like that."

"We gotta do something to keep you shit-kickers in line. We got a hit almost immediately off the prints. Alvin Cross is actually a fellow named Alvin Gortimer. We're still assembling information on him, but he was born in Hartsville, South Carolina. He's sixty-one and he has a jacket."

"He was in prison?"

"Did a two-year stretch in the eighties for indecent liberties. Seems he picked up some girl in a bar in Myrtle Beach and took her back to his hotel room for a spirited game of hide-the-cocktail-frank. Turns out she was only fifteen and had a big mouth. He was charged with statutory, but pled it down in court. The psychologist's pre-sentencing evaluation report makes for interesting reading."

He handed me a six-page document, stapled at the top left corner. I glanced over it. The first three pages were the usual gobbledygook, lots of test results and numbers. The second half was somewhat more revealing.

"Gortimer grew up on a farm," Mabry said, condensing the story. "His father was a holy roller who married a girl barely old enough to graduate high school. Alvin's mother got tired of a future of nothing but dirt, dashed dreams, and the calloused hands of her Bible-toting husband, so she split when the kid was four. She went from man to man like water in a bucket brigade. She died when Gortimer was sixteen, and only saw him two or three times after she took off. Gortimer told the shrink that he had always resented her for abandoning him."

"You think that, by taking in these runaways and murdering them, he's killing his mother over and over?"

"Oh, he did a pretty good job of that the first time."

I looked up from the report. "You better run that one by me again."

Mabry pulled another parcel from the stack on his desk, a tattered cardboard folder with a string tie around it. He handed me a wire-bound spiral Blue Horse notebook that looked about half a century old. It bulged in places, from items that had been stuffed between pages.

"The nightmare part," he said. "Gortimer kept a journal. It begins around the time he was fifteen, a year before he tracked his mother down and murdered her."

Mabry handed the notebook to me. I read the first page. It was a litany of hate and rage against a woman whom the author had plainly adored years earlier, but had grown to loathe. The first pages were a mixed bag of adolescent revenge fantasies and general rebellion. He described several different scenarios in which he envisioned what he might do to his mother if he ran across her.

Twenty pages in, a notation began with the portentous sentence: *I have found the whore and destroyed her!*

What followed was an account, in the awkward scrawl and syntax of a high school kid, of how he had located his mother. He had found a letter from her, written to his father, that included a return address. Using money he saved from an after-school job, he took a bus to Columbia on a Saturday in November and navigated the city by using the city bus system, until—sometime in the late afternoon—he found himself standing in front of a strip apartment building with an overflowing trash dumpster and car parts leaning against the dilapidated brick.

He had found her apartment and had knocked on the door. At first overjoyed to see him, and a little embarrassed for all the times that she had disappointed him, she begged him to come inside. It was a cold day and he had worn a sheepskin jacket and a pair of leather gloves. He removed the jacket. He kept the gloves on.

His mother asked if he wanted anything to drink and he asked her for a cola. She retreated to the kitchen, ducking around an ironing board that had been set up in the living room, the iron still standing upright next to a blouse.

Gortimer wrote that he had considered confronting her about all the promises she had made, all the visits she'd canceled, all the times she had simply not shown up without explanation or apology. He had come seeking answers. In the moment he saw her, however, his desire for closure was overcome by his rage and disgust. He had no need for answers. What he wanted now was revenge.

He slammed the iron into her face as she walked out of the kitchen. She didn't say a word, didn't utter so much as a shriek. She made a quick exhalation and staggered back, dropping the cola. She would have fallen straight away, but the wall stopped her. Her knees buckled and her legs wobbled. Her eyes glazed over and began to roll up in their sockets.

Gortimer struck at her again and again as she slid down the wall. With each blow, all the fantasies he had carried in his head ran like an endless video loop. He had dreamed of this moment for a decade.

Finally, his arm grew tired of wielding the iron. He stopped, his breath coming in gasps. He could see his mother's eyes dilated in the mess of her face, and he knew, even without checking her breathing or pulse, that she was dead.

Amazingly, there wasn't much blood. He had been spattered once or twice, just a light spray of droplets, but he was prepared for that. In his knapsack was a change of clothes and a plastic bag. He stepped back into the living room, out of the small circle of blood spatter, and quickly stripped down to his underwear. He bagged the soiled clothes, taking care to toss in the gloves, and sealed the bag with a secure knot. After pulling on clean clothes, he stuffed the bag into his knapsack.

Then he sat on the couch and admired his work.

When he had soaked up as much memory as he could store, he put on his jacket and another pair of gloves and left the apartment.

"Jesus," I said.

"There's more," Mabry said. "Keep going."

I glanced through the rest of the journal. A lot of it was the typical musings of an idealistic if somewhat misdirected youth. Some of it was violent and disturbing.

About a hundred pages after his account of killing his mother, I ran across the description of how he had killed his next victim, a runaway in Virginia Beach. A Polaroid photograph of the girl's naked, bludgeoned body had been taped to the facing page.

From that point on, the journal was nothing more than a catalog of spent rage and senseless brutality toward wayward girls, each story accompanied by a picture illustrating Gortimer's handiwork.

"Sick puppy," I said.

"This guy's a monster, but I suspect you already knew that," Mabry said. "This guy desecrates the surface of the earth just by walking on it. I don't want him sharing my air."

"I understand completely."

"The very fact that this vermin chose to park his bus in my town makes me piss blood. Makes me want to track him down and toss him under the jail, and then build another jail on top of the first one."

"And you've never even met him," I said, unable to pull my gaze from the horror I held in my hands.

"There's more. That's why I wanted you to see this in person. Skip to the back of the journal."

I riffled though the pages until I reached the last four or five sheets.

It began with a description of how Cross had "ministered" to a girl Ricky Chasen had picked up in Myrtle Beach. Her name, according to the book, was Jean Stark. The details of her rape and death were graphic and horrifying, but nothing compared to the picture Cross had stapled to the sheet.

The next picture appeared to have been shot inside a house. A woman lay naked on a loop rug on a hardwood floor. Ricky Chasen lay on top of her. She had a canvas or burlap bag tied around her head. Her fists were clenched.

"I bet that's Karen Craighead," I said. "If it is, this proves that Ricky Chasen abducted and raped her. I know a guy down in Prosperity who's going to be very happy to hear about this."

"His name wouldn't be Sussman, would it?"

"Yeah. How did you—"

"Keep reading."

I turned the page and saw a picture of Sussman's trailer and the skeleton of his new house in the background. Stapled to the facing page was one of the sex offender flyers I'd printed for Stu to distribute. On the following page, Cross described how he and Chasen had snuck onto Sussman's property, carrying cans of diesel fuel and magnesium sparklers, and had—in Cross's words—"burned the devil out of Prosperity."

"Arson," I said. "When we do catch this guy, he's going down for just about every felony in the statutes."

"Keep reading."

I turned the page and my heart stopped for a second.

There was a photograph of my house. I could clearly see Donna sitting on the wicker settee on the front porch, in shorts and a T-shirt, reading a book.

I felt the heat rise in my face. I held the book in one hand and gripped the handle of the chair with the other, fighting for balance. The room seemed to go eerily silent, as if all the air had been sucked out the ventilation registers. My eyes clouded over.

"He dies," I rasped. "Isn't gonna be any trial. When we find him, I'm going to blow him clear into the middle of the next century."

"I understand your feelings," Mabry said as he took the book from me before I could rend it—and the evidence it provided—to shreds. "But I'm going to pretend I didn't hear that last remark."

I tried to reel in my fury. I tried to recall who I was and why I was wearing the tin on my blouse.

I grabbed my cell phone and dialed my home number. Donna answered on the third ring.

"Donna," I said, trying not to sound irrationally panicked. "I need you to get in your car and get away from the house."

"Why?"

"I'm in Pooler, at Chief Mabry's office. I have reason to believe that you might be in danger. You need to get in the car and go. Don't go to your house. Drive straight to the Prosperity Police Station and tell Sherry to take you to my office. Wait there until I come for you."

"Judd, you're scaring me."

"You'll be safe at my office. Call my cell phone as soon as you get there, or get Sherry to radio me. Either way, I want to know when you get to the station."

"What's happening?"

"I'll explain later."

"Is this about Cross?"

"Please, Donna. Just go. I'll explain when I see you."

After pocketing the phone, I asked Mabry if I could see the book again.

"Remember, it's evidence," he said.

"Sure."

He handed it to me. I leafed through the pages again until I came to the picture of Sussman's trailer and construction site.

"This was taken after the fire," I said. "The first trailer was a doublewide. This is a single. That house frame was finished a few days ago. Some volunteers from Habitat for Humanity helped raise it."

"So Gortimer and Chasen returned to the scene to take this picture."

"I don't think they were there for carefree sightseeing," I said bitterly. "I get the impression that Cross doesn't like to leave a job half done."

"You know what you're saying?"

"Yeah," I said. "I have to get back to Prosperity."

FORTY-NINE

Twilight descended on the farm, and brought with it the onslaught of midsummer mosquitoes bred in the irrigation troughs in the father's fields.

The boy swatted at the bugs as they dove onto his exposed arms and legs, drawn by the dried sweat and the sweet lure of his exhaled breath.

Cars passed less frequently now, and as they did the boy noticed that they had switched on their headlights. A dreaded notion began to form in the back of his mind. It grew with each passing moment and each car that blew by his solitary lawn chair without stopping or even slowing appreciably.

Even if she shows up, *he thought,* it's too late to go anywhere. Even if she shows up, she'll only stay for a few minutes and then she'll go away again.

As the light of the Dog Star began to bore through the heavens, the boy gave up. He folded the chair and dragged it haltingly up the drive toward the front porch. His father sat there, waiting, as if he had expected that the boy, at some point, would lose hope.

"Ready for something to eat?" the father asked.

The boy nodded. The father took him by the shoulder and walked him inside. There was cold baked ham and biscuits and lima beans and new potatoes. The father had been boiling the beans and potatoes for some time. They had formed a frothy skin on the top of the water in the pot. The father skimmed the foam with a large spoon and took the vegetables off the heat. He sliced several pieces from the ham and placed a plate in front of the boy.

As the father crossed the kitchen to fill a glass with fresh milk, the boy started to cry. The father stopped momentarily and then finished pouring the milk.

"Why didn't she come?" the boy asked between sobs as the father placed the glass in front of him.

"I don't know," the father said.

But, of course, he did. He knew all too well the mother's motives, and her inconstancy. It was something he had come to accept in life, like drought and seventeen-year locusts. It was a test from God.

"Don't she love us anymore?"

"I think she does," the father said. "As best she can. Your momma understands love, and she fears it. She sees it as a yoke, and she don't take kindly to being tied down."

"So she just run off like she did?"

"It wasn't to hurt, son. Being here on the farm frightened her. I think maybe she's afraid of dying, scared that she might run out her time on earth without actually living. I don't think she saw what she had. Now that she's abandoned it, she can't bear to come back."

"So why'd she promise me she'd come if she knew she wouldn't?"

The father chewed on a piece of ham and thought.

"I think maybe she intends to come when she says she will. As the time draws nearer, though, she panics. The farm means something to her that she dreads, and she can't bring herself to come here. Then, I think maybe she's too ashamed to call and back out."

"I hate her," the boy said quietly, and then slapped the table so hard that he hit the fork and sent it flying. "I hate her!"

The father picked up the fork and, after wiping it off with his napkin, placed it back next to the boy's plate.

"I reckon you do," he said. "You're too young to understand the ways of some women. I reckon you hate her because you don't have enough feelings to choose from."

"Don't you hate her?"

"*I feel sorry for her. And maybe I'm a little angry at me for not understanding what she needed, and for letting her go. Not that I could have stopped her.*"

"*People who run of—people who hurt their families—they ought to be punished.*"

The father swallowed part of a new potato and pointed the fork at his son.

"*You're talking about your mother,*" *he said.* "*She may have done a lot of awful things, and she might have disappointed you today, but she's still your mother.*"

"*I don't care! She was going to take me to town, and we were going to eat lunch and maybe see a picture show, and she promised me ice cream! I waited all day for her. I waited all day!*"

The boy jumped from his chair and ran to his room. The father could hear his sobs through the solid oak door.

He finished eating, and he wrapped the boy's plate in wax paper and placed it in the refrigerator, and then he washed his own dishes and placed them in the drying rack, and by the time he was finished the boy had stopped crying.

The father quietly opened the boy's door, and saw him lying on the bed. His breathing was slow and measured and deep. A snail trail eroded by his tears coursed through the patina of dried sweat and road dust on his cheek.

The father considered getting the boy up to wash his face and put him in his pajamas, but decided that it would be better to let him sleep.

"*I'm sorry,*" *he whispered, as much to himself as to his precious son.* "*I'm sorry I wasn't a better husband to your momma.*"

He stood there for a while and watched the child snoring softly and imagined the tortures that the boy was inflicting on his mother in his grief-ridden dreams.

"*I'm sorry, Judd,*" *the father said again, and then he closed the door.*

FIFTY

One benefit of being a cop is that you don't have to screw around with rush-hour traffic.

As soon as I cleared the parking garage at the Law Enforcement Center, I hit the bubbletop and flipped on my siren. The normal trip from downtown Pooler to Prosperity, under the best of conditions, takes about forty-five minutes. I was shooting for less than half an hour.

After weaving through the worst traffic, I hit the main highway to Prosperity and kicked the speedometer up to the mid-seventies.

It was hard to keep my eyes on the road. Overhead, the storms that had brewed all afternoon were starting to coalesce into a tempest of Biblical proportions. Jagged tridents of lightning arced across the sky and down to the ground, each of them close enough for me to feel the pop of static electricity as they lit off, and the car roof rattled with the instantaneous peal of thunder, like standing inside a kettle drum. The wind bent centuries-old elms and oaks and tulip poplars that lined the highway every which way, twisting them to their limits and sometimes beyond. The highway was littered with broken twigs, many of them still sporting dozens of water-starved leaves.

It felt as if I was racing the gods themselves as well as time.

As I drove, I pulled out my cell phone and tried to punch in Carl Sussman's number. In response, the phone returned an ear-splitting three-tone signal and an announcement that the number was out of service.

Of course, I recalled. *The fire.*

When Cross and Chasen burned down Sussman's house and mobile home, they also destroyed the telephone lines. Odds were they hadn't been repaired yet.

On the off chance that Sharon Counts might be with Sussman, I called the dispatcher at the Bliss County Sheriff's Department.

"What's up, Chief?"

"I need to contact Sharon Counts. She's a CSI with the department."

"Not as of this morning. She tendered her resignation, effective immediately. Sheriff Webb was really upset. She's cleared out her locker and everything."

"Did she give a reason?"

"Nope."

"Do you have a cell phone contact for her?"

"The only number we had was for the department-issued phone. She turned that in with her badge and gun."

"Thanks. Oh, could I get you to send a deputy around to check on one of my residents in Prosperity? I'm en route to his place from Pooler, but I probably can't get there for another twenty or thirty minutes."

"I'll see what I can do, but we have a bit of an emergency up here in Morgan. The Outlaws and Vulcans are having a shootout over on the east side of the county. Most of our deputies have been dispatched to help put out that fire."

"Whatever you can do to help would be great. Send whoever you can muster to Carl Sussman's place off Bostian Road in Prosperity."

I gave her the address, signed off, and hit the speed dial for Carla Powers at the morgue. It took several rings for her to answer.

"I have a probable ID on the other dead girls we dug up over on Ned Murray's farm in Prosperity," I told her. "You got something to write with?"

"Constantly. Shoot."

"The first was probably Jean Stark. She was from Hialeah, Florida. The other is a girl named Kate Poore—that's p-o-o-r-e—from Rockaway, New Jersey. If you contact the police departments in those cities, they'll probably have missing persons or runaway reports on the girls."

"Great. How'd you find this out?"

"We got lucky. I'll check back with you after I take care of some other matters."

"Thanks for the tips," she said just before I broke the connection.

I had passed the exits for the Pooler outer loop, which meant that the traffic had dropped to practically nothing. I juiced the accelerator a bit more. Every second now could be critical.

Pea gravel scattered as I slid the cruiser into the parking lot at the Prosperity Police Station. I jumped from the car and dashed through the door. Almost without thinking, I locked it behind me. Across the street, the newsies quickly came to life and scrambled about, gathering their equipment. They smelled a story in the air.

As I bolted toward the station door, a blue-white streak of lightning flared from the clouds and connected with the steeple of the Baptist Church across the street. The ionized air, seared by the flash, contracted then boomed with an ear-splitting roar. The reporters ducked and glanced skyward, as if waiting for a second shot from the heavens.

I blew right past Sherry to my office, where I found Donna sitting in my chair, behind the desk. She stood as soon as I appeared in the door.

"Judd!" she cried.

I closed the door.

"Cross," I said. I walked to her and gathered her up in my arms. "He's been spying on you. The crime lab guys in Pooler found a journal with pictures of my house and you on the front porch. The guy is pure evil, Donna. I couldn't take the chance that he might make a run at you before I could get up here."

"Make a run at me?"

"He did it all. He killed and buried Nate Murray and those other people at Nate's farm. He burned down Carl Sussman's house. He and Ricky Chasen kidnapped and raped Karen Craighead. He killed that biker over in Morgan, and lit off the gang war between the Outlaws and the Vulcans. They only thing he didn't do was kill Steve Samples. His journal reads like a Bible of evil without a last chapter. I had to get you away from the house before he could write the ending."

"He isn't gone?"

"No. If I'm right, he's somewhere nearby, in Prosperity. There were pictures in his journal of Karen Craighead being raped. I recognized the room where it happened. They did it at Nate Murray's house."

"Call the Sheriff's office," she urged. "Get them to send deputies there to arrest him."

"I tried that already. The entire department is deployed to east Bliss County. The dispatcher thought she might be able to spare me a deputy to look after Carl Sussman's place."

"Carl Sussman? Why?"

"There was a picture in the journal of Carl's new house, the one he started after the first one was torched. Cross and his boy Chasen must know the net's getting tight around them. They only have a couple of unfinished jobs—Carl, and me."

I pulled away from her and crossed my office to the locker against the side wall. I stripped off my blouse, opened the locker, and took out my kevlar vest. Donna watched me in horrible amazement as I strapped it on.

"You're going after him, Judd? Alone?"

"I'm the law in Prosperity," I said. "It's my job to take him down. Slim's on duty. I'll call and have him meet me at Nate Murray's place after I stop by Carl's house to make sure everything is all right there. If Cross and Chasen are hiding on Nate's farm, maybe we can sneak around from the rear and take them by surprise."

"And if you can't?"

"Then I suppose we'll pin them down as best we can until we get help."

I saw the worried look on her face. I hoped that my own face didn't reflect it. Outside, I heard another flick of electricity, and the building shook under the blast of another explosion of thunder.

"Now, don't worry," I said as I embraced her. "I've been a cop for twenty years, man and boy. In Atlanta, I faced down drug dealers with full-automatic weapons and lived to talk about it. I should be fine against a sixty-year-old preacher and a Lumbee ex-con. Especially with Slim backing me up."

"Can you call Stu in for some extra help?"

I thought about it for a moment. Stu was scheduled to come on duty in an hour or so anyway.

"Sherry?" I called out.

"Yeah, Chief?"

"Call Officer Marbury. Tell him I need him to clock in early. Tell him to wear his vest. I'd like him to meet up with Slim over at Nate Murray's farm. Tell him he'll have to take his truck over, because both cruisers are going to be busy."

"Roger that, Chief," she said.

"There," I said, turning back to Donna. "Feel better?"

"No," she said.

I opened the gun locker and grabbed two boxes of double-ought shells for the Remington shotgun in my cruiser. I also stuffed two magazines of nine-mike in my Sam Browne for my Glock.

"You stay here," I told her after giving her another long kiss. "I'll call when it's all over."

I pulled on my Stetson and started to leave.

"This seems familiar," she said.

I turned back to her.

"I know," she said. "*Gunsmoke.* You're Matt Dillon, going out after the bad guys, and I'm Miss Kitty, staying behind and worrying."

I smiled and tipped my hat at her.

"I knew Miss Kitty," I said. "Miss Kitty was a friend of mine. Miss Kitty on her best day could never be Donna Asher."

"Don't get shot," she said.

The reporters were waiting for me when I stepped out of the station. I waded through their gauntlet, mumbled a series of "no comment, no comment," and slipped into the cruiser. I backed out without paying a lot of attention to whether a cameraman might be standing behind me. If he was dumb enough to get in the way, running him down would have been thinning the herd.

As soon as I was half a mile from the station, I pulled the cruiser over and checked the action in the Remington. There was a shell in the chamber and six in the extended magazine. My Glock was fully loaded. If I needed more than seventeen pistol rounds and seven loads of buck to bring down Cross and Chasen, I'd turn in my badge.

I toggled the microphone on my shoulder. "Prosperity One to Prosperity Two."

"Prosperity Two."

"Slim, rendezvous with Prosperity One and Officer Marbury at the entrance to Nate Murray's farm in about fifteen minutes."

"Two, Roger."

"Just stay there and wait for my arrival. Do not approach the farm."

"Got ya five by five, Prosperity One."

No other communication was necessary. If I told him to, Slim would have waited there all day. He was a good cop, and I was privileged to have him under my command. I hated like the dickens to toss him in harm's way.

I turned onto Bostian Road, headed toward Carl Sussman's homestead. I hadn't explained much to the dispatcher in Morgan, and I wanted to update the deputy I hoped she had sent on the situation and why I wanted him to keep an eye on the place.

As I pulled into the gravel drive, I saw the Bliss County Sheriff's Department bubbletop sitting empty, next to Carl Sussman's mobile home. He'd made good time. I'd only called the dispatcher a half hour before. I made a note to send her a thank-you card.

I parked the car and pulled the Remington free from its mount. After sliding my hat onto my head, I stepped from the cruiser and walked to the front door of the trailer. I didn't hear any construction activity on the house site, and, in fact, Carl would have been a fool to be out working with the storm overhead about to drop on our shoulders.

I rapped on the front door, expecting the deputy to answer.

Nobody responded.

Lightning flashed somewhere to my right, and four or five seconds later the air itself reverberated with the report of thunder. The storm was almost on me. I knocked again, even as the first quarter-sized drops of rain plopped in the dust next to my feet.

When nobody came to the door, I tested the knob. It rotated freely.

I have heard that, in moments of absolute peril, the senses are heightened to a point similar to that among the lower animals, who are forced to depend on instincts rather than reason. Unblessed by the convolutions of gray frontal lobe matter we humans have accumulated over the last million years or so of evolution, the lower species have to rely on chemical alarms prompted by dangerous smells.

Perhaps there was nothing waiting for me on the other side of the door. Something, however, some primal instinct, kept me from pushing the door open.

Instead, as the rain began to thicken into sheets, I stepped down from the door, and walked as quietly as possible around the hard side of the trailer, away from the deputy's squad car, through thickets of brambles and poison ivy, to a point from which any unfriendlies would never expect me to approach.

As I peered around the back corner of the mobile home, the sky directly over my head lit up with God's own fire, and a sound like cannons surrounded me from every direction. As I reflexively cowered to protect myself, I realized that a longleaf pine only thirty yards or so from me had taken a direct hit from the lightning. I heard the trunk of the tree creak and snap, and the smell of burning pitch stank in the drenched air. The rain now fell in waves and poured off the roof of the trailer, spattering in a pool two yards across, not far from my feet.

I looked up and my heart froze. A man in a Bliss County Sheriff's Department uniform sat against the back side of the trailer, the front of his shirt drenched in a black spread of blood. His unblinking eyes stared straight ahead as the water from the rain cascaded over them and down his face.

I toggled the radio microphone on my left epaulet and switched the radio on my belt to the Bliss County Sheriff's frequency.

"Officer down!" I said, as quietly and calmly as possible.

"This is Chief Wheeler, Prosperity Police. I have a Bliss County deputy shot, fourteen thousand block of Bostian Road. All available units respond."

I repeated the message once, and then toggled the radio to the frequency I shared with Slim and Stu.

"Prosperity One, all units respond."

The radio crackled once, but I couldn't hear it as thunder broke again over my head like clashing cymbals. I depressed the send button on my microphone.

"Slim, I'm at Carl Sussman's place. I have one dead deputy in sight. I need you and Stu to haul ass over here right now."

"Ten-four," Slim said.

I should have waited for them to arrive, but I had a dead officer just twenty feet from me, and no idea where Carl Sussman might be. I harbored a disturbing suspicion that, wherever he was, he wasn't alone.

The clouds overhead had grown so thick that it looked like half-night. Lightning crackled on every side of me, separated by mere seconds. Wind whipped through the trees, snapping off branches that fell to the forest floor in random piles. I faded back into the woods and began to circle the perimeter of the building site. One gust of wind grabbed at my hat, jerking it from my head. I let it go.

The back of Sussman's house came into view through the random tangle of tree trunks. I could see Sussman sitting against the foundation of his house, clutching his side. His hair had come unbound, and fell across his face and shoulders in sodden ringlets. Another person lay motionless next to him, curled into a fetal position.

Ricky Chasen stood over them, holding a shotgun. Next to him was a can of gasoline. His eyes were wide with adrenaline, his mouth frozen in a toothy grin.

He raised his face to the clouds as the lightning strobed all around us.

"Is that all you've got?" he screamed to the heavens. "Come on! Let it all out!"

He looked back down at Sussman and leveled the shotgun at him.

"What? You ain't gonna beg? I always heard you child molesters was just pussies. I figured maybe I put this barrel in your face, you gonna shit your pants and cry for mercy. C'mon, asshole, beg me not to shoot your fuckin' nuts off."

Sussman simply stared at him through the rivulets of water that fell across his brow.

I stepped out from the trees and brought up my Remington.

"Ricky Chasen!" I yelled. "You are under arrest. Drop your weapon immediately!"

Chasen's face turned, his jaw dropped, and he tilted his head the way a golden retriever does when you show him a power tool. He kept the shotgun trained on Sussman.

On TV, the hero might give the bad guy three or four warnings to disarm, while the villain tries to delay the inevitable. Real-world law enforcement officers, when facing an armed adversary, issue one warning only.

I counted to three, and when he hadn't dropped the gun I blew Ricky Chasen's shit all over the cement mixer behind him.

As soon as Chasen hit the mud, I rushed over to Sussman. His hands had been bound in front of him with cable ties.

"Check on Sharon!" he yelled over the din of rumbling thunder that now seemed to be a constant roar.

I lay the Remington on the plywood floor of the house frame and bent over Sharon. There was a nasty cut above her right temple. The blood had flowed into her hair, mixing with rainwater and matting her hair to the side of her head. I checked her eyes.

"She's alive!" I shouted. "What happened?"

"He was waiting for us when we got back from the store. He was inside the trailer. He put these ties on our wrists and walked us around here. The deputy came around the side of the house about ten minutes ago and this guy shot him twice. Sharon tried to stop him and he hit her with the gun."

"Okay," I said. "Let's get this tie off your wrists and Sharon inside the trailer. My officers are on the way—"

Something hard and heavy stuck my back and drove all the air from my lungs. I collapsed face-down in the mud, which filled my mouth as I tried to draw breath. Gasping and heaving, I pushed myself over, spit the mire out of my mouth, and saw Alvin Cross standing over me with a section of iron pipe.

"You had no call to kill that boy!" he yelled. "He was a good boy. He was doing the Lord's work, wiping out the evil that has infested your land."

Cross's eyes were glazed and wide, his pupils dilated. He was gripped in the fervor of some kind of Old Testament fury the likes of which I had never encountered.

"He who countenances evil embraces evil!" Cross shouted. "As the Good Book tells us, 'Ye shall chase your enemies, and they shall fall before you by the sword.' "

I tried to push myself up. Cross swung the pipe, and it caught me in the ribs. Agonizing pain rolled across my chest.

"For Ezekiel wrote, 'He cried also in mine ears with a loud voice, saying, Cause them that have charge over the city to draw near, even every man with his destroying weapon in his hand.' You have come to this place with charge over the city and the destroying weapon in your hand, and you have murdered a child of God, a servant of the Almighty. There can only be one punishment for that!"

Assured that he had crippled me, Cross had stepped away for a moment, raising his arms toward the skies that rippled with electric fire, as if preaching to the angels themselves.

What he didn't know was that the bulletproof vest had absorbed most of the energy of his blows. It had hurt, for sure, but by concentrating on my midsection he hadn't caused any lasting damage.

I tried again to get to my feet, to face him down on more equal terms.

" 'Be ye afraid of the sword: for wrath bringeth the punishments of the sword, that ye may know there is a judgment,' " he quoted as he slashed through the air with the pipe. It clanged against my holster, and I heard the polymer casing of my Glock crack and collapse under the impact. The force of the blow rippled through my midsection. I instantly felt my stomach contract with nausea. It was as if someone had inflated a basketball in my entrails.

I had only one chance left. If I tried to attack him straight on, he'd pummel me into hash with the pipe. If I could get to the Remington I'd left lying on the floor of the house, I could drop him in his tracks.

Every breath I took sent another spasm of agony through my torso. I tried to ignore the pain and attempted to roll to a crawling position.

" 'For I am the minister of God to thee for good. But if thou do that which is evil, be afraid; for I beareth not the sword in vain: for I am the minister of God, a revenger to execute wrath upon him that doeth evil!' " Cross shouted.

He swung the pipe another time. I rolled out from under it and tried to get inside its arc. Just as the pipe swept past my head, I leapt at Cross.

He stepped out of the way, grabbed me under the arms with a strength I'd never have imagined in a man his age and stature, and he threw me two yards away from the house. I hit the ground rolling.

Before I could try for my feet again, Cross swung the iron pipe and brought it down on my back. This time I saw stars as the air was driven out of me and the corners of my visual field began to close like a theater curtain.

" 'As the Lord rejoiced over you to do you good, and to multiply you; so the Lord will rejoice over you to destroy you, and to bring you to nought!' " Cross roared as he raised the pipe over his head.

With the last of my strength, I rolled and faced him, knowing that he meant to bury the pipe in my skull. I willed my arms and legs to move, but they flopped listlessly.

His gaze locked on mine, his deadly intent all too obvious. He held the pipe aloft, motionless, as if savoring his imminent victory.

At that moment there was a brilliant flash just over our heads. A blue-hot spear of lightning struck a pecan tree at the edge of the woods and a finger of naked electricity danced from the tree and lit up the end of the iron pipe clenched in Alvin Cross's bony fists. The arc instantly traversed his body into the sodden ground on which I lay. Both our bodies bowed involuntarily as the charge surged through our muscles, and in that instant I knew what it must feel like to sit in the electric chair when the warden slams the switch that knocks the fire out of your ass.

There was a tremendous explosion that seemed to come from everywhere at once and echoed inside my head over and over as my eyesight failed and darkness claimed me, and then I was aware of absolutely nothing at all.

FIFTY-ONE

"I think he's coming back," I heard someone say, far away, through ozone mists that swirled about me like moonlit smoke under water.

Something was rolling over my chest, over and over. My lungs burned like I had inhaled lye fumes.

I felt myself gasp, sucking in the sweetest air I'd ever tasted. Even so, I couldn't seem to open my eyes. I feebly raised one hand, then let it fall back into the drenched earth with a dull thud.

"Don't try to get up, Chief," someone said. The voice sounded familiar. I thought it might be someone I trusted, but for the life of me I couldn't figure out who.

"Where in hell are those paramedics?" someone said.

"They have to come all the way from Mica Wells. Give them time."

"We almost didn't have any time."

I gasped again, and forced my eyes to open. Immediately, drops of water flooded them and overflowed to my cheeks. I looked straight up from where I lay, and as my eyes focused I saw rain falling and clouds roiling like chocolate cake batter in a mixing bowl.

I found Carl Sussman's face to one side. I opened my mouth and tried to ask him what had happened.

"Don't try to talk," he said. "You were struck by lightning. Damnedest thing I ever saw. Cross was about to brain you with that pipe, and out of the blue came this bolt of lightning. Blew him right out of his shoes. You weren't grounded, lying in the water the way you were. You got quite a shock."

I rolled my head and saw Cross's body lying ten feet away. Smoke still rose in wisps from his charred clothing.

"Cross?" I whispered.

Sussman shook his head. "I can only do CPR on one person at a time. It wasn't his turn."

Far off, I heard the first wail of approaching sirens, a mix of the staccato whoop of police cars, and the mournful extended tones of the volunteer fire department rescue squad. It only half registered in my fried mind that they were coming for me.

"Glad you made that choice," I said. "I think I'll take a little nap now."

A week later, I sat in Dr. Kronenfeld's office. I had called him after they released me from the hospital. I said I wanted him to give me a onceover, to make certain there weren't any lasting neurological effects associated with having your wiring nearly melted by lightning.

"You seem fine," he said after he finished his examination. "I have to say, though, that you're one lucky fellow."

"Luckier than Cross!"

"Yes. I suspect you wanted to see me about more than a simple neurological checkup. What's on your mind?"

As usual, he had seen right through me. After our years exploring my cop's mentality, it was hard to hide things from him.

"I've been thinking," I said. "Cross and I weren't so different, when you get right down to it."

"How so?"

"He grew up on a farm. I grew up on a farm. His mother deserted him when he was a kid. My mother left my father when I was only six. His father was overtly religious. My father was the buckle in the Bible Belt. What happened? How'd he go his way while I went mine?"

"You're worried that, with only a little nudge, you might have wound up like Cross?"

"Something like that."

"Or maybe you think there's a piece of Cross inside of you, something you've denied all these years, refused to allow to come to the surface."

"When I was in Chief Mabry's office up in Pooler, he showed me Cross's journal. It had a picture of Donna sitting on my front porch, and I realized that he was targeting her, or me, or both of us . . . this is hard to say. I think I decided right at that moment that he was going to die. It wasn't a question of whether he should or shouldn't die, or whether it was the right thing to do. It was just something that fell into place in my head. The guy was scum of the lowest order, and one way or another I was going to plant his sorry ass."

Kronenfeld nodded, his fingers laced over his ample stomach in the classic therapist's nonthreatening repose.

"With Chasen it was easy," I continued. "He had a gun on an innocent victim. I gave him the opportunity to drop it, step back, and live. He made his choice and mine at the same time. I don't think I'll ever lose a minute's sleep over parking one in his hide. I wonder whether I would have done the same to Cross, even if he hadn't attacked me with that pipe."

"Are you disappointed that Mother Nature took that choice out of your hands?"

"No. Cross got what he deserved. Sure makes it hard to figure out what I might have done, though."

"There are a lot of theories," Kronenfeld said. "Since the birth of psychiatry, therapists have tried to figure out why people do such awful things to each other. Some believe that our personalities are fully formed from the moment we're born, that it's a matter of the way our neurons are arranged in our brains, or the size of the structures in our limbic systems. Other people say it's all about our experiences, and that psychopaths are created by the violation of elemental trust."

"What do you think?"

He mulled that one over.

"I think . . . now, don't go quoting me here. I think maybe we've spent so much time trying to measure human emotions and personality that we've forgotten about more primitive notions such as good and evil. I think maybe there is evil in this world, and sometimes—if you have the right combination of weakness and proclivities—you're just evil's sucker bait."

We talked for another half hour or so, and when we were done I felt a lot better about myself. I still didn't know whether I might have jammed Alvin Cross's spokes if he hadn't come at me with murder in his heart, but I also figured that—the way things turned out—it really didn't matter much.

Sometimes a thing is what it is. You can call it something else, but that won't make it so. Better to accept it and move on.

I stopped by the market and picked up some steaks and some sweet silver queen corn and a bag of baking potatoes and headed for my farm.

When I got there, Donna and Craig were waiting for me on the front porch. Craig had rushed home from Myrtle Beach when I was taken to the hospital. Soon he'd go off to college so he had decided to turn in his notice. I hadn't realized in the two months that he had been gone how different the house was when he lived in it. Somehow, seeing him and Donna on the porch made me feel more complete, in a way that surviving the closest of brushes with the Grim Reaper couldn't.

I parked the car, walked up the stone steps to the porch,

kissed my girl, ran my hand through my son's hair, and thought to myself how thankful I was to have whatever it was in my life that kept me from becoming the awful monster that had been Alvin Cross.

Later that evening, we had a big cookout. Slim and Jennifer came, as did Stu and his wife. Carl Sussman arrived last, with Sharon Counts, her head still bandaged to cover the twenty stitches it had taken to close her wounds.

We grilled steaks and corn on the stone charcoal grill, and ate at the cypress picnic table my father had built when I was just a whelp. We talked and joked and emptied a galvanized washtub full of iced beer, and I thanked each and every one of my guests for bringing me back from the brink of destruction, and we were all quiet until Slim said that he expected the same from me someday, and then we laughed and decided that late summer in Prosperity wasn't such a bad place to be after all.

ABOUT THE AUTHOR

Richard Helms is a retired forensic psychologist who now teaches at a local college. He has been nominated three times for the Private Eye Writers of America Shamus Award, and remains the only author ever to win Short Mystery Fiction Society Derringer Awards in two different categories in the same year. An amateur astronomer, gourmet cook, avid woodworker, and father of two adult children, Richard Helms lives—as he refers to it—"back in the trees," in a small North Carolina town that looks suspiciously like Judd Wheeler's Prosperity, with his lovely wife Elaine and an ever-changing number of cats.